Altai

WU MING is a collective of four Italian fiction writers based in Bologna, Italy. Wu Ming's books include *54*, *Manituana*, and the bestselling novel *Q*, published under the collective's previous pseudonym, Luther Blissett, and nominated for the *Guardian* First Book Award. The group's website is www.wumingfoundation.com.

Altai

Wu Ming

Translated by Shaun Whiteside

VERSO

London • New York

This paperback edition published by Verso 2014
First published in English by Verso 2013
First published as *Altai*
© 2009, 2013, 2014 by Wu Ming
Published by arrangement with Agenzie Letteraria Roberto Santachiara
© 2009 Giulio Einaudi editore s.p.a., Torino
Translation © 2013 by Shaun Whiteside

1 3 5 7 9 10 8 6 4 2

Verso
UK: 6 Meard Street, London W1F 0EG
US: 20 Jay Street, Suite 1010, Brooklyn, NY 11201
www.versobooks.com

Verso is the imprint of New Left Books

ISBN-13: 978-1-78168-167-1
eISBN-13: 978-1-78168-458-0 (UK)
eISBN-13: 978-1-78168-242-5 (US)

British Library Cataloguing in Publication Data
A catalogue record for this book is available from the British Library

The Library of Congress Has Cataloged the Hardback Edition as Follows

Wu Ming (Writers collective)
[Altai. English]
Altai / by Wu Ming ; translated by Shaun Whiteside.
pages cm
Translated from the Italian.
ISBN 978-1-78168-076-6 (hardback : alk. paper)
1. Italy—Politics and government—1559–1789—Fiction. 2. Istanbul (Turkey)—History—16th
century—Fiction. 3. Historical fiction. 4. Spy stories. I. Whiteside, Shaun, translator. II. Title.
PQ4923.U2A7913 2013
853'.92—dc23
2012047429

Typeset in Garamond Premier Pro by Hewer Text UK, Ltd., Edinburgh
Printed in the US by Maple Vail

To Valerio Marchi

Drifting on the sea go the swift ships.
Slacken the sails, there, loosen the ropes,
catch the wind and save your companions
if you want us to remember your name.
Stay far off, go not where the troubled wave rises.
Now it depends on you.

—Archilochus, seventh century BC

Prologue

Constantinople, 8 Muharram 977
(June 23, 1569)

From the rooms in the palace no sounds come. The smell of the Bosphorus and the muezzin's chant accompany the living into the evening, toward a semblance of peace. Beyond the open windows, the sky is ablaze with purple and gold. Fishing boats part from Asia and drift on the honeyed current.

A thought takes hold of Gracia: The greatest artists in the world—and she knew many of them when she was in Europe—can only imitate the beauty that the Lord has given us; they can never match his wonder.

She lifts the pen from the paper; now she is holding her hand in midair. Her eyes are closed as she listens to the chant.

As the last note fades away, she signs and seals the letter, and finally she relaxes against the back of her chair.

Dana watches her, studies her desk. The letters already sealed, and those awaiting a reply. She knows that the *Senyora* is exhausted. She won't be able to spend the evening writing, as she did until a short time ago. Her strength is leaving her, and there is still so much to do. Everyone is calling to her, from one end of the Mediterranean, and Europe, to the other. Fleeing exiles, persecuted Jews, Sephardic merchants, Ashkenazic rabbis.

"Help me," Gracia says. "I want to get up."

Dana tells her off: "You shouldn't stand up, my *Senyora*. You shouldn't even sit at your desk. You should rest."

Dana knows it's her part in the play, and she performs it every evening. Donna Gracia will repeat her order, her maidservant will obey, the *Senyora* will put an arm around her and take a few steps into the room, accepting with serenity the creaking of her joints.

The mirror on the wall is covered by a green cloth. For some time now, Gracia has relinquished makeup or any form of ostentation. She has given up admiring herself, but tonight she moves the cloth aside and looks at her own image. Over the past few years she has obscured herself. Dana takes care of her body every morning, with the greatest possible attention.

She is fifty-nine years old, and in the pane she sees the face of an old woman. Wrinkles at the sides of her eyes and mouth, the skin of her neck loose and pendulous, her nose pointed, her silver hair opaque. She studies

the folds in her face, seeks the girl who one night received a secret name, and the following day a Christian baptism to protect her from the Inquisition. *Beatriz de Luna Miquez.*

Looking into her own eyes, Gracia seeks the lights and shadows of the alleys of Lisbon, the house of her childhood and her earliest youth, little Yossef who called her aunt. Memories, the voice of his mother, the story of how the Miquez family fled from Spain.

Beneath the layers of time, in the curve of her eyebrow, is the girl who was married to Francisco Mendez, *el Gran Judio*, and who had to bury him too soon and found herself left with a little daughter and the huge family finances to fetch to safety.

This is what her life has largely been like: the life of a wealthy Jewish widow, in business, fighting against princes, kings, and emperors, first in the Low Countries, then in Venice, and finally in Constantinople.

In the face of the *Senyora*, Dana sees an ancient queen, whose devoted subjects are scattered from one end of the world to the other. Over the past fifteen years she has done her best to reunite them and drip them, drop by drop, inside the borders of the Ottoman empire. *As the shepherd pulls from the lion's mouth two feet or the lobe of an ear, so the Israelites will escape.* It's the first passage of a most ambitious project that among a thousand difficulties is taking shape down there, in Tiberias, where the *Senyora* wants to go to die.

Dana glances outside at the stretch of sea in front of the palace. She wonders if the letter will arrive. She knows that it is bound for a man far away—the *Senyora* mentions him from time to time, in phrases dense with love and compassion. Phrases from an intimate past.

Gracia lets the cloth fall back. Weariness is calling to her, claiming her, dragging her to itself, deeper and further away. Dana walks her to the bed and helps her to lie down, arranges the pillows behind her back, unlaces her dress, and then they sit there, looking at the waves and the vessels beyond the window.

"It's time for me to go down there," Gracia murmurs, her eyes half closed.

"Take me with you, my *Senyora*," Dana pleads.

She strokes her face, takes one hand between her own.

"No, my little one. You must stay by Reyna's side. You must live."

Then she juts her chin toward the desk.

"Take the letter. Send it to you know who."

Part One

Mi Star

September 13–December 10, 1569

1.

When the thunder came I was still awake. Sitting at the table, I was flicking through accusations and denunciations by candlelight. I was committing to memory the names and addresses of spies. Then my ears exploded, the floor shook, I was caught in a rain of glass and plaster. For days afterward I was picking shards from my hair.

I raised my head. The room was dark, but the shattered window framed a glare of light. It looked like sunrise, but it was the depths of night, and the wind carried the smell of cannon fire.

I got up and saw torches floating beneath the stars, behind the steeple of San Francesco. The *tezoni*, I thought. The dry docks, the Arsenal. The heart of La Serenissima in flames.

I dashed down the stairs. The main door of the palazzo had come off its hinges, but it was obstructed by a pile of rubble. I found a crack and pushed it until at last I emerged on the other side. In the *calle*, stunned faces quizzed one another in terrified silence. The more daring whispered the words *earthquake* and *Apocalypse*. Whole families were fleeing their homes, some leaping down from their balconies as if from the sides of a sinking ship.

The second explosion scattered the herd in a cloud of ashes and screams. I leapt into the middle of the *calle* to escape an avalanche of tiles, looked up, and saw them: two gondolas flying in the sky of Venice. They had wings of flame and they flew in uncertain arcs, like wounded birds. One crashed into the bell tower, which was sounding a constant fire alarm. The other disappeared from sight, beyond the rooftops.

In the hours and days that followed I would hear a thousand stories about what happened that night, and in each one it was a different object that was flying. Oak trunks came hurtling down, millstones for saltpeter, buckets of pitch, roasted corpses of men and horses, then dragons, comets, stellar explosions, the Madonna and Lucifer, Christ crucified and Christ resurrected.

I had to get to the Arsenal, join my men, stop and question as many people as possible. My legs started running as a gray veil fell over the city. It fell on the gawping crowd; it fell on the wounded, turning them into living statues. It fell on the wine carriers who came running with barrels and on the old people who stood speechless in front of the skeletons of their houses. It fell on the canals of Castello, so full of ash and rubble that the water itself seemed to be made of stone. It fell on the bodies on the ground, which looked like corpses but were not in fact dead, because only about twenty people had

died, and the rest were prevented from getting up by the fear that the sky might crash down on their heads.

To cross Campo San Francesco I had to step over men and women on their knees, busy singing the Psalms as they waited for the Lord's Judgment. I don't know if it was that suggestion, my weary, dusty eyes or the smoke-filled air. I know that I looked at the bell tower of the church and for a moment I was sure that it was rising into the air. I nearly fell to my knees myself, to shout out witness to the miracle and forget my duties.

Instead, I made for the Porta da Terra. The austere elegance of the marble framed a chaotic hubbub of people pushing, running and shouting. Above it, the Lion of San Marco observed the crowd with its jaws half open and its claws on the Gospel.

I shoved my way through the entrance hall. The fire was blazing at the far end, where the powder was stored.

I came upon a line of helpers passing buckets and leather bottles. There were splinters of wood and bits of scattered metal everywhere, but the main buildings seemed to be undamaged, and the wind had driven the fire beyond the outside wall toward the private dwellings and the Celestia Monastery.

I advanced toward the flames, drawn like a moth to a lantern. The heat burned my face; I was boiling inside my clothes and drenched with sweat. Smoke-blackened carpenters carried big wooden planks out of a workshop still threatened by the flames.

It was then that I heard someone say the name Giuseppe Nasi. It was the first time, that night, but it would become a refrain: the Swine of Judah, the Sultan's Catamite, the Archenemy of La Serenissima, the evil mind behind the catastrophe.

I reached the galley basin. The fire was still consuming two saltpeter mills, and one galley was ablaze on the still waters of the dock. The waves thrown up by the explosion had dislodged it from its moorings, and no one could get close enough to it to extinguish the blaze.

As I watched the galley burn, the outside wall of the dock began to crumble. The water of the lagoon was forcing its way in, as if inviting the ship to come away on a voyage. The galley set off slowly, the keel ablaze, and the flames seemed to be emerging from the sea and climbing up the masts, the stays and the sails, and then still higher up, like banners stirred by the wind.

Like an evil spell for the coming days.

2.

We floated slowly on a silent, funereal sea. The sheet drifted toward us on the surface of the water. An oar seemed to sink it but instead brought it closer to us. I leaned out of the dinghy and caught it between my fingers: the page of a book. The burned edges framed inky blurs. Only a single sentence was still legible: *Et tulerunt Ionam et miserunt in mare; et stetit mare a fervore suo.*

The Bible, the Book of Jonah, the storm-tossed ship. Jonah turns to the crew and asks to be thrown into the water. He is to blame for the storm, because he disobeyed the Lord. They take him and do as he asks, and the sea is immediately calm.

I too had to calm a storm, throw the guilty party to the Consigliere, free Venice from fear. I looked for fragments of the disaster, tiles to reassemble the mosaic. Perhaps this oracle would help me.

The galley canal was a graveyard, full of detritus. Wooden beams, smashed packing cases, whole oak trunks, scraps of sail, sheets, fragments of biscuit, ropes, the scorched and disemboweled carcasses of horses and mules. And the corpse of a man, his face and belly immersed in the water.

The scene was like a naval battle, when the ships have rowed or sailed away from the theater of death and all that remains is flotsam, bodies and the memory of the rage just passed.

On dry land, on the other hand, everything was in a state of agitation: dockyard workers, gawpers, people cursing and wailing, getting in the way of those with a task to perform. That was why we were in the boat. From the water I could look around, reflect and talk to my men as they rowed their way around the wreckage.

Silence. The sounds from the shore were drowned out by the waves. There was nothing but the lapping of the hull and the heavy breathing of Tavosanis the Friulian. My breath was the same, open-mouthed, as if I, too, were rowing.

"What an absolute disaster," murmured Rizzi from Rovigo. And it was true that the water seemed to have emerged from the Apocalypse, and yet you had only to look up to realize that the scene was not as tragic as all that. The fire had only consumed three warehouses. Pillars of black smoke were still rising from the rubble, but the other buildings around the dock were largely intact. Shattered glass, doors off their hinges, but not much more.

Perhaps the fire had been confined to the water, but I had to get a better understanding of what was going on, do things logically, check the site of the explosion in person.

The powder house, in the furthest corner of the Arsenal.

I came ashore just opposite the ruins of the three burned warehouses. To reach the powder store we had to pass all the way through one of them. Thank God it was empty, like all of the structures in that brand-new wing. Work on the galleys had not yet begun; the big merchant ships that were there to be repaired and refitted for the purposes of war rested calmly in a corner of the port.

Suddenly Rizzi pulled me by my jacket against what remained of the wall. Rubble rained from the blackened skeleton of the roof. We quickened our pace.

The powder monkeys were in a state of utter confusion. Tavosanis looked at them grimly and opened up a passage for us through the crowd. We found ourselves on the edge of a blackened crater, all that remained of the storehouse. All around, not so much as a stone, as if the explosion had thrown everything onto the moon. I asked to speak to the head armorer, and they pointed me to the saltpeter mill, now reduced to a pile of rubble.

Teams of dockyard workers were digging among the debris, carrying away rubble, drawing up inventories, trying to decide what could be saved and what had been lost forever. A big quern stone had got stuck upright in the ground. It looked like a wheel about to set off on a solitary journey.

The man I was looking for had a terrified expression on his face, a child woken by nightmares. "Signor De Zante, have you seen? A ruin. I'd said to myself, and you know it, too, and I've been saying it these thirty years or more, you can't make powder where you make ships. Now that at last the Senate has listened to me, the storehouses are ready on the islands. Look, over there. Luckily, half of the boats left yesterday."

He was scared, and the stream of his words couldn't hide it. He knew I was there to provide answers for the Republic, and he knew that the easiest way would be to accuse him of negligence.

"Calm down. I want to know what happened."

He spread his arms. "I don't know what to say. My men are all careful; I do the rounds of the Arsenal five times a day and everything's been fine for months."

"That's great, but you haven't answered my question. I want to know how the fire has spread."

He gestured beyond the wall, toward San Francesco. "Last night's wind drove the fire outside. The Celestia Monastery is ruined, and the houses all around it were destroyed. We had one only man dead here, a guard. Over there, though . . ."

"Boss, boss!" A dockyard worker was waving his arms around a few yards away. "Look what we've found!"

We joined him, already surrounded by an excited crowd. The name of Giuseppe Nasi ran from mouth to mouth, from lips twisted into grimaces of disgust, and on faces expressions of alarm appeared. Giuseppe Nasi, the Swine of Judah, La Serenissima's greatest enemy.

"It is no accident! The Turkish dog is waging war on us!"

We made our way to the front, Tavosanis just behind me, Rizzi to my left.

On the floor, in the middle of the circle of legs, were two black stains as big as the palm of a hand. The boy who had summoned us pointed to them with a beaming smile.

"Pitch, boss. It's pitch!"

I leaned forward and touched it, then sniffed my fingertip. Pitch, no doubt about it. Pitch in a powder store. Like stoat-shit in a chicken coop.

"What a spectacle!" Rizzi muttered between his teeth as Tavosanis pushed the boat toward the foundries. "You don't need pitch to set fire to a store of saltpeter. It only takes a spark."

"Right" I agreed. "And the motive for all this?"

He started counting on his fingers. One. "If it's pitch, there's someone involved." Two. "If someone's involved, it's not an accident." Three. "If it's not an accident, then they're not to blame for anything."

Well done, Rizzi, a good observation. But I still wasn't convinced.

"Tell me, what makes you think it was an accident?"

He pointed to the big chimney pots of the foundries—the area we were about to visit. "If the Turks wanted to damage us, they'd have started their fire somewhere more central."

"There's not just the Turks in this world."

"Thank God. But what I say about them applies to anyone: If I wanted to destroy the Arsenal, I'd strike at its heart, not its heel."

I nodded. "And you certainly wouldn't wait until half the barrels of powder had been taken somewhere else. Or choose a stormy night, so that the wind would carry the flames outside."

Tavosanis lifted the oars and took a breath, staring straight into my eyes. "Only chance is as precise as that."

"Chance, certainly." I lowered a hand into the water, as if the sea might give me a clue. "Or an enemy other than the Turks. An enemy who doesn't want to do too much damage."

3.

As I had expected, the foundries were unscathed, since they were far away from the site of the explosion. The first and second workshops were still bolted shut. Tavosanis and Rizzi slipped into the *calle* between one and the other and checked the perimeter.

The third door was wide open. A sound of hammering came from within. I stepped into the doorway and walked forward slowly, checking the various departments. In the carpenters' area there wasn't a tool out of place. The tree trunks that had already been shaped were divided according to caliber and type, in the usual meticulous stacks. Farther along, where the pressing was done, a certain chaos was only to be expected. Bags of lime, ox hair, wax presses for relief decorations: Everything was scattered around big tables or piled up at random in corners. The foul stench of tallow oil emerged from jars that had been left open. Only the clay shells were set down carefully, ready to receive the molten bronze. On the other side, the piercing frames were silent and no one turned the lathe, the wheels of the augers, the bow-drills for punching touch-holes.

The racks for the finished weapons seemed unmanned too, but again a metallic sound reached my ears.

My call of "Who's there?" received a faint reply a moment later, and a gray head appeared from behind a long, slender cannon. It was Varadian, the Armenian artilleryman who worked on prototypes. I was about to ask the man if he'd noticed anything when he suddenly spoke first: "Signor De Zante, it's a good thing you've shown up, you at least."

He looked shattered. The room was cold and the kilns were unlit, but his forehead was pearled with sweat.

"What's troubling you?"

He opened his eyes wide, as if a ghost had appeared behind me. I had to force myself not to turn round and check. "The Turks. Trust me, I've worked for them. This fire is just the start of it; they're going to attack us again. I know the architect Savorgnan is reinforcing the defenses at the entrance to the lagoon. Fair enough, a good precaution, but take a look, look around. There isn't anyone here yet this morning, no guards or workmen. The treasure that interests our enemies most is here, but no one's protecting it apart from me, and I deserve more protection than the others."

"What did the workers do?"

"They spent the night putting out the fire, they got a pay raise, and now they're resting on their laurels."

I tried to assume a reassuring tone. Varadian knew how much the Mohammedans hated renegades. He had been an engineer in Constantinople for years, before coming over to us. He had become a Christian because the Republic allowed him to work, financing his experiments into cannon recoil. In contrast, the Turkish vizier of war had considered them pointless and unworthy of attention. The Ottomans wanted only one thing from a fiery mouth: that it should be big, gigantic, colossal. They wanted the wide-open jaws of the Devil, bombards spitting out the whole of hell and making the world shake. Why worry about the recoil?

"I'll talk to the chief guard, Signor Varadian. Meanwhile I'll have someone sent over, right away, and I'll see to it that you and your work are given double protection. But don't worry—I have a feeling the Turks haven't got much to do with this business."

He gripped my hand between his own, and his voice dripped with gratitude. "Thank you, Signor De Zante. And trust me, I know them well: This is their work."

It was evening when we got back to the palace. Some of my men, keen to demonstrate their zeal and ruthlessness, had already got things started. They had assembled a handful of seditious wretches, people used to singing songs against the Doge and the noblemen: con men, provocateurs.

On the wheel, one arsenal worker had confessed to be Giuseppe Nasi and the son of the Devil. A blacksmith from Chioggia had sworn himself blind that he had always been a Turk, a janissary and friend of the Kapudan Pasha, who had personally issued the order to start the fire. A woodcutter from who knows where had started talking a language entirely his own, saying that it was the language of the Turks of Asia Minor, adding a few words in Latin that he had picked up from the Mass.

Spilled blood and the stench of excrement. Torture is pointless when you're looking for the truth. And in any case I was soon disgusted with it.

I made them stop. The foreman had given me a list of hotheads and discontented arsenal workers. I asked Rizzi to check if any of them were among the ones arrested in our absence. There were a few.

I ordered Tavosanis to start on the first one.

Usually I waited at least half an hour before coming into the room. Meanwhile Tavosanis asked general questions and got to work with his fists. This time I was more impatient: I had to end the day with a result, something to give the Consigliere.

The man's head was hanging over his chest. He was tied to the chair; he seemed to be still conscious. Tavosanis came over and whispered in my ear what he had managed to get out of him. Now it was my turn.

"What's that song you were singing at the inn a few evenings ago? 'Come, Turk, free us from our masters . . .' That was it, wasn't it?"

Silence. Tavosanis looked at me. I gestured to him to wait. "We know what you were singing; we know who you were singing with. We know what you ate, what you drank, when you got up to go for a piss. We know everything."

The man pleaded, "What do you want from me?"

I slowly circled the chair. The wolf isolating his prey.

"It'd be a good idea to speak now. Think of the magistrate. Think of the wheel. You'll miss this chair and my mate's knuckles." Tavosanis drew back his arm and hit the man in the jaw. "We know your friend Battiston kept saying 'I know a way of getting them to up our pay.' Isn't that right?"

"I was plastered. I don't remember a thing."

He didn't remember a thing, and yet he was crying. He was about to give up and he felt guilty for his friend.

"And in fact it looks as if you're going to get your pay raise, doesn't it? As a reward for putting out the fire."

He said nothing. I stopped in front of him. I lifted his chin. His expression was blank; the hatred had fled. He would tell the truth.

4.

The Consigliere's palazzo overlooked the Grand Canal, but shadows like me came by the land route. The waterside entrance was for the aristocrats. I'd only come in on that side once, with my father. A silk carpet guided our steps across the bridge to the marble sirens guarding the front door. I was to introduce myself to the head of the household. An audience with the pope himself would not have stirred me as much.

Some days later they showed me the back entrance, and from then on that was the only one I used: across the big garden, invisible from the street and protected by high walls. In the middle, the fountain and the stone angel, wings outspread, that never ceased to unsettle me. His face and body were tense, raptorial, as if he were about to take flight and seize his prey. One day I had pointed this out to my lord, and he had put it down to bad conscience, to my sinful soul.

Today, a servant walked with me into the palazzo, up to the threshold of the main hall. He knocked and ushered me in.

The Consigliere was standing by the window. He seemed to be observing the clouds reflected in the lagoon, but perhaps his eyes saw something entirely different. His soul was labyrinthine, his mind impenetrable. I looked at his tall, slender form, wrapped in a long robe that fell to his ankles; his black hair, sprinkled with gray; his back, still straight.

He beckoned me in. I already knew where to go and sit, and I knew that he would ask his first questions from a standing position, to dwarf me.

"You have a determined gait this morning." He stared at me, as if he were still trying to recognize me. "How do your inquiries progress?"

"We've questioned twenty-three suspects." I paused, to stress the number. "Most of them gave irrelevant statements, but two of the arsenal workers have confessed names and details that are extremely interesting."

"I am glad, De Zante. Just leave out the details. I know how scrupulous you are."

A long breath. The Consigliere didn't like excessive passion. I had to set out my conjectures coldly, as if referring to someone else's thoughts. "The caulkers have been asking for a pay raise for months. Some of them thought starting a fire and intervening to put it out again might be the best way to get one."

He bit the inside of his lip, a sign that he was displeased with this information. I had to find out why. "And these 'some,' how many might that be?"

"I couldn't yet say, Excellency. We have precise accusations against one

Erio Battiston. We've been looking for him since yesterday morning; he is said to be the man responsible for coming up with the plan. As to those who carried it out, we do not yet have sufficient evidence."

He started drumming impatiently on the wood with his fingers. I couldn't work out what was bothering him so.

"I will tell my men to put every effort into capturing Battiston, and . . ."

"Do you really imagine," he cut in, raising his voice slightly, "that a discontented arsenal worker could hatch a plot of this kind? Come on, De Zante. You're doing your own intelligence a disservice."

A shiver ran down my spine. I tried to follow my instinct and took some time to put my words in order. Impulsiveness leads inevitably to ruin. "Permit me to express myself better, your Excellence. Various clues suggest a provocation that got out of hand. The men carrying out the plan had apparently taken care to avoid . . ."

"Care?" This time he allowed me an enigmatic smile. "Our job is not to grant extenuating circumstances to the guilty men." He slumped onto his chair, emphatically, to show me how wearying he found my stupidity. Then he rearranged the pieces of paper on his desk, as if he needed to calm himself by performing a meticulous task.

"Listen, De Zante." he said, looking up. His voice had changed; he sounded as if he were about to have a man-to-man chat with me. "I know your zeal. I can imagine the determination with which you gathered this information. But that's exactly the problem: You are examining things so closely that you lose the vision of the whole, which all of Venice, apart from you, has seen from the very first."

I felt the muscles in my neck twisting like the strands of a cable.

"Let's admit that the workers have something to do with it, and they stand to gain financially. Would you agree to bring Venice to its knees for a few ducats? Would you risk your life for an extra slice of bread to dip in your soup? No, of course not, you'd want a higher prize. And who could offer you that?"

Now I could see what he was getting at. I said, "We've arrested various Turkish spies over the past few weeks. We've made them talk, and there was no inkling of anything like . . ."

"It's not the street spies you should be looking at, De Zante. We won't hunt down the eel by asking the shrimp. There must be a traitor somewhere higher up, one much more important than an arsenal worker or a mere spy. Someone who can influence, if you like, spies, agitators and Arsenal hotheads. Someone who can act as intermediary between them and Giuseppe Nasi's money."

Nasi. The name on everyone's lips, the people's word made flesh. If I'd written him off, it wasn't out of absentmindedness.

"Do you have any suggestions?"

"Someone high enough up to be able to hatch an attack on the Arsenal.

Someone sufficiently beyond suspicion to be able to do it. Someone holding a major post, but not necessarily a patrician. Someone with a secret, and therefore vulnerable to blackmail by the Turk. If possible, someone not Venetian by birth. I trust you, De Zante. Find a name appropriate to the task, and the Republic will derive greater glory even from this outrage."

"I understand." I tried to remain impassive. "The perfect culprit."

The Consigliere nodded agreement, then rose to his feet and, as if nothing had happened, returned to studying the gray vault of the clouds.

I reached the door. I knew he was listening to my footsteps on the floor, but however much I tried, I couldn't keep them sounding as confident as they had on the way in.

5.

I wandered aimlessly, in the places of the city I thought of as home, wherever my legs might take me. I thought of the people I would have to make pay, first with pain, then with their lives. I wondered about the meaning of the Consigliere's words, winnowing names and faces. I was determined not to disappoint him: No one would ever want to disappoint Bartolomeo Nordio. However, I had no name that matched the characteristics of the perfect culprit as they had just been outlined to me.

I set off, heading down the Ruga Rialto and cutting through the *calli*, impelled by the gravity of my thoughts. On the Riva del Vin I stopped to look at the canal, the boats, the chaos of people, and to listen to the voices. I had to solve the riddle. I had to come up with a name. As I walked, I realized that my feet were taking me in a precise direction. Arianna, like her namesake, had unspooled her invisible thread, and I, half unaware, had followed it.

I found myself in Calle del Paradiso, outside a door that I knew very well. I knocked until the maid opened up. She saw me, nodded in greeting and climbed the stairs. She was going to announce my presence to her mistress.

Arianna welcomed me with an expression of faint surprise. The smile on her freckled face was cheerful. "I wasn't expecting you. But your visit fills me with joy." She surveyed me from head to toe. "You look glum. What's up?"

"The whole of Venice knows what's up. But I will tell you afterward."

I wasn't the best of lovers that day. Too hasty, too brutal. I drank from her lips like a man parched by the August sun. I pounced on her full, heavy breasts like a hungry man on loaves of bread. I agitated her hips like a drunk shaking a bottle to get at the last drop.

My courtesan, besides, wasn't the best in the universe just then. Perhaps, I thought, she could sense my unease.

As God willed, the embrace came to an end.

"Now tell me what's wrong."

I looked at the woman. She was the most beautiful creature I had ever seen. Blonde, curly hair; dark, shining eyes. She had been one of the best-known courtesans in Venice before she became mine alone. For some years I had been the only one who paid for her services. My condition prevented me from visiting brothels, where rumors spread like wildfire. Arianna kept me out of trouble.

"I have to find a culprit for the fire at the Arsenal. Someone up to the job. It's irrelevant whether he really organized or committed the crime."

"A scapegoat," she said.

"Exactly."

"We're often called to do things we don't want to do," she said, or at least I thought she did. I was barely listening to her, thinking out loud.

"I need a perfect culprit to feed to the people of Venice. Consigliere Nordio is thinking of a man with a double life, because he says the man has to be beyond suspicion."

I closed my eyes and took a deep breath. I turned my boss's words around in my head, trying to enter them from all sides, to grasp their every implication.

Beyond suspicion.

Someone with a sufficiently elevated position.

Someone with a secret, an impostor.

I felt the warmth of my lover close to me.

Beyond suspicion.

I looked at Arianna. She smiled, uncertainly. Furtively, swiftly, she checked the door. It just took a moment. I looked down.

A secret.

My flaccid penis dangling to one side.

An impostor.

A penis without a foreskin.

A Jew.

A wave of horror ran through me. I suddenly turned to Arianna: she had hidden her face with her arms. I leaped to my feet and ran to the window that faced the *calle*. I glanced through the crack between the shutters.

Five guards were waiting outside the front door. I recognized two of them. My most trusted men. Gualberto Rizzi and Marco Tavosanis.

They owed everything to me. So, they were the most likely to want to get me. Men hate their benefactors. Do somebody a favor and nine times out of ten you'll make an implacable enemy.

My lover had withdrawn to the end of the bed and covered herself with the sheet. Fear assumed the garb of modesty. Her eyes were moist. "They forced me—they did, Emanuele. Against my very will." My lover, the only person I trusted, had sold the secret of my origins. Strip down Emanuele and you will find *Manuel*, the Jewish boy from Ragusa across the Adriatic.

They needed a culprit for the storm *et tulerunt me*, the Jew, the impostor, the liar, *et stabit Venetia a fervore suo*.

Hurry downstairs, confront the bastards in plain view. Counting on surprise and on my dagger, I could overpower two or three men, but not all of them.

Flight isn't running full tilt with other people after you. Flight is disappearance.

Arianna came a few feet toward me, letting the sheet fall. Her face was anxious, but resolute. "They won't get you if you do as I say. There's a passage-way that leads to the house next door, which is uninhabited. From there you can escape through the back way."

For a moment I stood firmly on the spot. Then I got moving.

6.

God had shown me at least a hint of compassion, in that I escaped the hands of Rizzi and Tavosanis. Hands that had acted at my command and now wanted to take my freedom and my life. Hands that were the fist and the claws of the inquisitor, as I had been the eyes, ears, and tongue on the cobbles and the water of Venice.

The sky was dark, the wind was coming in from the northeast and the summer was being carried away. I walked along the *calli* that I would no longer call home. As a piece of gravel forms a cyst under your skin after a nasty fall, and can only be removed with an incision, and the stone comes out along with blood—so Venice spewed me out.

People were noticing me. I had to stop walking so quickly, stop looking over my shoulder. I was a fugitive, and my body announced as much. Someone pointed at me, but I had already turned the corner, I was running, another corner, yet another, and at last I started walking again, because no one was coming after me. I had to keep a clear head and think.

I couldn't go back to my house. Without a doubt, they would be keeping an eye on it. No, I had to disappear very quickly. There wasn't much money in my pocket, just enough to leave the city, but I had a substantial sum at the Braun Bank, at the Fondaco dei Tedeschi. It was money set aside for a rainy day, and the rainy day had arrived. I had entrusted it to a German banker to keep it far from prying eyes.

I quickened my pace again and headed for the Rialto. The need to move toward the interior of the city did battle with my instinct to reach the sea, a boat, safety. I forced myself to stay calm, as cold as I was when I questioned suspects. I took a course through the less busy *calli*, and when I emerged near the Fondaco I waited for a few minutes before edging toward the front door of the building with my back to the wall. A few cautious steps and I froze again. Something was holding me back—a sensation, a premonition based on my years of experience in the field. How many times had I trailed a spy or a troublemaker? I flattened myself into a doorway, covered by the bustle of carts and porters. Amid the ceaseless movement of goods, the eye could spot immobility.

The first of them was standing in the corner of a *calle*, leaning against the wall. He was looking around very slowly, observing everyone who passed in front of him.

The second was right beside the entrance. A dark cape fell from his shoulders and covered him entirely, hiding possible weapons.

There was also a third. There's always a third. I hadn't noticed him imme-
diately because he was just a few feet away from me. He was checking the
length of street separating me from the front door.

I waited for him to turn his head in the other direction, then slipped from
my hiding place and turned back, into the dark innards of Venice, away, far
from the death that lay in wait for me, away, feet flying on the cobbles, free to
obey my instinct to flee.

A gold chain with a medal hung on my chest. A gift from my father: on
one side the Holy Cross, on the other the Lion of Saint Mark, with its book
closed and sword unsheathed. The war banner of the fleet.

War. The Republic had declared war on Emanuele De Zante, its faithful
servant.

Betrayed servant. Treacherous servant. Fugitive.

I could convert the medal into small change, wherever fate happened to
take me.

The most important thing was to flee. I would think of everything else
afterward.

I reached a jetty and bargained briefly, letting the gondolier have more
money than he expected. The gondola moved, while music from strolling
players drifted across from the land. We slipped around the long loop of the
Grand Canal into a leaden afternoon, harbinger of autumn. The ceaseless
activity that animated the city hadn't yet subsided. Boats plowed the water;
men busied themselves on the shore.

Nostalgia, regret and rage pressed my heart, gripped my throat and tied
my guts in a knot. The *palazzi* slipped past, half hidden in the darkness.
Rather than making them out clearly, I was merely aware of their massive
presence. Memory filled the gaps that the eye couldn't pierce. Every image
that appeared in my mind carved a furrow in my soul. The notes that had
greeted my departure rang out still.

So it was that I abandoned Venice, sure that I would never see her again.

7.

"*Ti volir cunciar partida, Tuota?*"

Those were the words, after days of rough silence spent in a corner of the world where the Po, as if drunk, twists and snakes before hurling itself into the sea. I accompanied them with a twisted smile on my weary, muddy face, my right hand seeming to ask for alms but in reality showing the dice—the things least expected in the middle of a bog. I'd fashioned them from the wood of a dead poplar tree, carving in the numbers with the tip of my knife: I, II, III, IV, V and VI. No more than a joke, a trinket, my notion of a comical greeting to the man I might meet. The man who had been like a father to me.

"You want to play, Tuota?" You want to play these dice with me? Fate, who carried me in the palm of her hand yesterday, now thwarts me, grips and squeezes me like a rotten apple. All of a sudden, I, a Venetian gentleman, find myself once more a fugitive Jew, and accused of betraying the Republic. My feet are in the mud and the phrase whirls around in my head. "*Ti volir cunciar partida, Tuota?* You want to play?"

Just like that, in the bastard language that foreigners used in every port on the Mediterranean from Genoa to Tripoli, from Smyrna to Gibraltar. The lingua franca of corsairs, merchants, smugglers; the language of every illicit trade, even here, among the reeds, to the hoots of the owls, on an island in the Po. In that marshland the river goes mad, on that last mile it touches the apex of desire, yearning to be extinguished in the great gulf's embrace. It loses its senses and loses itself in labyrinths, mad hybrids of land and water.

There, in a tumbledown shack, I had hidden after leaving Venice. I was as crazy as the river, and no less confused, but I knew that sooner or later a boat would come, and on that boat there would be outlaws.

I knew, because for a while I'd been with them. I'd been *one* of them.

And here I was, with those rough dice in my hand, in front of me the boat, a *batana*, and on that *batana* was Tuota. The moon lit it up to let me look at him, and he, too, looked at me.

"You're a mighty brave man to show your face here, in this place, in this way," the *vegliotto* said in his language. "I barely recognized you. You only just escaped dying like a dog."

He certainly couldn't have forgiven me, and the surprise, my appearance, my little joke, everything seemed likely to rake up old grudges.

"I'm a fugitive, Tuota. Venice wants me dead."

Tuone Jurman shook his head, as he did when I erred on the side of naïveté

as a little boy. Age didn't seem to have left its mark on his face, apart from his beard, now gray. Tuone Jurman. Tuota.

I wanted to tell him about the years when we had been apart, and about what had happened to me a few days before. Tell him about my secret life, my shady responsibilities.

Perhaps, at first, he would have listened to me while pretending to do something else: peer through the reeds, look for lights along the shore, mutter orders to the two men who were assisting him. I didn't know either of them; they were very young. Then, when I went into details about my second life—or was it my third?—who knows what the old smuggler might have done? Perhaps he would have thrown me into the water, after first cutting my throat with his fish knife. Or perhaps not. Perhaps he would have humiliated me with serious, silent contempt.

I told him nothing, and he asked no questions. He didn't ask why I wanted to go back to Ragusa, of all places—a city of memories and spies, of streets where eyes and ears might recognize me and of inns where mouths might give me away. I, on the other hand, had asked myself, during my days of solitude, Why Ragusa, still so close to the jaws of the lion?

The answer was him: Tuone Jurman.

My mother had arranged for me to be brought up as a good Jewish boy, faithful to the Torah, but things hadn't worked out that way. Even as a boy, I had preferred the port to the rabbi's school, and the coarse conversation of the dockers to the boredom of the *midrashim*. It was there that I had met Tuota, the only one who could make me feel like a man before I felt like a Jew. I had soon set out to work with him, sailing for the islands off the Dalmatian coast. Little deals, smuggling, and every now and again we had gone as far as the opposite coast, invisible landing posts between Venice and Ferrara, taking on board and ferrying across the sea someone who planned to deny Christ, or who had already denied him, and was going to the empire of the Turks in search of adventure. And besides, was it not on the shores of the Po that Heracles had asked the nymphs where the trees with golden fruit grew? In our own century, Muslim nymphs replied by pointing beyond the estuary, toward the great Orient. They spoke of caliphs and sultans more wealthy and liberal than the Italian noblemen. Artillerymen, doctors, sailors, weavers: Those who allowed themselves to be persuaded turned to people like us, and from Dalmatia the journey continued, southward or eastward.

I had dedicated myself to that trade, with Tuota and his colleagues, until my father had come back to the city—my real father, first by semen and then by surname, and my life had changed for ever. And now I was back with Tuone Jurman. The man who felt I had betrayed him, when I had never done any such thing.

In the years of service that I had given to the Republic, I had never said or done anything to stop the trafficking I myself had done as a young man. And now I needed him; I was the one who was fleeing, with a burned bridge, a

burned arsenal, in fact, behind me, and now I could make the journey in one direction only. Tuota would keep on going back and forth, back and forth, for who knows how long. I would just have to go, and that would be that, never to return.

We sat in silence, amid grim glances, tight jaws and the occasional snort, somewhere between impatience and resignation, that meant "Look what's happened to me this time."

Tuone Jurman. Who else could take me beyond the sea and allow me to start a new life elsewhere? We left the estuary, the Adriatic received us, and for a time the former ferryman became the ferried.

A short time afterward, we reached the *schierazzo*. The square sail, just as I remembered it.

As I climbed the rope ladder along the keel, I felt a twinge that made me falter. So many times, in that other life of mine, I had performed these motions. Now I didn't know how to go on. Tuota was below me. He became aware of my confusion and touched my calf. You won't fall, those fingers said.

So it was that I found myself at my point of departure. I was going back to Ragusa, Dobro Venedik, the Good Venice, as the Turks called it, mispronouncing the Slavic name, to distinguish it from the Bad Venice on the other side of the sea. A *porto franco*, neither Eastern nor Western, a midway city where everyone moored sooner or later, some in search of shelter from the storm, some chasing business deals, some pursued by their own destiny.

I sighted it in front of me several days later, at sunset, trapped within its fortresses that were like a clenched fist: Dubrovnik. From a distance, as we approached, I tried to understand what I was feeling. As I approached, I was moving away. Fleeing, I was coming home.

In my jacket pocket my fingers fiddled with the dice.

8.

I climbed the wooden ladder, and this time Tuota went ahead of me. The trap door led to the roof space of the old warehouse. As the stench of mold reached me from above, I hoisted myself toward the opening.

In the corner I recognized the straw mattress, the bowl, the worm-eaten table. It was there that we used to wait for the right time of night to go to sea. I remembered the first evening, my heart in my mouth, the feeling of expectation that devoured me, and Tuota telling me to get up and follow him. That was what I had done for years, and when I had chosen another destiny for myself, I hadn't been able to keep a scrap of my soul from being trapped there.

I had come back. I thought of my house in Venice, where I had lived at ease and in prosperity, and I smiled contemptuously. Tuota noticed and gave me a wry look.

"You know the place," he grunted. "If I were you I wouldn't show my face in these parts." He looked around and added, "I'll fetch you something to eat." He looked as if he were about to go downstairs.

"Tuota . . ."

He stopped, and for a moment I said nothing, looking at his sunburned face. He was still as powerful as I remembered, like a mooring post. I wanted to hug him as I never had when I was a little boy, to feel his muscles, the protective hardness of his belly.

I took the medal from around my neck and handed it to him. The medal with the warlike symbol of Venice. Intent as I was on hiding the truth from him, I wanted to buy the right to his help.

Tuota looked at the precious object, turned it around in his hand and then, without even raising his eyes, he handed it back to me. He disappeared through the trap door, which closed over his head. I heard the squeak of the rungs and the fading footsteps.

I went and stood by the only source of light, the little skylight in the roof. Ragusa was a clutch of fire-red tiles and white stone, between the green of the mountain and the green of the sea. When I was a boy, I had watched the ships coming into port through that opening. How many times, in the clear May days, had I daydreamed, looking for the outline of the Gargano. And how many nights had I spent admiring the constellations.

Many years before, one summer day, I had run to the port. I was shouting, "Tuota, Tuota," because I had learned to throw a knife and wanted him to see me. Some of the sailors standing around thought that "Tuota" was a

mispronunciation, my way of saying "Tuone," or Ante, Toni, Antumi, Antal. Everyone liked the sound of the name, and from that point on they started using it all the time, although the Dalmatians knew that *tuota* is a word from the island of Veglia and means the same as *baba* in Turkish, *tata* in Croatian, *pare* in Venetian and *papa* in Ladino, the Jewish dialect. That was what I had started calling him, *papa*, in the language of my mother and the Jews of Spain, but he had told me he didn't like the word, because "*il Papa*" is the king of all the priests and he didn't like kings or priests. So he had given me permission to call him Tuota, as he had called his father, and I, who was eight years old and didn't know who my father was, didn't need to hear him say it twice. At the port everyone knew that Tuone Jurman had no children, that he wasn't married, and, as I knew, the idea that someone might call him Father even made them laugh. So the nickname became official, and to close the circle they started calling me *el Feil*, and the dog that was always near me in those days was rechristened *Spirit Sant*. A fine paradox, for a little Jewish boy.

I lay down on the mattress, my mind caught somewhere between my memories and the uncertain present. I looked at the walls around me, the ruined objects. It took me a long time to get to sleep, and I entertained myself by throwing dice, playing against myself, losing even when I won.

I was wakened by the sound of the trap door opening. I instinctively brought my hand to my stiletto, under my cape. I didn't know what time it was, but the light outside the window was intense.

Tuota's gray head emerged from the floor, followed by the rest of his body. He was carrying a bag over his shoulder, and from it he took a bundle. Bread, sardines and a canteen full of water.

"I was hoping you'd offer me some of your grappa."

"It isn't that cold yet, and you don't need it."

There was no room for discussion with Tuota; age hadn't softened him. We sat in silence, chewing our food. He was the first to speak.

"You haven't told me where you plan to go."

"Because I don't know yet. Anywhere I can stay alive. Far from Venice, that much is certain."

"I'm trying to find a boat for you, but it's going to take a few days. You'll have to be very careful in your movements if the Venetians really are looking for you. You're hiding in their backyard."

I couldn't help provoking him: "When I left, the word *freedom* was written on the banners of Ragusa. The Sultan's still guaranteeing you protection."

Tuota hissed between his teeth. "Freedom. The more they write it on their shields the less they want it. I come from a line of pirates that has never bowed to anyone. My ancestors were enemies of Julius Caesar. The aristocrats of this city are as despotic as your Venetian friends; they're just a bit smaller."

"Age is making you bitter, Tuota. You used to be proud of the independence of Ragusa. You were the one who brought me to the castle of San

Lorenzo to read the motto carved above the door. Do you remember? It says Freedom isn't sold for all the gold in the world."

"And you've learned it off by heart to spit on it."

I couldn't hold my tongue. "You've never learned to see things from above sea level, have you, Tuota? Do you think Venice doesn't fight for its freedom? It's a little republic squashed between giants that would like to bend it to their will. On the one hand there's the Great Turk, on the other the Holy Roman Empire, and then the Church of Rome, which is hatching every imaginable plot to impose its power on the city. And yet Venice resists. In freedom."

"Then you could have stayed there," he said, and his words were like a tombstone. I was a fugitive, my old homeland wanted me dead, and yet my tongue went on defending it.

"I'll help you," Tuota went on, "but I don't want to know anything about what's happened to you, or about what you've done for the Venetians." He got up. "I'm setting off at dawn tomorrow. Over the next few days a woman called Dinka will bring you something to eat. If I were you, I would hole up here for a while. If you really can't resist the temptation to go down, remember to leave your dagger behind. In these parts they don't deal kindly with Jews who walk around the place carrying weapons."

He must have noticed the stiletto under my cape. His eyesight was still sharp.

"I'm not a Jew anymore."

He shook his head. "We aren't in Venice here. Lots of people remember Manuel, son of Sarah. That's enough."

9.

Very soon, boredom came to dominate my days. Time passed slowly and languidly, minute by minute, hour after hour. The next day, Dinka, an old woman who didn't waste her words, climbed up to bring me some food and empty the pot. She made me take off my Venetian clothes and replaced them with a pair of torn trousers and a jacket that had once belonged to who knows who. The signs of my previous life slipped away and I assumed a new appearance. I looked at my reflection in the glass of the jug, my beard longer than before, and prickly, my face pale, my eye vague. A different man. Flight was a chrysalis, but the caterpillar didn't turn into a butterfly, just a different caterpillar.

In that room I had nothing to do but look down upon the city of my birth, for ages, until it burned my eyes. The busy coming and going of ships was accompanied by shouts from longshoremen and the barking of dogs. The wind stirred the laundry that hung from the windows; the gusts struck the sheets, making them crack like gunfire. Observing and deducing were part of my job. I imagined those people's lives. On that white linen men and women had slept, the old and the sick had died, children had come into the world.

Inevitably, I ended up thinking of my mother, her black eyes, the old Spanish lullabies she sang to put me to sleep. From there my memory slipped as if in a puddle of grease, and I found myself in a November dawn, in the bed of my childhood, woken without patience or affection by the shrill voice of Old Abecassi.

Once again, everything exactly the same as before. She throws open the door and drags me from sleep, always with the same stupid phrase on her lips, one of the many Sephardic proverbs that I have learned to hate.

"Wake up! If you want to marry a *moza*, don't wait till you're old."

I give a start that shatters my beautiful dreams, try to grasp the tail end of them lest I forget them, but they vanish in a flash. By the time I've washed my face, there's nothing left of them. It's dark outside, the water is cold, my heart is thumping in my throat. I'm just seven years old.

Proverbs. Even on the point of death, as she entrusted me to Abecassi, my mother told me one with her very last breath.

"*Ke darse mi ijo, ke seyga en Teshabeav.*"

May my son preach in the temple, even if it's for *Tisha b'Av*, the Day of Conflict. Even in these dire circumstances, make sure my son grows up as a good Jew, in the observance of our rules, at the rabbi's school. So I, who until

that moment lived close to the port, have been moved to the ghetto, to Jew Street, to the house of an old witch, a friend of my grandmother's since the days of Spain—or so she says, although it's impossible. When they left Toledo, my grandmother was still in swaddling clothes.

The Cardosos had fled from Spain in 1492. Wife and husband, Aganbena and Baltazar, with a newborn daughter, Raquel, who would be my grandmother. The exact date had been etched in my mind, because Sarah did nothing but repeat it: the fifteenth day of Adar, 5252, the day after Purim.

On their way eastward, the Cardosos stopped in Ragusa, where a little community of Jews was starting to form. They never left. Baltazar began dealing in wool and fabrics. Their daughter was impregnated by the shop boy, a Romaniot Jew who died of bad blood even before the birth of her daughter, my mother, Sarah. It was 1515. Sarah was born, and was given the surname of her mother and grandfather.

Sarah's life, by a quirk of fate, began with an exile. That year the Jews were expelled from Ragusa, all of them, apart from the ones who had converted to the Holy Roman Church, or who let it be known that they had. The Cardosos moved to Spalato. By the time the Jews were able to return to the Good Venice, Sarah was seventeen and carrying a child. No one knew who the father was, and the child was born dead anyway. The big sister I never had.

Five years later it was my turn, another child of an unknown father. I was born alive and stayed that way. The surname of Baltazar, Raquel and Sarah became mine too. They called me Manuel.

In the evening, Tuota came looking for me in my attic refuge. I was middoze, and the sound of the trap door closing made me jump, my hand reaching for my stiletto. Tuota threw down his own so that it stuck in the floor. The thump shook the last residues of sleep from me.

"The difference between the sleep of the just and the sleep of the idiot is that the idiot doesn't wake up." The voice was the scrape of a ship's hull on rocks, but his mood was jollier. He clearly had good news.

I muttered something. I thought this rude awakening was worthy of Old Abecassi, but I wasn't a little boy anymore. I was a condemned man on the run. I got up, went over to the washbasin and tipped the jug of water over my head. When I took the towel off my face, Tuone Jurman was leaning against the table, arms folded.

"In Venice I was rich," I said. "I had a servant, and lived in a beautiful house."

"I told you before, I don't want to know what you've done. I'm not getting involved; don't tell me anything."

I rubbed my eyes. I didn't want to talk. A sea and ten years had interposed themselves between us, and I couldn't fill that distance.

"You'll be leaving soon. A ship is sailing for Durrës in a week. I've called in an old favor, and you'll have a place on board. From Durrës you'll be able to

take the Via Egnatia, and stop wherever you feel like it. Maybe in Salonika, where there are lots of your people.

I gave a sort of grunt. "My people? You're hard of hearing; I'm not a Jew anymore."

He gave one of his snorts and smiled. "As you wish. In the meantime, don't champ at the bit too much. Go out as little as possible. Don't look for women, whether alive or dead."

Having said that, he pulled the stiletto from the floor and put it back in his belt.

The Via Egnatia. Across the Balkans, eastward. All the way to Constantinople, if I liked.

I remembered the angel with the severe expression in the Consigliere's courtyard. I imagined it saying, "Clear off."

To spend weeks penetrating the empire I had opposed, whose agents I had had arrested, whose plans I had foiled, whose interests I had thwarted. I had dedicated ten years of my life to that opposition. There was something wrong about my escape plan, something obscene. Venice accused me of serving the Turks, and I was seeking refuge among them. It was like admitting I was a traitor. On the other hand, hadn't I perhaps betrayed them? I had deceived them. I and my father, old De Zante, had kept quiet, had hidden the truth, had erected an edifice of lies. Lies told to the Republic, and above all to the Consigliere. At what point had Nordio started to suspect me, to seek information about me? What could have put him on his guard? And how much truth had he managed to discover? I told myself it was no longer important, but I was lying. I was the umpteenth Venetian I had lied to. The wound was too recent, the suffering flesh still belonged to Venice, and Venice would reclaim it.

Hide out for a week, sit there like a stewing codfish, then board another ship, only to disembark and set off once more on my journey. By what means of transport, in whose company, heading where and living how? And money? I would have to sell the gold medal. I would do that in Durrës. No, I had to do it right away, the next day. Sell it, and later allow myself a glass of *rakia*. Go down, find the right shop, the right person. But not a Jew: There was a risk of them recognizing me. Go to the port, find a buyer among the commercial agents. No, too risky. The port was swarming with guards and informers. A week still lay between me and my journey, more than enough time for them to find out about me, trap me, sell me to Venice. The rumors about the traitor who had burned the Arsenal, the arrest warrant, all of that must have reached as far as Ragusa. That meant leaving immediately! Selling the gold and using part of the money to pay someone with a ship, a boat, to head elsewhere. Yes, and where could I go? I was surrounded by Ottoman lands, Christian Europe had spewed me out, and the Jews were the people I hated. I was nothing now. I was sweating and breathless, and sleep was out of the question.

At dawn I decided to go outside.

10.

The brief slumber of the port was already disturbed by traders and steve-dores. In the taverns that had just reopened, some people were already knock-ing back the first spirits of the day, while the whores sweetened their mouths with wine or mulberry syrup.

I walked past two big ships that were loading fabrics, and turned toward the fishing harbor, where I wouldn't risk meeting Tuota, or guards or inform-ers or Jews, who only hung around the merchant dock.

Piles of cases, full of giltheads and sea bream, obstructed the shore. An old man with only one leg was gutting the carcass of a swordfish. Cats and gulls were taking advantage of the fact to have their breakfast.

I wanted something to drink, but I knew that one wouldn't be enough, and the second would demand a third, then a fourth, and so on until I was left without a penny, or sitting on the floor in a pool of vomit. I tried to distract myself and think, staring at hands and knives cleaning piles of mussels in the seawater.

It was no use. If I stayed there, outside the inns, surrounded by the smells of *rakia* and fish, nothing and no one would save me from drunkenness. I trusted my own legs, and my legs, without much hesitation, led me up an alley squashed between white stone houses and inn signs.

The first stretch was all offices of scribes and brokers. Further up, a young carpenter empted a bucket of sawdust at my feet and apologized in Albanian and Turkish.

"*Me falni! Affedersiniz!*"

I climbed three flights of steps, slippery with moss and salt. Past the church I turned left and through a gap in the wall, up some narrow stairs leading to a wide square terrace. It was the roof of a dye works, crisscrossed with lines where clothes were hung to dry, in a pattern as orderly as a spider's web. I always remembered them full, sometimes with lots of different colors, others with an infinite range of blues, but that morning they were empty. Perhaps the gray sky and the half-risen sun had persuaded the dyers' boys to put off their work. I didn't have to push my way through the fabrics, or hold my breath to keep from inhaling the stench of indigo and pigments. After a few yards I reached the opposite side, facing a green door.

Knives had scraped from the architrave the carving of a seven-branched candelabra and the date: 5256. The mezuzah was still nailed to the right-hand doorpost. New owners had mistaken it for a flower bowl. A bunch of

dry buttercups occupied the place of the parchment with the lines from the
Shema.

The house of the Cardosos, built by Baltazar with the first money he saved.

Honeysuckle climbed on the wall, all the way up to the window of my
room.

The house where I had been born and bred, before moving to the ghetto.

I've just turned seven, I'm old enough to recognize human malevolence, and
I understand Sarah's reputation. No one would ever say it to her face, but
they see her as a woman not to be trusted. That summer day, I stop chasing
lizards, take my courage in both hands and ask her why.

She's sitting beside the front door, laying aubergines out to dry. The air is
still, and droplets of kermes and saffron drip from the fabrics. Her answer
leaves me baffled.

"Because I gave you life."

All I know about my father is what she told me: a sailor, dead at sea a few
months before I was born. A *goy*. A Venetian.

With time, as I grow up, I will understand the suspicion surrounding
Sarah. She fornicated several times with a gentile, perhaps a good-for-
nothing. She got herself pregnant, then was left on her own, without a
husband, without a man by her side—"but with many men around her," the
old women of the ghetto sneered, including the hypocrite Abecassi. Besides,
hadn't she been impregnated by who knows who, years before Manuelito was
born? And basically, isn't she the daughter of who knows who herself? My
mother is a devoted and observant woman, but she's young, beautiful and
alone, and such a combination is unforgivable.

At the age of seven, on this terrace, I don't understand absolutely every-
thing, but I absorb the acrid sap like a plant, a weed grown in a field of sulfur.
So, even though I'm part of them, I start to hate the people of the Torah, from
which my mother would never want to part. Each arm tied to a stout rope, two
teams of mules pulling me in both directions: a child, about to be torn in two.

Shortly afterward, my mother dies and is buried close to my grandmother,
in the Jewish cemetery just outside the walls.

Beyond the steeples of the city, the sun rose amidst the clouds, accompanied
by a flight of storks. I walked on among the white stones, my eyes low, read-
ing the inscriptions. I couldn't remember the exact spot. I'd been there several
times before, always dragged along by adults, in a ritual that had struck me as
macabre and empty.

There's nothing important about a grave, and hers was all I had left of her.
I would have preferred a thousand times more one of the yellow kerchiefs
she'd worn on her head, to plunge my face into it and smell once more the
perfume of her hair. But Sarah's few belongings had been sold, down to the
last scrap, apart from a little ring that Abecassi had kept for herself.

I looked up at the ghost of the moon and spotted a magpie among the yellow leaves of a lime tree.

You wanted to turn me into a good Jew, so that I would live in the ghetto, among the people who blamed you for having given birth to me. Today my feeling is not very different from theirs. I despise the life you gave me.

Ragusa is full of converted Jews, who pray in the cathedral on Sunday and recite the *Shema* every evening in their bedrooms. They are rich brokers, merchants; they frequent the noble palaces and recite the great Italian and Croatian poets by heart. I could have become one of them. And instead?

Grandmother Raquel wanted you to be a good Jew, and you weren't, whore of the gentiles. And yet you wanted the same thing for me. Guess what? I couldn't do it either.

I denied you. I denied Tuota. I betrayed Consigliere Nordio and was myself betrayed.

Recantation and betrayal: Those are my real parents, the only ones I have never renounced.

I stared at the gravestones with a shiver and regretted that Manuel Cardoso wasn't there too, buried in that ground, along with all the lies that had populated his life. The lies of Sarah, the lies of Old Abecassi, the lies of Emanuele and Gioanbattista De Zante.

My mother's last words, now that I thought about it, might have been another trick. That stupid old woman had reported them to me, and I had believed her. Perhaps Sarah hadn't actually wanted me to become a good Jew, and had asked instead that I be baptized a Christian.

Everything was possible, in the darkness that surrounded me, and I was nothing.

For that very reason, I had never hesitated to turn my back on myself. There was nothing true in me to turn it on.

11.

Old Abecassi is superstitious.

Almost a year has passed since my mother's death, a year wasted coming and going between the old woman's house and the temple, house and temple, house and temple, Abecassi and rabbi, Abecassi and her hag friends. Only every now and then a trip out of the ghetto, to the port, where I can breathe.

My rages are more and more frequent: I kick chairs over, I hurt myself by banging my head against a wall. It lasts for a few furious minutes, and then it stops, everything goes out, and I'm left in a state of lethargy.

One morning Abecassi consults our neighbors, an ancient couple who argue all day and even at night, because everybody knows you need less sleep as you get older, for one fine day you die and you're going to sleep forever. The shrieks from those neighbors inflame my brain; each time I hope it will be their last quarrel, that they will die soon, but it doesn't happen. Abecassi plots with them because, as I will discover later, she wants to cure me of my outbursts of rage, and she wants to do it as her mother did, and her grandmother and so on all the way back to the Babylonian captivity. She will cure me with the ritual of *indûlko*, because old Abecassi is superstitious. She will cure me with *indûlko*, and she needs the help of the neighbors. They were supposed to go away for a few days—perhaps to stay with the rabbi, their grandson. For *indûlko*, only two people may stay under the roof: the patient and the wise woman.

I'm the patient. And I'm scared. What does she want to do to me?

Old Abecassi announces her battle plan. She's going to take my books, put them in a bundle and give them to a friend. For *indûlko* there must be no Scripture, nor any mention of the name of God. And I will have to stop praying. An easy one, that, I say to myself.

Old Abecassi already has all the things she needs: grain, water, salt, five eggs, honey, a jug of milk, candied fruit. A few minutes before midnight, she will mix a little of each ingredient into a blob that she will spread around my bed, on the threshold and in the four corners of the little room. While doing that, she will recite some formulas and beg the demons infesting me to leave me be. In exchange she will offer them honey to sweeten their tongues, grain to feed the livestock (demons keep livestock?), water and salt for I no longer remember what. After that, she will go to the cellar, where she will break the eggs, prostrate herself, kiss the floor and do who knows what else. She'll do that for three nights in a row, and if necessary for seven, or even nine, until I'm cured of my rage.

Except that the neighbors refuse to leave. This produces a furious argument: Old Abecassi yells, the others yell, angry words are exchanged, dewlaps wobble.

Unnoticed by anyone, I slip outside.

"Worms, rats, that's what you are! You've spent your lives running away, hiding, flattering the powerful. You've bought your flight in gold. You've lied and dissembled, all of you. I have nothing but disgust for you!"

Old Abecassi, feeble now, hunches on her chair. Perhaps she's aggrieved about not having placated my demons, that day seven years before.

I yell my accusations in her face, in as loud a voice as I can muster. I shout at her, implicating my mother and with her all the other Jews. Guilty of so many things. Guilty of bringing me up with lies. I came back only for that. I'm almost fifteen years old and I'm with Tuota; the port and the sea have saved me from meanness, from narrow-mindedness, from the mold that coats the souls of the ghetto. But the separation has been long, and the road long and winding. I left Old Abecassi's house shortly after my bar mitzvah, master of myself according to the Law.

Lies. Gioanbattista De Zante wasn't an unknown sailor, but a Venetian *capo da mar* who one day, returning from a campaign against the Turkish pirates, cast anchor in the port and met my mother.

Perhaps they loved each other. De Zante stopped in Ragusa for some time, but in the end he had to go back to Venice, and when he did so he didn't bring the Jewish woman with him. The woman pregnant with his bastard. Sarah Cardoso, who would be known as *puta de los goyim*.

Lies. My father isn't dead. He isn't dead, and he has sent money several times a year, even after Sarah's death. He couldn't settle with a Jewish woman without giving up everything, but he could provide for his son. I sometimes wondered where the money Sarah had left to Old Abecassi came from. I thought of Grandma Raquel's jewels. The truth is that my mother didn't leave very much, and most of the money has always come from Venice.

And now De Zante has returned to Ragusa, to take back his son. The captain of the fleet is here again. I'm nearly fifteen, and he's offering me another life.

He sends someone to get me one morning in May. A boat takes me to Lacroma, the island that lies offshore from the city. Gioanbattista De Zante is a person of some standing, a guest at the Benedictine monastery there. It looks out on the Elaphite islands, on Šipan and Mljet and Srđ, the mountain that looms over Ragusa. My legs itch with excitement. Tuota doesn't know where I'm going.

We look at each other in silence, my father and I, for a moment that I will remember for a very long time. He's not a tall man, but his shoulders are broad. I have the same black hair, the same small and almost lobeless ears, the

same cleft in my chin. The rest came from my mother. He is wearing a red cloak, fastened at the shoulder with five round buttons. Gold buttons. Gleaming. On his head he wears a wide velvet beret, also red. My cheeks must be the same color. I'm only a boy, and I find myself panting for breath. It's the most important day of my life.

The captain knows many things about me, most of them dating back to when I was with my mother. Was it she who wrote to him, who kept him up to date? Did De Zante ever reply? Perhaps they exchanged letters filled with regret and remorse, but full of love, of unrealizable dreams. Or perhaps not; perhaps someone observed our life, our days, sending dispatches to Venice every now and then. I don't dare to ask him, and I will never find out. After his death I will find no letters among his effects, nor anything else to remind me of my mother.

Of course, after Sarah's death the glass grew cloudy. Of that part of my life he has only the vaguest information, episodes vaguely told to him.

"When I asked about you, I found out that you'd taken up with a gang of smugglers. You're my son, and you deserve better. Perhaps I've found out late, but not too late, and perhaps there's still time to start over again. In Venice."

Venice. Everything he says leads in that direction. He doesn't talk about my mother, or about why he abandoned her. He doesn't ask me about myself, about Old Abecassi, about life in the ghetto. Those things no longer matter. He looks forward, always forward. His voice is low and gentle, but his tone is firm, his meaning peremptory. I am his son; I will go to Venice.

He is advanced in years and without descendants: his two legitimate sons are both dead. That's the source of my new fortune: the void left in the heart of an old man.

12.

I gave a start, and resumed my journey into the past. I was still at Sarah's grave, and the sun had risen, faint and pale behind a veil of clouds.

Mother, who would have thought that we'd meet again like this?

Mother, I'm leaving again, this time bound for I don't know where. I will never see your grave again. I turned my back and walked away from the gravestones.

It happened all of a sudden. Four of them were waiting for me, hidden behind a low wall. They attacked me with sticks; I fell to the ground; I felt blood on my forehead. Then they dragged me off, into a whirl of shadows and muttered orders.

I drowned in the void that I had just evoked.

When I came to, the first thing I saw was a cockroach climbing the wall. It was escaping the floor, which was drenched with water. The walls of the cell were eroded with damp and salt. The only items of furniture were a bench nailed to the wall and a hole in the ground for the call of nature. The pain in my head and chest made even breathing difficult. How long had I been here?

I shut my eyes, letting the little dots of light flit about me like glowworms. My temples thumped. I touched my face: burst lip, swollen cheekbone, a big bump. I'd seen so many of them, beaten like this: spies, pimps, petty informers, hotheads from the Arsenal. I'd arrested lots of them. I'd even made some of them disappear. Not in person, of course. I had men willing to do that job; mine was to give orders. Or to take them, from the Consigliere.

The sounds of a key in the lock and chains rattling shook me from my reflections. Sitting up was a struggle. The door opened and a man appeared, dressed in the clothes of a wealthy Jew: a silk caftan tied at the waist and a conical hat with a yellow band. Slightly older than me, with black, black hair and a grizzled beard. He spoke in Ladino:

"My nombre is Yaakov Del Soto. I am here to favlar with you. I have been sent by a person interested in vuestra suerte."

I hurled insults at him in various languages, beginning with his own. I called him "Judas," I said his ancestors were dogs, I accused him and whoever had sent him of all the bruises on my body, all the pain, all the aches that took my breath away. I wished him plunged in a foul-smelling hole, as I myself had been. I told him to talk to me in Italian, because Ladino was a language of flies in shit.

He stood open-mouthed, stunned, then replied in a choked voice, "It wasn't . . . it wasn't us who had you arrested. We only found out about you a few hours ago." Then, as if he were suddenly seeing me for the first time, his face bore an expression of concern. I must have looked terrible.

"Are you injured?"

My hand went to my chest. At least one of my ribs was broken, but I said nothing.

"Do you know why they've locked you up in here?"

"Why don't you tell me?"

"The Venetians asked the people in Ragusa to arrest you and hand you over to them. The Council of Ten has charged you with treason and with selling state secrets, as well as with the death of various citizens in the fire that was started at the Arsenal." He paused to assess the effect of these words. "Ragusa insists on defending its own independence, but in a case like this, not to keep Saint Mark happy would seem like an act of defiance."

All I had left was sarcasm. "It'll be a lovely hanging. How could you deny that to the people of Venice?"

Del Soto took a step forward, but was driven back by the filth and the stench of shit.

"I can relieve Ragusa of the burden of that decision," he said. "I can help you escape."

I slowly rose to my feet, counting the twinges of pain. They appeared in my mind like the numbers on my dice: I, II, III, IV . . . I had to steady myself on the bench to keep from falling. I rummaged in my pockets, already knowing what I wouldn't find there. The medal had gone. The gift from my father. "Why should I do it?" I asked.

He assumed the most solemn expression he could muster. "The person who sends me has always used his wealth to help our people."

"Tell me the truth," I replied. "I'm not of your people." At that moment I regained all my lucidity. I remembered the man they were accusing me of serving.

The most feared Jew in the world.

The archenemy of Venice.

We were in a vassal city of the Ottoman empire. I was a trusted agent of Venice, who had suddenly fallen into disgrace, who knew the secrets of the Republic. I said, "You've been sent by Giuseppe Nasi, haven't you? The enemy of Venice wants to buy the renegade."

If there was one thing I was clearly skilled at, it was taking him by surprise. He opened his eyes wide, then stopped to reflect. He had thought our discussion was going in a quite different direction. "Think about it," he said at last. "If you're accused in Venice of having been sold to him, Don Yossef Nasi is the only one who can protect you."

"Did he have me arrested so that he could buy me?"

"Why would he do that?" the man replied. "He could have had you

kidnapped without spending one coin. No, before you were arrested we didn't know you were in the city. Then they got you, and the information fell on the right ears."

My grin reopened the wound on my lip, which started bleeding.

Del Soto went on, "If they send you back to Venice you'll end up with a rope around your neck. But first they'll torture you, to make you confess even if you're innocent."

I knew the method. And I knew how enthusiastically they would apply it to me, Emanuele De Zante, who had made the guilty confess without torture. The faces of Rizzi and Tavosanis, intent on putting me through hell, had populated the previous nights, along with the image of the Consigliere coming toward me with a smile, with a sword in one hand and a book in the other.

I approached Del Soto until his back was pressed against the filthy wall. I raised my fist to smash the mask he was wearing. He closed his eyes in terror.

When he cautiously opened them again I was inches away from him. The scent of spices contrasted with the foulness of my breath.

"I know your kind. Pimps of the worst order. I've been fighting you for years. What will you do when I refuse to return the favor? Will you torture me, too? Will you have me quartered in front of the Sultan?" I stepped back, and immediately my thoughts returned to my pain, so intense that I had to support myself on the bench again.

Del Soto regained his composure, and suddenly he seemed surer of himself. "Your fate outside of Ragusa does not concern me." At last, he was sincere.

"How do you plan to get me out of here?" I asked.

"One of the jailers is willing to accept a bribe."

"When?"

"Tonight."

13.

Where did they plan to take me? The question swelled and filled all my time until the end of that day. Where did they plan to take me, to turn me from a spy hunter to a fleeing spy?

The empire of the Turk was big, vast. They could take me to Constantinople, or to the coast of Africa, or to a remote island in the eastern Mediterranean. The centers from which they ordered plots against Venice were scattered from the north to the south, like colonies of poisonous mushrooms. Perhaps they would take me to Naxos, the island of which Giuseppe Nasi had become duke when the Turks took it from Venice.

I put my right hand in my jacket pocket. There was a hole at the bottom. I slipped two fingers into that hole, rummaged in a twist of the fabric and, after a few attempts, was able to fish out my companions. I'd had them with me for less than two weeks, but they seemed like old friends.

Sitting on the mattress I threw them, perhaps in search of a response. The faces showed me two sixes: VI and VI. It was an order. "*Vivi*—live."

The most important thing was to escape the gallows.

I thought of the executions I had seen—men hanged, mutilated, cudgeled, decapitated, sometimes quartered after their death. People still talked about the death of Pietro Leone of Valcamonica, sentenced almost twenty years before. He was a debauched chaplain who had impregnated lots of nuns and then forced them to have abortions. That day the blade had lost its edge, or perhaps the priest's head refused to come off, and the executioner had to enlist the services of a hammer, striking the blade until it sank in and severed all the tendons. After thirty blows, he finished the job with a butcher's knife.

My father was there that day, and had been disgusted by the spectacle. He had fought in the war, against Ferrara and the League of Cambray; he bore scars from the battle of Polesella; he had seen bodies pulped by the artilleries of Ippolito d'Este, embarkations by Ottoman pirates, throats slit, corpses with half a face and one wide-open eye. And yet he couldn't stand the sight of the state killing in cold blood. Let them do it, but not where he could see it.

"As long as I live, Emanuele, I'll never take you to see a fellow getting the chop. If you really want to, you can go on your own." He had said that to me shortly after I arrived in Venice. A few years later, he would launch me on a career. The kind of career—it was almost funny—that amounts to sending people to the gallows.

I had been with him during the last years of his life, but I had never managed to see him as a father, nor had he managed really to treat me as a son. Too great a distance separated us, but he had been generous to me. He hadn't just pointed out my new path, he had smoothed it, too. My origins were hidden at first, then skillfully erased. Gioanbattista De Zante, a naval officer and a hero of the Republic, could not have a *marrano* son. I had acquired his surname; I had been baptized and confirmed; I'd taken communion. I'd learned the Christian prayers; I'd studied Greek and Latin. I'd been given lessons in fencing and pistol shooting.

Once his career in the navy of La Serenissima was at an end, De Zante had dedicated himself to politics. He had introduced me to the Consigliere and asked him to take me on. Within two years, I was launched on my new career in the secret service.

When my father died, I found myself the master of a well-kept house in Cannaregio, with a servant and a cook. For eight years I hadn't wanted for a change of clothes.

I had also discovered my talent. The Consigliere had spotted my anger and translated it into his language, a tongue of deceptions, mysteries, and murders, all for the security of the Republic. De Zante had given me a name and a new faith, but the Consigliere gave me a cause to fight, kill and die for. That man was a superior mind, a genius of his time. I had never wavered. Until he had asked me to frame myself.

I didn't touch the revolting soup that they passed me through the hole in the door, and I watched the darkness filling the cell until no light entered from the little window at the top. It must have been a moonless night, for I could hardly see my own hand.

After hours of stillness, I heard a rattling sound from the lock. I shrank back against the wall and slipped behind the opening door. No light, no word came in from outside.

For a while I waited for something to happen, and then I tiptoed toward the threshold. I thought I could hear someone breathing, and I froze. I went on listening, and finally I decided to take a step forward. I was in total darkness and had no idea where the exit was. I walked down a narrow corridor, always staying close to the wall, with one arm outstretched. I advanced slowly, for fear of suddenly finding myself at the top of a flight of stairs and tumbling down.

My sense of smell came to my aid. A light breeze reached me, carrying a breath of the sea. I followed it as a dog follows a scent and found myself by a half-open door. I opened it. In front of me the glimpse of a path, a piece of night sky, a faint lapping sound. Not a soul.

I leaned out through the doorway, in search of the fresh night air. A blade stung my throat. Someone pronounced my name.

"*Ti star Emanuele De Zante?*"

"*Mi star.*" I replied in the same lingua franca of the ports.

The sword lowered, but it didn't disappear. I became aware of a dark outline at my side, and another one on my other side.

"You have to come with us," said the voice. "If you try to escape, *noi ti massar.* Understand?"

We must have been below the southern walls, near the docks. I was sure they were going to take me somewhere else, far from Ragusa; they must have a boat ready and waiting.

Instead, we headed toward the heart of the city. My ribs were hurting, and soon I found myself panting for breath. Things got worse when we turned into a street that rose between the houses towards the eastern bastions. I had to stop a few times, but the two shadows gripped me beneath the arms and forced me to go on.

By the time we reached the top I was breathless. I slipped to the ground, and they picked me up again, pushed me into an alleyway, then into a courtyard. I smelled horses and found myself resting against the seat of a cart.

A familiar outline came toward me from a doorway. The dawn's light was starting to appear above the hills, just enough for me to recognize Del Soto.

"You're out of jail, but you're not safe yet."

I'd got enough of my breath back to speak.

"Where are you taking me?"

He sighed. "I can't tell you."

"Go to hell," I hissed.

"It's just a precaution," he reassured me. "You'll be going to a safe place, where the Venetians won't be able to get you."

A stitch in my ribs made me bend double with a groan, and he helped me back up. I felt an instinctive impulse to shrink from that contact, but discovered that I didn't have the strength. He nodded to the servants, who took me and hoisted me onto the cart.

"Why not a boat?" I murmured.

"Venice will be looking for you in all the ports of the Adriatic. You're going to be leaving by land. Good-bye, De Zante."

He gave his men the order to set off, a whip cracked, the wheels creaked. I slumped beneath the heavy tarpaulin they'd used to cover me, and stayed like that, with my throat tight and a hole where my heart should have been, an abyss that sucked everything in: the pain in my ribs, the bruises, the thoughts, my past, the help that Tuota had given me, the crossing to Durrës, everything. Even my name.

14.

The multicolored strip of houses grew larger with each stroke of the oars, until it filled my eyes. The city I saw was as splendid as a bride, lying outstretched on green slopes mottled with gaudy colors, red, yellow, indigo, beneath a sky that the northwesterly wind had turned a clear, deep blue.

I turned back to look for the estuary of the river that had impelled us into the gulf. I turned to one of my guards, a hairy little man armed to the teeth who spoke a Greek dialect to his colleagues. "*Poia poli ine afti?*" I asked, hoping the question was comprehensible.

He didn't reply. No one had spoken to me during the entire journey, even though I'd asked the men several times where they were taking me. Exasperation started battling with patience again. I wanted to gesticulate, to insult him in various languages, but I didn't do any of that. Then, all of a sudden, I heard him utter a single word.

"*Thessaloniki.*"

I studied the line of houses again. I must have imagined it. Fate was taking me where Tuota had said it would. Salonika. The Jerusalem of the Balkans. That was what they called the old city of Saint Demetrius, the capital of the Sephardim in the Ottoman empire. One of the fortresses of Nasi, from which his long hand drew innumerable threads.

We were arriving here after weeks of traveling. The first had been infernal. Leaving Ragusa, we had entered the interior on a dilapidated road. The creaks of the cart sounded like the wails of a cat in heat, and the jolts hadn't done much to heal my ribs. Across mountains and narrow windswept valleys we had reached Podgorica, where a doctor had visited me and bound up my chest. I had a fever, but there was no time to stop. The cart had set off again for Skopje, and Del Soto's men had handed me over to a new set of guards. The journey had continued on the water, on board a long barge, to the great relief of my bones. Now, I realized that we must have sailed the river Axios across Macedonia to the estuary that feeds into the Aegean. The water around us was the Thermaic Gulf.

After we moored in an inlet in the port, I was pushed into a cart and driven toward the place they had decided I was going to stay. The streets were crowded, the smells were strong, the jerks and jolts were dizzying. Luckily for me, I hadn't eaten for hours, or I would have thrown up.

"*Mi ozo en tu kulo!*" I heard someone shout. The memory of the same oath on the lips of old Abecassi struck me like a slap.

The journey had exhausted me, and nausea dealt me the final blow. I was in Salonika for the first time in my life, and I was arriving with my soul bowed.

In Salonika's low city people lived cheek by jowl. Their world was foul-smelling: the stench of urine kept in tubs to tan hides, the stench of those tanned hides, the stench of rubbish and rot. Above that rottenness there floated perfumes of cooking and lust.

The words exchanged from one house to another invaded the room where I was being kept. The Ladino of the Spanish Jews, the language of my mother, fixed me in the past. A landlord whose manners were pleasant but firm fixed me to the present, a present that was always the same, day after day.

He said his name was Efrem Del Burgo. He was a short, round man with the face of a mastiff, the son of Jews who had taken refuge in Salonika fifty years before. His father had come from Puglia, his mother from Granada.

Efrem was the owner of a tanning works and of the house where I was imprisoned, or so he said. He spoke a melodic Ladino, as rounded as his body; his Italian was dry, made up of crisp, short phrases. Every morning he knocked at the door and entered my room, to ask me how I had spent the night and exchange civilities.

My questions about Nasi or about my confinement bounced off a wall of politeness and smiles. I knew how the world of spies worked: He wasn't the one who was going to question me. The ingredients used to prepare for an interrogation were always the same: waiting and uncertainty. I wondered how long I would have to wait.

Efrem himself brought me my breakfast and dinner: beans with meat, chicken croquettes, desserts of dry fruit, but no wine or *rakia*. Perhaps they wanted to keep me thoughtful and alert. In that state of constant lucidity I could only look at the world through the grille of the window and listen to its voices.

As the first days passed I didn't see anyone apart from my "jailer." I addressed him mostly in Italian, sometimes in my rusty Ladino.

"*Kuanto tiempo tengo ke estar aki?* What are we waiting for?"

Efrem replied only with smiles and shrugs.

One day, he brought a servant into my room carrying a tub, jugs of hot water and a bowl full of some kind of perfume. Efrem touched his nose and pulled a face: "It might be the custom in *Venesia,* but here we wash."

When I was washed and dressed he nodded, but he still didn't seem satisfied. "*Pareses un papas,*" he said comparing me to a Greek priest. He meant that it was time to shave me and cut my hair. The barber he sent to me the same day was the third person I'd met between those walls, but he had been given instructions not to talk to me—a difficult task for someone of his profession.

Like almost all of the Jews in Salonika, the man wore a yellow turban. Like Efrem, the servant, and the passersby that I glimpsed from the window, he struck me has having a refined and cultivated elegance.

I was genuinely dumbfounded when I saw, down in the street, women walking around covered with ornaments and jewels, proud in their brightly colored garments. The care they devoted to their clothes seemed to contrast with the neighborhood's intolerable stench and filth. I had never seen Jewish women dressed up like that, apart from my mother. For hours, as a child, I had watched her making herself pretty, painting her face, decorating her neck and ears with gold and precious stones inherited from her mother and grandmother.

In my captivity, which had lasted a week, I desired those women as I had never desired anyone. Even the oldest of them. In Ragusa I had stayed away from women, perhaps because my lover had betrayed me, or perhaps because the memory of my mother was everywhere around me. I had looked for liquor and wine, and even now I missed them, certainly, but not as much as I missed intimacy with a woman.

In Venice I had once seen a monkey in a cage brought from Africa. It jumped around, shrieking, its member stiff and erect as a pen. That was how I felt, alone, in that room. Five times a day, the muezzin's chant drifted down from the upper city. The elongated, vibrant phrasing sounded like a hymn to my desire.

Early one morning, out in the corridor, I heard a female voice. It must have been a servant. She passed by, humming to herself, and making my heart leap. When Efrem came in I confronted him. I demanded wine and a woman.

"*Kero una muyer!*" I shouted. "*Y kero vino!*"

I tried to put my hands around his neck, but was immobilized by two huge servants. They shoved me against the wall and pinned me there until I calmed down. Efrem came toward me. "It's fine, Venetian," he said. "I'll see that you're taken outside."

The men locked the door behind them, leaving me sitting on the floor.

15.

In the field of yellow turbans there was the occasional white one, indicating a Muslim, and more rarely a blue one, signaling a Greek Christian.

I had trouble believing what I saw and felt. A Jew disguised as a Christian dressed up as a Jew, my soul turned inside out like a pair of trousers, I was walking around a little Oriental Spain that reminded me, even though it was different, of the world of my childhood. Perhaps it was a multiplied version, a thousand times more powerful and intense. The sound of Ladino filled the streets and my head, causing an unsettling euphoria, a feeling I had never had before. I had never heard that language spoken by so many men and women at the same time.

For a reason that struck me as obscure, the Sephardim who had been chased from Castille and Aragon, from Portugal and Granada, from Sicily and the Kingdom of Naples had chosen that city, of all cities, for their new life. A city of trading and business deals, of tanners and weavers, carders and dyers, multicolored crowds and strong smells. The Jews of Salonika made the uniforms of the Ottoman janissaries, and sewed other garments that were appreciated and sold around much of the empire. Silver gleamed in Salonika, more silver than I had ever seen: It arrived every day from mines nearby, to be worked on by Jewish craftsmen who turned it into jewelry, the same that I saw on the necks, wrists and earlobes of the women around me—women drenched in perfumes that made my head spin, whose movements shook my body from top to bottom. My desire to fornicate pawed the ground. Impatience tempted me, with every step I took, to set off in search of a whore. But I couldn't do that. I was escorted by three men, one on each side and a third bringing up the rear. I wondered whether they had orders to kill me if I tried to escape. How much time and money had Nasi invested in me? Too much for him not to go all the way with me, or too little for me not to be expendable?

We turned into an alleyway, and things suddenly changed. In a moment we had passed from the noise and color of the main thoroughfare to the shadow and quiet of a short, narrow backstreet of houses crammed against one another. One of the guards knocked on a little door. It was opened by an even littler man, a dwarf, with a blue turban and a long beard, white jacket and trousers, red slippers.

The man who had been tailing me until then addressed the little man in Greek, in a tone that seemed curt and contemptuous. The man let us in.

Inside, another surprise: an elegant residence. Light from chandeliers fell on fine carpets; trays with glasses of tea rested on low tables beside cushions and divans; and on solid wooden surfaces were tastefully arranged objects, decorated bowls and statuettes. Beyond that first room, an open door led to a flight of stairs.

The little man gestured to me to go up. I looked at my guards, one after the other. They glanced at me with impatient agreement, as if to say, "What are you waiting for? We haven't got all day."

I practically ran up the stairs, reaching a corridor at the top. In a doorway, with the light behind it, a female outline. I narrowed my eyes and saw that she was already undressed, as naked as the day she was born. I walked over to her and pushed her down on a wide, low bed. The sheets smelled fresh, and so did she. A lamp to my right, a tumble of dark hair, skillful hands unbuttoning and gripping me. I spread her thighs, but too late.

I cursed in a low voice, looking down at my member, flaccid and empty, at semen smearing my belly and my cock. Semen that had spurted quickly and furiously, just giving me time to take my pants down. Semen that had freed itself without waiting for me. It had freed itself, leaving me in chains. While the woman got up I felt embarrassment and doubt speaking to one another, saying something to each other, or slipping away, suddenly, vanishing.

I was still wearing my turban. And beneath my turban, inside my head, the echo of a shriek. The cry of a monkey, or a guffaw.

Someone, somewhere in the depths of my mind, was laughing at me.

16.

My return to captivity was slow and pathetic. My guards jeered at me silently, taunting me in their thoughts, and so did the women who crowded the street. I felt hundreds of eyes on me, as if they knew where I came from and how little of a man I had proved to be.

As on the way there, my escort baffled me with twists and turns and dead ends, until I got home exhausted. Home, I said, because that was what I thought by then. Efrem's house was my only refuge, prison though it was.

Once I was through the door, Efrem gestured to me to be quiet and follow him. He led me across the internal courtyard, opened a side door and stood in the doorway waiting for me to come in.

A dark, strong-looking man was waiting for me on a high-backed chair. Bearded, unturbaned, dressed as powerful men dress the world over. "*Salud i Beraha*," he said. "Sit down, we have to talk."

In front of him were a little table and another chair. In the room around us, everything was vague. I could have spent crucial hours there, without remembering a single detail, whether it was luxurious or plain and bare. Reluctantly, I sat down.

"I call myself Moisés Navarro. I hope you like this city."

I remember that he kept his hands in his lap, resting on the elegant fabric of his gown. On his finger he wore a little ring, a ruby the color of blood. The light from the window bisected his face, so that his eyes stayed in the gloom and his mouth seemed to belong to someone else. I watched it moving and formulating words. "Efrem will bring us coffee."

"Spare me the formalities," I replied in Italian. "Tell me exactly what you're interested in, and let's get it over with."

Navarro clicked his tongue with disapproval. He lifted one hand a little, Efrem left the room, and the door closed. We were left on our own.

"Such ingratitude, Messer De Zante. If it wasn't for us, you would be dangling from a rope in Venice now, or perhaps with your guts scattered in all directions. Don't you think you owe us something?" He spoke without rancor, but his feigned politeness was at most a thin veneer.

"If I wasn't who I am you would have let me die."

"You're wrong," he said. " We saved you because we don't know who you are. Or rather, we don't know who you'll want to be from now on. Because the man you were in Venice no longer exists, or am I mistaken?"

I didn't reply. I was expecting an argument with the Sphinx and I knew the game very well. I couldn't afford to give him an excuse.

"Oh, plainly, some things we do know," he went on, his lips barely curling into a smile. "Trifles, like the fact that you were an agent of the Venetian secret service and that you're accused of setting fire to the Arsenal."

"And nothing new so far," I spat contemptuously. "Tell me something I don't know. For example, what you want from me."

He stroked his moustache affectedly, then folded his hands in his lap again. "I told you: gratitude. Like the gratitude of the shipwrecked man for the sailors who pick him up. You were floundering in the water, traps awaited you at every landfall, along with people ready to stab you in the back. Venice wants your head, and she's telling the four winds."

"Get to the point," I snapped.

"Very well. Then let's go back to the beginning. How did a Jew from Ragusa end up protecting the secrets of La Serenissima?"

I was taken aback by my own reaction. I wanted to be honest. I had often imagined a plight like this: kidnapped by the enemy, grilled, tortured. Every time, in my head, I imagined myself concealing or twisting the truth, throwing my questioner off the track, serving him up some intriguing blend of reality and lies. And in fact, now that the moment had come, I wanted to tell the truth. But why? I tried to contain my thought, give it some sensible motivation. I convinced myself that openness was appropriate. Spill the beans, and see what happens. Before I had finished reasoning thus, already my lips were moving.

"I'm not a Jew anymore."

Navarro looked interested. The movement was tiny, almost imperceptible, but I saw him leaning forward. And then I went on.

"I left Ragusa when I was very young, because I didn't want to be like you. I was fed up to the back teeth with this hypocritical clique, with meanness, with fear. Fed up with cultivating a rat-like soul." I paused, waiting for a reply that didn't come. Navarro looked at me in silence. He was definitely thinking about the intention behind my words. At last he said, "Go on."

"My father was a gentile, a Venetian. One day he returned to Ragusa to redeem my wretched life. He took me with him to Venice; he made me study. He concealed my origins; he gave me his name and his faith. Once my studies were over, he introduced me to Consigliere Bartolomeo Nordio."

There was no need to add anything else. Just as Jupiter is lightning personified, Nordio's name embodied the secrets of the Republic.

"What tasks did you perform for him?"

Still I held my cards close to my chest: "At first, I followed people who came to Venice from the Levant. I collected rumors about possible spies, I tailed them, I checked up on what they were doing."

There was a knock at the door. Efrem came in with a tray and two steaming little glasses. "I don't want coffee," I said. "Bring wine."

"You'll have that later," Navarro reassured me. "For now, I need your mind to stay alert." He waited for the door to close again, and then he gestured to me. "Go on."

I sipped the black brew, scorching my palate. I cursed under my breath. "After a few years, I was promoted. The Consigliere gave me the task of unearthing anyone who might be undermining the order of the Republic. Spies, heretics, insurrectionaries . . . crypto-Jews."

Navarro moved very slightly, spreading his legs and brushing a bit of invisible dust from his cloak. "What exactly did your responsibilities consist of?"

"I was in charge of a handful of trusted men. We collected evidence, we interrogated suspects, we made them confess."

"Why were you, a man so devoted to the state, accused of setting fire to the Arsenal?"

I took a deep breath. "They discovered my secret. A missing half inch of skin where the sun doesn't shine. I had lied to the Republic and to Nordio. They ordered me to find the perfect culprit. And the perfect culprit was me." I laughed. "I, who fought for them for years, written off as a man in Nasi's pay."

He let me savor those words without batting an eyelid. "Do you have any idea who it was who caused the fire?"

"The workers at the Arsenal themselves."

"What evidence do you have for that?"

I recapitulated the facts I had uncovered along with Rizzi and Tavosanis during the first two days after the act, and concluded, "All they would have had to do was set fire to the powder store the previous evening, and half of Venice would have sunk. I deduced that it wasn't the work of an outside enemy, but of a Venetian expert who knew the place very well. The *arsenalotti* are a very solid corporation. Someone very high up in the Republic thinks he can bring them to heel, and they wanted to send a loud, clear message."

He seemed to meditate on what I had just said, then got to his feet. "We'll continue tomorrow," he said, and pointed to a little desk against the wall. "In the meantime, here are paper, pen and ink. I want a map of the Arsenal and a description of the damage done in the fire. Do it calmly, there's no hurry. *Asta amanyana*, De Zante."

I didn't return his farewell. Without saying another word, the Sphinx took his leave.

17.

Dawn came like a deliverance, after a dull, sleepless night. I raised my head, and it was as if a homunculus had started hammering on it from inside. I had gone to sleep with my clothes on, and the smell of wine still hung heavily in the room. The bottle, a kind concession from Efrem for good behavior during my questioning, lay empty on the floor. Rather than carrying out the task assigned to me by Navarro, I had chosen to get drunk, to dodge the boredom of confinement or, more probably, to fog my mind and remove the nagging doubts that I had brought with me from Ragusa, from Venice.

The Consigliere had betrayed me, he had thought I could be sacrificed to the greater glory of La Serenissima, and yet I felt no desire for revenge. Was that what they had trained me to do? Sacrifice everything to the cause, even myself? No one had ever said as much explicitly, but in the secret service we had always known it.

It wasn't revenge that I sought, but a way out. A way to lift myself out of the bog, or perhaps a reason to do so. The Sephardim had brought me to safety, but they had nothing to offer. Good wine and coffee, a visit to a brothel. When I had told them everything I knew, what would happen to me? They might kill me or send me back to Venice. They could, in fact, keep me a prisoner here forever.

I slipped down from the bed and reached the window. I threw it wide open, as if the air of the room were poisoned with lime.

Outside, the light was still faint, but I needed to move; I wanted to get out of there, even if it meant getting my guards out of bed. I walked over the door, determined to knock loudly. Before I did, I instinctively tried the handle.

The door opened.

I poked my head into the inner courtyard: no one. The house was still plunged in sleep. I held my breath; there was no time to thank fate or a lucky star. I walked down the pathway lit by the light of dawn and reached the front door. I lifted the peg that held it shut, then pulled the big iron chain, and the outside world was there, just beyond the threshold. All that was left was for me to start walking, quickly, but without running, so as not to draw attention at that time of the morning.

The streets already breathed with the hubbub of *Parasheve*. The eve of the Sabbath was dedicated to concluding the most urgent deals, salting the meat and the fresh fish, using up the supplies of fruit and vegetables. Come on, I had to get as far away as possible. How long did I have left before they

discovered my escape? Storekeepers and vendors were already opening their shops, arranging their goods on stalls, and craftsmen were getting ready for work. I could recognize the Jews from their way of bustling about—small rodents preparing for hibernation, the chosen people leaving Egypt. It was as if the habit of packing their luggage and changing countries was relived every week in the ritual of preparations for *Shabat*. There was something irrevocable in their gestures, a haste unknown to Greeks and Ottomans, because all activity had to cease at sunset. The next day, performing any of these actions would impede the coming of the Messiah, since it is written that he will come when all the Israelites have observed the Sabbath two weeks in a row.

As I crossed the city, my childhood memories reemerged at every street corner, in every face, as they had in Ragusa. The market already echoed with the cries of the vendors.

Berendjenas! Guevos! Aubergines! Eggs!

I understood these cries better than I had in Campo San Polo, where a Slavonian or a Brescian might have uttered familiar words in an obscure way.

Poyo! Sevoya! Chicken! Onions!

The ingredients of the *chamin* echoed from one stall to the other; they filled cloth bags, and already I thought I could smell them as they cooked with chickpeas and rice, all night long, to be ready and hot for lunch the following day with no need for cooking on the Sabbath.

I kept on walking blindly, my only aim to gain ground, to increase my distance from my starting point. They must have discovered my escape by now. Gaining distance on your pursuers in a market is impossible, I knew: hunting people down was my trade. Or at least it had been.

I recalled the escape attempts of a trafficker in forbidden books, a Slav by the name of Gigek, suspected of spying for the Turks. When he realized he was being followed, he had started running through the stalls. Catching him had been easy. A cry of "Stop, thief!" and the crowd itself had immobilized him.

I left the market behind me, my senses alert. My ribs still ached, although they were getting better. A single punch would have left me breathless on the ground. I couldn't afford to be caught; I could never manage to wriggle free.

I glimpsed the sea, the pennants of the ships standing out against the sky like pennons on the tips of lances. Without thinking, I made for an open horizon, toward a means of transport to take me away from there.

It was at that point that I saw them: Efrem's two guards, his henchmen, who had come out in search of me. I just had time to hide behind a tarpaulin that had been hung out to dry. I spied on them as they eyed the comings and goings of the port, checking that I hadn't turned up there in search of a boat.

Again I imagined the past, when I had made others flee. I remembered the face of a man who had managed to get away from me, thanks to a flash of genius, a brilliant intuition. His name was Baldan. He had pretended to stumble, toppling against my men before diving into the water of the canal. I had stopped short of the water's edge so as not to ruin the fine gown I was

wearing. I had seen Baldan swimming to the opposite bank, a few strokes away, and hoisting himself out, dripping, with a grin of triumph on his face. I had taken aim and fired my pistol and shot him in the leg.

Now I could expect a similar fate, if not a worse. I quickly set off again. I chose a street off to the right, then one to the left, like a throw of the dice, realizing too late that it was a blind alley. Turning back was too risky. In front of the wall at the end of the alley there was a cart. I slipped underneath it and crept over the mud until I reemerged in the narrow space between cart and wall. A stench of piss and rot. All I could do was wait. Leaving the city in darkness would be easier. I lay down on the ground and stared at the thin strip of sky.

The sound of children singing came from the high windows. Perhaps it was a synagogue.

If I forget thee, O Jerusalem, let my right hand be forgotten.

Again, my childhood memories. The song came from a psalm, the one about the rivers of Babylon. I, too, had learned it at their age. The song became clearer and more confident.

May my tongue cleave to the roof of my mouth if I do not remember thee, if I do not consider Jerusalem my highest joy.

They were the voices of children born here, children of parents who had fled from who knows where. Here, in the greatest landfall of refugees that I had ever seen.

My mother's face emerged as if from a dream.

Si me olvidaré de ti, oh Jerusalem, mi diestra sea olvidada.

I have forgotten, mother.

Something burned in my chest until it hurt, something that only now appeared in all its clarity. Escape.

To go where? Drifting, like a beggar, a tramp.

For the Venetians, I was a traitor in the service of Nasi.

For the Jews of Salonika, I was still a Jew.

For a fleeing Jew there was no safer refuge than this city.

I stayed like that, lying in the dirt, letting time pass above me. An hour passed, two, who knows. Then, without haste, I got up and returned to the street. I didn't need to take my bearings. The street was on a slope and I knew my way was uphill.

When I reached the door, Efrem opened it in person. He let me in without a smile, and I had a sense that he had been waiting for me. He fetched me coffee and clean clothes, with the solicitude normally reserved for someone who has just suffered an accident.

18.

It was a rainy day, the sky outside the window was a grey veil, and yet Navarro seemed gaudy, as if light were emanating from under his clothes. The colors that covered him were excessive, the red of his ring was a heart torn from his breast. Even his words seemed to me to have a color: a bright blue, they floated in the air along with the steam from the coffee. Such miracles brightness performs: Before trying to flee I had been confused and irresolute, certain of nothing. The realization that I could only go forward had blown the fog from my eyes.

"You must really like this city, if you felt the desire to take another walk," he said as I sat down.

"Salonika is only a bigger ghetto than the others. In fact it's a collection of little ghettos. Calabrians and Spaniards, Romaniots and Portuguese, Puglians and Dalmatians."

Navarro took a sip of coffee. He kept his eyes half closed, the better to enjoy the savor of the drink, and to take his time. The muscles in his neck moved slightly, he sighed with pleasure, and it was only then that he spoke.

"The ghettos are in your mind, De Zante. For a Jew in Christian Europe, the ghetto is the only place. Things are different here, you will understand with time."

I didn't reply. I would have thrown out my words at random and cut a poor figure before a man who always found the right words. "Time." The time I had ahead of me. The time allotted me. "You could have escaped and you didn't. Why not?"

"To balance the books, Navarro."

He gave a start: I had done well with the little I had, obtaining the result of startling him. I had put a question in his head, and for the first time I had uttered his name, bringing us closer together. It was his turn now. I watched him thinking, struggling and finally surrendering. He gestured to me to go on.

"That's enough about gratitude, and about how much I owe you. I could have escaped, and instead here I am. The books are balanced. So far, you've told me what will become of me if I don't help you. It's time to tell me what I will gain."

His eyes narrowed slightly. From the start Navarro had studied me like a book; now, at last, I saw him turning the page.

"You're a clever man, De Zante, congratulations. The truth is that you

didn't escape because you hadn't the faintest idea where you could go. And yet you present it as if it's a choice and you want to give me something in return."

"Then I've passed the test. I'm a good Jew."

He laughed to himself, snorting through his nostrils. He said he would give me money, a lot of money, if my revelations were useful to him. And a house, in a safe place of my choice. The chance of a new life. I asked why I should trust him.

Navarro replied, "Aren't we all good Jews?" And he had my back against the wall again. From that point onward, I couldn't move without giving him a shred of what he wanted.

He asked me about the Arsenal, about the damage caused by the fire.

I told him what I had seen: three burned galleys, some flooded docks, the collapse of the surrounding walls, the destruction of the powder grinders. A severe blow, but damage less severe than one might have imagined.

He asked me about the new wing of the Arsenal, the recent expansion. He wanted to know what went on in there.

"The dry-dock basins are used for the repair of old galleys, big merchant ships," I replied. "Someone decided not to let them go on rotting in the port. In the event of war, they could be useful as troop carriers."

Navarro handed me the coffee that I hadn't yet touched. The glass was tepid, the liquid no longer steaming, I took a great sip. "So Venice is preparing for war," he observed. "Do you have any idea what its goal will be?" The question was uttered in the same neutral tone as the others.

"Don't pretend you don't understand. The Sultan is preparing for war; he has been ever since he came to the throne. Some people say it will be against the Portuguese, to chase them from Hormuz. Some are convinced that he wants to support the revolt of the *moriscos* of Granada. Others say that he will besiege Tunis, Heraklion or Cyprus. The Doge, in Venice, fears a direct attack on the city. He has even recalled the architect Savorgnan from Cyprus to reinforce the whole defense system of the lagoon."

That name produced a barely visible reaction on Navarro's face, and made him even more alert and watchful. He leaned toward me slightly.

"Giulio Savorgnan? Did you know him?"

"Yes. The Consigliere employed me to ensure his personal security and the secrecy of his projects." Cat's eyes flashed in the gloom. You could almost hear him thinking.

"Do you know if he planned to return to Cyprus?"

I shrugged. "He didn't say as much, but I shouldn't imagine so."

"And what sense did you have?"

"He was very out of sorts, even though he had made every arrangement for the work to be completed in his absence. The money had run out, so before he left Nicosia, he come up with the idea of a competition between the aristocratic families of the city: the one offering the most money could give their

own name to one of the eleven bastions. It was the result of that lottery that constantly troubled him."

"And in Famagusta?"

"He only managed an inspection there. He said the defenses were very antiquated."

Navarro paused for a long time. It was clear that he was making a decision. When at last he got up, I realized that he had resolved the dilemma.

"I'm sorry, De Zante," he said, "but I've decided to send you away. You will leave tomorrow."

"What?" My alarm was like a long flaming branch that had been passed from hand to hand for an hour, growing shorter and shorter, until it was finally scorching my fingers. "You said I could choose where to go!"

"And that's true," he said without batting an eyelid. "You will choose, but not today. Other people must hear what you have said to me. You will go to Constantinople. Don't worry, you'll like it." He waited for a moment before adding, "Even more than Salonika."

Then he bade me farewell and left. I peered out of the doorway, still stunned by the news, and I heard him say to Efrem, "Tomorrow *el mansévo* will leave for Konstantinopla. You're going to go with him, *apronta todo*."

In my right pocket, my hand touched my dice.

19.

I was on the deck, still under guard, but I didn't feel like a prisoner. Exposed to the south wind, which fills the sails and makes men skittish as horses, I felt alive, ready to take on anything, lucid and alert. Efrem brought me food and we swapped some words in Ladino. The sailors talked to each other in lingua franca, and increasingly often in Turkish, as we approached our destination. I had spoken the language since my childhood in Ragusa, and I hadn't stopped in Venice, but what I heard now sounded strange to me, mixed with Greek, and I imagined that in Constantinople they spoke yet another variant. Or rather, a hundred variants, and more.

Off the coast of Lemnos, the sailors hauled a tunafish on board. It died in the sun, struggling under their blows, amid the victorious shouts of the crew.

The first time I saw a big fish dying, I was still a little boy, in the port at Ragusa. I saw it opening its mouth and its gills, twisting and leaping. It was impossible for it to turn both eyes to the sky. One eye was dazzled by the sun; the other was pressed against the stone of the dock. Perhaps it was screaming, but its scream of death could be heard only in the world of fish, under the sea.

Or perhaps it really was mute, as they said, and this, along with having its eyes on either side of its head, was a very sad fate to endure.

When we entered the Sea of Marmara, the wind changed direction. What we Italians would call the *bora* began to blow shards of ice all the way down to the lower deck, and if you ventured up to the top it sliced the skin of your face. In Istria they say that the *bora* is born in Segna, gets married in Fiume and dies in Trieste. I didn't know where that wind coming down from the Black Sea was born, but it seemed less tense and fierce than the furious breath of Aeolus that I knew so well, and that, in the Adriatic, would have prevented us from sailing.

The ship struggled on, impelled by oarsmen, battling against the waves and currents. The walls creaked, like scaffolding about to collapse. In the midst of this cacophony of wood, wind and foam, I could barely hear the curses of the crew, and it seemed to me that everyone was speaking incomprehensible, alien languages. I was grateful for the excellent manufacture of the Turkish clothes I had been given in Salonika: a raw-wool cap, thick breeches that reached below the knee, thick stockings. When the temperature fell still further, Efrem gave me a fur coat.

One December morning, the outskirts of Constantinople came into view. I climbed on deck, only to be welcomed by a dense blast of rain and frozen

snow. Then, all of a sudden, the wind ceased. Snowflakes started falling slowly, sparse at first, then gradually in greater numbers. It was as if the running sand had slowed in time's hourglass. I watched the snow melting on the rocking surface of the waves, then I looked at the coast, keen to give a name to places and palaces that Efrem had pointed out to me on a map.

In spite of the inclement weather, boats of every style and size clogged that stretch of sea. They were seeking shelter, heading toward the Golden Horn, the only safe landfall along the shores of the Bosphorus.

We passed by a fortress, the seven towers that gave their name to the suburb of Yedikule. A brackish stench caught my nose, a stench of death and human waste. I was being given an appropriate welcome. I looked at Efrem, who was standing beside me on the deck. He replied without waiting for questions, through a handkerchief with which he was protecting his nostrils. He said it was the tanning works. And the rope works. And the abattoirs.

The ship ran alongside the imposing walls that had enclosed the city for more than a thousand years. A veil of snow was starting to cover the roofs of the wooden houses, but even on that leaden day the gilded domes gave off light. Minarets, towers and steeples, walls enclosing seraglios, gardens were all coated in white. I caught myself counting the hills on which the Second Rome stretched, to check whether there really were seven. I counted only five, but thought it might depend on my observation point.

After rounding the tail end of Europe, the home of emperors, divinities and sultans, the ship slipped into the Golden Horn. It looked like a river estuary, so sheltered and protected, it seemed a work more of art than of nature. It was crowded with vessels of very kind. Big merchant lighters, round-bowed caïques, European carracks. On the left bank, where the Turkish city lay, ruins, the remains of a big fire, appeared like ghosts on the water. Behind them, a huge black swath of charcoal and ashes slashed through the dense network of warehouses and palaces, trees and mosques. The first layer of snow on these burnt carcasses made the scene an Apocalypse painted in black ink. Judging by the ruins, the fire at the Arsenal had been a trifle compared to this catastrophe.

I turned toward the opposite side, Galata, the Christian city, and nostalgia hit me like a sudden whiplash. I wondered if I would ever see St. Mark's again, if I would ever again walk down the *calli* and canals of the city to which I owed everything, not least my downfall. I thought of my house, of Arianna. I saw Galata reflected in the sea, and below the surface of the water everything was transfigured. The reflection was Venice, and I had a lump in my throat. Beside me, Efrem smiled and stretched out a hand toward the quay.

"*Sobre este mar, todas las sivdades son la misma sivdad.*"

Yes, on this sea all cities are the same city. His words consoled me. As the ship approached the dock, Galata seemed to be slipping into the sea: Even though my feet had not yet stepped on dry land, by now I felt I was inside the

city; I was aware of its comings and goings, the smells of its inns, the move-ments of its stevedores, the streets, febrile even under the falling snow.

The impression of opulence and relaxed grandeur that I had received from a distance was replaced by disappointment. The houses were small, dirty, made of wood, few of them taller than a single story, and the streets were narrow.

As the crew got to work on the cargo, Efrem asked me to follow him—me and the two guardian angels, who didn't take their eyes off me. He had to deliver a number of letters in person, and he had to hurry before the alley-ways turned into a bog.

Rough streets, dark and encased. The houses looked as if they wanted to crush us. We continued on foot, up and down exhaustingly steep slopes. Carts and coaches couldn't pass that way, and the few horses to be seen were forced to adopt a gait even slower than ours. Now I understood the agitation of the inhabitants: They had to get their business done before the snow blocked those filthy streets entirely. Struggling along in the sludge, we met men from all parts of the world. Groups of Italians, Venetians and Genoese, red-faced Dutchmen, Frenchmen, Muscovites wrapped in fur. And turbaned Bosnians, Gypsies, Persians and Arabs, Greeks, Turks, stout Armenians. I was at the foot of the tower of Babel, just after God had confused our minds and tongues. The only people missing were the savages of the Americas.

The street opened into a square with a church looming in the middle. It struck me that there were as many churches here as there were in Venice. We passed by a group of men building a house. They went on working even in the snow, since their method of construction allowed them to do so. They had prepared a wooden framework, as you do with ships, and now, after putting on the roof, they were placing boards like ribs between one pole and another. It didn't look very solid, and I couldn't see whether there were stone founda-tions, but at least the men were working in shelter.

Efrem did what he had to do, and we went on, soon reaching a dock just outside the city, where a four-oared boat was already waiting for us. Again I found myself on the sea. The snow fell and fell, but there was no wind. Ahead of me, Asia: the place they call Üsküdar, beneath a white pall. The crossing was brief and silent.

We landed. All I could see were wooden houses, exactly like the ones on the other shore, but less densely crowded. I was led into one of these, which leaned out over the water from the top of a slope. The interior was comfort-able and well decorated. Efrem got to work lighting the brazier to heat the room. After a few attempts, the faggots caught fire. He turned his usual smile on me, but this time I knew he was saying good-bye: "I have other business to attend to in town before I go back." The idea of being left on my own wasn't entirely consoling.

"And I'm stopping here, really?"

Efrem shook his head. "You're not quite there yet," he said. He walked to a

side door and threw it open, revealing a covered terrace. I joined him in the doorway, looking out at the white flakes that were still falling. Beyond the gray water stretched the city. Efrem pointed to the right, where the straits continued towards the Black Sea.

"The Palazzo Belvedere is on the far shore. The Nasi residence."

The cold forced us back inside.

"Will I meet him?"

He turned and looked at me. "If that happens, listen to him." He nodded good-bye. "*Suerte . . .*"—he paused very slightly—"*amigo mio.*"

I didn't know what to say, so I said nothing. I had learned to appreciate his sympathetic expression, but I certainly couldn't call him a friend. He had been polite with me, more like a landlord and a traveling companion than a jailer. But he left the room and my life as lightly as he had entered them.

I was alone. I didn't know whether there was anyone down below who might be keeping an eye on me, and I didn't care. I stretched out on the bed, fully dressed. I felt ill, exhausted by my journey and my uncertainty. I was in the snake's nest, close to the greatest enemy of Venice.

Giuseppe Nasi. The Damned. The Cursed One. The Devil in person. The Sultan's favorite Jew. Also known in Europe as Juan Micas or João Miquez. I had listened to more gossip and collected more information about him than I had about the Great Turk. For years I had fought, unearthed and punished his agents. Now I was in his hands.

The bed was too high, and too soft.

I fell asleep just as dawn was breaking.

Interlude

The world traveler
Out of Europe, Rabi'al Awwal–Shabban 977
(September 1569–February 1570)

The old man rereads the letter. Marks on paper, entrusted by a woman to a commercial agent. Words that have traveled from Egypt at the bottom of a rucksack, then to the Red Sea by camel, then again on a fast ship, propelled by favorable currents, before finally reaching the shores of Arabia Felix, 2,000 miles southeast of the waters of the Bosphorus.

Mokha. City of coffee, a crossroads contested and shared by Arabs, Turks, Abyssinians, Portuguese. Mokha, theater of a rebellion, occupied for months by insurgents. The imperial fleet has just reestablished the authority of Selim II, and the rebels have fled to the high plains. They aren't warriors; they're coffee planters who have taken up swords and the Shi'ite faith, weary of the theft and corruption of Ottoman functionaries. A peasants' revolt once again. Once again, the religion of beggars . . . and business.

The old man has remained. Packing up and leaving belongs to his earlier lives. At least he thought so before this letter arrived.

He looks at the signature once more, he observes its uncertain line, not firm as it once was, back when he imagined he would be by that woman's side until the winter of his life.

Hard to say when their paths began to diverge. He remembers the day he asked her if he could follow the Nasi family's trades from that staging post deep in Arabia. She raised no objections. She knew, she had always known, that the world traveler can't stop, that there's always another place to see before you close your eyes, an unknown place to be buried. That old Ismail should have taken the coffee route was written in his fate. And yet now she is inviting him to travel that same route in the other direction. *Before it's too late.*

Can words move a mountain? Because that's the old man, a block of rock eroded by time, whom the letter wants to tease from his lair in the remotest corner of the empire.

The old man will move, but he will have to wait for winter to come, and with it the monsoon that blows to the north. The coffee caravans will come down

from the mountain like snakes attracted by water, and Yossef Nasi's ships, laden with merchandise and lined up along the jetty, will wait for the moment to leave. The pointed sails of the feluccas will travel back up the Red Sea to Suakin, the city of coral, where the barges of Suez will take on board slaves and precious spices.

Wait for the monsoon. Does that wait alone impede the journey? Or is there also the fear of confronting the past, the weight of balancing the books of a life, the fear of seeing in the death of the beloved the fear of one's own memories?

Winter comes, and the old man can dedicate himself to his luggage. When he was younger, that ritual marked out his days.

He puts in a bag the pages written by his own hand, and impulsively touches the middle of his chest. Beneath the fabric that covers it he feels the outline of the ancient coin, carved with the credo of the kingdom of the mad: "One God, one faith, one baptism."

His past lives are fading and he doesn't know what awaits him. The outlines around him are blurring. So he carries his words with him, all the words he has written over the years.

That's not enough. He also takes a fragment of mirror, to be sure that he recognizes himself at the end of the journey.

He takes his pistols and the twins, Hafiz and Mukhtar, silent and sharp as blades.

Ali Hassan announces that he will go with him. The ascetic friend of God has prepared his bag for him.

Having reached Suez, they entrust the cargo of coffee to the local agents of the Nasi family and then set off again, with a caravan of camel traders heading for Arish, where the ships set sail for the Holy Land.

At the oasis of Elim, a staging post for the Israelites fleeing the pharaoh, the old man falls ill. Ali keeps watch over him for three days and three nights of fever and delirium, and when he thinks has finally lost him, his friend recovers and they resume their march.

The journey by boat from Arish to Haifa restores his strength. God spreads out clear water and propitious winds. In Haifa they buy dromedaries, paying twice their value. Ali tries to protest, but the old man shrugs: The money is his, and fever has already made them lose precious days; there's no time to haggle.

It's a silent journey, as if the old man's taciturn nature has infected everybody else.

Tiberias appears like a mirage, softened by the haze of morning. Behind the city, the lake reflects the gray of the sky. Beyond the mirrored surface of the water, the Golan Heights lead the eye to the horizon.

Outside the arch where they enter the city they have to declare their names

and places of origin to a squad of janissaries, who look them up and down suspiciously. Other soldiers guard the walls and the market. The travelers leave their mounts and accept the water offered to them.

The old man climbs down from the saddle, and grits his teeth to keep from groaning. He summons his strength, grips his stick and, accompanied by the others, starts walking, surrounded by the voices, languages and dialects of every corner of the Mediterranean and the Levant.

He finds the house of Gracia Nasi without having to ask for directions. A Spanish-style building on the edge of the square stands out. At a window, a man watches them approach. The old man calls to him from the street, introduces himself, says he has come to visit Gracia Nasi.

The man narrows his eyes and looks at him for a long time, as if to assess the meaning or sincerity of these words. At last he replies, in a voice thick with sadness.

"The *Senyora* said you would come. She waited for you till the very end."

Only a rough and wordless piece of stone marks the little mound.

The face of Yossef Ben Adret, the man who welcomes them, the administrator of the colonies, is marked by recent grief. The *Senyora* wanted this anonymous grave in the middle of all the others, so that her tomb wouldn't become an object of veneration.

It was the peasants of Tiberias who issued the invitation, he says. When they discovered that she was ill and that God was preparing to receive her into his peace, they asked her to come and die here, in the valley where we will rise again together when the Messiah comes to save us. Recently she detached herself from the world; her thoughts were for God alone. When she passed away, a crash of thunder shook the Sea of Galilee, and a storm struck the earth with unexampled force.

"Never again will our people know a woman like her."

The old man kneels by the grave and murmurs incomprehensible words. Ben Adret asks Ali what language he is praying in.

"He isn't praying. He's speaking the language of ghosts."

Incredulous, Ben Adret asks him who the old man is. The Yemeni replies, "He is the stories he tells. When he feels like it, which he seldom does. Usually he prefers to write them down."

And why on earth have the others come with him, all the way here? Ali points to the two Indians. "He bought them from a Portuguese galley, then freed them. They follow him everywhere." The reply is incomplete. Ben Adret waits.

Ali puts a hand on his heart: "I'm with him because God, the Merciful, the Compassionate, gave me the task of converting him to the true faith."

Ben Adret hasn't time to be startled, because the old man turns and calls to him. He asks him to recite a Jewish prayer. In the silence that follows, Ben Adret utters the words. Flowing sounds, pure sounds, and even those who

don't understand them bend their heads. As the words rise towards God, they will become everyone's words.

> . . . ul'assaqa yathon l'chayyey 'al'ma
> ulmivne qarta dirushlem
> ulshakhlala hekhleh b'gavvah . . .

The boats move calmly on the lake, toward the bare hills on the opposite shore. The orchards of the plain can be seen in the distance.

Once the simple ritual is over, they return to the home of the Nasis. For a long time, the old man remains locked in a dark silence. When he opens his mouth again it is to ask why it was, as they approached the city, that they saw more soldiers than sheep in the fields.

Ben Adret tells him how things are. The inhabitants of the region treat the Jewish colonists as unwelcome guests. Before the siege there were mostly Christians and Muslims there. Yossef Nasi bought their lands, their plots, their pastures. He built houses and moved the colonists into them. Recently there have been raids against the farms, and fires and threats. Don Yossef persuaded Sultan Selim to reinforce the garrison.

"If our security depends on the janissaries, sooner or later they will end up in charge," Ben Adret concludes bitterly. "We will have to be able to defend ourselves on our own. Don Yossef should get hold of weapons, not guards. But he doesn't want to contradict his friend Selim, and if the rumors going around are true, things can only get worse."

Ben Adret says nothing more, but the old man presses him. What rumors? What are people saying? Ben Adret hesitates, sighs, then replies, "They are saying that Yossef Nasi wants to make himself king."

Gracia's room contains only a bed, a carved wooden chest and an armchair upholstered in damask, luxurious enough to look out of place. The air smells of sandalwood and incense.

"The *Senyora* wanted to give away all her surplus furniture, her clothes, her books. And her tapestries."

Ben Adret is on his feet, standing by the door. He lets Ismail come in and touch the deathbed of the woman who let him hope for a new start many years before.

The old man moves slowly, as if afraid of colliding with invisible presences. He stops in front of a shelf on the wall that holds a Hebrew Bible and a Talmud. The latter volume looks familiar. It was printed by Usque, a bookseller in Ferrara, many years before. The name makes him smile. He limps, without using his stick, to the chest and opens it. Inside, an old brocade blanket covers a few ornaments, a rolled-up carpet and a bundle. He picks this up, unties the knot that fastens it, and takes out two volumes: a Christian Bible written in Greek and the Koran. As he puts them back in, the spine of a third,

much smaller book attracts his attention: *Trattato utilissimo del Beneficio di Gesú Cristo Crocifisso, verso i cristiani.*

In the evening, Ali finds the old man sitting in the doorway, covered with the cloak adopted by the Moors, the same color as the night. He doesn't look sad, but weighed down by thoughts and memories. The Yemeni has never asked about the letter that has brought them there. He does so now. What was written on it?

"That she was dying," the old man replies. *Beatriz*, as he calls her, was summoning him to Tiberias. She wanted to see him one last time.

"That's all?"

The old man chews over his reply before giving it to his friend. Beatriz exhorted him to help her nephew Yossef at a difficult moment. Ali understands: the old man has made a decision. "We aren't going back, are we?"

The old man huddles in the cloak. There is a debt to be honored, he says. Many years ago, the Nasi family brought him to safety when his fate was decided. At any rate, he adds, Ali is not obliged to follow him. The Arab studies the Crab fixed to the zenith of the sky.

"Well, here I am," he murmurs. "I, too, have an undertaking to honor. To God, the Sublime and Munificent. Now you should sleep, old man. Constantinople is still a long way away."

Part Two

Tikkun Olam

2 Rajab 977–21 Safar 978
(December 11, 1569–July 25, 1570)

1.

When I woke up, light was flooding in through the window. It must have been late morning. Someone had stirred the fire. By the brazier there was a wooden tub full of steaming water—an explicit invitation. My last bath had been in Salonika, two weeks before.

I pricked up my ears, but the house was entirely silent. I threw open the shutter and an enchanted picture presented itself to my view. A fabulous city stretched out before me. Houses, trees, boats, streets, domes, minarets were the warp and weft of a big sheet of white silk lace shot with threads of silver and gold, glittering under the sun, so bright it almost hurt the eyes.

The warmth of the bathwater made all thoughts evaporate. I stayed motionless, eyes closed, lulled by the crackle of the fire and the scent of burnt resin, until a voice made me start. "*Buenos dias.*"

I turned around sharply. The new arrival leaped backward to avoid being splashed. We stared at one another, bewildered, and then the other man smiled and addressed me in Italian.

"I hope it's still hot. I was careful to see that it was boiling, so that it would be the right heat when you woke up. But I hadn't thought you would sleep so long. The journey must have been very tiring."

I guessed that he must be about fifty. He had a thin moustache and a pointed beard. The fox-skin robe that reached to his knees opened over a leather waistcoat and a belt with an engraved buckle. On his feet he wore fur-lined boots. On his head was a black velvet hat with a blue feather. Of course, Nasi's men never skimped on clothing.

"Who are you?"

"Your Charon," the other man replied with apparent amusement. "I'm here to take you to Palazzo Belvedere." He took a package from under his arm and set it down on the bed. "But not before dressing you appropriately." He untied the strings, revealing the contents: new clothes. He handed me a towel to dry myself with and stood waiting for me to put them on. They were well made, heavy and warm. "Are you ready?"

"So Nasi's very keen to meet me? I'm sure he isn't worried that I'll escape, given that I'm a pistol shot away from him now."

He was silent for a few moments. Then he said, "The answer to the question is yes, you are expected at the palace for luncheon. It would be discourteous to keep the other guests waiting. As to fears that you might escape,

we trust that you made your decision in Salonika. Efrem Del Burgo has given us a detailed account of your stay with him. But now come, we must hurry."

Outside the house, three men wrapped in heavy cloaks waited to escort us to a little jetty. We climbed on board a slender boat, and the helmsman issued an order to the oarsmen, who propelled the boat into the middle of the current. My eyes were lost again among the whitened domes of the big mosques. There was something sensual in those shapes, and in their clear contrast to the minarets, erect toward the sky. Instinct called Arianna to mind, her smooth and sinuous body. Blasphemous thought, but since my coarse humiliation at the brothel in Salonika I hadn't touched a woman, and desire chooses strange ways to manifest itself.

Our boat slipped by the hills of Pera, below the sumptuous villas of the foreign noblemen. One in particular drew my attention with the richness of its facade.

"The residence of the Venetian bailiff," my companion said, winking, without adding anything else.

We made quickly for the opposite bank, aiming toward a large building, one both magnificent and menacing. Thinking about it again, I see in my mind the image of a many-eyed monster, squatting on the strait preparing to grab the vessels as they crossed. Hard to forget that all goods between the Mediterranean and the Black Sea passed before its jaws.

The boat reached a flight of stairs that descended from the garden of the palace and plunged into the water. The submerged steps were covered with dark weeds, stirred by the waves like sirens' tresses.

"Welcome to Palazzo Belvedere."

My guide walked ahead, past snowy flower beds and cypress trees, until he reached a second entrance. We went in, walking down a short corridor, then climbed a flight of steps and emerged into a loggia that led to a big drawing room dominated by a white marble menorah that rose from a pool full of water-lilies. Jets of water representing flames spouted from its seven branches. Then another loggia like the one that had welcomed us opened up before us, this one punctuated at regular intervals by a large number of doors. Wooden panels carved with floral motifs decorated the walls.

The floor of the drawing room was decorated with a mosaic depicting the Mediterranean surrounded by the shores of Europe, Africa and Asia.

The Strait of Gibraltar was covered by a long low table, where at least fifty people, squatting in the Turkish manner, waited with empty bowls for their food. There were old men, their faces weary and bewildered, and children, who bit into loaves of bread and munched handfuls of dried fruit. Around them stood the women, passing the bowls back and forth, dishing out soup, dipping their spoons into copper pots.

The smell of coriander and artichokes rose thickly to our nostrils.

"During the feast of Sukkoth," the guide explained to me, "the oldest

Jewish quarter in the city caught fire. It was opposite Galata, on the shore of the Golden Horn."

I thought of the blackened ruins I had seen from the sea on the first day. A big fire in the Jewish quarter, opposite the Frankish city, in the capital of the Great Turk: It all suggested an act of revenge on the part of La Serenissima for the damage done to the Arsenal, but thinking about the dates, I realized this couldn't be so.

On the day of the explosion, the Jews of Venice had been celebrating. Many people had accused them of gloating over the ruin of the Republic, but they were only celebrating the Jewish New Year. There were just two weeks between Rosh Hashana and Sukkoth—too short an interval for any news, however urgent, to get from Venice to Constantinople.

"Hundreds of families," the voice beside me continued, "lost all their belongings: houses, beds, clothing. We put them in all possible shelters, but some of them remained outside, and with winter at the gates we couldn't let that happen."

I watched an old woman wiping the bottom of her bowl with a piece of bread. The accurate and meticulous gesture reminded me of old Abecassi, forever shouting at me not to waste my food. The woman got to her feet and hobbled across the drawing room. Before disappearing from view, she stood in the doorway of the internal courtyard, her eyes turned upward and her hands joined as though in prayer. Her eyes were staring at a painting, just above the architrave. A full-length portrait of a woman, seated, her opulent robes falling softly to her feet, her hand resting on a desk. Her eye proud, her brow wide, her hair arranged in an elaborate style.

"Donna Gracia Nasi," said my companion, as if introducing me to a flesh-and-blood person. "I imagine that in Venice she is still known by the name of Beatriz de Luna Miquez."

Although merely a painting, the woman was awe-inspiring, like certain portraits of saints or emperors. Our Senyora of the Sephardim. I had heard Jews invoking her name under torture, and recommending their souls to her before being executed. She was the matriarch of the family, the widow of a wealthy Jewish banker from Portugal. She had lived in Antwerp and had escaped the designs of the emperor before taking refuge in Venice. Her nephew João was her most trusted servant. The one who, in Constantinople, had assumed his own Jewish name: Yossef Nasi.

Some months previously, news had reached Venice that Donna Gracia Nasi was dead. Consigliere Nordio had been delighted.

"We are still in mourning. We all loved her very much. She was our beacon. Our queen." The man lowered his head and sighed. "The past year has been very unhappy. Two months before Donna Gracia, from one day to the next, Samuel passed away."

He didn't explain who that was, nor did I ask. He must have been Nasi's younger brother, known in Venice by the name of Bernardo.

The woman in the painting attracted my attention again. Now a devout little procession passed below her. Men and women bowed in front of her image before they left. Only the children lingered in front of the sumptuously laid table. I let my eye wander around the vast sitting-room. To me, this soup kitchen for the poor looked like the palace halls where European aristocrats display their trophies of war and the hunt. It wasn't possible that there wasn't another place in the whole building in which to give food to the evacuees. Nasi wanted his guests to see how great and good his heart was. He was like those Pharisees criticized in the Gospels, the ones who strike their chests in front of everyone when doing penance and ostentatiously give generous alms in order to be admired.

The guide took two steps back and reached the wall behind us. With a mechanical click, he released a wooden panel that covered it, revealing a concealed opening.

"This way, please."

I entered a narrow, dark room, smelling of dust and wood shavings. There was just enough space to accommodate a bench, and we sat down side by side, facing the wall. My companion lifted a strip of wood and a blade of light struck my face. He beckoned to me to peer through the crack, just wide enough for the eyes.

A big hall opened up below us, the walls occupied by hundreds of bound volumes. We were in a secret chamber, built so that a watcher might observe the library without being seen.

"It's better that you take a glance at the guests before meeting them."

He spoke the advice in a smug and irritating tone, so irritating that I immediately wanted to leave off this spying game. But I rested my forehead against the wall and counted four people, composed and elegant, conversing in front of a big clock. The clock's face, framed in a tall, narrow case, was filled with numbers, letters and smaller squares, above which needles of various lengths rotated, quickly or slowly—some so slowly that they looked as if they weren't moving at all. Charon spoke close to my ear.

"They are impressed, and they're quite right to be. That machine is a genuine marvel. Besides the hour, it shows the day of the year according to the Christian calendar, the Hejira, and the Jewish calendar. It arrived from Egypt a few days ago, a precious gift from its maker, the famous Takiyuddin."

I had never heard his name, but then again, I wasn't here to talk about clocks.

"Let me guess what's about to happen," I said. "I'm going to ask you who these gentlemen are, and you're going to explain. Or do we have to talk about pinions and gear-wheels?"

The man maintained his dreamy tone. "Don't underestimate machines, Senyor. Not even as a topic of idle conversation." Then he settled himself more comfortably on the bench and began to describe the people there for my benefit.

"The thin gentleman all dressed in yellow is the French ambassador,

Guillaume de Grandchamp, Monsieur de Grantrie." The color of the Frenchman's clothes, together with his build, made me think of a canary.

"An agreeable conversationalist, but also an unscrupulous businessman, when it comes to drawing up agreements with the Grand Vizier to the detriment of rival powers. Next to him, the great blond bear being strangled by his collar is the Voivode of Sandomir, the envoy of the king of Poland. A good fellow, but with the unforgivable defect of preferring beer to wine. He has it sent from home in barrels." He touched my shoulder with a hand. I instinctively shrank away.

"The man sipping tea is Solomon Ashkenazi, secretary to the Grand Vizier Sokollu and personal physician to the Venetian ambassador." I spotted a lean man with an alert expression, busy having his cup filled by a servant. "He came to Constantinople three years ago, when Selim ascended the throne. He likes to call himself a subject of La Serenissima, and he was actually born and bred in the territories of Venice."

An increasingly bizarre picture was forming in my mind. Not only was Nasi the Sultan's favorite, not only did the Grand Vizier have a Jewish secretary, but that secretary called himself a citizen of Venice. In Constantinople the world was turned upside down.

"He's famous for his memory," the voice went on. "They say he can recite the whole Torah from memory. Anything said in his presence might as well have been written down."

I still had to examine the last guest, sitting slightly apart from the others, absorbed in studying a book. A young man with reddish hair, in simple, dark clothes without aristocratic furbelows.

"Mr. Ralph Fitch, a subject of the English queen. He arrived a few days ago. He traveled here from London to consult the book he is holding in his hand, an extremely rare and precious text written in the time of Tamerlane. But come, now, we've kept you waiting long enough. The conversation will be in Italian, which is the lingua franca among the Europeans, but you don't have to speak it if you don't want to."

I followed him out of the little room. The drawing room seemed even bigger now. At the bottom of the staircase we reached the door to the library, but before he opened it I stopped. "Where is the master of the house?" I asked impatiently. "Doesn't Nasi receive his guests?"

"Normally he does, yes. But on this occasion he went and brought the most important guest to his own lodgings."

I was quite exhausted by the way this man had of posing as a great friend. "And who might that be? The Grand Turk in person?"

He smiled, not at all bothered by my sarcasm. "It's you," he said, before throwing open the door, ignoring my amazement.

I watched Giuseppe Nasi enter the library and display himself in an act of reverence toward his guests.

"*Shalom aleichem*, gentlemen. Welcome to my house."

2.

Nasi didn't introduce me to my fellow guests, and throughout our meal he behaved as if I didn't exist, except to show me to the seat to his right, where I was to sit. I didn't say a word, but simply observed the others, and gradually, as the courses followed one another, I realized it was precisely what Nasi wanted. I was the enigma.

I saw the glances the others were darting at me, unsettled and doubtful, and I imagined how satisfied he would be. Fish was served, then game, sweets with mint, oranges and fruits I had never seen before. All washed down with wine from Naxos.

I ate and drank without much of an appetite. I felt acid in my throat and my stomach squeezed in a vise. I was sitting less than three feet from Venice's greatest enemy, and rather than killing him I was listening to him like an old friend.

"On the feast of Hanukkah, the children of Israel celebrate the victory of the Maccabees over the Seleucids and the new consecration of the Temple of Jerusalem. I wanted to take this opportunity to welcome Master Ralph Fitch, hoping that his stay here will be both lucrative and pleasurable."

The Englishman thanked Nasi with a nod of his head. The Grand Vizier's secretary reclaimed his attention with a little coughing fit.

"May I ask you what struck you most when you arrived in Constantinople, Signore? Sometimes first impressions contain immediate truths."

We turned toward the Englishman, who took his time, wiping his mustache with his napkin. Then he replied, with the air of someone who is sure of himself but doesn't want to make a great show of it, "Not so much an impression; more of an observation. It seems incredible that so many people and faiths can live together in the same place without coming into conflict."

Ashkenazi smiled sardonically. "That's an answer worthy of a diplomat."

At that moment Nasi cut in. "If you stay here long enough, as I hope you will, you will discover that the secret is called tolerance."

Fitch seemed really curious. "Do you think we could draw a universal rule from that? When Her Majesty, Queen Elizabeth, wanted to show tolerance to her Catholic subjects, they rewarded her with a conspiracy, and England flowed with rivers of blood."

The French ambassador's mirthless chuckle was chilling. His cheeks colored for a moment. "*Unicuique suum, monsieur.*" The voice was a croak. "The same thing is happening in France, to the Huguenots, and, I assure you,

in the Ottoman empire too. Don't be deceived by our magnificent host's fine words. I am aware that in Yemen the Sultan's troops have just crushed a rebellion by Muslim heretics." He turned toward the Grand Vizier's secretary and received a nod of confirmation. "A tolerant sovereign is a weak sovereign. What keeps states united is the exercise of terror. The Ottoman peace is due more to the fact that subjects live under the vigilant eye of a single limitless power, that of the Sultan, without an aristocracy competing for titles and the throne. You have to agree, Don Yossef: Tolerance is nothing; power is everything."

The master of the house raised a hand in an enigmatic gesture, while he had his glass filled by a servant. "My lords, I sense that we are giving the same name to different concepts. You speak of sovereign power and its exercise. I am referring to the life of the subjects. To what in Turkish we call *tahammül.*"

Everyone's eyes were on him. In his youth he must have been very handsome, and that attractiveness hadn't faded. Nasi was fascinating, there was no point in denying it. It's not for nothing that Satan is the great charmer.

"You must know that the houses of Constantinople were built by mixed teams of workers. The reason is clear to see. Turkish carpenters are very good at working and sawing wood, but they can't carve stone. And a house without stone foundations is an unstable house. That's why we turn to Armenian, Greek, and Arab stonecutters. So some of the people dig a foundation; the others build the upper stories and the roof."

The French ambassador took advantage of a pause to reply. "I don't see that masons have anything to do with tolerance."

"Oh, they do, they do, Excellency . . . Of course you know the Bible story of the Tower of Babel. Well, many people think the Lord scattered the tongues of men to punish them, but it's exactly the opposite. He saw that uniformity made them proud, dedicated to enterprises as excessive as they were useless. Then he realized that humanity needed a corrective and he made us a gift of differences. So the masons, of different customs and faiths, have to find a modus vivendi that allows them to conclude their construction of the building. And for that you need not a conceded, flaunted tolerance, like the tolerance of the powerful, but an experienced tolerance, lived out every day, lived with the awareness that if it is lost, the house will fall down and you will be left without shelter. *Tahammül*, gentlemen."

It was Nasi's turn to address a reverent nod to the Grand Vizier's secretary, who replied with a forced smile. This new interpretation of the biblical passage mustn't have been greatly to his liking.

A faint clap of the hands made us turn toward Fitch. The Englishman was paying amused homage to the rhetoric of the master of the house. A moment later, the Polish voivode burst out laughing all by himself, at the sight of the pale face of Monsieur de Grantrie.

3.

By the end of the meal, the meaning of that bizarre meeting was clear to me. Basically, that was my trade, working out who was doing what and why. The presence of those people must be significant. Nasi had wanted me to be a spectator at this drama, so it was up to me to decipher the roles.

The Grand Vizier's secretary represented the Empire. France and Poland were the Catholic friends of the Grand Turk. The English bibliophile might have been there only for a book, but for some time his queen had certainly wanted to gain favor with the Sultan and open a trade route in the East. After all, Nasi was the guarantor of the soup kitchen, the referee in the diplomatic game, and I was the advantage point that he held over the others.

But I had no intention of being his amuse-bouche, the surprise dish to serve to the guests after the sea bass and roasted kid.

I told him as much later on, after he had said good-bye to his guests and we were left on our own. Not alone, as we had been that morning, in fact, because when we went back to the library, he introduced me to David Gomez, Satan's right hand. Gomez was a sturdy-looking man, with an olive complexion and distinctive features. He must have been about the same age as Nasi; his youth was behind him, but his physical and mental health were still intact. He inspired awe, although it would not be he who held a blade to my throat a few moments later.

I refused the tobacco that Nasi offered me and observed him as he lit up a roll of it, taking dense mouthfuls of smoke in the manner of the natives of the New World.

"So, what did you think of the meal?"

"Your cook serves you well. And so does your cellar keeper."

He smiled. "I was actually referring to the guests."

"Listen," I said to him through gritted teeth. "Moisés Navarro sent me all the way here from Salonika to give you some information, not to answer your riddles. In exchange, you promised that I would receive money and a house where I could rest."

"Everything under the sun takes its time. For a time, you will be my guest here at the palace, if you don't mind."

That really was the final straw, and I could barely refrain from insulting him.

"Use words to mean what they mean. I'm not really your guest, I'm a prisoner."

His surprise seemed sincere. He looked at me as if I were a chaffinch that had suddenly started braying. Then, with a slow movement of his arm, he invited me to look around. "Does this look to you like a cell?"

I didn't move my eyes; I kept them fixed on him. The smell of tobacco made me want to vomit. "How long am I going to have to stay here?"

"Long enough for us to get to know each other," he replied. "Today's meal has shown you who I am." His keen eye lit up with a strange light. "A Jew at the top of the world. Would you have thought it possible?"

He got up and set the roll of tobacco down on a little plate. "You can circulate wherever you like except for the north wing. That's my wife's chosen refuge." I thought I spotted some sadness in his eyes. "David will show you to your lodgings. *Ásta luego,* Senyor De Zante."

He strode out, leaving me prey to a mute rage. I breathed deeply and looked around at the hundreds of volumes that filled the walls. It was then that I noticed the open chink. Dark eyes were studying me from the secret room that I had occupied with Nasi.

Almost as soon as I spotted them, the chink was closed.

4.

A big room, a bed overflowing with pillows. A small table, a chair, a desk. Broad carpets on the floor and the walls. Warmth from the stove and the perfume of sandalwood from the candles. I looked around, and remembered Tuota's hovel, the cell in the backstreets of Ragusa, Efrem's house in Salonika.

Time, when it builds up momentum, changes a man's conditions quite quickly. Even the conditions of his imprisonment.

Gomez looked at me in puzzlement. Perhaps he didn't understand the smile that had just vanished from my lips. I imagined him serving Nasi all his life, and then a memory took shape. An old list of names. The eminent wanted men, the list of Giuseppe Nasi's acolytes and agents.

Duarte Gomez. Yes, Duarte was his *marrano* name; David was his Jewish one.

He picked up a bell from the desk and made it tinkle faintly. A young woman appeared in the doorway, her raven hair piled up under a mantilla, a tanned complexion. She was wearing wide breeches and a wool jerkin.

"If you need anything, you know what to do," Gomez said before taking his leave, leaving me alone with the girl.

I asked her for her name.

"Dana."

I stared at her. Memories of my body wrapped around Arianna's. I stepped forward, letting my eyes caress her features and the curves of her body. I framed her eyes with my hands and felt her freeze. Her eyes were light green, like the patina on copper pots.

No, they weren't the eyes that had been spying on me through the chink in the library wall.

"Why does Nasi's wife stay in hiding?"

She hesitated, the reply already on her lips, perhaps to weigh the words she was about to say. "She isn't hiding. She's still in mourning for the death of her mother, Donna Gracia."

There were other questions I would have liked to ask, but her body claimed all my attention. The shape of her breasts. The curve of her hips. The swelling between her legs.

She began straightening the bed, which was perfectly tidy already. Nervous gestures to overcome embarrassment, waiting for me to dismiss her. I sidled up to her until the fabric of my trousers touched hers. I took a deep breath, filling my nostrils with her perfume. She smelled of almonds and . . . a blade

pricked my throat. The woman's eyes were keener than the dagger that she was pressing to my neck. She waited for me to step back before returning the weapon to her belt.

"This isn't the Sultan's harem, and I'm not a concubine. Remember that, *kofer*. Do you need anything else?" I shook my head and watched her slip out of the room.

I needed air. I went over to the window and discovered that it looked out over the Bosphorus. The stars of Leo kept an eye on Asia.

Here I was, risking having my throat cut because of my baser instincts. What a grotesque end, after the journey I had taken. But certainly it was even more grotesque that I should have found myself there, that I had a room assigned to me in Palazzo Belvedere, the source of all conspiracies.

Later, Dana came back with a tray. As she set the plate and glass down on the little table, I noticed that she avoided catching my eye. Before she left, I called to her.

"Please forgive me," I said.

She nodded slightly, made not even the hint of a bow, and immediately turned to leave, but I held her back once more.

"Please, stay. I haven't spoken to a woman for weeks."

She knelt down reluctantly on the carpet, a few feet from the door.

Dinner was yellow rice with pistachios and raisins, then aubergines in yogurt. As I ate, I asked her to tell me about life at Palazzo Belvedere, to have an idea what awaited me.

Dana had worked for the Nasis for four years. She told me of the habits of the household, the names and jobs of about fifteen servants, the layout of the rooms on both stories of the building. She listed each detail rather mechanically, but when she talked about Gracia Nasi her voice filled with love and devotion. She had been her personal chambermaid, and she had treated her as if she were her old mother, until she began succumbing to illness.

"She wanted to die in the land of our fathers, in Palestine."

"Were you with her?"

I saw her face darken. "The *Senyora* didn't want me. She ordered me to stay with Donna Reyna, her daughter." She looked at me impatiently. "May I go now?"

I didn't want to stay on my own. I knew already that I wouldn't sleep. I remembered that when I was a child, to keep my mother by my bedside I used the excuse of my fear of the dark. Then my mother had been replaced by old Abecassi, and I had had to conquer my real nightmares on my own.

I thought of holding Dana back again, but it was clear that my presence irritated her.

It was hard to blame her: I was a spy of Venice, a renegade Jew, and I had just brazenly importuned her. I dismissed her with a word of thanks and prepared to fill my night alone.

I blew out the candles; the embers in the stove were my only source of

light. For at least an hour I stayed on the bed, crushed by my thoughts, trying to impose a different rhythm on my heart. But none of it was any use: I couldn't sleep, and anxiety drove me out to the loggia. Through the windows in the ceiling the moonlight fell on the mosaic floor, illuminating Spain, Italy, the Balkans. I heard faint sounds, apart from the murmur of the fountain. I leaned in, but the hall was deserted. Only a strip of light under the library door indicated that there was anyone there.

All of a sudden I felt my skin prickle, and realized that there was someone else there, a few feet away from me. The figure came forward, holding a candelabra.

A woman.

The flickering flame revealed a pale face and big, dark eyes. I was looking into the face of the ghost of Gracia Nasi, but she was a woman of flesh and blood.

"He is locked in there every night," she said, "Studying maps. Cherishing his dream."

My senses in a state of alarm, my throat dry, I watched her white fingers brushing a pillar. She stared, her big eyes boring into mine, and made me flinch.

"I don't know what to wish for you. Love him unconditionally or really get to know him one day."

She raised her hand as if to touch my face, but at the last moment she stopped.

"Dana is right," she said. "You have honest eyes."

Then, without another word, the woman disappeared into the shadows.

Again I dipped my memory in the spring of the long lessons I had learned in Venice. Donna Gracia's daughter, Reyna, had been given in marriage to her cousin Yossef. Consigliere Nordio had taught me the story of the Nasis very well. He had always fought against them; it was his mission, and he had trained me to fear them and to defend the Republic against their traps. He had trained me so well that I still felt at fault in spite of everything. From one corner of my mind his feeble voice told me over and over again that I wasn't equipped for the extreme sacrifice. I had failed in my mission. I hadn't known how to do anything but end up in the arms of the enemy.

In the belly of Leviathan, or on top of the world.

5.

A hole in the ground smeared with honey, a sweet and sticky trap. I might never get out of it. Gradually, with smiles and jokes, lavish meals and riddles, they would take over my soul and Nasi would add it to his collection.

Lying among the pillows, on that excessively soft bed, I could hear, beyond the wood of the doorway, the echo of little movements, as of a body settling down, assuming new positions to conquer stasis and tedium and thus to bring an assignment to its conclusion. Someone out there, someone, was keeping watch over me. I thought I could hear his breath, and I was like that, too, listening, my limbs aching, unable to sleep. My mind's eye scoured the palace, to see if escape was possible. My soul wandered, tethered to my body by the leash of weariness, and my ears tried to catch every sound. The splash of the fountain in the palace drawing room. Distant voices. The creak of wooden boards, the soft clatter of feet.

I cursed the person I had been in Salonika, the one who had had the chance to flee and hadn't done it. The one who had felt the shadow of affinity with his jailers. I cursed myself for not having tried to kill Nasi. For not killing the enemy, finally within arm's reach.

I saw the scene. I clutched the man's throat and tightened my grip. Rage and contempt sustained me. I felt the bones of the neck yielding, and then I started on his face. I wanted to wipe that ambiguous, self-important expression from his face. I wanted to erase Yossef Nasi from the category of the living, from my life, from my future memories. I struck at him doggedly, drowning his features in a lake of blood. I plunged into an uneasy half sleep.

It must have been the middle of the night by the time I stirred again. I felt my clothes burning. Something was running along my skin. Agitatedly, I undressed, and in the candle-light I tried to inspect every recess, every nook of myself, but I found no parasites, no fleas in my clothes or lice on my head.

It was only a sensation, a sign. I was in a Procrustean bed, and this was a portent of the suffering to come. I wouldn't stay and wait for it.

I assessed all the possibilities. Only flight would make me free, but I would have nowhere to go. To return to my earlier life I would have to turn my fantasy into a plan: bring Nasi's head to Venice, return to my responsibilities and, in fact, be the savior of the Republic.

Nordio would be proud of me, and his power and influence would

increase, because one of his men would have got rid of Giuseppe Nasi, bringing an end to his sordid intrigues.

Yes. Having the Jew's head. Killing him was a task within my scope. But going back to Venice?

It wasn't impossible. Just difficult. A disguise, a ship. A basket with a head in it, salted, to keep it from stinking. Kill Nasi. Flee, perhaps in disguise. Reach the port. I had to get hold of some money, there must be plenty in the palace . . . yes, even that was a problem that was easily solved. I would be meek. I would sting like a serpent in the breast. Yes. But first I had to rest. Rest.

I closed my eyes, and the inanity of my plan struck me from behind, like when you're a child and one of your friends jumps out from behind a corner and shouts *Boo!* and you turn around and see him laughing. A thousand variables had to be aligned, like a favorable astral conjunction involving all the planets and the fixed stars. And even if everything went according to plan, if I reached Venice with my trophy in the basket, it wouldn't change my nature. To Venice I was only a Jew. My place was the ghetto. Or rather, my place was under the ground. But not in the graveyard, not in consecrated ground.

And then it would no longer matter if I got away. What I needed wasn't an escape plan, but the strength to act and forget myself with my final act of redemption. Kill the Jewish Dog and allow myself to be torn to pieces by his brigands. Show him that I was capable of making the ultimate sacrifice.

My mind ceased its intense conscious activity. I fell back into dull, dark sleep, peopled by voices and faces: Nordio, Arianna, my father. Those accents, Tavosanis's from Friuli, Rizzi's from Rovigo. Old Abecassi's rough speech. The mute censure on Tuota's face.

Then voices and faces became bodies and faces, lined up on a stage like actors in a play, masks lowered. They were calling to me to climb onto that stage, and all around were the loggias that opened onto the drawing room of Palazzo Belvedere. I struggled and managed to get up there. I wanted to join the masks; I walked towards the proscenium arch; but I discovered that I was still in bed, half asleep, unable to move a muscle, oppressed by a terrible weight, while the masks laughed at me and mocked me.

All this went on for a long time: I dreamed about getting up and saw myself asleep, useless, defenseless, while the audience laughed, until I felt drawn upward, toward the ceiling, and I awoke.

I didn't know how long my stupor had lasted. No light entered the room; the air came in through little openings above the architrave of the door, which had been closed for the night. Now I could move my body, and I raised it up, fearing this might only be a new episode in the nightmare. But no, I was me, alive and awake.

I closed the window halfway and washed my face with water from the basin, then tipped it over my head. I dried myself, got dressed and leaned against the door.

"I know you're there. I want to leave."

No answer.

I cautiously opened the door. There was no one there. The light hurt my eyes. The day had begun long before.

The smell of food rose from the courtyard of the palace; someone among the Jewish refugees was having breakfast. I felt pangs of hunger, and that forced me to go downstairs.

A group of men were sitting around a low table. I didn't know what language to speak to them, but the oldest of them anticipated me, talking to me in Italian.

"You look like someone who hasn't slept well, Signore."

A strange answer came to my lips: "The bed is a hard battlefield."

I had spoken under my breath.

"I'm sorry?" He was a serene-looking old man.

"I was saying I had a troubled night."

He gestured to me to sit down next to him. "Please meet my brothers and sons-in-law." I sat down without thinking and was offered bread, cheese and olives. "Where are you from?" the man asked. The question left me dumbfounded, and my reply came instinctively: "Venice." They all nodded, to show that they understood. "Don't worry," the old man continued. "Here you find sleep. This place will protect you."

I didn't say a word, with last night's thoughts still echoing vaguely in my head. I bent my head over my plate and, along with the others, ate the bread of the man I saw as an enemy.

6.

I couldn't think when I had last had a good night's sleep. I'd spent the night of the Arsenal fire awake, and since then Morpheus had vanished, to be replaced by Cerberus, the three-mouthed dog, guarding the threshold to keep me from leaving hell.

Weeks of horrible dreams, sudden awakenings, pain from the beatings I had received in Ragusa. Then everything changed. After dining with the refugees, I went back to my room and it was a relief to realize that I was going to sleep, calmly, without fighting. As in the *Aeneid*, someone had thrown Cerberus "a sop, in honey steep'd, to charm the guard," and now "long draughts of sleep his monstrous limbs enslaved." Virgil, my father's favorite reading. That was my last conscious thought after I crossed the threshold and left Hades behind me.

I slept, slept, and slept again.

The next day passed slowly, drifting on a lazy breeze. I watched it floating above me like a white cloud, one of the dense, clear, nimbus type, ice vessels floating in the blue of the sky, on those afternoons that you spend in a field with your nose in the air and a blade of grass between your teeth. Afternoons that seemed endless to me as a boy. How long had it been since I had had one like this? My mother took me to play outside the walls, we ran together, we picked flowers.

For the whole of that day I didn't see Yossef Nasi or David Gomez. Dana made a fleeting appearance, just a flash and a trail of perfume. She left my dinner in my room, but I took the tray and went back down with it into the drawing room, to share a table with the old man and the other refugees.

It was there that Nasi found me, less than an hour later, when he bustled in with Gomez, followed by a troop of servants. He stopped in the middle of the room and spoke in a loud voice: "Listen to me. Some of our brothers and sisters need help from whoever is capable of giving it. It's not far from here; please come with us."

With the exception of the infirm, the aged, and mothers nursing babies, almost everyone moved right away. Little knots of people dissolved, people who were sitting down got to their feet, even children left their games. Gomez walked toward the door along with the servants, and everyone else followed after him. Before setting off himself, Nasi

glanced at me. I was still at the table, startled by the turn that events had taken.

"You come too, De Zante," he said. "It'll do you good."

Flights of gulls, low, risky parabolas among the masts of the mooring barge and the roofs of the houses by the water. We approached, and the ship slowly came alongside. I began to make out the faces of the people on the deck; on land, the men responsible for mooring the boat were organizing two gangways. Nasi and David Gomez quickened their steps, followed by the little crowd. I stayed behind, confused.

We hadn't exchanged a word. The sense of expectation was palpable, and the loquacity and affability of my fellow guests seemed to have vanished in the cold air of Ortaköy. Nasi was bustling about on the dockside, issuing orders. Gomez helped him to set up a gangway, and the first people prepared to disembark in the lashing wind.

The men's faces were ashen. An old man came forward, supported by his children and grandchildren. Nasi had a word of comfort for each of them, and pointed to a building behind us. "In there you will find hot tea, dried figs, and bread." His firm tone was reassuring. "There are also beds where you can rest. If one of you is ill or in pain for any reason, a doctor will be called."

I heard people speaking Ladino and Italian, as the servants distributed water and blankets. A middle-aged man who had just come down the gangway stepped forward.

"*Shalom*. Are you Don Yossef Nasi?"

"I am."

The man, his features distorted with fatigue and excitement, leaned forward and kissed his hand. In my mind's eye I can still see the image of his dirt-blackened fingers gripping Nasi's white ones. "What they say of you is true," the man said. "May the Lord allow you to protect us at all times."

Nasi smiled at him and led him to the shore. "You're safe now. Go and warm yourselves. Later you will be accompanied to your lodgings."

In front of me was the Great Enemy, concerned about people he didn't know, people he had never seen before, as if they were his children, parents, cousins.

Then I saw the woman and the child. Among the last to disembark; the little one, six or seven years old, clutching his mother's skirts. They walked cautiously, and there was profound weariness in the woman's eyes. The child was very fair, and looked around in terror. On the last step, just before they touched dry land, they stumbled.

I leaped forward and gripped the woman's arm. The child hurried to hide behind her.

The words came to my lips unbidden: "*No tened miedo*, you are safe."

The woman thanked me and was helped on her way. I stood where I was, looking out toward the sea, filled with a surge of emotion that swelled my chest and veins. I had just witnessed an ancient scene. I had played my part in

a performance that had been going on for centuries, for more than a thousand years.

I felt tears trickling down my cheeks, all the way to my lips, and tasted their bitterness. A hand fell on my shoulder. I still remember the sound of Nasi's voice, which brought me back to the present, amid all the noise of the ship's landing.

"Welcome back, Manuel Cardoso."

7.

The window frames the roofs of Cannaregio. I'm sitting at the table, waiting for the servant to bring in the braised meat, but instead Rizzi comes in with his favorite kind of game: well-roasted Jews on a spit.

"They call them Aaron and Asser. They're young, they've just entered the house of catechumens so they can become Christians. One of them's from the ghetto; the other one's from Poland."

A report in tiny, neat handwriting. Rizzi hands it to me smugly. I swallow my mouthful and clear my throat. "Is there anything urgent, Sior Rizzi? Some Jews who have only just come to their senses want to become Christian and live in the grace of God. Nothing too dreadful so far. What else have they been up to?"

"That's easy. It seems that it's the fault of this guy, a porter they call the Cunt. He's set the two catechumens to work and cursed the Madonna." I nod. Rizzi goes on. "Then that one from the ghetto, on Saturday he gets on his clean Sunday shirt, and he goes around saying as how when he's a Christian he'll have a fine set of clothes, and it'll get him a long way."

"A cheeky fellow, then. But blasphemy and scandal is none of our business."

But the cook Rizzi has saved his finest course for the end: "They're both workshop assistants to a printer from the ghetto. His name's Zanetti."

I stand up uneasily; that meat will have to wait. Books and printers are always our business.

Facing Tavosanis and Rizzi, the two of them are on their best behavior. They deny the insults to the saints and the Madonna. They confirm their intention to have themselves baptized, although perhaps not right away. Tavosanis conducts the interrogation. Not badly, but all too predictably. The first boy has ready answers.

"So why did you change your shirt that Saturday?"

"It was dirty, so I put on a clean one."

"They say that in the house of catechumens you're always quarrelling with the prior, that you plague him with questions."

"And where's the sin in that? I ask him all those questions so I can understand the truth."

He's a clever young man; he defends himself well. You don't need to press such people, you don't need to keep on at them. Better just to let them talk. Scare them a bit and keep listening.

I tell Rizzi to warm his hands, and gesture to Tavosanis to say that's enough.

A little while later, we know where the books are hidden. Zanetti didn't present them to the Office for examination, and that's enough for confiscation and a bonfire. Three hundred copies of the same text. On the frontispiece, Hebrew characters that I read instinctively, without noticing.

מחזור ספרדים

And now here they are, in front of my eyes, in the library of Palazzo Belvedere. *Mahzor Sephardim*. The collection of rites and prayers of my mother's people.

In Venice, the name Sephardim had slipped away among my thoughts. Back then I was Emanuele De Zante, Venetian, member of the apostolic Roman Catholic Church, and these were Jewish books. "Sephardim" had a faraway sound, like the name of a remote population of the Caucasus.

"A very rare copy you're holding in your hands," said someone behind me. I turned around and recognized the Englishman, Ralph Fitch, dressed as he had been on the evening when I first saw him. He pointed to the shelves around us and said, "Many of these works escaped the flames, the fanaticism that is intoxicating Europe."

Again I lowered my eyes to the *Mahzor*. Meanwhile Fitch went on talking, in his singsong, slightly gloomy Italian. I wasn't listening to him, it was just a sea of syllables, but eventually he stopped and I became aware of the silence.

I looked up again. "Forgive me, you were saying?"

He laughed faintly. "I was saying that this place is precious," and again he looked around, before adding, "It's a refuge for runaway books."

8.

I read greedily, as if to satisfy an ancient hunger. Every day I spent in the library was a new apprenticeship on a long trajectory that urged me toward its conclusion.

I looked at the walls filled with books and they seemed to me a mountain I must climb, to glimpse from its summit a horizon I had never seen before.

I thought of my mother and heard in my ears the echo of her voice. Around me, lined up on the shelves, there were volumes that a good Jew should love. Some of them I had struggled through during my schooldays, others I didn't know, but they all attracted me like treasures. Perhaps fate had chosen an intricate path to fulfill Sarah Cardoso's last wish.

I soon found myself remastering the Hebrew letters, even if the meaning of what I was reading sometimes escaped me. I found a Hebrew-Latin dictionary, compiled by a Dominican friar, and this discovery helped me considerably.

I started studying the *Moreh Nevuchim*, the *Guide for the Perplexed* by Moses Maimonides. I realized that I knew the Torah as a donkey knows the carter's whip. I plunged into the commentaries on the Zohar, which many people held to be equal to the Talmud. Speculations, visions. My mind opened.

I spent whole days in there, while outside it had started snowing again and the garden of the palace was reduced to a narrow passage between white cumulus clouds and icy fountains.

In the morning I was always alone, but during the afternoon, I often met other users of the library, and gradually I began talking to them about what they were reading. Apart from Ralph Fitch, I met a kabbalist called Meir, a poet of Azeri origin and a calligrapher of the Sultan's, who was devoting his skill to copying out an ancient Mohammedan text.

One day the master of the house came to see me. I was concentrating so hard on the meaning of a sentence that I didn't notice him entering and suddenly found him standing behind me.

"I see that you like reading, Manuel," he said, peering at the pages from over my head. "My Aunt Gracia was a keen reader, too. She said that books have only two shortcomings." He reached out his hand and tapped the cover of a big volume lying on the table. "They're heavy," he said. Then he looked up at the walls covered with shelves. "And they need space."

"Then this room solves both problems," I observed.

He shook his head and settled into the armchair next to mine. "Five hundred and eighty volumes is a troublesome legacy. Gracia also said that a Jew should never unpack his bags, but always keep them ready beside the door."

"And does that apply even here?"

He narrowed his eyes as if trying to spot something in the distance. "Since I disembarked more than fifteen years ago, not a day has passed when I haven't asked myself that very question. The Ottoman empire is safer than any other territory, but do you think it's easy? Our business deals, our movements, our way of dressing. Everything falls under the control of the authorities. We aren't free to cultivate our dreams. Have you ever had a dream, Manuel?"

The answer came out like a sob. "Yes: not to be Jewish. It was my father who fulfilled it."

My frankness didn't seem to bother him. "I understand you better than you imagine. Why be weak when you can become strong? But I'm not just content with transforming myself. I want to transform a people. From weak to strong. From divided to united. From unwelcome guests to masters of their own destiny. From fugitives to protectors of the fleeing. We've been running away for fifteen hundred years. The time has come to stop."

That man went on disorienting me, as when a light enters a room and little by little the corners are illuminated, revealing it as different from the way we imagined it in the gloom.

He slipped a big key into one of the panels that ran along the base of the bookshelves. From the space behind it he took a roll of parchment and spread it out on the table in front of me. It was a map, showing the portion of the world that extends from Crete to the Holy Land, from the coasts of Anatolia to the sources of the Nile.

"Years ago, my aunt received from Suleyman the concession to found a colony on Lake Tiberias." Nasi's index finger stopped on a little patch of blue between Jerusalem and Damascus. "It was her dream, and it has been mine, too. Palestine is the land promised to Moses, our land. But things haven't gone as we hoped, and the colony can't provide for itself." He looked up from the map and turned towards me.

"Over time I've understood our mistake. I am a merchant and a banker; I invest money in commercial enterprises. Very many Jews have the same vocation, because the sovereigns of Europe have forbidden us to practice any other trade. We need not a lake, but a sea."

His hand, outstretched and with its fingers spread, stroked the Mediterranean.

"But you already have possessions in the middle of the sea," I said, pointing at a spot on the map. "You are duke of Naxos and the Seven Islands."

Nasi sighed. "The Cyclades are a handful of little rocks. Beautiful and polished, and it's nice to hold them in your hand and shake them like a rattle,

but I have something bigger in mind." He gestured with his hand, and the Cyclades were swept aside. "I imagine a land where we will be able to live in peace, do our business deals, and cultivate the vine, the olive and tolerance. A place where you could choose the residence that we have promised you. A free nation, a refuge for all of us, for the books hated by the despots, and for everyone who is persecuted. Will you help me build that place, Manuel?" It was a sincere question and I felt like answering with one that was equally candid.

"Do I have an alternative?"

"You can leave here and walk all the way to the gate," he said. "No one has orders to stop you."

"Why are you giving me this opportunity?"

"Because I'm not Consigliere Nordio. He asked you to be true to Venice. I'm asking you to be true to yourself."

I swallowed. If the time I had spent at Palazzo Belvedere was supposed to allow us to get to know one another, Yossef Nasi had used that time to great advantage. In only two weeks he seemed to have plumbed the depths of my unease. "How can I choose, if I don't know what you want from me?"

He looked satisfied. I still hadn't left, and that was a good sign. He got up and walked around for a moment, brushing the spines of the books with his fingers. "You told Navarro that the architect Savorgnan left his work in Nicosia unfinished. Is that true?"

"Yes."

"Do you remember in detail what he said to you?"

"That there wasn't enough money to reface the bastions of Constanza and D'Avila. All eleven fortresses of the city are made of earth, then covered with stone. If they aren't refaced they're little more use than sand castles."

I paused. I lowered my eyes to the map and saw the name of Nicosia, just off the Ottoman coast. "Cyprus . . ." I murmured to myself, and then raised my voice as I looked at him. "The sea, of course, and a big island. Vines, olive trees, commercial ports. That's how you plan to take your vengeance on Venice. By taking Cyprus away."

"I have a score to settle with Venice, that's true. But it isn't vengeance that inspires me, and not even the Sultan wants the ruin of La Serenissima." He put his hand in his pocket and took out a gold coin. He held it between his thumb and index finger, so that I could recognize it: a Venetian ducat. "In Constantinople the most important business deals are done with this, and no one wants to stop doing them."

He approached me again and lowered his voice, as if to lend additional weight to every single word. "The score that needs settling is with history, Manuel. I have the money to do it and I have the support of the Sultan. He promised me the crown of the island, when it is in his hands." He looked me straight in the eyes. "Thanks to your information, I will soon have a fleet." He set the gold coin down on the map, in front of me, right on top of the outline of Cyprus.

9.

On the two shores of the Adriatic, and doubtless elsewhere, too, they say the eyes are the mirrors of the soul. Of all the emissaries of our emotions, they are in fact the most sincere, the hardest to manipulate. For the same reason, others say that you can know a man by his way of laughing.

In my people's books, on the other hand, it is the voice that testifies to the soul of a man. Indeed, voice, soul and breath and life are one and the same. In the first two chapters of the *Bereshit*, in which the story of the Creation is told, the voice of God rings out ten times, the same number as the Commandments.

Shemà, Israel. Hear, O Israel.

Our daily prayer invites us to welcome the words of the Lord.

I had begun to recite it again, twice a day, but now no one was forcing me to do so. And lo and behold, my voice had changed. I heard it vibrating sonorously, like a well-tuned instrument, and I couldn't work out whether it was the effect of the Hebrew, with its guttural consonants, or because my soul was expressing its change in that way.

Nasi explained to me that soon, with my new voice, I would have to address the most eminent men in the Ottoman court. Perhaps the Great Admiral, or one of the viziers, or even the Sultan himself. He wanted to hear the information about Nicosia from me. He wanted them to ask me their questions, to convince himself that Cyprus could be conquered, with little effort and in a few months.

The wait for that meeting began disturbing my nights again. I dreamed of finding myself in the presence of the Sultan, incapable of speaking, struck by sudden muteness. I imagined Consigliere Nordio sitting on my chest and trying to pull my tongue out with his hands.

Days later, at the first sign of a clear sky, I decided to shake off those visions with a long late afternoon walk. Often certain stale thoughts need wind and fresh air to blow them off into the distance.

The palace garden was at its finest at that hour. The sun, low on the horizon, played in the branches, and the blackbirds hopped silently among the patches of snow. A group of women were collecting the refugees' laundry, which had been hung out to dry in long, billowing lines.

I left the central avenue and took a muddy path toward the furthest corner of the park. Beyond the duck pond, a hedge formed a high barrier. I walked along it, and after a few steps I found the entrance to a kind of labyrinth, or rather a sequence of green rooms, with the sky for a ceiling and a grass floor.

After a few twists and turns, I found myself in a round clearing dotted with shrubs. The thorny branches of a climbing rose climbed an iron arch and framed a bare stone bench that resembled a great boulder. Directly behind it, a white drystone wall, no more than ten feet long, and a tree with a slender trunk.

Beneath the dark green foliage, Dana was trying to hang a goldfinch's cage. The bird greeted me first, then she turned round and froze, like a deer surprised while grazing in the depths of the forest.

"Welcome to my garden," she said at last, with a hint of pride. "Everything you see here was planted by me."

Only then did I realize that Dana, too, had changed. She no longer addressed me in polite phrases and forced replies, and when she brought me my food, the brief glances that we exchanged said that the task wasn't entirely unpleasant to her.

She gestured to me to sit down, as if I were a guest on the doorstep of her house, then sat down beside me on the bench, and it was the first time we had been so close to one another since that first night.

"It's growing quickly," I said, pointing to the little tree. "You've been here for four years, and you'll be able to enjoy its shade this summer."

She laughed, lifting her chin and revealing her throat. I felt a desire to kiss her, but then I remembered the dagger. She wrapped herself up in her woolen cloak, tugging it up under her chin, perhaps because of the cold wind, or perhaps so as not to throw other temptations my way. Then she started to tell a story, accompanied by the song of the goldfinch.

On the coast of the Morea, in a fishing port, there was a corner of the world identical to this one, with wild roses, the bench and the wall of white stones. The only major difference was the size of the carob tree down there, which was rough-barked and centuries old.

It was in that port that a Jewish child called Dana had spent the first ten years of her life, until a corsair had taken her away from home to give her to Prince Selim.

In the harem of the future Sultan, Dana had soon attracted attention because of her personal qualities, and had entered the group of *jariye* taking care of the favorite, the Princess of Light, Nurbanu Sultan.

They dressed her, they combed her hair, they prepared her hot bath and, every day after dinner, they served her a sherbet of carob and lemon peel. It was her favorite drink, and to make sure she never went without it, at the end of every summer they had to peel thousands of carob berries, extract the pulp and prepare the syrup. Dana always set aside a few seeds or, more often, she found them on herself, stuck in a fold of her gown, and enjoyed planting them in the four corners of the garden. But with the first frost, the shoots that had just appeared died of cold. Only one managed to survive, for three winters, protected by the wall of the stables and the giant umbrella of an oak tree.

During the fourth winter, after his father's death, Prince Selim moved from Kutaya to the capital, and Dana made the journey in a cart, with her little tree between her knees. The festivities for the new sultan went on for weeks, and Nurbanu granted freedom to her most loyal *jariye*. She arranged a marriage for each of them, and Dana was matched with an old provincial bey, meaning an even worse form of slavery than before. But thanks to a Jewish woman who supplied the *harem* with fabrics and perfumes, Dana had made sure that Don Yossef approached the Sultan and saved her from that unwelcome marriage. A few days afterward, she and the little carob tree were settled at Palazzo Belvedere.

A trill from the goldfinch embellished the end of the story like an inky flourish.

So I was sitting in the replica of a memory, the clearest one that Dana had kept of her own land. Perhaps every now and again, when her memory restored a detail to her, she added it and enlarged the picture. I asked her if she hadn't ever thought of going back home, of seeing the village she had been torn from.

"They didn't tear me from it," she replied. "I think my father agreed. I don't remember any violence, just my sister weeping."

I remembered some prints I had seen in Venice, with Turkish-looking corsairs dragging women onto ships. I had been sure that the Sultan's female slaves came only from war and piracy. I said this to Dana, and she corrected me.

"Not all. The harem is more like a monastery than a private brothel. You learn to read and write, to sew, play music, dance, prepare a bath, cook. You become ideal wives for the Sultan's pages and administrators. Many fathers couldn't offer a daughter anything better."

I had never heard this account of things before. "Are you trying to tell me that it's a kind of school in there, that you had happy years?"

"Not by a long way. I had to forget I was Jewish, learn the Muslim prayers, obey rigid rules, stay afloat on a sea of envy. But most of all, they accustomed me to thinking that a whim on the Sultan's part might improve my life."

"And did that happen?"

"No, but you know that it might happen any day, so each day is the child of his will, and cancels your own."

She stopped there and, in silence, began pulling up blades of grass and throwing them in front of her, as if trying to tell her own fortune.

I said that I, too, had been a child in a Mediterranean port. Then my father, a corsair-hunter, had taken me away to offer me a better life. I, too, had had to change my faith, and, I too, had displayed myself in a kind of harem, albeit a masculine one, where the Sultan laid claim not to the obedience of sex, but the obedience of death.

"And perhaps I, too," I concluded, "managed to escape thanks to Yossef Nasi."

The last phrase drew a shiver from me, and the twilight air prolonged it. I had come outside in my shirtsleeves, and the damp cold was already slipping under the fabric and into my skin. The smell of a storm and wet earth rose from the Bosphorus.

Dana noticed that I was trembling and unhooked the cage from the carob branch, and together we went back toward the palace, beneath the white sickle of a still, lifeless moon.

10.

I'm getting to know you, capital of the empire. I'm adapting myself to the way you punctuate your time.

Twenty-eighth day of the month of Shabban, nine hundred and seventy-seven winters after the Hejira.

I'm getting to know you, Byzantium, New Rome, Rūmiyya al-Kubrā, Qostantiniyye, Istanbul, city of damp, heavy air. On mornings when the sky is clear, I dream of rising into the wind and flying, seeing you from above, but the wind is heavy, thick with smells from the tanning works of Yedikule, the glue factories, the guts being turned into ropes. Every city has a background smell: Venice is mold and brackishness; Salonika reeks of piss; Constantinople breathes wet earth and weariness and dreams.

I'm getting to know you, frozen city with the narrow, dirty streets along which cruel winds blast. Pyraz blows from the north, Karayel from the Balkans, Lodos from the south. They take turns like a team of flagellators, they rummage through your clothes, they beat your bones mercilessly. When it rains, the streets turn into pools, and feet and legs sink into the mud.

I'm getting to know your men and your veiled women, to catch allusions and double meanings beneath the dirty crust of your Turkish, to imagine dreams and smiles behind the thin linen veils.

As we walked, David Gomez and I, we tried to avoid the most treacherous of the puddles. We left Palazzo Belvedere often, and from Ortaköy we headed southwest. Reaching Galata, we went inside a *kahvehane* a few steps from the Golden Horn. I treasured the sounds, the smells, the warmth of the place. A new experience for me, afternoons spent in a coffeehouse. I had never devoted myself to idleness. My days had been made of orders, men to follow and interrogate, detailed reports, weapons training. I felt the need to act, but Nasi's plans required more time than expected. Time spent getting the Sultan drunk, reassuring the Treasurer, discussing matters with the viziers, bringing gifts to the Great Mufti and the most influential imams. So all I had to do was wait, and my curiosity about the thousand faces of the capital was the secret diversion that kept me from dying of boredom.

Even in its cold season, Constantinople knew how to flatter you and lend you affectations. You just had to see the effects of its bustle on Gomez: solid as a tree trunk and well on in years, and yet light in his movements, able with a single step to look like a dancer, like a pen drawing in the air. He walked

ahead of me along a street that flowed with torrents and impromptu water-falls, and his trousers didn't even seem to get damp.

The voices from the *kahvehane* came closer. In a minute, I would plunge into the scents and vapors, the music played on flutes and violins, the thousand tongues and dialects of the city. I was getting to know you, Tzarigrad, Konstantinopla, city of the five thousand mosques, of *peramas* and caïques that carried you from one shore to the other, of people who arrived every day from every corner of the empire, of Jewish businessmen, of Jewish craftsmen, of Jewish merchants dealing in slaves from Russia or the Caucasus, city where I never met a single beggar but saw a thousand sellers of nightingales, city of *eskici*, strolling rag-and-bone men who defied the wind and rain with barrows filled with rubbish.

Outside the benches were empty. It was still cold. Inside, between windows that framed the gray of the day and walls painted with blue and red motifs, there squatted men of the most varied appearance, origins and ages. Genoese, Jews, Arabs, Frenchmen . . . Most numerous of all were the Turks, their heads shaven and topped with the *topolan*, their slightly yellowed mustaches smelling of yogurt and coffee. They played *tavla*, sitting facing one another and sipping drinks of every color.

I exchanged a few words with Yassir, an Egyptian who claimed to make majolica. He lived in a street in Galata that abounded in taverns, but *hic meliòr ke illic*, he announced in a kind of crazed Latin: better in this café than in dives full of janissaries *ke solum volunt fornicar cum putas*. Yassir talked to me about drinking sprees, brawls that had broken out among soldiers over the aforementioned whores. His face was filled with revulsion.

In a corner at the back, a flautist was playing a sorrowful tune, weaving it into the carpet of voices and noises. Gomez, leaning against a wall, began listening to the tale of a Genoese merchant who had just returned from Persia.

With the entrance of Meddah Masun, the storyteller, everyone fell silent. The son of a Turk and a Circassian, this old man had blue eyes and beneath his turban his locks, though thin, were still fair. There was no one who did not respect Masun; no one was a match for him when it came to recounting the legends of Nasreddin Hoca, the sage who had lived in Anatolia three centuries before, about whom there were dozens, perhaps hundreds, of moral tales and funny stories. He told them in a language that was fascinating but obscure to me, mingling words from every country and sometimes turning into pure sound. It was Gomez who translated for me, murmuring in my ear. That afternoon, accompanied by his violinist, Masun had just launched on a story about when Nasreddin, to find a bit of peace and silence, had withdrawn to the desert, and one night . . .

"Senyor David, Effendi . . ." said a voice behind us.

We turned around. It was a young servant from the Palazzo Belvedere, whose name I had never known. He was panting. He beckoned us to follow him outside.

"What's happening?" Gomez asked on the threshold.

"Don Yossef asks you to come back to the palace as a matter of urgency," the young man replied. Then he stopped, confused and thoughtful.

"Go on," Gomez prompted him, his brow furrowed.

I remember everything about that moment, everything: the cold, damp air, the hubbub coming from inside the café, the boy's hesitation, my curiosity . . .

"So, Effendi . . . 'We're going to see the giant.' That was what Don Yossef asked me to say to you. 'We're going to see the giant.' "

11.

Imagine a village in the heart of the Balkans and a little boy called Bajica grazing the family herd. He's only ten years old, but everyone around knows him, because of his giant stature and his alert mind. So, when the moment of the blood tax arrives, the Ottomans come and find him on the mountains and carry him away, or perhaps it's his father who points him out to the Sultan's officials, to spare his intelligent son a future of hunger. Be that as it may, Bajica is brought up by a family of Muslim peasants. He learns the language, converts to Islam and takes the name of Mehmed. At the age of fifteen, when he is sent to Adrianopolis to become a janissary, he is already more than six feet tall. At thirty-seven he commands the imperial guard and three years later he is made the Great Admiral, replacing the legendary Ariadeno Barbarossa, lord of Algiers. He is then appointed governor of Rumelia, the province where he was born and where once again he hugs his mother, who says she recognizes him by a birthmark on his face. At fifty, he is third vizier, then he becomes second; finally, when he is on the brink of sixty, Suleyman the Magnificent appoints him Grand Vizier.

So it is that a Serbian child has become the most powerful man in the Ottoman Empire after Sultan Selim II, one of whose daughters he married. In the course of his incredible rise he led the army against the Hapsburgs, the Shah of Persia and the Tsar. He repressed revolts and thwarted plots. He designed a canal between the Red Sea and the Mediterranean and another between the Volga and the Caspian Sea. Now his emissaries keep him in contact with the whole world, from the Moriscos of Spain to the Sultan of Aceh on the island of Sumatra. He speaks Serbian, Turkish, Štokavian, Arabic, Persian, Italian and Latin. He is Sokollu Mehmed Pasha. The Giant. The man who summoned us one winter day to appear before the Divan.

At that time, much about Mehmed Pasha was still unknown to me. But I did know the legend of his destiny, and I couldn't help comparing it to mine. Both renegades, converts, loyal to those who had given us a new life. Except that I had had to conceal my origins, because the Repubblica Serenissima would never allow them. By contrast, the Great Turk, who in the eyes of the Venetians was a cruel tyrant, had had no difficulty entrusting his empire to a convert. Nasi told me that Sokollu, for his part, maintained excellent relations with his brother, who, thanks to him, had become a patriarch of the Orthodox Church.

With that thought in mind, I climbed into the carriage that awaited us at

the Fishmongers' Gate. In Constantinople, Nasi was one of the very few Jews who were allowed to use carriages or sedan chairs, or even move around on the back of a mule. He owed that privilege to his own influence, which had won him a dispensation from the Sultan. We sat in silence, and soon we arrived at the Seraglio.

The walls of the palace were so long that they looked like another city, separate from and protected by the first. The impression became even stronger once you had entered the first courtyard, where craftsmen, dockyard workers and petitioners formed a long and orderly queue to obtain a colloquy with the vizier of the Dome.

We got out of the carriage near the stables and proceeded on foot toward another door, yet more imposing than the first and flanked by two stout towers.

Beyond that threshold, which only the Sultan could cross on horseback, there was a second courtyard, entirely enclosed by a colonnade. Peacocks and gazelles wandered among hedges and cypress trees. On the right, the kitchen chimneys gave off smells of roast mutton. A central meadow, gleaming like a silk carpet, had four paths running across it. A single path of black cobblestones traversed it lengthwise, leading to a third portal. Instead, we took one of the side paths, which brought us to a spot below a marble loggia, where we were told, with a gesture, to wait.

We sat down on a long porphyry bench softened by comfortable cushions. Absolute silence reigned, a silence that would have made any speech sound vulgar and disrespectful. And yet speech would have been a great help to me. The instructions that Nasi had given me did not seem sufficient to face such a crucial trial.

I knew that the Divan had been in deadlock for years on the question of attacking Cyprus. I knew that there had been provocations, periodic visits by the Turkish fleet, some artillery fire supposedly aimed at pirates. I knew that the Divan was divided into two factions. The one opposed to war was the smaller, but its chief supporter was the Grand Vizier. The larger party, led by the Great Admiral and the viziers who came from the army, was seeking a definitive argument for war that would overcome all objections at a stroke.

Supplying that argument was my task for the morning.

I stirred myself: Nasi was approaching me and beckoning me in. I hadn't even noticed that he had got up from the bench and had already accomplished the formalities decreed by etiquette.

The room we entered was rather bare, intimate, and protected by a dome. The light entered through a big window screened by a shutter, and a red fabric sofa ran along three walls. On this divan sat the ministers of the Ottoman government. They wore turbans of different shapes and styles, some high and long, others puffy and round. The differences clearly were significant, but I was, sadly, unable to interpret them. The central place, raised slightly above the others, was occupied by a bearded giant, who was

rendered still more majestic by a turban that sprouted from his head like a great white tulip. Higher up, a golden grille covered an opening in the wall. Nasi had explained to me that the Sultan often followed the viziers' meetings from there.

I tried to spot a shadow through the golden mesh, but caught only a very vague impression. I bowed deeply and kissed the hem of the Grand Vizier's robe. He welcomed me in my language, calling me "Signor De Zante."

A man on my right, who must have been the chancellor, began reading from a register in a neutral, formal voice. The dragoman translated his words for me, because the language used by the dignitaries is very different from that of the people, stuffed with archaic Arabic and Persian terms. There is as much difference between plain Turkish and its Ottoman form as there is between the dialect of Chioggia and Cicero's Latin.

"In the first instance, the Imperial Council wishes to know from the gentleman convened the extent of the damage done to the Venice Arsenal by the recent explosion of a powder house and the fire that followed from it."

Nasi had predicted this request, and had advised me to stick to the facts. Certainly, to say that the fleet of Venice had been destroyed, as many patrons of the café maintained, would have helped the case for war against Cyprus. At any rate, four months after the event it was unimaginable that the Ottoman viziers had no clear information on the matter. So I had to prove myself to be honest and trustworthy. I described in detail what I had seen in my investigation. When I finished, the chancellor read again from his register.

"Secondly, the Imperial Council wishes to know the information in possession of the gentleman convened concerning the defenses of Nicosia and their alleged inadequacy."

I described the map of the city that I had seen drawn by Savorgnan: a star with eleven bastions and three gates. I told them what I knew about the hundreds of families forcibly moved to make way for new barrages and the big trench. I said that Giulio Savorgnan had finished the work in the incredible time of eight months, and when he returned to Venice all he had left to do was the refacing of the bastions.

Here one of the viziers interrupted, in a fluting voice that matched oddly with the thick black mustache that framed it. I imagined he must be the Great Admiral, Ali Pasha, known as Muezzinzade, or son of the muezzin, because that was the profession of his father and it had been his own as well for many years, in a mosque very close to the Seraglio.

"Do you believe," Muezzinzade asked, "that these bastions are still unfinished?"

"Savorgnan told me that he had made arrangements for them to be completed in his absence, but that for want of funds at least two of them had been left unfaced: Constanzo and D'Avila."

The Great Admiral smoothed his mustache and smiled with satisfaction,

exchanging a glance of agreement with a bearded old man who, judging by Nasi's description, must have been Lala Mustafa Pasha, the fifth vizier, general of the land forces.

"We will have to hurry," murmured another vizier, striking his hands on his knees, "before they have time to collect additional funds and properly complete the job."

Sokollu turned toward him and gave him an icy stare. "Haste is never good advice, Piyale Pasha. This information is precious, but we need to assess the cost and the time needed for this campaign. Remember Malta."

As soon as the Grand Vizier finished speaking, three sharp blows rang out against the golden grille above his head. The Giant froze, and so did the other dignitaries.

Then Sokollu Mehmed Pasha dismissed me with words of thanks, to which Muezzinzade added a personal encomium, in Italian, for the "*straordinario servigio*" that I had rendered the Sultan. Seven other viziers showed their approval, nodding their turbaned heads vigorously, like a clump of crocuses bent by the wind. And so ended my audience below the dome of the Divan.

When we were outside again, a radiant and emotional Nasi hugged me.

He explained that on a few occasions the Sultan resorted to striking the grille, to suspend the meeting so he might speak in private with the Grand Vizier. About what the two men were speaking to one another as we climbed back into our carriage, Yossef had no doubt. It was not within the power of the Grand Vizier to oppose the war, but he could still delay it.

"Sokollu knows full well that it is not such a simple matter to unleash this conflict. There is a peace treaty between Venice and the Ottoman Empire, signed by Suleyman and confirmed by Selim. At least two things would be needed to break it. First of all a *fatwa* from the Grand Mufti, justifying the war on religious grounds. Then they would need a *casus belli*, a political pretext. The island of Cyprus pays a regular tribute to the Sultan. No Ottoman subject has been mistreated or offended. The only excuse seems to be the pirates."

"What pirates?" I asked in surprise.

"In the peace treaty," he explained to me, "it is written that when the Cypriots capture Muslim pirates, they must send them for trial to Constantinople."

The carriage passed through the outer walls of the palace and set off down the hill toward the Golden Horn.

"I have never heard of such a practice."

"Indeed. That demonstrates how seldom the clause is honored. It is a feeble pretext, but the only one there is." He cracked his fingers. "The game has begun, Manuel," he said, with a complicit glance. "Let us prepare our moves."

12.

That night, I didn't hear Dana when she came in to bring me my evening meal. I was looking at the sky, turning the constellations into a firmament of thoughts. Orion and his dog Sirius were confronting the Bull, and I wondered what hunting strategy Nasi had in mind, and what my intended place was in the chase. I had revealed the information in my possession to the Divan, and at least on paper, my job in the city was done. And yet Nasi's words after the audience seemed to allude to new prospects. I didn't know the city well, I spoke its language with an Italian accent, and I was a foreigner, a Jew, forbidden to carry weapons. What use could I be to him now?

Dana's voice distracted me from the stars.

"I've brought you something to eat." She had already set it down on the desk and poured wine into a copper beaker. In a bowl I noticed some sweets that I had never seen before, like the ones that the Turks call *halva* but with a more spicy, pungent aroma.

Dana's eyes gleamed with mischief. "After a day like that, I thought you might want some comfort to calm your mind. These sweets will help you to find it."

I thanked her for her solicitousness and sat down to eat. She went on, "It's very cold tonight. Do you want me to revive the fire?" I gave another gesture of agreement and started soberly eating, as I always did in the evening. Dana knelt in front of the stove, filled it with wood and blew on the embers to encourage the flames. I saw her breasts swelling beneath her blouse. The curve of her buttocks on her heels made me sigh, and without realizing I was doing so I found myself stroking the table as if it were the smooth skin of a woman's back.

When she had finished, Dana stood up and made as if to leave.

I asked her to stay and invited her to come and sit next to me. She looked me in the eyes and made herself comfortable on the cushions. We divided the sweets that she had brought, savoring on our tongues the taste of pistachios and a resin with a strange relaxing effect. My body was filled with languor, a light, diffuse intoxication. The effect of the drug on Dana seemed less intense.

Our eyes met again. Like men at arms following orders in perfect concurrence, we approached one another. I embraced her; our mouths met. Filled with a delicious frenzy, we began freeing ourselves of our clothes, which in the land of the Turks are rather more easily and quickly unlaced. The wide breeches fell, and the shirts. I heard a metallic sound. Something had slipped to the floor. I gave it a sidelong glance.

The dagger, which the skin of my throat had felt weeks before. The bronze handle glinted blood-red.

Dana. Through her strong, myrtle-scented flesh, I reached a place that had long been closed to me, an earthly paradise where I had dwelt with Arianna in a past life.

Our bed is green with leaves, the beams of our house are of cedar, our walls are cypress trees.

The rise and fall, the dip of the groin, the mounds of buttocks and breasts: I enjoyed Dana, her every facet and gesture, her voice and her taut, young, lithe body. Sweet war, whose gestures are acts that some would call bestial. In the end I discharged my male burden with a long groan. Dana put her hand over my mouth.

"Don't make too much noise. No one must know."

I reassured her and rested her head on my chest, then began to stroke her, my mind empty, as our breathing subsided. I let my eye wander over her body and mine. Her left leg concealed my manhood. It was the first time I had lain with a woman of my people.

It was the first time I hadn't paid for a woman's favors.

I studied the dagger, abandoned among the clothes, on the floor. "At our first meeting, you threatened to kill me if I touched you. Today you should take a thousand lives from me."

Dana smiled, and without saying a word, she roused herself, collected her clothes and hastily dressed. When she reached the door, before closing it behind her, she turned.

"I was a thousand times more harmless to you when I held my dagger."

13.

Five years earlier, in 1565, the fleets of the Turk had laid siege to Malta. At the head of that expedition had been the same men now seated at the Divan: Muezzinzade, Lala Mustafa and Piyale Pasha. They had thrown the whole of the Ottoman fleet at the bastions of St Elmo's Fort but could not bring it down. Under the protection of Saint John, the Knights Hospitaller had resisted for four months, until the Turks had finally been forced to give up.

That failed enterprise was a serious humiliation, the specter raised by Sokollu, the same ghost that Nasi had to exorcize from the mind of the vizier. He said he was convinced that for the Sultan's troops Cyprus would not be a second Malta, it was too big for that. Neither would there be any great bloodshed, because once Nicosia had fallen the Turks would push their way inland, forcing the Venetians to negotiate a surrender.

"Six months at the most and it will all be over. But the invasion will have to happen soon, before the summer."

It was late winter, so there was no more time to lose.

Palazzo Belvedere was a hive of activity in the weeks that followed. Sometimes Nasi invited me to sit in the little secret room with him, to show me some of the new guests.

"The thin man with the long beard is Emin Mustafa, a former member of the Ulema Council and cousin of the Grand Mufti. His wisdom is boundless, and so is his vanity. On his right, the old man with the cataract is Eli Ben Haim, our chief rabbi. A tough old character. You'd better have him against you than on your side. And never behind you."

Ralph Fitch, the English guest, was among the most assiduous users of the library. He had a deep liking for books and read them unselfconsciously, many pages a day.

The news came early in the spring. The envoy from the Sublime Porte had sent Venice the order to cede Cyprus. The excuse used was pirates, as Nasi had anticipated.

The event was celebrated with a bottle of the finest wine. But our anxieties did not diminish, not even when, after the Doge's refusal, the Grand Mufti appealed to the Muslims to reconquer Cyprus "because peace with the infidel is legitimate only when one derives from it use and advantage for the generality of Muslims." Even the Prophet, in the eighth year of the Hejira, had broken peace with the infidel to conquer Mecca.

During those feverish days, the Venetian ambassador to Constantinople was arrested in his residence.

"The die is cast," was Nasi's first comment.

He had brought me with him to the Bosphorus, on one of those outings that he said helped him to think. We had taken the smallest boat, with four oarsmen. David was sitting in the bow, and Nasi stayed with me in the stern. It was a bright, hot day, the first really pleasant one since I had come to the city.

"Last year, Pope Ghislieri expelled our people from the territories of the Church. He ordered that all sign of our presence be erased from the city, even from the cemeteries. There are families who escaped from Ferrara with their dead on their backs. For some time he has wanted to unite the Catholic powers for a new crusade. For a bulldog like him, the dispute over Cyprus is excellent news."

The picture was beginning to take shape as the boat slipped on, and Nasi kept adding details. France and Poland would not take sides. As to Spain, Philip II had no intention of investing his money in an expedition to help Venice. On the contrary, he would pay any sum of money to see St. Mark's sink into the lagoon. Still, the Catholic world could not oppose the pope's invitation. They would take their time, trying to guide the war toward Algiers or Tripoli rather than committing themselves to the defense of Cyprus.

"If I know the Catholic sovereigns at all, they will never reach an agreement," Nasi said firmly. It wasn't their alliance that concerned him for the time being. He pointed to the building on the coast in front of him, on the slopes of Pera Hill. It was the same one he had pointed out to me the first time I had come to Palazzo Belvedere, on that same boat: the residence of the bailiff, the Venetian ambassador, Marcantonio Barbaro.

"We know for certain that he is communicating with the outside world, and that his messages are reaching Venice."

"You mean his imprisonment is a farce?"

"It saves face, given that Venice and the Sultan are now in open conflict. But as I have already told you, in Constantinople the party of the friends of Venice is a strong one. And if Venice and Constantinople reach an agreement, our plan could still go up in smoke."

"Are you referring to resistance on the part of the Grand Vizier?"

"The vision of Mehmet Sokollu is broad and deep, and he has grand projects that might turn out to be useful to us as well. He wants to dig a canal connecting the Red Sea and the Mediterranean. Can you imagine? You could get to India with ten thousand miles' less sailing. Cyprus would become a hugely important port of call. But Sokollu likes to take his time, and he doesn't like risky undertakings. He's a strategist, not a merchant."

By now we had reached the city, and the Imperial Seraglio loomed magnificently on the edge of the promontory.

Nasi explained to me that Sokollu could count upon support inside the

palace: "Nurbanu Sultan, Princess of Light, Selim's favorite wife. She was raised Muslim, but she is also the niece of Admiral Venier. She certainly wouldn't be too pleased if her husband declared war on La Serenissima."

I knew her story; she was the daughter of a noble Venetian family, captured by Turkish corsairs.

"Fortunately for us," Nasi went on, pointing at the palace, "she is locked up in her rooms, although that doesn't mean she is cut off from the world. The hall of the Divan and the imperial harem are divided only by a small court-yard, and the head of the Black Eunuchs has intimated to me that Nurbanu sometimes goes and sits behind the grille that you saw, above the head of the Grand Vizier, and secretly listens in on the meetings of the Council."

We sat in silence until the shores of the Bosphorus began to widen and the outlines of an archipelago appeared clearly beyond the prow, in the middle of the Propontis. Nasi ordered the steersman to turn back. That day seemed inspired by signs and clues that he alone perceived. He waited until we were back below the bailiff's residence before he spoke again.

He said he could imagine how the ambassador communicated with the outside world. The expedient was a simple one. Barbaro complained of deli-cate health, and received frequent visits from the doctor to the Venetian community, one Solomon Ashkenazi.

"The Grand Vizier's personal secretary?" I asked in amazement.

Nasi nodded. It was only a hypothesis, without any proof. No one could understand how Ashkenazi got the messages out, given that the janissaries searched him at the entrance and exit of the bailiff's house. But certainly Sokollu was informed of the communications between the ambassador and Venice, and secretly served as their bondsman.

Now the picture was almost complete. All that was missing was me.

Me, the Venetian. The spy hunter.

14.

If patience is a virtue, waiting is an art. I had learned it in my Venetian years, lying in wait for spies and conspirators. Staying in the same place for hours, beguiling the time without letting the time beguile me into lowering my guard, had been a crucial part of my job. Perhaps that was why I felt so much at my ease hidden in the shade of the poplars, not far from the villa of the bailiff Marcantonio Barbaro. The prisoner couldn't have been having too bad a time in there. Seen from the land side, his residence looked even richer, surrounded by a well-tended garden, but above all well guarded, kept under constant surveillance by two orders of watchmen. Inside, I counted four armed men, servants of the bailiff. I imagined there might be a few more inside the house. The janissaries were stationed on the outer circle, by the doors. Grim faces and drooping mustaches, as the code of the Sultan's chosen bodyguard decreed.

I spent my days studying every detail of the building from different angles. I examined the windows and the balconies, because I knew that sometimes guards communicate with mirrors or little colored flags. I also kept a close eye on the movements of the birds around the building, looking for messenger pigeons, but saw only swallows and crows.

Provisions arrived on a cart on the morning of the second day. Every basket, wineskin and bag was opened and examined before the servants brought it into the building. The janissaries were highly efficient sentinels. No one went in or out—with one sole exception.

It was not until the morning of the fifth day that I saw a sedan chair arrive, and out of it climbed the doctor I was waiting for. I remembered the thin outline of Ashkenazi from the Hanukkah dinner on the day of my arrival at Palazzo Belvedere. He greeted the two janissaries at the main entrance and allowed them to search his clothes before they let him in. They did so without hesitation or compunction, leaving him bareheaded and half naked in the cold of the early morning. Ashkenazi said nothing, got dressed again and crossed the threshold. He stayed in there for half an hour, and when he left, he resignedly submitted to the same procedure all over again. I narrowed my eyes, paying a great deal of attention to the movements of their hands: I had to be sure that Ashkenazi wasn't actually using the janissaries as couriers.

The doctor climbed back into the sedan chair and was carried down the hill toward the heart of Galata. I watched after the vehicle for as long as I could, then let it go its own way.

What would Consigliere Nordio have thought if he had seen me at that moment, discovering the method by which the bailiff was able to evade surveillance? One of the first things that he, of all people, had taught me was that by choosing simple solutions you reduce risk and error. Sokollu must have been of the same school.

I had already ruled out the possibility that the medium for the message might be Ashkenazi's prodigious memory. The Venetians would never have trusted the *flatus vocis*, and certainly not if the voice belonged to a Jew. They would certainly demand a letter written and sealed by the bailiff's own hand.

A different detail had attracted my attention.

The janissaries had missed something.

His shoes.

Ashkenazi, as a privileged Jew, traveled in a sedan chair. Indispensable if you wanted to keep your babouches out of the mud and the puddles, without putting at risk their precious contents. I left my post and set off rapidly toward Palazzo Belvedere. I had just demonstrated to myself that I was still a good hunter.

15.

Two dark-skinned boys were washing their arms in the fountain. They looked like Asians from the East Indies and were so similar that they could have been twins. When one of them released a pin and let his hair fall to his shoulders, I was startled to realize that "he" was a woman. Her breasts were hardly visible under her masculine clothes.

A little way off, a Muslim was finishing his prayers. His robes, his amber skin, his reddish beard all suggested that he was an Arab. He got to his feet and rolled up the carpet on which he had been praying. He also picked up a scimitar. He saw me and nodded his head—a cautious and barely perceptible greeting.

Coming back from the day of investigations and surveillance, I certainly hadn't expected an encounter like this. The last refugees had returned to their homes, and the drawing room at Palazzo Belvedere was almost always empty.

Last of all, I saw the old man. He was standing beneath the portrait of Donna Gracia and staring at it in silence. The big painting loomed over him. I, too, had often contemplated that picture; I had admired its strength. The *Senyora*'s black eyes looked like lunar eclipses. Her arched eyebrows were bridges hanging over precipices so high, it took the breath away. Her sharp nose was the prow of a ship.

The old man was dressed in the Moorish manner, the darkness of his tunic and turban broken by his white beard. I studied him from a distance, at the edge of the hall. It was impossible to tell how old he was, but his body was still straight, in spite of the stick that he held parallel to his leg.

At that moment a door opened and a servant came rushing into the room. He barely deigned to glance at the other foreigners, but headed straight for the old man. When he was close to him, he slowed his step as if he didn't want to frighten him. Or perhaps he was the one who was scared.

"Don Yossef is at the Seraglio, Effendi. A guest of the Sultan," he said in Turkish, his voice full of bitterness. "We have managed to warn him, but you will understand that it's difficult for him to be here before evening."

"Duarte Gomez?" asked the old man.

"You mean . . . Don *David*? He was with Don Yossef."

The old man spoke the name of Donna Reyna, and it was like a revelation to the other man.

"Yes, of course, Effendi, right away, Effendi." He nodded his agreement

and flew toward the stairs. The old man stared at the painting again. Less than a minute must have passed when his voice broke the silence.

"Tell me, you who are observing me: Is it only indiscretion on your part, or have you some other motive?"

I froze. I was sure that he hadn't turned his head in my direction. In spite of the clothes he was wearing, he had spoken in Italian, and in an accent that was clearly European.

"Might I know who is asking?" I replied.

He turned and walked toward me. I stared at him, keeping the others in the corner of my eye. We found ourselves face to face, and I met his gaze, more out of curiosity than defiance. His eyes were gray and piercing. For some reason the memory of Tuota flashed through my mind.

"I am Ismail al-Mokhawi," he said. "I deal with the Nasi family's affairs in the Yemen."

My sixth sense told me there was more to this than he was letting on. I didn't yet know the extent to which my presentiment was correct. "Arab name, German accent," I observed.

"Congratulations; you have a good ear. And your name?"

"My name is Manuel Cardoso." I gave a slight bow that the old man didn't return.

"Spanish name, Venetian accent," he announced, as if we were having a riddling competition. "Are you a businessman, too?" he asked. "Are you in business with João? I don't think so, or I'd have heard your name mentioned." He touched my right hand with his stick. "Of course you don't work with those. No recent marks, only old scars."

I brushed his stick away. "Your eyesight is enviable, in spite of your age."

"Indeed. If I'm not mistaken, what you have on your jacket is poplar pollen." I instinctively checked my sleeves. On the green of the fabric, some barely visible filaments had appeared, the tiniest pinch. "I don't remember poplars in the park at Palazzo Belvedere," he went on. "But there are many in Pera."

A secret agent should never be dumbfounded, so I maintained my self-control. I don't know how our discussion would have continued, because we were interrupted by a voice from above: "Don't upset our man Cardoso, Messer Ludovico. He's Yossef's new pupil."

It was only the second time that I had seen her, and I was very struck. Not an ostentatious woman, but pride shone from her eyes. The old man smiled. He seemed already to have forgotten me and what had just happened.

My mind, meanwhile, was working quickly. He was German. He had introduced himself as Ismail, and Donna Reyna had called him Ludovico. He called Don Yossef and David Gomez by their Christian names. It was clear that he knew the Nasi family well, perhaps since before they had arrived in Constantinople.

With one hand, Donna Reyna pointed to the woman in the painting, her mother.

"Are you paying homage to one who is no more, Messer Ludovico?"

"I am paying homage to one who lives in my heart, Signora." With these words he touched his chest and bowed to her.

Reyna vanished, reappearing in the drawing room a moment later. Once they stood facing one another, they held each other's hands for a long time. I looked at the Arab and the two Indians, who remained impassive. I wondered if they had understood even one of the words that had just echoed around the room. In all likelihood they didn't know Italian.

"It's still hard to believe you're here," said Reyna, without letting go of the old man's hands. "And yet you are. How much time has passed?"

"Eight years," he answered, with a half smile. "And they have been a little more kind to you than they have to me."

It was as if I had ceased to exist.

"You are exactly the same as the man I remember," said Reyna. "And you have survived a very long journey. You will want to rest and refresh yourself."

"What my friends and I need more than anything is a hot bath and a bed." He smiled. "But I'm no longer used to the comforts of a palace. Tell João I will wait for him at Uskudar, in the house where I used to live."

The woman seemed disappointed, but not very surprised. "You're not staying here? Yossef will be mortified." The last sentence sounded like a distant formality.

The reply was a whisper: "Between these walls, memories would keep me from resting."

"I understand that very well," said Reyna. "They keep me awake too, every night. And there is nowhere one can go to seek refuge."

The skin below one of the old man's cheekbones twitched. I thought that beneath his beard he had clenched his jaw. I wondered what was happening, and what messages were being passed, hidden in their words.

Reyna called a servant. "See to it that our guests are escorted to the other side of the Bosphorus."

"Thank you, *mia signora*, but that isn't necessary." The old man bowed briefly, then turned, saw me and gave a start, as if he had only that moment remembered my existence. He collected himself and walked quickly across the room, using his stick occasionally, followed by the rest of his strange retinue.

The first to catch up with him was the Arab, who immediately addressed him in his own language. The Indian youngsters were slower, glancing around, moving with soft and even steps. They drew up alongside the other two and all four walked on like that, in a row, all talking together, on the path that led through the middle of the garden. Seen from behind, they looked like friends who had just emerged from an evening of drinking and idle chit-chat.

When they had disappeared, I turned back to Reyna.

"Who is that man?"

"He is the past," she replied. "The past knocking at the door." She took her leave with a nod of her head. We were left alone, I and the eyes of Donna Gracia. As if those presences had been mirages, the voices the ravings of a lunatic.

16.

"You've found your place at last."

Dana was resting her head on my chest. Before she spoke, I thought she had fallen asleep, and I was lost in reflection. My thoughts were rough wool that needed to be carded and spun, and they began with Ashkenazi's slippers. I would have liked to communicate my suspicions about how the bailiff's dispatches traveled, but Nasi and Gomez hadn't yet come back, even though the sun had set an hour before. My thoughts returned to the meeting I had witnessed a few hours previously, with the weird old man and his entourage. Ismail, or Ludovico. Who knows where he and the Nasis had met. Maybe in Venice. I found myself thinking about Braun's bank, at the Fondaco dei Tedeschi. My money was still there, the money I hadn't been able to withdraw after fleeing from Arianna's house.

After that brief deviation, here I was again at Palazzo Belvedere. I guessed that right under my nose, and without my understanding it, something important had happened that day.

"My place? What do you mean?"

"By Don Yossef's side."

It wasn't strange to see things in that way. Nasi had given me the chance to return to my job. Basically it was the one I was best at: collecting information. I said as much to Dana. She lifted her face and folded her hands under her chin.

"Information? About Don Yossef's enemies?"

"Particularly."

"And who are the most fearsome of them?"

I let her hair glide through my fingers.

"Some of them are Jews like us. Envious men. They don't support Don Yossef because he sees a hundred miles beyond their horizon. To avenge themselves on his intelligence, they prefer to serve the Venetians, or the Grand Vizier."

Gusts of wind stirred the leaves in the park. A dogfight began in the distance.

"It was because of his dreams that the brothers sold Joseph to the Ishmaelites," observed Dana.

Her words startled me. The similarities between the biblical Joseph and Yossef Nasi now struck me as obvious. Both had won the favors of a foreign sovereign. They had both obtained government positions, aristocratic titles,

huge wealth. But not the trust of the family they served. Not immediately, at least, and not without a great deal of effort. A question came to my lips, the thin tail of an elephantine thought.

"Why are your mistress and Don Yossef barely talking to each other?"

"You must have noticed: Don Yossef doesn't appreciate the attentions of women."

It was true: I'd never seen him in the company of a woman, not even his wife. I hadn't seen Gomez with a woman, either. In Venice Yossef Nasi was known as the Sultan's catamite. In the secret service he was spoken of in low terms. On the streets of Constantinople I had heard similar allusions and obscene jokes.

"Incredible that such a man should be destined to live without heirs."

"You could be his son. You're the right age."

In a different situation, the words might have irritated me, and I would have given a harsh reply, but I found myself saying something quite different. "My father was much older than Don Yossef."

Just as the spinning of wool is followed by the doubling of the yarn, when two threads are twisted together to make one stronger one, in my mind the figures of two old men were superimposed upon one another, I still didn't know to what end. I said, "This Ismail al-Mokhawi, the old man who arrived today . . . What do you know about him?"

Dana shook her head and let her eye wander along the walls. "Not much. He left Constantinople before I got here. I know what Donna Gracia told me."

"Down in the drawing room, he spent a long time sitting in silence by her portrait."

"They loved each other," said Dana. She must have seen me looking startled, and took advantage of it. "Do you love me?"

I didn't know what to reply. I stammered something; I felt very stupid. Dana smiled and felt sorry for me. She picked up the story where she had broken it off.

"Before she died, Donna Gracia wrote him a letter. I was with her that evening. At sunset, the Bosphorus was beautiful." She lost herself in her memory, and I avoided disturbing her with any further questions. A little later, it was she who broke the silence. She sat up in the bed, as if talking about Donna Gracia called for a more respectful posture. "She wanted to see him one last time before she died. She asked him to join her at Tiberias."

"Why on earth did he leave her?"

"Donna Gracia never explained that to me. She once told me that, faced with a desert, a river has two choices: to hurl itself into the sand, determined to pass through it and irrigate it, at the risk of drying up and disappearing for ever, or else to evaporate and become a cloud, to fly above the desert and, raining down on the mountains, become a river again. She said that Ismail was the river that becomes a cloud."

I was struck by the simile. "Was Donna Gracia the river that wanted to irrigate the desert?"

"Perhaps. Or perhaps she was referring to Don Yossef. What do you think?"

I replied impulsively, "That irrigating the desert is a difficult enterprise, but it's worth trying."

We said nothing more. We lay there side by side, waiting for sleep to overtake us.

"Ismail!"

The shout came from the drawing room and made us jump. Dana leaped to her feet, dressed in a flash, said good-bye to me and rushed from the room, swift as a fawn. All that remained was her scent, her perfume. Once I had put on my breeches and my shirt, I crossed the threshold. There was no one in the loggia. I leaned against the balustrade to look down and saw Nasi in the middle of the drawing room, which was lit only by a servant's oil-lamp, with David Gomez next to him. They were talking to the manservant who had received the old man and called Donna Reyna.

Mulier in fabula, that was her, a dark outline below her mother's portrait. Nasi saw her, and pointed at her, followed at a distance by Gomez. From the loggia I couldn't make out every word; their conversation reached me in scraps.

. . . staying here at the palace?

The tone couldn't be misunderstood.

. . . his old house in Üsküdar . . . with his retinue . . .

Bitterness, detachment.

. . . miles to get here . . . he was supposed to be our guest . . .

Resentment, aged fury.

. . . you know yourself why he doesn't want . . .

Then they stopped talking. A lull of silence settled in the room. Then Nasi bowed to his wife and turned on his heel. "Let's go," he said to Gomez.

I saw them leaving like arrows in flight, fired from the bow in the direction of Üsküdar.

17.

The Palazzo Belvedere was abuzz with voices. Servants and sutlers, general dogsbodies, gardeners, wood suppliers and whoever happened to be passing through, everyone was coming and going, questions required answers, little knots of people clustered rapidly before scattering like ears of wheat when duty called and reassembling elsewhere, in the drawing room, in the kitchen, in the pantry, in the corridors and even outside, in the park, at the start of the tree-lined avenue. The women tidied up the rooms, talking about the German, *el Alemán*, back from Arabia after all these years, *kon una barba blanka ke lo faze pareser un profeta*, with a white beard that made him look like a prophet, and accompanied by three Moors *ke tienen fachas de lókos*, with the faces of madmen, it would have frightened you to look at them, but if they're friends of his they must be decent people. A cook said that *el barbarroja* had asked her for five cups of boiling water, and then he'd put some nutshells into them, offered a cup to each of his friends and the last one to her, to try this drink, because apparently they weren't actually nuts, but a kind of coffee. And it was so good that the woman had asked them to give her a handful, and if anyone wanted to try it she could make it in a moment, *kishir*. The two Indians, meanwhile, had beguiled the time by dancing in the park. What do you mean, dancing, it was a fight, didn't you see when they drew out their shields and whips? What agility! Did you see when one of the two jumped the other with his feet pressed together?

I turned round, slightly puzzled, in the whirl of voices and stories. No one seemed to be paying me any attention; the day's news was the reappearance of the old man. Everyone who had known Ismail before he had gone to Mokha—which is why he was known as the Mokhan—seemed to hold him in great esteem, and there was a certain solemnity in the way they talked about him, replying to the questions of new arrivals, boys and girls who had served Don Yossef and Donna Reyna for only a few years, some for only a few months. They listened with admiration to the stories that danced their way from mouth to mouth. They nodded and returned to their tasks filled with more curiosity than before, anxious to see *el Alemán*, when someday soon he would come back to the palace.

I followed these stories, too. They announced themselves as vague references, two sentences thrown there as if to say *pay attention to me, I know what's going on*, and then they were referred to, commented upon, provided with the kind of glosses applied to ancient poems, and through those glosses

they merged together and poured into one another, assuming new forms and consistencies. The old man appeared now in one country, now in another: He had been in Africa and France, in Chipango and Cathay. He had known Martin Luther, I heard a cook saying to a young scullery maid in the doorway to the kitchen. I was listening from behind a column, my back resting against the cool marble, my eyes closed. The woman spoke an enchanting Ladino that reminded me of my childhood, every sentence ending on a high note, a bit like when in Italy you hear people from Ascoli or Ancona talking. Her voice was intoning the story of Ismail and Luther, luring new people to stop and listen.

The old man hadn't just known Luther, he'd been with him that day when they nailed a big piece of paper on the door of a church in some German city, a paper that was read by lots of people and infuriated the pope. And what had he written on it? That the relics of the saints are nothing but filth, bones to be thrown to the dogs. Such courage! Certainly, but what foolhardiness! Indeed, but such love of truth. But when did Luther die? The replies came flying: Luther's still alive. No, what are you talking about, he died twenty years ago and he was over a hundred—*el Alemán* is old, certainly, but not *that* old; pay no heed to such nonsense. But it's true that the papists pursued him halfway around the world, because he's a heretic of the first water. I've heard all sorts of things being said about them. And who told you? Lots of people. I've also heard them being told to Don Yossef. I just know that he was Donna Gracia's lover, a male voice said at last, in the tone of someone bringing castles in the air down to the ground. It's true, a girl added. They say that she died in his arms, down in Tiberias.

At the mention of Gracia Nasi and her last moments, the listeners became lost in thought, the speakers' voices grew more serious in tone, and the conversation thinned out. In a few minutes, the cluster of people had dissolved and everyone had returned to their own tasks.

I opened my eyes. Standing in front of me was Yossef Nasi.

"Did you hear them?" he said. "The world traveler has returned."

18.

Nasi was in a strange mood, melancholy and thoughtful. The event everyone was talking about, Ismail's strange secret meeting with Reyna, the trip to Üsküdar at dead of night . . . My mentor wore it all stamped on his face, on his forehead and around his eyes, in the wrinkles at the sides of his mouth, in the shadow of a beard that covered his cheeks. All stamped in plain sight, but in characters that I didn't yet know how to read.

I told him that I had something to report: I had worked out how the dispatches were leaving the bailiff's house. "Let's go to the library," he replied. He told a servant to call David Gomez, and off we set.

In the doorway to the book-lined room, we met the kabbalist Meir, pale in the face as I had always seen him, the black velvet *kippah* covering his bald skull. "The German has returned, hasn't he, Don Yossef?" asked the man whose mind revolved around permutations and calculations.

"Yes, master. Ismail is back amongst us."

"So, this is a sign, and it will need to be interpreted."

"What do you see in it?"

"The man with many names defies the Gematria," said Meir. "Which letters will we match up with a number?"

"You know, everyone has called him Ismail for years," Nasi replied.

"Yes, *Ishmael*," repeated the kabbalist, pensive and gloomy, pronouncing the name in Hebrew.

The story of Ishmael is well known to my people. The son of Abraham and the servant Hagar, he was removed from Sarah along with his mother, for mocking his stepbrother Isaac. In the desert, mother and son were helped by an angel, who showed them a spring and urged them not to be afraid, because a great people would be born of the boy's loins. The Moors saw him as their prophet and the father of their tribe.

If a German heretic had taken that name, did it mean he had turned Muslim?

Anyway, in those letters—*Yod, Shin, Mem, Ayin, Aleph, Lamed*—there must have been something more, because Meir remained silent, plunged in who knows what computation, his eyes fixed on nothing, and Nasi coughed, in an attempt to bring him back among us. "Don't weary yourself, master. If you had to ruminate like this on all the names that man has had, you would keep yourself busy for a very long time. When I knew him his name was Ludovico, to others he was Tiziano, and yet others remembered him as Gert. Just leave it; *el Alemán* has always defied all calculations."

I remembered what Dana had said to me: Ismail was a river that evaporates and becomes a cloud, to cross the desert and rain on the mountains.

The kabbalist stirred himself and took his leave. At that moment we were joined by David Gomez. The three of us came into the library at the same time, and stood around the big table. At last I told them my suspicions about Ashkenazi and his slippers.

"Ingenious," said Gomez. "Precisely because it's trivial."

"Stay glued to Ashkenazi's shadow," Nasi broke in. "I want confirmation. Discover who the letters are passing to and how they are leaving Constantinople." Then he left.

"Why is he so troubled by the arrival of this German?" I asked Gomez. Rather than replying, he began nosing around among the shelves, examining the backs of the books. He said, "You know that the first printing press was brought to Constantinople by the Sephardim, in 1493? Jews and books always go together."

He pulled a book that sat on the shelf at eye level, and set it down on the table with a theatrical gesture. A small yellow volume. I picked it up, studied it and recognized its title. It was a forbidden book, one that had caused a scandal in Venice and throughout the whole of Italy many years before. I opened it at random and read a few lines.

> . . . the righteousness of Christ will suffice to make us righteous, and sons
> of grace without any of our good works, which cannot be good if, before
> we do them, we are not first made good and righteous by faith.

Calvin's heresy, *justificatio sola fide*. Words that came from a world now far away. Gomez said, "*Il Beneficio di Cristo*. Do you know it?"

"Of course. It's the most famous heretical text of our times."

"It was we who printed and distributed it, to sow discord among the papists."

" 'We,' who?" I asked him. Meanwhile I was mulling over a phrase I had heard a moment before.

When I knew him his name was Ludovico, to others he was Tiziano.

"The Nasi family paid the typographers. A bookseller by the name of Perna worked in the field, and with him a great expert in the field of troublemaking. Someone who knew how by spreading certain ideas you can throw things off balance. And that was the old man whose return everyone is talking about."

When I knew him his name was Ludovico, to others he was Tiziano. My mouth had dried up. When I joined the Consigliere's secret service, the older agents still spoke of a heretic, a mysterious character who, years before, had passed through northern Italy, practicing blasphemous baptisms and driving the inquisitors mad. His name was often associated with the *Beneficio di Cristo*.

"Are you telling me that Ismail al-Mokhawi is Tiziano the Anabaptist?"

"The very same. Then events gathered speed, the Inquisition began to tighten its grip, and Ismail escaped from Venice along with Gracia. Yossef, Samuel and I attended to some unfinished business, then joined them here. Ismail loved Gracia, but he soon realized that he was different from her, from the Nasis, from all of us. The fate of the Jews is to defend one another against the perils of the world. Often we are obliged by circumstances to befriend powerful men, but Ismail is a wanderer by choice, and for all of his life he has tried to bring the powerful down."

I had never heard David Gomez talking at such length. That day, everything was going in the opposite direction. I looked at Takiyuddin's clock. I was reassured to see the hands turning clockwise, as they always did.

19.

Following a sedan chair along the byways of Constantinople is an easy business. The narrow, muddy streets force the vehicles to adopt a slow, uneven pace. And anyway, people who use them don't do it to go faster, but rather to shelter their heads from inclement weather and keep their shoes clean—two advantages that I couldn't help envying as I walked along, drenched by the storm. In the morning, when I left the palace, a tepid sun was shining. Shrubs and bushes were putting out their first flowers, and the scent of jasmine sweetened the air, like a drop of honey in a spicy brew. Then all of a sudden the wind had risen, and while Ashkenazi lurked in the bailiff's rooms, a curtain of clouds had covered the blue.

The sedan chair passed down along rivers of mud until it reached the coast at Galata, where I lost sight of it in the crowd. Boatmen harried by the rain called out the price of a crossing to the opposite shore. Pickpockets, thanking the precipitation, robbed the passengers distracted by the cries. Taking care not to be among their victims, I boarded a *parema* and had myself ferried to the peninsula, sure that Ashkenazi would have done the same. And indeed, I found him at the Fishmonger's Gate, ready to climb into a new chair.

We left the warehouses and fish stalls behind us, crossed the Imperial Road, and came back down toward the district of Kadirga, on the shore of the White Sea, the site of one of the city's three arsenals.

The sedan chair passed through the entrance to a big building set into the city wall, revealing still more gates and courtyards above a sequence of three terraces. From without, the structure's appearance was imposing but plain, typical of Ottoman seraglios, which surprise visitors with the contrast between their simple facades and elaborate interiors. I sheltered from the rain beneath the closed balcony of a house and asked a passer-by who owned the residence in front of me. Sadrazam Mehmet Pasha, was the reply.

The Grand Vizier Sokollu.

Over the next few days I pondered this discovery, until I realized that I hadn't resolved a thing. From Solomon's journey I could deduce that the bailiff's letters very swiftly ended up in front of the eyes of Sokollu. But I had no proof of their transit, and besides, I didn't need any. My aim was to work out how those letters reached Venice, and I was sure that the Grand Vizier was not the courier I was looking for. Too reckless, for him, to act as a direct

go-between in this correspondence. It was one thing to read the enemy's messages, quite another to help them reach their destination.

Don Yossef had talked to me for a long time about Ashkenazi's dealings. The doctor's properties were on the island of Crete. Vines, olives and lemons. His ships regularly came and went from Candia. Nothing better than a Venetian colony to deliver the bailiff's letters to the right people. If my idea was correct, I had to work out *who* would bring them to the island, and when.

I plunged into the depths of Galata like a pearl fisher, hoping to come back up with the treasure in my hands. I lingered in the taverns till late; I unloaded bales of silk on the planks of the jetty. I spoke Turkish, Dalmatian, Italian, Ladino. I won the words of gamblers at dice, I bought them from merchants, I forced open the silence of drifters. I lent an ear to whispers and tall tales, to the conversations of barbers and cries in the street, to the gossip and secrets of the port. I reacquired the taste for an activity congenial to me. I felt gratified.

In the end I got hold of three names, all commercial agents working for Solomon Ashkenazi.

The first was a Greek. I managed to meet him in a tavern during a shadow play, and without too much difficulty I got him drunk on raki and mulled wine. He told me his life story, listed the lovers he had had, and finished off by accusing himself of several murders. I couldn't imagine Ashkenazi entrusting such a man with the task of passing on secret messages.

The second came from the Crimea. A silent, discreet character, rather more suited to the task. Still, obeying an old instinct from my days on the lagoon, I paid more particular attention to the third candidate, who looked the least likely.

His name was Bernardo Traverso, and his ship was due to set sail at the end of the month. He was Genoese, his every fiber filled with hatred of Venice. I had met him before on several occasions, at the *kahvehane* on the Golden Horn, the one I frequented with David Gomez. He said he had been to Goa and Brazil and that always, in every corner of the world, he had met a *galuscio* Venetian who was ready to squeeze his *cuggie*. He even complained that the Venetians who lived in Istanbul lived in a district that had been built, stone by stone, by the Genoese before they surrendered it to the Sultan. I was struck by his resentment, because that, ostentatiously displayed, might act better than anything as a screen for secret activities in favor of Venice.

I became convinced that he was the pearl I was diving for.

20.

Bernardo Traverso wasn't one of those Europeans who live confined in Galata, as if it were an Italian or French city, eating the same food that they would eat at home, not learning a word of Turkish and despising all Ottoman practices, even the most pleasing and wholesome.

Instead, he went often to the Old City, where he applauded the acrobats in the local markets, played dice, bet on the ram fights and greyhound races at the hippodrome. He was an equally assiduous visitor to the nearby baths at the Seraglio, so much so that some people wondered whether cleanliness was the only reason for this deep attachment.

Each time he went into the hammam I waited outside, pretending to take an interest in the shops selling herbs and syrups, before tailing him again as soon as he came out, guided by his fragrance of cedar.

On the fourth occasion of this kind, driven by boredom, I discovered a welcoming and not very crowded *kahvehane* down the street. From the benches outside, resting against the wall, you could keep an eye on the entrance to the baths. As soon as I sat down I took off my slippers, ordered a coffee and, not even thinking about it, started listening in on the conversations of the other patrons.

Two bearded old men, sucking on the rims of their cups, were loudly commenting on the news of the day. The Doge had ordered the arrest of all the Jews and Ottomans living in Venice. Now it was time to pay back the favor and do the same with the Venetians in Galata. No, quite the contrary. Precisely because they were treated well in Istanbul, they should demand that their compatriots do the same at home with the good Muslims. And the Jews? They needed putting down here too, not freedom. They needed sorting out, them and their wives, always jeweled up like queens; who knows how much they enjoyed humiliating the good Muslims. That was why God, the Merciful, the Compassionate, had punished their arrogance by setting fire to the Jewish quarter some months ago.

I ordered a plate of cakes while a toothless young man, his face covered with scars, recommended the services of a prostitute to two others. A fourth, older than his companions, dismissed the youth's tedious advice and suggested instead blond Mursel, a Bulgarian *tellak* at the baths, who could pleasure you three times in a row with his mouth. This boy, most importantly, was also a good poet, and liked to recite his erotic verses and love lyrics. The toothless boy screwed up his nose and said that only an ignorant

heretic like the Shah of Persia would write his poems in Turkish. The truly literate and the great sultans wrote in Arabic or in Persian. Yes, of course, everyone agreed, but no one understood Persian, and if you don't understand erotic poetry how on earth are you going to get a boner?

I paused with my cup in midair. Then I finished my coffee and ate the last baklava. For a few minutes I contemplated a flight of midges, until I saw Traverso coming out of the baths and walking away. I paid what I owed, my fingers still sticky with honey. I quickly put on my slippers and headed for the hammam.

Inside, beneath the great dome, stood a white limestone fountain. The water that poured from it, slipping from one basin to the other, filled the silence like the voice of a stream. All around, cushions and carpets accommodated a dozen clients; on the seats along the walls the same number of men were taking their clothes off. Daylight imprinted the colors of the stained glass on their faces.

A freckled servant came toward me to hand me clogs and a bath towel.

"Mursel?" I asked.

"I'll get him for you right away, Effendi; he's just come free. Meanwhile you can get undressed and have a drink."

Mursel was a bony young man, almost beardless, with curls so blond they looked white. Like the other *tellaks* he was naked to the waist and wearing a blue cloth skirt. He was holding a pot of aromatic oil. He talked to me in a low voice.

"If you want a poem, Effendi, it's three aspers for a short one and five for a long one."

Having pocketed the three coins, Mursel beckoned to me to follow him into the hot room. We passed under one of the arches and sat down in a tub, alone, sheltered from the eyes of the other bathers. When he knelt down in front of me and made to lower his head between my legs, I stopped him with a hand on his forehead.

"No verses, Homer. What I want is information."

Over the next few days, still on Traverso's heels, I made a bet with myself. I put twenty aspers on the meetings he would have before he set off for Crete, while his men loaded the final cases onto the *mahona*.

First stop: Solomon Ashkenazi, to receive from his hands the bailiff's letters, guarded like relics in one of the Jewish doctor's secret drawers.

Next: his sweetheart, to take final leave before he boarded the ship, like any self-respecting seafaring man, with her perfume still on him.

That was exactly what happened that last afternoon, the only difference being that the sweetheart was a fair-haired boy.

Once more I followed the Genoese to the door of the hammam. I counted to one hundred, to keep myself from being overimpetuous, and then stepped inside.

I was greeted by the same servant as usual. He asked me politely if I needed Mursel, because unfortunately, just a moment before . . . I told him not to bother Mursel, but to show me where the man who had requested his services had left his clothes. Five silver aspers appeared in the palm of my hand.

The boy replied that for any kind of theft in the dressing rooms he would be given twenty lashes, and that twenty lashes were worth at least five more coins.

"I'm not a thief," I told him and added one more asper, promising him a cruel death if he spoke of my visit to anybody. The young *tellak* brought his fingers to his mouth and pinched his lips as if gluing them together. He gestured to me to follow him. In no particular hurry, I set my slippers down on the mahogany shelf, put on a pair of clogs and complied.

The boy turned the key in the lock and half-opened the door. I quickly rummaged through Traverso's bag and clothes. The bailiff's letters were folded and hidden between the lining and the leather. I recognized the seal with the Barbaro family crest, a shield with a disc in the middle. Then I put the papers back where I had found them, having no need for anything else. I hurried to retrieve my shoes, returned my clogs and towel, and headed for the exit.

21.

I arrived at Palazzo Belvedere as evening fell, keen to tell Nasi what I had discovered amid the steam of the hammam. I was told that he had just locked himself away in the library, with Gomez and Master Fitch, and that he had given orders to be left in peace.

Perhaps it was fate, that I had to wait every time before passing on my discoveries. In fact, Nasi was always busy, always meeting someone or making some sort of decision. I would have taken advantage of the fact to enjoy a hot bath, but as soon as I got to my room the sharp scent of wine changed my mind. The night before, Dana and I had poured it from the flask, mixing it with opium juices left to dissolve in the bottom of our glasses. Now I served myself the nectar that remained in the jug and tried a sip. It was still good, but I didn't want to drink it on my own, lying in the bathwater talking to the wall. I washed her glass, hid it under my jerkin and went down to the garden with mine in my hands.

I walked along the central avenue, trying to remember the names of the trees. Dana had taught them to me, pointing them out from the bedroom window. Pomegranate, Judas tree, ash, perhaps a plane tree. She said that Adam had contributed to the Creation by giving names to the things of the world. All of mankind's other works were the fruit of the Fall. I, not to be outdone, had shown her the constellations and told her the legend of Queen Cassiopeia.

Past the duck pond, I slipped between the box hedges and emerged into the circular clearing, where Dana gave shape to her memories.

I knew that at that time of day I would find her there.

White and red roses peeped from the arch above the stone bench. She was hoeing the ground around the carob tree and singing, in a language that sounded to me like Greek, although its melody reminded me of a Sephardic song that I had heard a thousand times in my mother's voice. Lullabies unite the shores of the Mediterranean more than do the ancient routes of the Phoenician merchants.

"Are you already preparing to take it to Cyprus?" I interrupted her, pointing to the little tree. Dana raised her head and set the hoe aside. She came lightly toward me, barefoot, and stroked my cheek. Over the past few weeks I had stopped trimming my beard, which had grown luxuriant. I wanted to walk around the European city without danger of being recognized. "Your eyes look happy," Dana said. "Won't you tell me why?"

I gave her a clue. "One of Don Yossef's enemies has an Achilles' heel, and I've exposed it."

"And who is he? One of the Jews you were talking to me about?"

I didn't reply, even thought I would have liked to tell her about Ashkenazi and Traverso, to give her a better understanding of my job and my contribution to Nasi's enterprise.

"I understand," she said in a singsong voice. "The usual secrets between you and your boss." She slowly shook her head, as if to rid herself of some strange thought, but I asked her to welcome it, and not to keep it hidden from me.

"I was thinking I'd know more about what you did if the *Senyora* were still alive. She and Don Yossef consulted one another about everything—they took all their decisions together. And she often told me; she trusted me. But now I only know that my master could become king of Cyprus. Donna Reyna told me that, but she, too, complains that she knows too little."

I marveled at her way of talking about things. I said, "I don't think she was really very interested in Don Yossef's plans."

In the cage hanging from the carob, the goldfinch hopped about and chirruped pointedly. "Who knows?" Dana translated. "I don't think he ever asked her opinion."

"And you?" I asked quickly. "What do you think about Don Yossef's plans?"

Dana shrugged. "I told you, I'm just a lady-in-waiting, to a queen who doesn't know her own kingdom. I can only hope that the new palace has a corner where I can plant my garden."

"Of course you'll have a garden," I said. "Don Yossef promised me the residence of my choice."

It took her a few moments to work out what I was referring to. A house for both of us, where we could live together. And it took me a few to realize what I had just done. I was wracked with doubt, and my thoughts were a blur. My days at Palazzo Belvedere had been a succession of metamorphoses, discoveries, frenetic activity. Three months previously I had been a different person, lost, drifting. How could I be sure that I had finally berthed? How could I give someone else any kind of certainty?

And yet, I drew joy from indulging Dana. Thinking of us both, of our life together, granted me a youth that I had never had. Emanuele De Zante was dead, and I, Manuel Cardoso, had gone back to my bar mitzvah, as if I were fifteen years old again.

Except that I was thirty-one, and covered in scars.

I banished the bad thoughts as if they were irritating insects. I slipped the second glass from under my clothes, poured out a little of the wine still left in mine, then handed it to Dana. She raised it slightly and recited a phrase in our ancient tongue: *Barukh ata Adonai Eloheinu melekh haolam, bo're p'ri hagafen.*

It was the prayer of thanks for the fruit of the vine, and it was also the first

of the marriage blessings that come before the libation by the bride and groom.

We kissed for a long time, swapping sips of wine. I found it very hard to resist the desire to take her and lie down there, on the grass, beneath that carob tree that made her a child again, but I didn't want to risk anyone discovering our secret.

We drained our glasses in a final sip, and then I told her I had to get back. I had to talk to Nasi about Bernardo Traverso's sea crossings. We exchanged one last kiss, only brushing each other's lips, and then she got up and let me out of her garden.

22.

"Bartolomeo Nordio must have been proud of you." Nasi received my account with these words, then asked me to help him assess what needed to be done. We had to get our hands on the bailiff's letters and at the same time unmask Ashkenazi, while making sure that Sokollu didn't get his clutches on our net and free the prey. That was why I hadn't seized the letters at the hammam; if I had, the Jewish doctor would have coped, and his dealings with Traverso wouldn't have come to light. Besides, Don Yossef added, we couldn't carry out a large-scale action in the city, where we had neither men nor weapons. We had to make careful preparations, wait for Traverso's first voyage and strike him on the sea.

"On the sea?" I asked. "How?"

"We'll force Ashkenazi's ship to make an unscheduled stopover. The ship will be inspected, and the rest you can imagine."

"How will we force it to make a stopover?"

"Pirates. The waters between here and Candia are full of them."

At first I thought he was joking. Just as when you're a child and you make up a story, adding one character after another, Nasi had introduced sea-robbers into the tale, the same ones who were to act as a pretext for the war on Venice, the same ones that my father, Gioanbattista De Zante, had fought on countless expeditions. That Don Yossef could resort to pirates if necessary was a piece of information out of nowhere as far as I was concerned.

I showed my surprise, and the future King of Cyprus nodded with an inspired expression on his face. "Fortune willed that an old friend would decide to come back to town. Someone who has spent his whole life in the worst possible company. Ismail al-Mokhawi might be able to help us."

Pirates and Anabaptists. That remark left me more baffled than ever. I remembered my mentor's saturnine mood the day after his nighttime visit to his old friend.

Nasi guessed the nature of my reflections. "I know David talked to you about Ismail. You see, the man is a gentile, but to me he's a brother. Have you ever had a brother?"

No, just a stillborn sister. "Not that I know of," I replied.

"There are a lot of proverbs about being brothers, but they say everything and its opposite. It's a bond that no one can explain. '*Amor di fratelli, amor di coltelli,*' they say in Italy. 'Brotherly love is a matter of knives.' 'An offended brother is more unyielding than a fortified city,' it says in the *Mishlê Shlomoh.*"

I found the image appropriate: thick walls of stone. I was ignorant about too many things, and the bond between Nasi and the man from Mokha was impenetrable to me.

"Ismail's return filled me with joy, and yet knowing that he is here torments me. He's a rock hanging above my head."

"Why did he come back?"

"Gracia wrote to him."

I didn't tell him I knew about that already, for I wanted to keep Dana out of our conversation. Nasi went on, "She asked him to help me with one last mission. She said no more than that, and she's no longer here to put our doubts to rest."

The explanation struck me as obvious, so much so that I couldn't help myself.

"Perhaps she wanted to see the two of you together at the conquest of Cyprus, building up the kingdom."

Nasi shook his head doubtfully. "Ismail hates kingdoms, sovereigns and princes. Gracia knew that better than anyone. I set out our plan for him, but his heart remained cold."

"If that's the case, why do you want him to help you now?"

"Chiefly because he's the right person. And because the rock's hanging there. We know it's going to fall, but we don't know where or when. I don't want to leave these decisions to a gust of wind. I want to be the one who does the pushing."

"Will he agree?"

"There are two things *el Alemán* has never held back from: favors to friends and pranks played on the powerful."

23.

The caïque bound for Üsküdar, propelled by four oars, was thin and pointed as a gondola. The Bosphorus looked like the Grand Canal of a vast rural Venice. The villages on the Asian shore were colored jewels, linked together by a chain of villas, *yali*, stilt-dwellings, wooden jetties. The dark water welcomed dozens of other fishing boats, as well as freighters, big merchant *mahonas*, a galley armed with cannon, feluccas, and punts that looked empty but concealed lovers busy swapping sweet endearments.

Once they had reached the opposite shore, the oarsmen moored the boat and we jumped out onto the uneven planks of the dock.

In the last light of day, the fishermen sat mending nets against upturned hulls. A group of children ran about between the waterside and the alleyways, and women pulled in the clothes they had hung out in the morning. No one paid us much attention.

We reached the house where I'd spent my first night in Constantinople. Don Yossef called Ismail's name from outside without getting a reply, and then the Indian girl appeared on the terrace. "Ismail?" asked Nasi.

"Over there." She stretched out her arm, pointing to a spot in the distance. "At the top of the street."

A cluster of houses climbed the side of a hill. We set off, and when we were behind the dwelling I saw the red-bearded Arab leaning against a wall. Beside him there was a door, closed only by a piece of blue fabric.

"*As-Salaam 'Alaykum*," he said, poking out first his chin and then his forehead.

"*Wa 'Alaykum As-Salaam*," Nasi replied. "We're looking for Ismail al-Mokhawi."

He leaned inside, and the old man's head appeared a moment later. He barely glanced at me, greeted Nasi, and asked us to wait. Then he disappeared into the house again.

"What's happening?" Nasi asked the Arab.

The other man replied in a foreign accent, "A child has a high fever, and his parents have sent for Ismail."

We waited for half an hour, until the curtain opened again and the old man re-emerged from the darkness, followed by a short, squat man. They exchanged a few words, then said good-bye.

"So you became a sawbones as well, down in Mokha?" Nasi asked.

"I just got old," Ismail replied in Turkish. "These people think my advice

lengthens your life." He turned to me. "Good evening, Sior Cardoso." I replied, and he introduced the red-bearded Arab to me: "This is my friend Ali Hassan al-Najib, the man who promised God he would convert me to the Mohammedan faith."

The Arab greeted me again with a nod of the head. Ismail asked him to step into the house ahead of us, and warn the others that there were guests for dinner.

On the open terrain by the water we bumped into a fisherman who gave the old man a few big sea bream, and an old woman with her face veiled handed him a basket of apricots. Ismail thanked her, exchanged a few words and chased away a gang of begging children, pretending to run after them with his stick. Then he turned on his heel and we went into the house.

The old man knelt down on the carpet, beside the brazier that had warmed me too. He put a pile of cushions between his back and the wall and gestured to us to make ourselves comfortable. He pointed to the Indian twins: "These are Hafiz and Mukhtar. They come from the Malabar coast of India."

Hafiz, the boy, said something to him in Arabic, and the old man thanked him, using the only word I knew in that language: "*Shukraan.*" Then he returned to Turkish: "I'm listening." I realized that he spoke that language instead of Italian because his friends were there and he didn't want to exclude them from our conversation.

"The other evening we were left with a question," Nasi announced, also in Turkish. "It concerned the last letter my aunt wrote to you. Perhaps it won't be the answer you're looking for, but here it is. A few days have passed, and already your help would be invaluable to me." With a gesture of his hand he attracted my attention. "Master Cardoso will tell you what it's about."

I was careful not to be caught off guard by this investiture, and talked about the bailiff's letters, the Jewish doctor's slippers, Sokollu's intrigues, Traverso and his voyages. The German listened in silence. When I'd finished, Nasi made one last remark: "Manuel has done an excellent job, and to bring it to the best possible conclusion we need a gang of pirates to board Ashkenazi's ship and put it off course. I remember that you used to keep company with certain people, and I know that you could find them again."

Hafiz set down a tray with three steaming cups in the middle of the room. It was the drink I had heard them describe at Palazzo Belvedere: shells that looked like nuts, but with the flavor of coffee, left to infuse in boiling water.

We each took one, being careful not to burn our fingers. Ismail al-Mokhawi smoothed his white beard and cleared his throat.

"If I've understood correctly, it's a matter of putting the Grand Vizier, his secretary and the Venetian bailiff in check all at once." Nasi nodded, the old man burned his lips with *kishir* and started talking again. "Wouldn't it be enough to denounce Traverso as a spy and have him captured by the janissaries on Ashkenazi's ship before it left the harbor?"

"I don't trust the janissaries, my friend. Sokollu could easily manipulate them, get rid of the evidence."

"And yet," Ismail remarked, "before I came here I was in Tiberias and I saw janissaries on every street corner. And your kingdom of Cyprus, won't the janissaries and Selim's troops be the ones to conquer it?"

This time Nasi spread his arms in a gesture of impatience. "And how could it be otherwise? We Jews, in the Ottoman Empire, can't even go around with a razor blade. That's why we need the Sultan and the janissaries. At least for the time being."

I tried to work out what he could be talking about, but Ismail's words started troubling me again.

"Isn't that how it started, the enslavement of your people in Egypt? A Jewish dreamer who was a friend of the Pharaoh, covered with honors and prestigious duties? Then the Pharaoh died and the Jews were enslaved for four hundred years."

The reference to Joseph hit me like a slap. A few days before, I myself had superimposed that image over Don Yossef, like a grid over a coded message, but I had stopped at the first lines, and the message I had drawn from it was totally different.

"I like it when you quote my people's history," Nasi replied. "Joseph was a man of God, but I hope to do as Judith did, when she went to Holofernes's banquet and cut his head off. If you like, you could help me sharpen the sword."

Nasi was playing a game of chance. I thought of the time, in the stinking cell in Ragusa, when I had thrown my rough dice and they had replied, "Live." Here, every phrase from my mentor was a throw of the dice. Pause, check the result, roll again.

That last throw clattered away down the room, without giving any sign of stopping.

"Fine," the old man said at last. "I just hope you have a firm grip on your sword."

Nasi moved his hand up and down as if to say *Give me time, have trust.*

Ismail summoned Ali and the twins. He asked if they'd understood what we'd asked them to do, and added that we'd need a few days of research and may even have to leave the city.

The three of them consulted in low-voiced Arabic, then signaled their agreement with a nod of the head. Nasi thanked them, and then turned back to his friend.

"I'd like you to take Manuel. It's thanks to his intuitions that you've got this far."

"Yes, and you have to keep an eye on me." The old man stung him, and I couldn't work out whether he was joking or not. Then, looking at me, "I was right, about that poplar pollen and the hill of Pera. Well, the appointment's fixed for tomorrow, after the first prayer, at the caravanserai of the Suleymaniye Mosque. I'll show you ambushes of a different kind."

24.

We left the caravanserai on five haggard-looking bay horses. I was wearing Muslim clothes, to get round the law against infidels riding horses like everyone else. To my right was an Indian girl disguised as a man, then a man who looked like a girl, and finally a German in a cloak and turban. I wondered if the Moor Ali, behind his red beard, mightn't be hiding unexpected features.

We went down the third hill of the New Rome, the one upon which stood the Suleymaniye Mosque, and reached the Imperial Road. In spite of his age, Ismail sat straight in the saddle and rode at a good pace. I spurred my horse to catch up with him.

"Where are we going?"

"Out of the city," he replied crisply.

We headed westward, the only direction on the peninsula that doesn't lead to the sea.

"We're visiting a pirate, not a peasant," I said, in a bid to melt the old man's reticence.

Ismail raised his chin. "We're not going to see him, we're going to see the man who can tell us where to find him."

By now we were near the Column of Arcadius, and the voices from the Grand Bazaar drowned out our words. As we crossed the square, I noticed with surprise that they were female voices, and that behind the stalls and shops selling henna, candles, flowers and yogurt, there were veiled women, most of them peasants, and that the clientele was made up of women, too.

Once we were out of the crowd, I learned from Ismail that this was *Avrat Pazari*, the only market in the city where Muslim women could buy and sell in peace, without servants or brothers keeping an eye on them.

Our riding party carried on past the Cannon Gate, leaving the Byzantine walls behind. We passed through the suburbs and found ourselves in the open countryside. Low hills followed one after the other, run through with waves of green. I saw snakes darting in and out by the side of the track. Ali told me not to worry, because none of them were poisonous. And the horses remained calm.

Then the countryside assumed tones of yellow and ocher, as sunflower fields filled the horizon. Sparrows and bee-eaters chirped on the branches of the few trees. Their rainbow feathers filled me with unexpected joy. At about midday, Ismail made an announcement.

"Here we are, Cardoso. Nearly there."

The landscape was unchanged. Grass and sunflowers as far as the eye could see; nothing else. We crested a hill, and on the slope of the next one I spotted a group of men on horseback. Around them, a dance of birds flying in high circles and plunging in dives. They were falconers.

Years before, I had been the guest of a nobleman in the Trevisan marches, carrying out a task for my old bosses. Hunting with falcons was his great passion, but I could hardly say it was mine. I was pursuing different prey. On that occasion I had been bored, and had soon tired of standing with my nose in the air following the movements of the raptors. The nobleman had then bored me further with a long litany of complaints about the decadence of *tempora* and *mores*, which put such distinguished birds of prey on the forearms of unworthy priests and courtesans, though they were meant only for men of quite different status. In the end, thank God, he gave me the information I was looking for.

Ismail raised his right hand in greeting and called out a name in a loud voice.

Young men with thin beards replied with profuse salutations and low bows. One of them said he was the son of the man we were looking for, and that his father would be delighted by our visit.

So they guided us to his presence. He was a man of Ali's age, tall and handsome, who towered above his mount and emanated a calm, mild strength. He got off his horse and we did the same. The hooded falcon perched on his right arm stayed obediently in its place.

From the tone of the greetings and the brief allusions to old memories, I understood that Ismail had been close to the man who was welcoming us. As he introduced him to us, he listed all of his titles, and at last I knew who he was. Hassan Agha, the Great Falconer and second chief huntsman to the Sultan. That evening, back in Palazzo Belvedere, I would discover that he was the husband of Princess Shah, daughter of Selim, and remember with surprise his simple, cordial manners. His friendship with Ismail was doubtless the true motive for that attitude, but perhaps another factor was his habit of living among fields and bushes, in close contact with animals, and not in the halls of a lordly palace, surrounded by deference and submission.

It was thus that I learned that Ismail, during his years in Constantinople, had taken part in Hassan Agha's hunting parties, along with some illustrious lovers of the sport, one of whom was the fifth vizier, Lala Mustafa, whom I had met at the Divan.

We got back on our horses, and reached the top of a hill, the highest in the area. Below us, beyond a grove of willows and flowering bulrushes, the calls of ducks and toads revealed the presence of a stretch of water.

The falconer removed the hood from his bird, and the creature took flight with a nervous flutter of wings. It soared to a high altitude and began playing in the gusts of wind. Hassan Agha's men came down among the marsh grasses, beating the ground with their sticks. A flock of ducks rose from the depths.

The falcon flew a few more turns, then fell in a vertiginous dive upon its prey, which it grabbed with its claws. The victim's flight was cut short in a cloud of down and feathers. The young horsemen hurled themselves toward the spot where it had fallen, and came back to us bearing the falcon, which still gripped the duck in its claws. Hassan Agha drew it to his arm with a big piece of meat. While the falcon was eating, he slipped the prey from its clutches and put it in his bag.

"You Europeans like the company of dogs," he said, stroking the bird with a finger. "Submissive creatures, anxious to please man, as devoted servants desire to please their master. Hunting with a falcon, on the other hand, is a matter of trust and mutual self-interest."

The bird's bright white plumage was streaked with a rainy pattern of dark grey patches. I had never seen an animal like it, and as politely as I could I asked the falconer what kind of bird it was.

"They say that its mother comes from the icy marshes at the edge of the world," he replied, "and its father from the deserts of central Asia, the cradle of our people. Two different breeds, but similar enough to be able to mate, laying the eggs on the slopes of the Altai, the Mountains of Gold, which give their name to this hybrid."

I thanked him for the attention he had given me, but he went on talking, as if the answer were a very long one. "He's a very robust falcon, faithful, easy to train. You don't have to do anything with an Altai, and a good falconer does as little as possible. It's the falcon's nature that impels it to fly and makes it grip the prey with its claws. If you want him to do that for you, you just have to show him why it's to his advantage."

The Great Falconer paused again, and then told the story of Prince Temujin, who after losing a battle came home across the desert with a friend. The two men hadn't eaten for days, when they saw an Altai falcon flying high above them. The friend suggested that Temujin keep an eye on it, to take its prey away from it. The other man replied that you have to earn your food, and caught the falcon to teach it to hunt for them. Two years later, the princes finally came home. If they hadn't trained that Altai they would have died of hunger and the world would not have known Temujin, or Genghis Khan, the greatest leader of all time.

At the end of the tale he bowed deeply, as Ismail complimented his friend on his storytelling gifts. A little way away, the young men were whirling quail carcasses on a long string to train the falcons to seize them in flight. Hafiz and Mukhtar observed the scene carefully, as if committing to memory the gestures of a ritual.

At that point, Ismail judged that it would not be impolite to pose the question that had brought us all there, half a day's ride from the old walls.

"I was wondering, my friend, what happened to Mimi Reis. I lost trace of him, I have had no news of him, and I would like to see him as I have seen you."

The falconer nodded. "He had a few problems, so he decided to leave the city. You will find him in Bandirma, on the Sea of Marmara, doing exactly what he has always done. Mimi Reis will always navigate the sea, even if he has only a cardamom pod as a boat and a cup of coffee as the only available sea."

The two men laughed. I had never heard Ismail's laugh. It was sonorous, and sounded like the laughter of a young man, but it left a melancholy echo behind.

I would have liked to know more about the past that linked the old man to our host and to the pirate we were looking for, but instead the two friends' words flowed together into rumors about imminent war.

"They say our Sultan wants to terminate the construction of the Edirne mosque," the Turk explained. "He needs lots of money, and the Grand Mufti has told him that for the glory of God it is better to use the booty from a holy war than the taxes of subject Muslims."

That was an opinion that I hadn't heard before. The vox populi said that Selim needed to inaugurate his reign with a conquest, lest he be seen as inferior to his predecessors.

Ismail's comment was somewhat broad, and I tried to work out what he was trying to imply. "The men seem to be going off to war like dogs crowding around a carcass. But the causes are complex, hard to discern. That's why the humble people experience wars as natural disasters, like floods or plagues. They see cannons of bronze, not the gold that originated them. In the lands I come from, the cannon smelters and the money coiners were the same people."

"The point of view of the humble folk is not ours, Ismail," said the falconer. "You know what impels the powerful men of this city. And it's the ambition of powerful men that drives wars. There is no need to seek other reasons."

With those words, he gestured to his attendant to summon the others. The hunting day was over, and Hassan Agha invited us to his palace, which was not far away.

As we road among the grassy hills, I felt free, just as I had felt when I arrived in Constantinople, when I saw the city from the deck of the ship.

Even in the saddle, pages and boys made their raptors fly. The little ones, sparrow-hawks, kestrels and honey buzzards, perched on the arms of the youngest boys, sped into the air until they had a good view of the ground below, and then, with the wind supporting their wings, stopped in midair, waiting to plunge down on their earthly quarry. I remembered that this attitude was called, in Italian lands, the Holy Spirit. Like Tuota's dog, in Ragusa.

Then, once again, it was the moment of the falcon that Hassan Agha had called an Altai. I was drawn to the creature; it had a fierce and noble appearance, and yet it was serene, as if its fellowship with man came from the very

distant past, as if it had always known the voice and arm of its wingless companion.

The Altai flew high over the countryside. We went on, each in his own disguise, still not suspecting the carnival that would see us dancing together.

25.

The midday sun erased the shadows from the dock at Uskudar and scattered drops of gold in the puddles left by the nighttime rain. The reflections dazzled the eye. It was hot, perhaps for the first time since I had come to the city, and the sea's bright hues spoke of summer. Men and goods crowded the big open space on the Bosphorus; products from Asia and Europe went up and down between carts and holds, unloaded from the backs of stevedores and the humps of camels. Nothing seemed to stop for as long as a breath.

We took shelter from the light and the crowd beneath the big loggia of the mosque, which loomed over the slipway from the top of a platform.

I had grown used to asking the names of Muslim temples, because in Constantinople they tend to be named not after saints and prophets, but instead after the people who financed their construction, powerful men and women—the more influential, the more remarkable the architecture. Knowing the *kulliye* of the city is a way of knowing the personalities of the empire, whether past or present.

Ismail told me that the person responsible for this particular mosque was Mihrimah Sultan, a name famous even in Venice, where I had heard various rumors about her. Some said that her father, Suleyman the Magnificent, had besieged Malta just to make her happy, and they hinted at incestuous love. Some maintained that Mihrimah was an odalisque, an unscrupulous concubine, whose beauty had so bewitched Suleyman that he was impelled into that ruinous military campaign.

I asked Ismail if he knew which of those stories was true, and he laughed. "None," he replied. "The princess herself financed the expedition against Malta." He added that Mihrimah, Selim II's big sister, was the oldest woman in the Sultan's family. The siblings' mother, the legendary Roxelana, had in fact been dead for some time. So, along with Nurbanu, Mihrimah was one of the most powerful women in the empire.

"In Europe, no one can imagine the women of the harem capable of moving money, fleets, armies. This demonstrates how little we know about what's happening here." He shrugged. "Besides, the matter is reciprocal."

The boat that awaited us, a felucca with a lateen sail, was now ready to set off. Ali beckoned us over. We climbed on board and the sailors hurried to pick up their oars. The boat bore us off, away from the hubbub of the port. Soon we found ourselves on the open sea, heading south.

As evening fell, I realized that I hadn't exchanged a word with a living soul since we had weighed anchor. The sun set slow and red. Everyone stopped to pray. After that, each of us returned to his own place, waiting.

All but Mukhtar. The young woman traced a geometrical figure on the planks of the deck with a piece of white chalk, then aligned her feet with some of the marks and began to move in a dance that appeared to be simulating an act of combat. Her body seemed that of a reptile, or a lynx. I had seen great fighters and fencers practicing their movements bare-handed, and although the girl's were much more graceful and less direct, her limbs seemed to contain a strength not unlike that of a coiled spring, or a serpent ready to strike.

Ali must have noticed my puzzlement and imagined my reflections. He came over and said in a low voice, "In the land from which she comes, it is not unusual for girls to be sent to fight. They are trained in places like convents, under the direction of a sheik who also understands medicine and astrology. It is a skill practiced by idolaters, but also by those who have embraced the true religion. You see the figure she has drawn on the floor? In their language, that is called *kalam*. It conveys the precise steps and effective angles of attack and defense. In the language of the Book, *kalam* means 'the word of God.'"

"So Mukhtar's movements run through the word of God?" I asked him.

Ali thought for a moment before replying, "Yes, I think you could say that. But you could say it about any one of our movements, because everything that happens is the fruit of His creative will."

The figure danced on, with the sea all around and the sunset in the background.

That night, beneath a sky with stars clustered thick as cherry blossoms, I struggled to fall asleep. The placid rhythm of the boat would have encouraged rest had I not been enchanted by that dangling moment. We were far from land, in perfect equilibrium between the vast mass of water and the dark blue vault of the sky, sometimes barely distinguishable from one another. The two young Indians had recited their prayers along with Ali and were now sitting back to back, they, too, enchanted by the spectacle of the night, while the other lay down on his mat.

Ismail crouched downwind, in the prow. I studied his dark silhouette and thought of Tuota. Who knew what had become of him. It was fate that put the men in my way who led me out on the sea. I went and sat next to Ismail, and we said nothing for a while, as if we were afraid to disturb the silence of the night. It was he who spoke first.

"There's something you want to ask me and something that's keeping you from it."

His insight made me smile. "You know what I used to do for a living. I don't know how you would interpret my curiosity." He in turn gave me an amused glance.

"You were a policeman. Who's to say that I haven't done even worse things than that?" He was right. I knew little or nothing about him, and that was precisely the reason for my curiosity.

"You told the Great Falconer that the causes of the war are an impenetrable tangle. Have you fought?"

He stared at the dark expanse ahead of us. "In Germany, many years ago."

"Were you a soldier?"

I thought he wasn't going to reply, and sat counting my breaths. As I drew the fifth, he spoke: "Have you ever heard of the city of Münster, in Westphalia? I was there, in the year of our Lord 1534. And before that I was with the insurgent German peasants, at the battle of Frankenhausen."

Münster. All kinds of stories were associated with that name. It was a kind of curse: "Münster" summed up the madness of the world. It was said that the Anabaptist heretics had abolished all the sacraments there, all traces of religion, of human and divine order. It was said that they were guided by the devil himself, in the false guise of a new David. It seemed impossible that I found myself in the presence of a witness of such far-off events. This man came from another world, the horrors of which I had heard talked about in Venice.

I stirred myself and tried to resume the thread of my questions. "You wanted to found the kingdom of God on earth, didn't you?"

He looked into the distance again, drawn by the darkness, as his fingers slipped along his chest and rummaged under his shirt. "We wanted justice. And a reason to live and die. I had the good fortune to come out of it alive and meet people who explained something about the world to me. Something you don't find written in the Bible or the Koran, but in account books and registers." He fell silent. The weight of his memories couldn't have been easy to bear.

"I suppose that one of those people, the ones who opened your eyes, was Yossef Nasi."

He nodded, running his fingers through his beard. "I met him in Venice, after lengthy peregrinations, and when the Inquisition forced us to leave Europe, we chose Constantinople, where Yossef and Beatriz, or Donna Gracia, obtained an audience with Suleyman the Magnificent and offered him their services. I was there too that day, at the Seraglio. A heretic in the presence of the Sultan." He turned to look at me. "Satisfied?" Then he wrapped himself up in his cloak, stretched his legs, leaned his back against the wall and closed his eyes.

"That was only the prelude," I pressed him. "And after that? You left the capital, your allies . . ." I paused for a second, before finishing the sentence. "The woman you loved."

"You're not one for letting things go, are you? You must have been very good at your job. If we'd met somewhere else, at some other time, I wouldn't have hesitated to cut your throat." The unexpected words chilled my blood. "I have spent my life fighting alongside the humble folk," he continued. "That

is my vocation. The vocation of people like Nasi, on the other hand, is to do business with princes and emperors. My place is not at Palazzo Belvedere. I sensed as much that day, after meeting Suleyman, but I chose to wait, to put myself to the test. At my age it's difficult to give up the love of a woman, to give up having her beside you on the last stretch of your life. And when you decide to do it, you have to put a great distance between you."

"You've talked to me about what you've lost. What do you have left?"

My words, spoken on impulse, must have penetrated the shell that protected him, touching him at a sensitive spot. The old man turned to look at the others. Two of them were already sound asleep, but Mukhtar was standing as straight as a figurehead, defying the sea to unbalance her. Or perhaps it was Hafiz.

"Just them."

"Why do they always go with you?"

The night breeze hissed among the sails, made the joints creak, and together with the breaking of the waves against the keel it seemed to be composing a tune.

"I bought Hafiz and Mukhtar from a Portuguese slave trader who wanted to be rid of them. He thought he'd found a stable boy and a concubine, but when he worked out what kind of warriors they were, he took fright. I gave them their freedom, and since then they've called me 'Baba,' as if they were the children I never had." He paused, as if to keep a hint of emotion at bay, and again I thought of the man I had for years called father, even though he wasn't. "Ali came back to Mokha five years ago, after being away for a long time. His sheik died in Mecca while on the pilgrimage, and he headed south. He is a dervish, a Sufi. He was a great help to us during the rebellion last year. Perhaps you have heard that the rebels were heretics. They say that about all rebels. The truth is that they were peasants who were weary of being robbed by Turkish officials, and those religious men gave them a voice. Thanks to Ali, I was able to go on buying coffee from the insurgent tribes. Between us, we convinced the Zaydis to leave the city just before the Sultan's fleet arrived. We avoided a bloodbath in Mokha."

Far from appeasing my curiosity, his stories aroused it still more, if possible, but now the old man began preparing for sleep, adjusting the mat he was sitting on and arranging his traveling bag as a pillow. I had just enough time for one last question, and decided to come out with it.

"The other day, at your house, I understood that you disapproved of Don Yossef's project. So why did you decide to help him?"

"I don't really disapprove of it," he said, resting his head on his bag. "But, you see, if you want to catch a hare, whether you hunt it with hounds or with a falcon, on foot or on horseback, it will always be a hare. Freedom, on the other hand, never remains the same; it changes according to the way you hunt. And if you train dogs to catch it for you, you may just bring back a doggy kind of freedom."

I thought I understood what he was getting at, and tried to cloak my understanding under the authority of a famous piece of writing, one that the Consigliere had wanted all his subordinates to know by heart: "Machiavelli wrote that you must keep your eye on the end, not the means."

"Yes, Yossef often used to say the same thing." He closed his eyes and arranged himself on his side. "Over the years, I've learned that the means change the end."

He wished me a good night's sleep. I watched him drifting off, then, exhausted, I decided to lie down as well. Before closing my eyes, I looked up. The silhouette of Mukhtar, or perhaps Hafiz, was still there, watching motionlessly over everyone's dreams.

26.

We put in at a teeming little town. The ships en route for the Aegean, toward Smyrna, often moored at those docks. When storms lashed the White Sea, the boats and their cargoes sought refuge there. From the inland regions of Mysia and Anatolia came foodstuffs on their way to the capital. Judging by what Ismail said, the man we were looking for was a spider in the middle of this web, and the town, Bandirma, was his nest.

A unit of janissaries stood guard by the lighthouse, amid the fishermen's stalls and the cases and barrels ready for lading. Their feathered hats were visible above the heads of the crowd. And as we walked along the quay, I saw their eyes watching our every step.

"Stop!" the captain ordered us.

Above his bushy mustache his expression was icy. A scar furrowed his face. Instinctively, our company closed ranks. The janissaries came closer. The captain narrowed his eyes. "Who are you and where do you come from?"

"I'm a coffee merchant and these are my colleagues. My name is Ismail al-Mokhawi."

"Mokhawi?" The captain's piggy eyes fixed on Ali. "Are you Yemenis?"

"Damned dogs, get back to your homeland!" muttered someone behind him.

Ismail remained impassive. "We are all subjects of the Sultan, God have mercy on him, and we are under his protection."

The captain of the janissaries clicked his tongue and said, "He looks like a renegade Frank to me, and as to your friend," he pointed at Ali, "we've seen plenty like him, down in Yemen. Heretic dogs, ready to cut your throat while you sleep."

I noticed that the activity in the port had ceased. The people had formed a sort of circle, roping off the arena where the cocks were about to fight. I noticed Ali slipping his fingers around the hilt of his scimitar. Hafiz and Mukhtar had their hands on their belts. Ismail raised a hand, asking for calm. "These men aren't rebels. If the Sultan's standard is flying over Mokha again, it's down to me. It was I who ensured that you could come in without paying a blood price."

The captain didn't seem very interested. He spat on the ground, as the onlookers pressed in behind the janissaries, who struggled to contain them. A leg appeared out of the scuffling crowd and kicked at the old man's stick. Ismail managed not to fall. Mukhtar stepped to his side, shielding him.

The soldiers were irresolute, torn between their duty to contain the crowd and their desire to settle their scores with those whom they perceived as enemies. The captain of the janissaries drew his sword and spun about, threatening all the people around them. Meanwhile we retreated. Hafiz and I now faced the janissaries, while Mukhtar clung to Ismail and Ali, her hand on the hilt of her sword, opening up a path behind us. The captain barked at us not to move, while the people, who continued to rage at us, seemed ready to overwhelm his men. Then Mukhtar put her hand to her belt and drew a weapon that I had never seen before: a hilt from which long strips of steel protruded, supple and twisting. These, when whirled in the air above our heads, gave off sparks and a sound that chilled the blood. The crowd fell silent, and the captain of the janissaries froze where he stood. Ismail rested his hand on his pistol. Time seemed to stop.

Then the captain moved toward us, breaking the spell. The crowd roared. Ismail leveled his weapon, and the Indian girl prepared to bring hers down so that the steel blades first shredded the soldier's hat, then did more serious damage below. I waited for the tragedy to happen.

Suddenly I heard an agitated voice calling out a name that must have been the captain's. Another group of janissaries appeared, this one more tightly organized, and began to move the crowd back with more conviction.

A squat man, dressed in the Turkish style, pushed his way through with short but certain steps, accompanied by a janissary, who seemed to be a high-ranking officer, followed by other soldiers. They came straight toward the middle of the arena and interposed themselves between Ismail and the captain.

"*As-Salaam 'Alaykum,*" said the senior officer.

"*Wa 'Alaykum As-Salaam,*" the captain replied, without taking his eyes off us.

"You were about to commit an unpardonable error. Luckily Mimi Reis, here, requested that I intervene. This man," he said, pointing to Ismail, "enjoys the esteem of illustrious people. He even knew Suleyman the Magnificent. Many in Istanbul respect him like a father. Touching a hair on his head, or the heads of his companions, would mean finding yourself on the Persian border in a very short time, and for a very long time."

The squat man interjected, "May that never transpire, Captain. We want you here to defend us and ensure the safety of our trade."

The captain decided to take his eye off Ismail. He took his leave politely, and retreated quietly with his janissaries in the direction of the lighthouse. The senior official turned back to Ismail. "I would like to have you as my guest, Ismail al-Mokhawi, but I know you are traveling on important business. I hope that God may allow us to meet again."

"If God so wills."

Then those Turks took their leave as well, in a more formal and courteous way, and we were left on our own with the short man. He turned toward Ismail. "It's really you! I thought you'd been dead for ages," he said.

"I wasn't far off it."

They smiled, hugged, and kissed each other's beards.

"But I see that your habits have not changed. You're still in trouble. Yes, but you travel under a lucky star. That star, today, is Mimi," he said, patting his chest with his open palm. "Come, all of you come to my house. You are my guests."

We had come in search of a man, and he had found us.

So it was that I met Mimi Reis.

On reaching Mimi Reis's house, we went upstairs and sat on damask cushions on the floor. Two windows lit the room: One looked out onto the street and the other onto the garden.

Our guide's accent was familiar to me; that of the inhabitants of Puglia, opposite Ragusa, which made me like him, not least because he was almost a compatriot of mine. We asked him to speak in Turkish so that everyone could understand.

Two maids came in, carrying a huge metal tray upon which lay half a roasted kid. They set it down on a stool, and together the two objects became a table. All we had to do was move our cushions around it and start eating.

"I've brought my sisters specially from Bari, to teach the maids to cook," said the master of the house. He sang the praises of his native dishes, listing all the ingredients of dips and sauces. Ali asked if the animals had been butchered in the *halal* way, and it was only when he had received that reassurance that he and the Indians began to eat. Meanwhile, my attention was drawn to a Byzantine icon, right above a table beside the fireplace, surrounded by candles. Mimi Reis noticed my interest, and raised his right hand.

"*Sanda Necole*, patron saint of sailors."

With these words, he pulled up his shirt to show us his chest and abdomen. Drawn just above his sternum was a bluish crucifix. Further down a group of women, and on his belly a sailing ship, manned by sailors carrying a trunk.

"You see?" he said, touching his ribs, "these are the three virgins of the miracle, and this one in the middle is my ancestor Benuzzo, who came back to Bari along with his companions, bearing the bones of the saint. They came to get them right here in Turkey, in Myra, on the coast opposite Cyprus."

Ali couldn't conceal a certain disgust at this spectacle, perhaps because of the nakedness on display, or perhaps because of the sharp smell emanating from the Italian's chest. His expression didn't escape our host, who suddenly looked contrite.

"Now I know that having your body carved is an insult to God's work," he hastened to say as he lowered his shirt. "But the Christians in my part of the world say it's proof of faith, and also a protection, because if someone has these drawings on him it's harder for the Turks to take him away; he's like a rotten apple."

"And what about you?" Ali asked curiously. "How did you become a Muslim?"

"The Turks took me anyway; they weren't picky. I was eighteen, and my name was Domenico, Mimi to everybody. Since then I've been Mehmet."

"So your faith was imposed upon you," Ali said with regret.

The other protested: "Not at all. The pope is a tyrant, God is great and Mohammad is his Prophet. Saint Nicholas was born before him, so we can't blame him for not being a Muslim. In my crew, when I was a corsair, the Albanians and Bosnians venerated him as much as I did: They called him *imam*, and if the sea swelled we prayed to him together to keep us afloat."

The arrival of a tray of cakes interrupted his story. I was full by now, my head was heavy, and the warm air that day wasn't helping me to stay awake. I missed a few lines of conversation, and perhaps I even closed my eyes, until the scent of coffee reached my nostrils.

"Of these people's recipes, the only one we should imitate," our host announced, bringing the cup to his lips, and when we had emptied ours, he asked us if we wanted anything else. The request was polite but superfluous, after the mountain of food that he had served us.

"I want to talk business," said Ismail.

Mimi Reis stretched his arms out along the edges of the big pillow behind his back. He said, "It must be important business if it made you come back from Yemen. Or was it the Zaydi rebellion that dislodged you?"

Ismail smiled. "Rebellions don't scare me; you should know that. And besides, what should a man who has reached my age be afraid of? On the other hand, what made you leave Constantinople?"

The Pugliese tightened every muscle in his face, assuming an expression that was the quintessence of regret. "Aaah, a lot has changed since you were there. There are a lot of things that you wouldn't recognize. Some people worked their way up the ladder, and some people got stuck. And then there are the people who had to leave. Particularly the ones who didn't have saints to help them to Paradise, as we say—*senza sande nan s'va en 'mbaravise*. We also say that *'u pèsce gruesse nan pote sci mmocch'a cudde peccenunne*—the big fish doesn't fit in the little fish's mouth. The little one has to go and swim somewhere else, you understand?"

"I understand," said Ismail. "Anyway, I've come to suggest a transaction on behalf of a big fish. Yossef Nasi."

Mimi Reis narrowed his eyes and scratched his chin. "And I'm listening to you because you're you."

"Are you still in touch with your Greek friends?"

The Pugliese nodded, his nose tilted upward as if sniffing every word. Ismail gestured to me to speak.

"At the end of the month," I explained, "there's a ship bound straight for Crete. It has to go off course and put in somewhere else, on the island of Naxos."

The Pugliese pondered the request. "Whose ship is it?"

"It belongs to Solomon Ashkenazi."

Mimi Reis pulled a disgusted face. "This is a *rott 'n cule*, a filthy trickster, servant of the Venetians. The Venetians are impostors. They tried to take Saint Nicholas's bones, and when we got them back, rather than accepting the fact, they launched a crusade all the way here to tell us that we'd made a mistake and they'd found the real tomb." He struck his chest and shook his head. "Infidel dogs."

He stayed like that, with his hand on his beard, as if oppressed by that ancient injustice. Then he stirred himself, called for a bottle of raki and offered it to everybody, but of course Ismail and I were the only ones who accepted.

"This is no *sganuffa*," said Mimi Reis, after sipping the spirits. "It's no trifle. And people who engage in this kind of thing aren't easily satisfied. It's a big risk. It'll take a lot of money."

"How much?" I asked.

Again that contrite expression. "Let's say at least six thousand aspers."

"Fine," I replied firmly. I had Nasi's mandate to offer the necessary sum. "Half in advance and half once the business is concluded."

"No," Mimi insisted. "I need all the money up front."

I exchanged a worried glance with Ismail, and he spoke up: "You used to trust me."

The Pugliese sighed. "It isn't a matter of trust, my friend. It's that Yossef Nasi is more exposed than a sheet in the sun. They're preparing for war, everyone knows that he's up to his neck in it, and I don't want any problems. And then you know that *'u uacejiedde pisce 'u llejiette e 'u cula iave mazzate*." He stopped and translated for everyone: "The cock pisses the bed and the arse gets the kicking. I'm going to have to cover my arse . . ." He spread his arms. "Payment up front or I can't help you."

I looked at Ismail. The old man had no intention of replying. I wondered if he was silent out of kindness or whether he thought the objection was reasonable.

As we took our leave I was still filled with doubt. The Pugliese kissed us all and said he would send someone to get the money from Scutari. "Right then, Ismail," he said before he left us. "You're about to unleash a whirlwind, and troubles are going to come pouring in. It's better for the old boats to stay in the harbor."

The old man looked at him with laughing eyes. "Thanks for the advice, my friend. But you know me: I only stay in the harbor as long as I absolutely have to. *As-Salaam 'Alaykum*."

"*Wa 'Alaykum As-Salaam. Statt' bun.* Take care."

28.

It's on moonless nights that misdeeds are done, when only the stars sparkle on the black cloak of the sky and the pilots choose their routes with their noses in the air, their hands firmly on the tiller. It was on a moonless night that Mimi Reis's trap was sprung.

The merchant ship bound for Candia was passing calmly through the Cyclades when an alarm was raised on board. The black shadow of a sail had suddenly appeared from behind the island of Delos, on a collision course with the Cretan vessel. The bell on deck rang out, torches were waved, but the ghost ship pressed on until it struck the side of the merchantman, level with the prow, making it list to the left and spin on its own axis. Then it was clear to everyone that a major collision was unavoidable. The oarsmen were recalled to their benches, and the captain turned the ship's tail and fled with sails unfurled.

The pirates' slender galley, lighter and faster, pursued its quarry to Naxos. It was only at dawn, in view of the harbor, that it vanished again.

As Ashkenazi's boat moored it was welcomed by the island's militia and the keeper of the harbor, who in the name of the Duke of Naxos, that is to say Don Yossef Nasi, put the ship under the protection and custody of his master.

The captain's protests were futile. The militiamen climbed on board and inspected the ship and its crew. Bernardo Traverso was missing from the lineup. After a long search, the Genoese was found in the hold, his breeches round his ankles, trying to stuff some rolls of paper into his rear orifice. Caught *in flagrante*, he commended his soul to the Holy Virgin and prayed on his knees to be spared. The keeper of the port took charge of the precious rolls of paper, but not before he had cleaned them of all traces of Genoese jitters. At last, along with a detailed report, he entrusted them to a messenger and sent them to Constantinople. A few days later, the letters of Marcantonio Barbaro, addressed to the Doge of Venice and the Council of Ten, were in the hands of Yossef Nasi.

I imagined that Nasi would send the proof of Ashkenazi's betrayal to the Sultan in person. He didn't, in fact. He knew he held the winning cards, but he also knew how to play them. He went not to the Sultan but instead to the Grand Vizier. He brought Sokollu proof of his personal secretary's betrayal, having first taken the precaution of making the contents of the documents public. Thus he held Sokollu to his responsibilities, and linked him to his own conniving. I couldn't say if it was a flash of genius or a premeditated move, but it certainly put the Grand Vizier in great difficulty.

The events of the following week marked the victory of Nasi and the decisive step toward war. Sokollu couldn't keep Ashkenazi out of prison and had to use all his influence to save the Venetian doctor from the gallows. By so doing, he reinforced suspicions that he too had an agreement with La Serenissima. Selim was obliged to demonstrate his disapproval of that same Grand Vizier, and the advocates of war within the Divan were given a free hand to proceed with military operations against Cyprus.

Throughout this time, Nasi appeared strangely calm. Only his eyes gave away his excitement, his awareness that his plan was coming to fruition, one step at a time.

So it was that one day in early summer we all found ourselves in the big Roman hippodrome, which the Turks called Atmeydani, watching the Ottoman war machine get moving, to the sound of horns and drums.

29.

The Sipahi noblemen passed in serried ranks, their horses' steps perfectly synchronized, their lances pointed toward the sky, a forest of glittering pines. On the arm of every horseman was a round shield, and carved quivers and short, curved bows hung from their saddles. The Sultan's six cavalry divisions reminded everyone that the Turks had conquered their empire on horseback. They had galloped down from the steppes of Asia, passing through the Middle East with the violence of barbarians. The Sipahi represented the true heart of Ottoman power.

But they were not the backbone of the army.

The march of the janissaries was a triumph of red and green; the pennants and standards of the regiments fluttered in the morning breeze; the halberds and arquebuses shone in the sun, sabers and hatchets clattered in their belts.

Instead of weapons, one squadron carried big drums, pipes, trumpets, bells and cymbals. The sounds they made enfolded the soldiers and spurred them on, like a magic shield and an invisible force, capable of repelling projectiles, laying enemy forces low and reducing Cypriot fortresses to rubble.

A marvelous spectacle. Nonetheless, I recalled what Ismail had said to me during the crossing to Bandirma. The means change the end. How would the new kingdom of Cyprus resist that vast military apparatus? I thought of the army of the twelve tribes of Israel, the Ark of the Covenant, the seven ram's horns that had brought down the walls of Jericho. More than two thousand years later, Yossef Nasi was entrusting the conquest of the Promised Land to the Turkish imperial army, not one of whose soldiers was Jewish.

My people's only contribution to this war was the uniforms of the janissaries, sewn by the Sephardim of Salonika. The men who wore them were Slavs, Albanians, Bosnians, Greeks, Bulgarians, Hungarians. The Turks had torn them from their families as children and brought them to the imperial barracks to receive a training worthy of the ancient Spartans. They had converted to Islam, under the iron control of the *bektashi,* the spiritual instructors who were now going with them into battle. Forced to remain celibate, they formed a solid fraternity, like an order of knights devoted to a single father: the Sultan. They were his children and his slaves. For him alone they passed along to the rhythm of the music.

Selim-sani, Sovereign of the House of Osman, Sultan of Sultans, Khan of khans, Caliph of the faithful and successor of the Prophet. Guardian of the

holy cities of Mecca, Medina and Jerusalem, Caesar of the Roman Empire,
Padisha of the three cities of Istanbul, Edirne and Bursa, and of the cities of
Damascus and Cairo.

That was how the pages had announced Selim's arrival, following the titles owed to him with a list of his possessions, from Abyssinia to Hungary, from Mesopotamia to Algiers.

How that pompous introduction clashed with his most famous nickname—Sarbosh, the Drunk—and the gossip about his dissolute habits. The subjects who acclaimed him from the benches of the hippodrome knew very well that Sultan Selim, the shadow of God on earth, had obtained those titles only thanks to the death of his brothers, Mustafa and Bayezid, eliminated during his father's reign after years of plotting and lies.

With a gesture that looked like a blessing, Selim rose to his feet and saluted the people and the troops. Thousands of heads bowed and eyes stared up at him from below, because the Sultan's face was a rare thing to see. I strained to see, too, wanting to know whether he was really repellent, swollen and light-headed with spirits, as some of the dispatches I had read in Venice said he was. But I was too far away, and the Great Turk immediately went and sat in the shade, on the covered balcony of the great palace of Ibrahim Pasha, which looked out over the ancient Byzantine arena.

The other windows of the building, some of them covered with grilles and shutters, were reserved for members of the imperial family. On either side of the façade, big wooden triple-tiered galleries rose. On one of these sat Yossef Nasi, and David Gomez beside him, a short distance from the dignitaries and the Grand Vizier. The European ambassadors were on the other side. I recognized the Polish voivode, seated beside the Seigneur de Grantrie.

I had taken my place with Donna Reyna and her entourage in a covered stand right in front of the Sultan's balcony. That put me a few feet away from Dana, who accompanied her mistress, although my attempts to meet her eye had been unsuccessful.

"There's our Don Yossef enjoying his triumph," said Donna Reyna, by my side. "He has managed to make everyone submit, and exploited the Sultan's thirst."

I didn't catch the phrase then, and went on watching the parade. Passing below the obelisk of Thutmosis at that moment were the Azabs, the ill-defined troop of irregular infantrymen and those responsible for general field duties, while the higher imperial statesmen paid their respects to the Sultan and received the greetings of the Grand Vizier. In the front rank of senior officials I recognized Kapudan Pasha Muezzinzade Ali, the Great Admiral of the fleet, and Lala Mustafa Pasha, commander-in-chief of the army.

"And here are the Sultan's champions, who will have to bring about his victory, so that he can show himself worthy to be his father's son." Donna

Reyna fluttered a crimson fan in front of her face. "But Suleyman would have marched at the head of his soldiers, like a true warrior. Selim prefers to toast their success from the cellar doorway."

I couldn't help glancing around, worried that someone might hear her. I tried to meet Dana's eyes again, but Donna Reyna interposed herself between us, and I had a sense that she did so quite deliberately. Lest I seem rude, I resigned myself to replying. "You don't seem to have much confidence in the success of this enterprise, Donna Reyna."

Another red flutter. "On the contrary, Signor Cardoso, I think it will be a real triumph. How could it be otherwise? On one side is Selim, displaying all the power of the Ottoman Empire, and on the other is an undefended island, far away from any possible ally." She pointed with her fan. "Look at Don Yossef. Look at him carefully, because he is the true author of all of this. And most importantly, he's the one who's paying the bill."

I turned toward her; she was pleased to have attracted my attention.

"The Nasis are bankers, and the only art to which they have ever devoted themselves is finance," she said. "We pay for the wars of the sovereigns. This time, instead of a useful percentage, it would seem that we are going to receive a crown."

Nasi wasn't merely dedicating himself to the most powerful army in the world—he was financing it. Perhaps that was his hope: to move his credit to a more resonant coin than gold and silver. To buy the freedom of the future kingdom. It wouldn't be the Israelites conquering Jericho, but at least a Jew's money would make it possible. Watching that great destroying machine pass by, I wondered if it would be enough.

"So it seems that I am about to be a queen," Reyna went on. "Melancholy and alone."

"You seem to be neither of those things, my lady," I lied.

"You couldn't possibly understand. All women who are forced to live in the shadow of a great man have something in common: hushing up his weaknesses, weaving tapestries in the empty silence of a palace. I'm sure the Sultan's consort would agree with me."

"And I'm sure that many women would like to be in your place."

Rather than turning toward me, she let her eye fall on Dana. "And yet sometimes a servant has more freedom than a queen."

She said nothing more, but that was enough to spark my suspicion, and suspicion, in a man of my profession, is as vast as a mine and more inflammable than pitch. Those words, addressed to me as she referred with her eyes to Dana, were a precise allusion. I remembered Dana's words after the first night that I had spent with her. She had told me repeatedly not to tell anyone what had happened between us.

I was a thousand times more harmless, for you, with a dagger in my hand.

I had to discover whether Reyna knew, or even merely imagined, that her chambermaid was spending almost every night in my room.

The cheers of the crowd drowned out my thoughts. A long line of cannon, pulled by oxen and escorted by companies of artillerymen, had entered the hippodrome. There were cannon of every size, caliber and style, embellished with a thousand ornaments, with mouths shaped like the jaws of lions and wolves. Culverins, bombards, mortars, serpentines, siege cannons and half-cannons. A black snake whose tail I still couldn't see even when the head had traveled halfway around the arena.

Leading the monster was a piece of artillery that would never see the coast of Cyprus, but which the Ottomans venerated like a talisman. It was the huge bombard of the Hungarian engineer Orban, used during the siege of Constantinople. I counted thirty pairs of oxen forced to pull it, and judged that it was at least fifteen feet long. In spite of its size, I suspected that during the siege it had been more of a hindrance than a help. You couldn't fire it more than twice a day, and that had allowed the Byzantines to rebuild during the night what the cannonballs had destroyed during the day. And yet, more than a century later, that basilisk more than anything else bore witness to the superiority of the Turks over the European fortresses.

Now the guilds of armorers, foundry men and other war-related trades were preparing to close the parade. Out of the corner of my eye I saw Donna Reyna handing a note to Dana and whispering something in her ear. Dana nodded a few times, and then slipped away.

I saw her emerging among the crowd, and a few moments later I excused myself too, to go and join her outside the hippodrome.

When I found her, she was walking quickly along the Imperial Road. I stepped forward and gestured to her to follow me into an alleyway, because in Constantinople it isn't thought seemly for a man and a woman to stop in the street and talk.

The burned-out ruins of an old wooden house offered us shelter from the eyes of passers-by.

"What's going on?" she asked me impatiently.

"I'm worried that Donna Reyna knows about us."

She laughed, not troubled in the slightest by that possibility. A rat-squeak from a pile of rubbish echoed her laughter. "If she knew, she would have dismissed me already."

I wasn't satisfied. "Have you said or done anything that might have alerted her? Think very hard."

"Certainly not. Calm down." She stroked my cheek with her hand. "Now let me go, I'm in a hurry."

"What do you have to do that's so urgent?"

She tried to push past me, but I stood in her way. "Donna Reyna's business."

"Business!" I tried to smile, but I couldn't. "What kind of business?"

"None of yours, Manuel. Let me go."

I pushed her away so that I could stare into her eyes. "You know what my job is at Palazzo Belvedere. Don Yossef has chosen me to collect rumors and clues. There is no business within the Nasi family that is not my business too."

She gave me a glance that I couldn't interpret. It might have expressed annoyance, surprise or disappointment. A drop of sweat ran down her forehead from under her veil.

"Has the frenzy of battle gone to your head, Manuel? Perhaps seeing all those janissaries in a row, ready to crush the enemy, has made you want to do the same?" And with those words she pushed me aside and returned to the street.

Panting, I waited for my breathing to slow. The air was hot and smelled of ashes and carrion. With no particular haste, I stepped into the Imperial Road, recognized her yellow kerchief and started following her toward Santa Sofia. A pack of unhealthy-looking dogs decided to do the same to me. I hoped their barking wouldn't make Dana turn round, before a few lobbed stones persuaded them to shut up and go somewhere else.

Past the ancient church, now turned into a mosque, was the Augustus Gate, the chief entrance to the walls of the Seraglio. I saw Dana dart inside and decided to follow her. No particular formalities were required to enter the first courtyard. As soon as I was inside, I slowed my pace and kept my distance, concerned that I might be noticed. Unlike the first time I had been here, there wasn't much activity along the avenue, but I certainly couldn't hide myself behind a cypress tree, nor could I go another way: This was the only possible route. On the other hand, for the same reason, it wasn't hard for me to keep my eye on my quarry, even from a distance. Dana stopped at the second gate, chatted with the guards and was allowed in shortly afterward.

I experienced a moment of indecision. My eye fell on the fountain to the right of the entrance, where the hangman is said to wash his hands and his sword once his work is done.

Taking care not be too hasty, I turned around and went back where I had come from, hoping that no one had noticed my strange behavior. I had come in, I had walked to the middle of the courtyard, and now I was turning on my heel, all for no clear reason. I remembered the stories I had heard in Galata, of merchants beaten on the spot, just for having raised their voices or ridden their horses too quickly.

Once outside, I thought about what I had seen. I tried to remember which buildings opened onto the second courtyard. I recalled the kitchens, the stables, the Sultan's harem, the Council Chamber and the rooms leading off it for the private audiences of the various viziers.

I thought that Donna Reyna's message must be meant for a member of the Divan. And it couldn't have been an innocent one. Otherwise, why would Dana have been so reticent? Couldn't she have told me quite straightforwardly what was going on at the Seraglio?

I had just blocked one dangerous correspondence, and already another was requiring my attention. I felt the blood quickening under my skin, and then I turned into the street that ran down to the Golden Horn and allowed myself to be filled by the hunting instinct.

30.

Somehow, Nasi had got ahead of me. I found him in the central hall, beneath the menorah, confronting a bent old man. I immediately realized that I had seen him before, but it was a few moments before I recognized the chief rabbi, Eli Ben Haim. The contrast between the two men was apparent. Nasi stood splendidly in his brightly colored ceremonial robes, and his resolute expression took years off his age.

The rabbi didn't seem to notice my arrival. He opened his toothless mouth as if biting the air. "I am just warning you, Don Yossef," he croaked. "Remember the Proverbs of Solomon: 'Pride goes before destruction, and haughtiness before a fall. It is better to be of humble spirit than to share plunder with the proud.' You want to buy the kingdom of Zion, but only the Lord can give Israel its due."

Nasi looked fearlessly at him. "In the Proverbs it is also written that 'a wicked man listens to evil lips, a liar pays attention to a malicious tongue.' I am neither malicious nor a liar. I want the welfare of our people, and I tell the truth."

The old man raised a finger and shouted, spraying saliva. "Remember the *Shir ha-Shirim Rabbah*: 'And do not rise from exile as a wall is raised. Indeed, why will the Messiah come? To bring together the exiles of Israel.' "

Nasi walked around him, his hands behind his back, as if he was thinking, then stood in front of him again. "Tell me, Rabbi Eli, why the Lord should punish those who want to give a land back to His people? For centuries they have persecuted us, chased us, killed us. They have burned our sacred books, they have called us deicides, murderers. I want to put an end to all this, and for you it is an outrage against God. Or do you not mean rather that it is an outrage against you? Against you rabbis who taught us to pray and stay in our place, with our heads bowed."

The old man's furrowed face wrinkled still further in a grimace of contempt. "You think you can do business with emperors, when it was an emperor who dispossessed our people and a pharaoh who kept us enslaved in Egypt." He exploded in a fit of coughing. Nasi came closer and spoke to him without rancor, almost smiling.

"I want to repair the world. That is why I observe the commandments, recite the prayers, perform the rituals. That is why I want to give the Jews what you rabbis are not able to give them. A new Zion where they can live in peace and safety. An example of justice for humanity, because we were slaves

in Egypt and we will have the fate of every slave on earth within our hearts. This is *tikkun olam*, my contribution to the return of equilibrium."

The lids of the old man's glaucous eyes quivered within indignation, and a thread of slobber flowed from the corner of his mouth. "Blasphemy! You think you are the Messiah!"

Nasi shook his head. "No." He leaned forward until his nose almost touched the rabbi's. "But I would be a good king. That's what scares you."

Rabbi Eli gave a sort of roar, as if he wanted to plunge his fangs into his adversary, and then all of a sudden he turned around and limped out of the building, still chewing on his curses. At that moment, Donna Reyna appeared behind me. She must have been there for some time, enjoying the finale of the scene. She stepped forward to the middle of the room, and passed by Nasi with a half bow. "Majesty," she said in a simpering voice.

The future king of Cyprus didn't even seem to notice.

31.

I started keeping an eye on Dana and following her discreetly every time she left Palazzo Belvedere. At the Monday market, hidden behind a pile of dried apricots, I saw her buying a bag of grain for her goldfinch.

On Tuesday evening she entered a run-down building in Kuruçesme, where she stayed for a few hours. I discovered that it belonged to a Greek woman; she, too, had been freed from Selim's harem and was now the wife of his stable master.

On Wednesday afternoon she sold a pile of her embroidered blankets to a cloth merchant, and with the proceeds she bought two brushes and a box of oil paints. That evening, I decided that I might have to change my strategy.

I would have preferred to talk to her calmly, to persuade her to tell me what she knew, but the memory of her reticence offended my pride. If she hadn't yielded right away, after the parade, to my first request, it meant that at bottom she was more devoted to Donna Reyna than she was to me. On Thursday morning, when I bumped into her in the drawing room, I told her not to come to my room that night. I said nothing more, and went in search of Don Yossef.

During those days I had thought often about how alone my mentor was. Reyna, the Grand Vizier, the Ashkenazic rabbis and even his oldest friend—none of them believed in him. And yet thousands of Jews owed their lives to him. And yet I was there, a living proof that it was possible to change everything. You just had to want it, and with the help of the Lord things could be turned upside down, chaos canceled, balance reestablished. *Tikkun olam.* That was what Nasi had called it. Righting the world, healing the wound that our people had borne for fifteen hundred years, just as it had healed my own wound, hidden for half my life.

Nasi needed allies, and I intended to tell him as much. The Sultan's friendship and the money spent on the Cyprus adventure were solid guarantees, but that investment also exposed him to great risks and for many people was a cause for suspicion. It had been Dana who had reminded me of the story of Joseph, whose brothers envied him because of his dreams and sold him to the merchants.

When I found him, he didn't give me time to speak, and once again he was ahead of me, reading me as you read a book, perhaps one of those rare copies that had attracted Ralph Fitch in the library at Palazzo Belvedere.

He dragged me outside, and with just a few servants escorting us, we lost

ourselves in the hubbub of busy humanity in the Christian quarter. He spoke at length as we walked, and it was as if I had transferred my anxieties to his mind without even opening my mouth.

"The Grand Vizier is very strong, even though we have put him in the minority in the Divan. And above all, and never forget this, Mehmet Sokollu is highly astute. By obstructing Ashkenazi we have stayed one of his hands, but he is like an octopus; he has another seven. As for the Ashkenazic rabbis, don't worry too much. They've been holding us hostage forever. They sow uncertainty among our people; they say that Cyprus is a personal whim, a reward for services given to the Sultan. You understand? They use the divisions between Eastern and Western Jews to undermine our project. They say a Sephardic kingdom will arise in the east, when they know very well that I intend to offer a home to everyone, without distinction. A safe refuge for the wanderers of the earth: Jews, *moriscos*, heretics, slaves. As I did after the fire; you saw the people in my house. They weren't only Sephardim, and not all of them were even Jews."

I slowed my pace, overwhelmed by the freight of those words.

"The poor people are with me, but how will we overcome the mistrust of the wealthiest families?" Nasi noticed that he had left me behind, and stopped. "And that's why we're here."

Around us, Venetian and Ottoman accents met: We were in the heart of Galata. "Where are we going?" I asked.

Yossef pointed to a house halfway down the street. "To find ourselves a new ally. Someone who has nothing to lose and everything to gain from joining with us. Come, he's waiting for us."

Even today I can't imagine my face as we stepped inside that house and were invited to sit down in a spacious room, on comfortable cushions, in the presence of the man I had tailed for days.

Solomon Ashkenazi observed us carefully, sipping the coffee that his wife, Bula, had poured into our cups. The Venetian doctor's clever little eyes darted between Nasi and me. It was clear that the letter that Nasi had sent ahead of him had not revealed the reason for the visit, but Ashkenazi wasn't a stupid man and he must have guessed something. Perhaps for that reason, when his chief adversary offered to appoint him treasurer of the future Cypriot Jewish kingdom, he didn't bat an eyelid. At that moment, he was finished: He lived as a recluse. Nasi was giving him the opportunity to climb back up from the abyss into which he had plunged himself. His genius was a blinding light. Bringing the doctor over to his cause and giving him a job in the future government would send a powerful message to the Ashkenazic Jews: It would announce that the new kingdom of Zion was theirs as well.

The master of the house called his wife and told her to prepare lunch, because the guests would be staying. Then he came back and looked at us. We would talk business on a full stomach.

32.

I am walking in a rocky desert, beneath a brilliant golden sky. I'm thirsty, my mouth is dry, my clothes are sticking to my back. I walk wearily toward a lonely, black mountain in a range that stands out on the horizon. The outline of the range recalls the towers of a castle. Around peaks pointed like needles, falcons fly.

Having reached the foot of the mountain, I study the obsidian cliffs in search of footholds. I climb, to conquer the peak, but the mineral cuts my fingers, and I think I'm about to plummet when above my head I suddenly see a stone balcony. With a final effort I hoist myself up and find myself in front of an ivory door, set in the side of the mountain, protected by two warriors. They grip metal scourges like the one I saw Mukhtar using, except in place of whips there are bronze-scaled snakes. I want to escape, but the door opens and the two warriors let Dana through, and she comes toward me, takes me by the hand and leads me inside. "*T'estan asperando*," I hear her saying in the language of my mother.

We pass through identical rooms, one after another. They all look like the hall of the Divan—all that changes is the color of the carpets. In the red room, the Grand Vizier Sokollu is presiding over a meeting of dignitaries and pashas, but no one is speaking, no one is moving, they all look stuffed. In the yellow room, two janissaries, half naked, are fighting with hatchets, their bodies ragged with cuts and wounds. In the turquoise room there is a gigantic cannon that merges with the features of a male member. In the green one, we plow through a sea of praying Muslims, and only when we are surrounded by them do I notice that they are all women, prostrate as they worship the Sultan.

"I'm not a concubine," Dana says to me in a mechanical voice, and then repeats that they're waiting for me and pulls me by the arm toward the last room, which is dazzlingly white. On the couch that runs along the walls, woman sit winding huge skeins of thread and nursing children. I look at the babies sucking the breasts, and they resemble adult men, all of them the same, with beards and turbans, like the figures in Turkish miniatures. Other women, in the middle of the hall, form a dancing circle, hand in hand. I think I recognize some of them, but really they all look the same: my mother, Arianna, Reyna. The circle opens up to admit me, and I want to dance with them—the steps look simple, except that I can't hear the music, I can't catch the rhythm, and the intention of the movements escapes me; I can't work out if they're solemn or sad, macabre or grotesque. So I remain motionless, and I

feel my legs are hard, stuck, until Dana kneels in front of me and moves them with her hands, to show me what I'm supposed to do. Behind me, another woman takes hold of my arms and suggests the correct moves, her body pressed against mine. I have to struggle not to be aroused, to concentrate only on the dance, understand the steps, listen carefully to the music. In the end, after many attempts, I manage to follow the dance, first moving on the spot, then back and forth, then in an ever faster pirouette that turns the room into a whirlwind and swallows everything up, drags me away, while Dana approaches a golden grille high up in the wall, slips a hand between the metal meshes and hands something to a long-haired shadow. A woman's shadow.

I woke up rested, surprised to remember the details of my dream. Usually, oneiric visions and real life occupy different rooms in my head, and the first vanish as soon as I open the door of the second.

I washed and chose my clothes carefully: This wasn't a Saturday like any other.

In the atrium of Palazzo Belvedere a real procession was under way. Servants, family and acolytes abandoned their rooms, came down flights of stairs and crossed corridors to flow together in front of the big portal. Nasi was the last to arrive, dressed in crimson and cobalt, and took his place at the head of the cavalcade.

When the elderly guard opened the door, at least fifty people were ready to descend into the street, arranged in two groups, men at the front and women behind. Along the road, a much larger, disorderly crowd had gathered, ready to join the procession.

We walked along the streets of Ortaköy, savoring the pleasant warmth of that summer morning. The snake of bodies becoming increasingly relaxed, as we approached our destination, the synagogue of the *Senyora*, the favorite temple of the Sephardic Jews.

We surged into an internal courtyard, protected behind a wall and an iron gate and shaded by an old plane tree. Donna Gracia had had the synagogue built ten years before, and it was said to be our people's only place of worship planned and financed by a woman.

The sound of many voices reached us from the patio and grew beyond measure to greet the arrival of Don Yossef Nasi. The synagogue would never be able to hold all those people, not even if they climbed on each other's shoulders. There weren't only Western Jews there, from Spain and Portugal, like the Campos, the Mendes, the Hamons. Crowding into the courtyard were Romaniots from Greece, Jewish families who had lived in the city since the days of Theodosius, goldsmiths from Balat, weavers from Galata, merchants from Eminonu whom Nasi had helped in the days of the great fire, rabbis of tiny communities who had come from Tripoli and Syria, from the Caucasus and Yemen.

Nasi shook dozens of hands, hugged and stroked, promised money and

justice. He was a new Solomon, a new David, the man who had brought the tribes of Israel together, who had reassembled that which had been divided and scattered. Some people definitely thought he was the Messiah.

He had summoned them all with messengers and with gifts, with fascination and seduction. He wanted the chosen people to pray together, celebrating like a single body the news that was coming from Cyprus. The Sultan's army had disembarked at Limassol, and was marching unopposed toward Nicosia. The generals expected to lay siege by the end of July.

A servant appeared breathless and spoke into the ear of Don Yossef, who immediately interrupted his greetings and turned toward the gate, in a solemn pose. The crowd did likewise, and silence quickly spread.

I understood then, even before I saw them appearing behind the gate, that the last guests, the most important, were arriving.

I closed my eyes, overwhelmed by the power of what I saw happening. Yossef Nasi's money and genius had accomplished a marvel.

When I opened my eyes, Solomon Ashkenazi was entering the courtyard beside his wife, followed by a multitude of men and women got up in their finest clothes.

33.

We entered the temple, leaving doors and windows open, because a huge number of people were still outside, and no one must feel excluded. The women sat down in the loggia that opened halfway up, on three sides of the hall.

We got to our feet and intoned the psalms and blessings of the morning service. My Hebrew was now more fluent than it had been in my schooldays.

Yossef Nasi, the worthy man, opened the doors of the Sacred Ark. Solomon Ashkenazi removed the wooden cylinder that held the Scroll of the Law and handed it to the cantor, who passed with it among the faithful.

When the ark set forward, Moses said, "Rise up, Lord, and let your enemies be scattered."

Ashkenazi closed the doors of the holy cabinet and joined Nasi in the little procession as it moved through the synagogue and then back toward the pulpit.

Yours, Lord, is the greatness, the power and the glory, the majesty and the victory.

They walked among the benches, across the central corridor and along the walls, as the children leaned forward to kiss the Torah scroll with the tips of their lips.

Yours is the kingdom, Lord; you are exalted above all things.

I looked up at the army of women above me, seeking Dana's face. She was observing the ceremony with a worried expression, as if the gestures of the three men were not the right ones. Perhaps she wanted to correct them, as she had corrected my dance steps in my dream. Beside her, Donna Reyna was whispering complicitly into another woman's ear. I asked David Gomez who she was.

"Esther Handali," he replied. "She's a Sephardi, but she doesn't usually frequent our synagogue, because she lives in the Old City. She takes care of the affairs of Nurbanu, Selim's favorite."

My eyes slipped to the seat to Esther Handali's right. It was occupied by Bula Ashkenazi. I reflected on her husband's words when he'd introduced her to me: "She visits servants and concubines, she tells me the symptoms, prepares and sells remedies." She, too, frequented the Sultan's harem.

Exalt the Lord our God and worship at his footstool.

Two Jewish women, among the very few who had direct contact with the

favorite without living inside the harem. As far as I knew, the only other women with a similar right were the three princesses, Nurbanu's daughters: Ismihan, Geherhan and Shah, the wives of the Grand Vizier Sokollu, Piyale Pasha and the Great Falconer.

Exalt the Lord our God and worship at his holy mountain.

Nasi and Ashkenazi sat down side by side again, in the front row, on the bench next to mine. The cantor climbed onto the *tebah* and unrolled the Torah on the big lectern.

Sokollu, Piyale Pasha and the Great Falconer. All three *damad*, sons-in-law of Nurbanu and the Sultan. The first was an enemy of Nasi and an open opponent of the war against Venice. The second had been a grand admiral and was in command of a flagship in the expedition to Cyprus. The third, for his part, had expressed a sibylic opinion to Ismail about the attack on the island: "Wars are driven by the ambition of powerful men."

Blessed be the Lord, king of the universe, who has chosen us of all peoples and given us his Law.

I looked again toward the ladies' balcony, and I felt as if the ceiling of the synagogue had begun to spin. Bula Ashkenazi, Esther Handali, Donna Reyna, Dana. The first and the second frequented Nurbanu, the favorite of Selim, sister-in-law of the Grand Vizier. The fourth, Dana, had been Selim's personal servant before she arrived at the Palazzo Belvedere.

I had seen her carrying a message from Donna Reyna into the second courtyard of the Seraglio, the one that granted access to the Hall of the Divan. And to the harem.

Follow justice and justice alone, that you may live and possess the land that the Lord your God is giving you.

Reyna had spent her girlhood in Venice. Bula was married to a Venetian, the personal physician of the bailiff Marcantonio Barbaro, merchant and shipowner on the route to Crete, a Venetian island. Nurbanu, too, the Princess of Light, was Venetian by origin, kidnapped by Turkish corsairs from an island in the Mediterranean. Like a little Jewish girl by the name of Dana.

A second lector took the place of the first and began to recite in an uncertain singsong voice.

When you have entered the land that the Lord your God is giving you, and dwell therein, you will think, I will set a king over me, like all the nations that are around me.

Nasi muttered an *Amen*. I couldn't take my eyes off the balcony. Reyna, Dana, Bula, Esther, Nurbanu, Shah, Ismihan.

You may indeed set above you as your king one of your brothers, and he shall not take many wives for himself, lest his heart turn away.

The words of Ismail, in front of the mosque of Mihrimah Sultan, before he left for Bandirma: "Back in Europe, none of you can imagine that the women of the harem capable of moving money, fleets, armies."

The words of Donna Reyna, at the military parade in the hippodrome: "There's something common to all women who are forced to live in the shadow of a great man, weaving tapestries in the silence of a palace."

If what the prophet proclaims in the name of the Lord does not take place, that is a message that the Lord has not spoken. The prophet has spoken presumptuously, so do not be alarmed.

Don Yossef feared Sokollu, poured wine for Selim, offered a place to Solomon Ashkenazi in the aristocracy of the Island of Zion. He had managed to block communications between the bailiff, the Doge and the Grand Vizier, but he was too much enthralled by them to notice that very similar messages, rather than in the shoes of a Jewish doctor, could travel among the belongings of a Jewish doctor's wife, with the fabrics and brocades of a Jewish businesswoman, between the breasts of a chambermaid, on the lips of a princess, between the fingers of a queen, in his own wife's bedroom.

Dana's words, when I had asked her about the strange relationship between Donna Reyna and her husband: "You must have noticed, Don Yossef doesn't appreciate the attentions of women."

Perhaps he had no idea how many women were devoting their attention to him.

34.

That night, in bed, Dana's hand slipping under my clothes repelled me. I was irritated by her caresses, and pushed her away. It was an instinctive movement, completely uncalculated, but it fired my suspicions about the day just past. The worm was gnawing at my mind, even though it was my body taking the initiative.

She mocked me, saying that I had been wrong to refuse the halva with the cannabis resin. Over the past few days I had been in a dark mood, I needed to let myself relax, to set aside my nagging doubts.

I said no, this wasn't the moment to set them aside, and she must have noticed something in the tone of my voice—something that troubled her and put her on her guard.

Part of me was unwilling to yield to suspicion, afraid to open a door that might reveal my nemesis waiting on the other side. But the worm needed to be crushed.

"Some days ago, after the parade, you told me you had to take charge of some matters for Reyna, but when I asked you what they were, you wouldn't tell me."

She nodded, surprised, as if that episode had already slipped into a corner of her mind, amongst unimportant memories, ready to be erased.

"I know you were carrying a message. I saw Donna Reyna hand it to you, and believe me, it's very important for me to know what it was." I looked her straight in the eyes; she grew increasingly bewildered.

"It was a letter for Nurbanu Sultan. But you . . ."

I gritted my teeth, fists clenched. I had been right. Dana was yielding, and I mustn't ease my grip on her. "No buts: Listen to me carefully. The next time Donna Reyna gives you a message of that kind, you bring it to me right away, you understand? Even if it's sealed I know how to open and close it without anyone noticing, without suspicion falling on you."

"I can't do that, Manuel. Do you realize what you're asking of me?"

I did realize, yes, and it wasn't anything very terrible or dangerous. I insisted, and she refused again. Once, twice. "Come on, don't tell me you're the only serving girl in the world who doesn't read her masters' correspondence."

"I'm not a serving girl," were the only words she managed to say, but I realized that by now she was neither startled nor frightened. She was defying me, and that gave me a pang in my heart, right in the spot where my self-love lay.

"You know why Donna Gracia denied you the honor of going with her when she went to die?"

"She wanted me to stay with her daughter," she said in the irritable tone of someone who is being forced to repeat herself.

I gave her a joyless smile. Once I would have accepted that explanation, but now it was not enough. Not if I wanted to discover the truth. "Wasn't it more that she didn't want you beside her?"

She drew herself up in silence. The moon lit her face. "It's too late to ask."

I had struck home, I had hurt her and I was pleased. She turned again, ready to flee. I jumped from the bed and joined her. I gripped her shoulder and forced her to look me in the face. "Perhaps she didn't trust you. Perhaps she thought you were unworthy."

She pulled herself free. "Stop it, Manuel. I haven't done anything to deserve these insults."

I pretended not to hear. "Or did Donna Reyna tell you stay?"

Again she tried to leave, and again I held on to her, with both hands. "I've already told you," I shouted into her face, "in this palace everyone has to answer my questions. Anyone who doesn't deserves my suspicion, even if they stuff me with drugged cakes and slip into my bed every night."

I studied the effect of my words. Dana looked at the floor, and didn't resist when I raised her chin. Her black hair smelt of almonds, as it had the first time I had smelled it.

"I don't believe in your devotion to Donna Gracia. You told me that Yossef Nasi saved you from a marriage you didn't want, to a fat provincial bey. Since when has a harem slave chosen to be a chambermaid rather than the wife of an important imperial functionary?"

Now her eyes were filling with tears of rage, and I realized that I had crossed a line.

"Marrying a Muslim would have meant converting," she said in a harsh voice. "Christian servants happily barter God for an easier life. I don't change my faith as one changes one's clothes." She was talking about me, she wanted to return the barb, but she couldn't hurt me. These allusions to my past life now sounded strange and distant to my ears.

"Yes, you're not one to betray, you are true. The point is . . . to whom have you been true for all this time? Donna Reyna? Nurbanu Sultan?"

She turned her back on my sarcasm, but I held her back once more and pushed her against the wall. She slipped down and crouched with her knees against her chest, like a deer surrounded by dogs. Quivering, I bent over her, drenched in sweat and struggling to overcome my desire to strike her.

She wept in silence, not sobbing, just tears slipping down her face, bent double as if she had been dealt a fatal blow. I nodded to myself.

"Both, of course. Nurbanu sent you here to plot with Yossef Nasi's wife. Those letters aren't full of ladies' gossip, are they?"

"You're mad," I heard her murmur.

I walked over to the window and sought comfort in the air of the Bosphorus, but it was as thick and dense as a mildewed wall. "Perhaps. And perhaps this city isn't all that different from Venice. Back there I was betrayed by a woman. That isn't going to happen again here."

I heard her getting up and I didn't turn around. She left without a sound, leaving me prey to my obsessions, my eyes lost in the night.

35.

Whatever your hand finds to do, do it with all your strength. The kabbalist Meir interpreted that line of the *Qoheleth* as an invitation to completeness.

The will is not enough, he said, to bond with an important task. You need a soul that is all of a piece. My own had been much mended, but I hoped the Lord would grant me a new one. The soul of a raptor, which would plunge down on its prey, its instinct incorruptible by doubts or hesitations. A creature capable of seizing the body and the mind for an enterprise that waited only to be accomplished: defending Yossef Nasi from the perils that surrounded him.

When I joined him in the big drawing room that morning, he gave me a worried look. I must have looked as if I'd slept on an anthill. I set out my deductions in the clearest and most linear way that my fatigue allowed. I said that there was a chain of distaff-side relationships linking the Imperial Palace, the palace of the Grand Vizier, Ashkenazi's house and Palazzo Belvedere. Through Dana and Esther Handali, Nurbanu had allied herself with the Jewish gentlewomen who favored Venice. We had been harboring the Lion of Saint Mark within our own walls.

Nasi listened with great attention and few questions. Then he pointed to the painting that hung above the door. The woman in the portrait looked down at us like a wise queen.

He said that he, the nephew of Gracia Nasi, would certainly not have been one to underestimate the power of women. Over the past six months, through Selim, he had given Nurbanu dozens of presents, jewels, precious books, Italian fabrics, mirrors. Anything to soften her resistance to the war. As to Reyna, he added that her rancor was fundamentally comprehensible, and she had no choice but to support him. Perhaps I was right. Perhaps she and Nurbanu were plotting behind our backs, but the war had started now, and female diplomacy was no longer a crucial weapon.

As he said this, he lowered his eyes to the mosaic of the Mediterranean that filled the whole floor. Right beneath our feet was the outline of the island of Cyprus. I asked him what he planned to do with Dana, and his reply left me flabbergasted.

"Nothing. The cannon are speaking now."

I was speechless, and a queasy sense of unease took hold me. I took my leave and strode away.

Above the garden, a sky full of clouds. At any moment I expected to hear

thunder exploding over the hills, but the storm seemed reluctant to break, and flies buzzed crazily around over the grass. My mind echoed with Arianna's voice. "They forced me, Emanuele. Against my will."

No, no one had forced Dana. I knew that her kisses weren't false, or her embraces or the fluids that we had exchanged. And yet suspicion had dug an unbridgeable gulf between us. Doubt and suspicion were my vocation, but that part of me wasn't the one I felt getting the upper hand; it was the part of me that was frightened by what I had surmised.

And there was another passage of the Scriptures, buried in memories of my life as a Christian, where Jesus says that he doesn't pour new wine into old bottles, because the new wine bursts them and you lose both bottle and wine. I clenched my teeth in rage and turned on my heel. The rain had started falling, but I didn't care about that. I stopped under a plane tree, holding my breath, drenched through by the summer storm, staring at the houses of Scutari and the forests of Asia.

A servant informed me that Donna Reyna didn't want to be disturbed. I shoved him aside and stepped in. She was sitting at her desk. She wore a mauve dress, and her hair was coiled up on her head, revealing her neck. She merely stared at me, as if taking note of my presence, not even slightly surprised. She had the expression and the posture of someone who wants to get back to her business as soon as possible and will not appreciate superfluous words.

I decided to oblige her. "Did you send her to me?"

She didn't move. "I told you: sometimes servants are freer than their masters."

The voice was hers, but her face and body were so expressionless that it might have been another woman speaking.

"So it was her idea?"

"No, it was mine." She leaned into the back of her chair and gave me an icy look. "Because I couldn't come myself."

I didn't try to reply, I didn't care and I didn't want to help her read my mind.

"This is the plot that you have discovered, Signor Cardoso. The envy of a woman forgotten, forced to look at life through the eyes of a chambermaid. You men see a plot behind every coincidence, a threat behind your every uncertainty, and perhaps you're right. And yet you need only look in the mirror to discover the weaknesses that will bring you down."

I wanted to turn around and go, but her eyes held me back. She spoke her words clearly, as if firing arrows at my pride. "He has asked me to go to Tiberias, and I will certainly not object." She paused, to enjoy the effect of this information. "Why are you pulling that face? By fleeing, one admits one's guilt. You should be pleased."

I cursed her in silence, and found the strength to leave. My soul was a fistful of shards.

36.

The water of the Bosphorus was cloudy and agitated, stirred by the wind that passed up the straits from the south. The dock at Ortaköy echoed with shouts, orders given in Turkish and Ladino. Gulls wheeled between the sea and the clouds, in the hope of taking advantage of the gathering.

I took up my position behind a salt-encrusted shed, a storeroom for nets and sails. At the end of a wooden walkway I recognized a *mahona* belonging to the Nasis, the same one that had dropped off a cargo of refugees on this shore months previously.

She wasn't there. Perhaps she had already boarded her ship, and I was too late. I had followed a different road from the usual one, slightly longer. I had calculated, or rather hoped, that I would get there just as Dana had emerged from the labyrinth of streets into the open space in front of the slipway. But there was nothing. I stopped to contemplate the scene of dockland life, as if it were a memory.

Then, on the other side of the open ground, a crowd began arriving. Servants from the Palazzo Belvedere were pushing a cart. Lying on it, its roots wrapped in a jute bag, Dana's carob faced its second move.

She came after it, a leather bag in one hand and the goldfinch's cage in the other. She was dressed in her smartest clothes, a highly embroidered, sand-colored dress and a silk shawl that covered her shoulders. I admired her proud bearing, not very appropriate to the life of a chambermaid, or a peasant girl in a remote colony. I wondered why she was wearing such a sumptuous dress, and the answer passed through my mind.

If the stuff of which your limbs are molded is good, if your heart and mind are sound, the vicissitudes of fate will be received like guests of honor. That was what Dana was saying.

She climbed onto the ship and cast a glance around, her last before she left the capital. I had a sense that she had seen me, and instead of hiding, I took a step forward, into the open, but she had just disappeared behind a curtain that was to serve as a shelter for her, stretched between a bulwark and the mainmast.

I stood there motionless, trying to imagine her behind that veil. Was she sitting down, or kneeling in prayer? Was she looking to the south, toward the sea that the Turks call White?

I wondered what our fate together might have been. A house, a serene

existence, far from the struggles that consume the world. The goldfinch chirruped, suggesting my reply.

Amid a salvo of curses, the *mahona* pulled away from the shore. Someone on the jetty was waving. The cries of the gulls became shriller, a screech, as if something had been taken away from them.

37.

I endured gloomy days, forcing myself to think about what awaited us. Ahead of me lay a great task, but having lost Dana, I felt as if I were facing it after shedding a limb. I had to stir myself. The generally unfocused enthusiasm of the people around me was impressive enough to overcome my feeling of deprivation and discomfort.

The Sultan's troops had to be below the walls of Nicosia now, in the teeth of Marcantonio Barbaro and Sokollu Mehmet Pasha. It would all be over soon, and then there would be a kingdom to be governed. We needed to prepare.

Solomon Ashkenazi was studying the revenue of Cyprus, the income from vines and olives, for the future king of the island. Nasi seemed to live in his carriage, between the Palazzo Belvedere and the Seraglio. There had been no sign, on the other hand, from Ismail, since he returned from Bandirma. Nasi told me the old man was writing his memoirs.

Because of my somber mood, the doubts that the German had instilled in me were about to spill out with great violence. They dampened the enthusiasm that I needed to cauterize my self-inflicted wound. That weird old man from a far-off place had placed a little wedge in Nasi's great edifice, enough to open it up a crack. The story of Joseph began to torment me again. Showered with honors by the pharaoh, he had made the Jews prosper in Egypt, but when that pharaoh died, his successor had enslaved the people of Israel.

What would happen if Selim were suddenly to die? What guarantees did we have that the new sultan would go on protecting us? We didn't have a Jewish army; we had no weapons. How could we defend the new Zion?

When I set out my doubts, Nasi heard in them my cry for help. I wanted him to startle me again, to take me up a mountain and let me see even further. And my mentor did exactly that.

The place he took me to was the laboratory of the greatest inventor on earth. Taqi al-Din Muhammad ibn Ma'ruf al-Shami al-Asadi, whom the Turks called more simply Takiyuddin. He was a Syrian who had grown up in Egypt, a man of faith and science, a judge and mathematician, an engineer and astronomer. He had come to the city on the invitation of the Sultan. Selim intended to finance his studies and his inventions, and there was already talk of a huge astronomical observatory, even bigger than the one in Samarkand.

The gray beard and the wrinkles beside his laughing eyes revealed that

Takiyuddin was even older than Nasi. I noticed how similar the two men were, though very different in feature. The affinity was intellectual: two geniuses confronting one another.

The precise order that reigned in Takiyuddin's laboratory did not seem dictated only by practical considerations. Mathematics and geometry also desire to enchant the eye, as happens in the most successful architecture. The desks, the equipment and the machines formed an arabesque that filled the vast room, made of wheels and pulleys, hoists and ladders. Forming a colored backdrop were shelves filled with jars, boxes, powders and liquids. Takiyuddin welcomed us, and with his arms spread wide he introduced us to his creations.

"Just look, my friends. These machines speak for themselves."

Immediately twelve chimes confirmed his assertion. They came from a clock to my right, the size of a double-doored cabinet, like the one I had seen in the library at Palazzo Belvedere. Judging by the inscriptions, this one was capable of recording not only the hour and the calendar date, but also the time of day, the phases of the moon, and the positions of signs of the zodiac.

It reminded me, though much smaller in form, of the clock that dominates Saint Mark's Square, with the two Moors striking the bell.

Takiyuddin came up beside me, holding a glass ball the size of an orange. A thin gold chain held it around his neck like a pendant. He looked first at it and then at the clock, and at last he nodded with satisfaction. Within the sphere I glimpsed a numbered dial. I had heard of clocks so small that you could wear them on your person, but I had assumed they were legends. Now, on the other hand, I was seeing one close up, and I couldn't work out how weights and counterweights could be contained, going up and down, in such a tiny space. Neither could I understand what use such an object might be. Perhaps to a country squire, because in a city like Venice or Constantinople, church bells or muezzins were more than enough to help mark out the day, the same for everyone.

Takiyuddin opened a door below the wall clock and took out a peg the size of a finger. Then he slipped it into one of many holes that ran around the main dial and said only that in a quarter of an hour, at the sound of the alarm bell, he would have to say good-bye, having been summoned to the Sultan's palace.

Spellbound, I stared at the numbers and pointers. I imagined that the metal arrow that told the hour would continue its course around the dial until it struck the peg inserted by Takiyuddin, setting off the alarm mechanism. I would have stayed there watching for the whole quarter hour, to see whether my hypothesis was correct, but a strong smell of roasted meat drew my attention toward the fireplace, where a spit laden with chickens was turning over the embers, without anyone there to move it.

Suspended just behind the birds, where the flames were high, was a big copper teakettle with a narrow spout. Above that was the chimney flue, and

if you lowered your head a little, you could see a paddle wheel right in the opening. The kettle, with an impetuous puff, shot steam from its spout, and the hot, powerful exhalation struck the paddles. They turned, and a system of arms, serrated wheels and pulleys communicated that circular motion to the spit. "Would you ever have thought that a teakettle could roast chickens?" remarked Don Yossef. The sight of such ingenious machines had a cheering effect, and I certainly needed that, but I was beginning to wonder why Nasi had brought me there.

Before I could ask him, he put in my hands a metal tube with a lens fixed in each end. He told me to put it to one eye and look through it, out of the window, toward a faraway object. I chose a minaret on the Mosque of Suleyman.

The effect took my breath away. I could see the little window from which the muezzin summoned the faithful to prayer as if it were only a few feet away from us. I instinctively thought of how useful and at the same time how dangerous such a tool would be if it were made accessible to everyone. Spies would be able to look into people's houses from a comfortable distance. Governments would be able to control the activities of their subjects. An invention of this kind would change the practice of my trade completely.

I was about to convince myself that this was the reason for our visit, when the bell of the clock started striking over and over again, making a diabolical racket.

Takiyuddin apologized, saying that he couldn't keep the Sultan waiting. And besides, he knew that we, too, had another appointment.

It was only then that I became aware of the presence of a person in the darkest corner of the big laboratory. I recognized the amused expression of Master Fitch. That day he was wearing his usual leather jacket and dark breeches, but he had allowed himself the affectation of a white feather in his hat.

Coming forward and bowing, the young Englishman invited us to approach an object covered by a gray cloth. I couldn't imagine what new contraption it might be.

"This is the proof you wanted," he said in his comical accent. He lithely slipped the cover off to reveal an ordinary piece of artillery mounted on a wooden gun carriage.

38.

"The scale is reduced," Fitch said, "but the proportions are correct. The iron was smelted in Takiyuddin's foundry, as you requested. He himself can guarantee the success of the propulsion and the resilience of the weapon."

"Good," murmured Nasi, stroking the gun carriage. He slipped his hand and the whole of his forearm inside the mouth of the weapon, exploring its inner surfaces. "Very good," he repeated. Then he turned to me.

"This, my friend, is the answer to the doubts that are gnawing at your soul." I was about to say something, but he raised a hand and stopped me. "A kingdom cannot say it is free until it is capable of defending its own freedom. That is an incontrovertible truth. But where the strength of an army cannot reach, ingenuity can."

The ceremonies were starting to get on my nerves. In my life, I had always taken the trouble to ensure that I was not left in the dark about anything. Perhaps in returning to my trade I was also reacquiring my old obsessions. "How many cannon do you think it would take to defend an island the size of Cyprus?"

The tone of the question betrayed my state of mind, but Nasi didn't turn a hair.

"Hundreds."

The reply had come from Fitch. His pointed moustache and the beard on his chin looked like sharpened swords. "Please, Master Fitch, do continue," said my mentor.

The Englishman thanked him. "Do you know where Sussex is, Signor Cardoso?"

"In England, I suppose."

"Indeed it is," he agreed. "It is a region of forests, oak for the most part, with land rich in iron and springs. Water, wood, metal: even the ancient Romans smelted swords and coins over there. But they didn't know that the iron in Sussex is of a particular kind." He struck his hand on the breech of the cannon. "Very malleable. The first person to notice this peculiarity was the Reverend William Levett, vicar of Buxted, a man who has spent the whole of his life cultivating two great passions: Jesus Christ and artillery."

It occurred to me that the juxtaposition wasn't too bold. The foundries of La Serenissima chiefly produced bells and cannon.

"The Reverend Levett," Fitch continued, "wanted to resolve the age-old problem of iron cannon. Unlike bronze, which allows guns to be forged in a

single casting, iron can only be turned into smoothed bars, which are then pressed together into a series of rings. Obviously, with wear and tear cannons of this kind tend to fall apart after a short time."

What the Englishman said was true, as I myself had witnessed. I had been present at the forging of cannon at the Arsenal in Venice, and at shooting tests on the Lido beach, under the direction of the engineer Varadian. The Armenian's practice was to try out different guns of various lengths and calibers. Iron cannons were the worst: They cracked, and sometimes they exploded. One bombardier had had an arm sheared off by a flying splinter.

Fitch walked around the cannon and then rested his hand on it.

"As I am sure you will know, bronze is an alloy of brass and copper, two minerals that are in short supply in Europe. This makes bronze cannons extremely expensive. The Reverend Levett, God bless him, wanted to find the perfect match between resilience and convenience. And he managed to do so, thanks to this iron from Sussex—" and he repeated the strange gesture of resting his hand on the cannon as if introducing an old friend. "After a series of experiments, thirty years ago he produced the first English cannon in cast iron, in the royal foundries at Newbridge. A weapon made all in one piece, at a cost five times lower than any bronze cannon. Thirty years of experience since then have allowed our craftsmen to discover all the tricks for improving these weapons. The lifetime of these cannons remains shorter, in fact, but that doesn't mean they are not advantageous, given the reduced cost. One could arm an entire fleet with these, were it not for the recoil that prevents them from being used on ships. And as to their weight, it is a hindrance if they have to be transported, but not if they are placed on a rampart and not moved from there."

He paused, as if waiting for a question, but I was still too confused. From clocks with alarms to a tube that intensified eyesight, from a self-propelled spit to cast-iron cannons, that morning my journey through the world of machines had been a headlong trip.

"Her Majesty Elizabeth I," Fitch continued, "is so jealous of the Sussex cannons that she is thinking of preventing them by law from being sold to Catholic states, but there is no prohibition on their being purchased by a Jewish king."

A masterpiece of diplomacy. England was looking for a commercial outlet in the East. England had excellent cannons at the lowest prices on the market. Yossef would become king of an island in the eastern Mediterranean. *Do ut des.*

Fitch resumed his thread. "The future kingdom of Cyprus will receive an annual supply of one hundred cast-iron cannons, in exchange for exclusive commercial capitulations for English vessels in the ports of Larnaca, Limassol, Paphos and Famagusta."

"What are your credentials for such an agreement?" I asked.

Fitch remained unflappable. "The word of Her Majesty Elizabeth I, whose

envoy I am pleased to declare myself. And I guarantee, Signor Cardoso, that Her Majesty does not waste her breath. She is willing to seal the agreement as soon as Yossef Nasi is king of Cyprus."

A long silence followed, after which it was Nasi who spoke. His words were directed at me alone. "When everything is concluded we will continue to maintain good relations with the Sultan. We will pay the annual tribute and fill his cellars with the most excellent wine, but we will defend ourselves on our own, and remain independent. Cyprus will become the commercial base for trade between the Ottoman Empire and England. And when Sokollu's plan to cut a canal through the Isthmus of Suez is realized, our kingdom will be the crossroads of trade between three continents." He rested his hand on my shoulder. "Wealth, strength, freedom. We should put it on our flags."

I looked down at the cannon and touched it with my fingers. Yossef Nasi had just shown me that his plans were not molded from the stuff of dreams. They were forged from English iron.

At last I understood the true difference between the two men who had guided my steps as an adult. Consigliere Nordio had forced me to hunt for him like a bloodhound, muzzle lowered along the narrow *calli* of Venice. Nasi, on the other hand, had made me lift my head and fly like a falcon, like the Altai that I had seen taking flight from the arm of Hassan Agha and soaring proudly above the fields. He had put in my hands one of those tubes invented by Takiyuddin, and with it I could see Cyprus and the world, and read fate in the stars.

Interlude

Three days of fever
4–7 Rabi'at Thani 978
(September 5–8, 1570)

The old man kneels on the mat, in front of his writing board. Evening is falling outside, but enough light is still filtering through the window, and the lamps are out. He has spent the whole afternoon in the room, leaving his pen only to drink *kishir* with Ali and receive a merchant from Scutari in search of advice on a cargo of coffee.

He dries the page and stacks it on the pile to his left: It's a hand's span high, ten years of memories for each finger. Worn-out paper, ink scars, written in a Latin that is by now threadbare, patched by the old man with Turkish, Arabic, German, and Venetian terms. Saints Jerome and Augustine would not recognize their chosen language.

He rereads his last words, his head heavy, then gets up and stretches his back. He needs to move, to smell the salt, silence the voices and listen to the sea.

In the doorway, Mukhtar holds him back by his shoulder. "You look like you've seen a ghost, sheik. Are you sure you don't want to lie down?" Ismail touches her hand with his fingers and shakes his head.

Leaning on his stick, he slowly walks up the hill. As he does every evening, he punctuates his walk with greetings and quick visits to people's houses, he eats a *borek* stuffed with mince, quenches his thirst at the fountain of the big cemetery of Karaca Ahmet. The scent of hundreds of cypresses fills his lungs. When he comes down to the shore, near the site of Chalcedon, the profile of the old city is already a dark shadow against the purple of the sky. Flocks of storks fly down along the Bosphorus, migrating toward a place that they call home.

In the twilight breeze, the old man is prey to long bouts of shivering, not just from the cold. He feels a subtle unease traveling down his bones; his legs are frail as plaster. He has walked for more than two miles, and now he's wondering if he'll get home before dark.

His feet sink into the sand, his stick gets stuck. He falls, gets up, falls again.

He shuffles over to a little fishing boat, clutches its edge and drops into it, seeking shelter under the fabric of the sail. His teeth chatter like a crazed

machine, a sign that the fever has returned. The same fever that made him late in reaching Tiberias.

The fever of the oasis of Elim.

The sandy course of the wadi *opens and narrows, the first channel between rocky highlands, then stretches, leveled by herds, wide enough for the dromedaries to proceed along it several abreast. I take a little sip from my flask, and the water turns my body's interior into a garden in bloom. There is no wind, but effort is a dull pain that tries to stay hidden.*

Silent days, an incessant march, eating on the hoof, pausing only to sleep and pray, men and animals as old as the desert, as the oasis we must reach.

Elim, among the rocks of Sinai, halfway between the Red Sea and the Mediterranean.

In that place, the morning dew turned into manna, to appease the hunger of the Israelites fleeing the pharaoh.

The palms of Elim sway over the fiery sand.

Unloading the dromedaries, preparing the fire, drawing water from the wells.

We eat cooked food, after many days of nothing but dates.

I struggle to swallow a few mouthfuls, then collapse exhausted, without finishing my meal.

"Ismail, *shayk*!" Hafiz's face is framed by stars, the smell of damp sand and night.

"Ali, Ali, we've found him." Mukhtar's voice, choking in her throat.

Sturdy arms lift him up, supporting him under the armpits, gripping his legs.

"What's happened, old man? Is it the fever again?" The Sufi rests his rough hand on the sick man's forehead.

Ismail feels the fresh, dry palm caressing his skin. "I'm home now," he whispers, before closing his eyes.

This is the place where the head will be severed. The wheels groan, the donkeys lower their heads, the cart comes to a standstill. Around us, a pack of rabid dogs has been following our course, and now it is approaching. A vicious gang, barking and foaming at the mouth.

The heretic's swollen face attracts blows and spittle. There isn't a shadow of repentance in his face. Only a huge crow spreading its wings.

His neck is on the block. The crowd points and comments, shouts insults, throws mud and rotten vegetables and pots of piss. The sun is halfway through its course.

The executioner spins the axe, tests the blade, looks around so that the pack of dogs has a clear idea of who's been given the job.

The condemned man shouts his heresy: "Freedom!"

Bones shatter, but one blow is not enough.

It takes another, then another.

Through the first day, Ismail trembles like a leaf. During the night he talks in his sleep, groaning and shouting. Ali stays close to him at all times, practicing the *dhikr*. The repetition of the divine names is powerful, but Ali also thinks of covering the old man with additional blankets.

Hafiz recites the Koran from memory. From the Sura al-Fatiha to the Sura of men, he can chant every verse of the sacred text.

Praise be to God, the Lord of the Worlds, the Compassionate, the Merciful, King of the Day of Judgment.

Mukhtar picks up shield and *urumi* and fights, until dawn, the shadow of death.

Beatrice is lying on the bed, much thinner than I remembered. Her eyes are hollow, her cheeks sunken. Her shoulders sink into her pillows as she sips a glass of water with unsteady hands.

"The first and last letter of the word Torah *joined form* mother. *The last and the first form* heart."

I come slowly forward into the room, as though approaching a frightened puppy. It's eight years since I last heard her voice, eight years that I've reconstructed her face from memories no longer true.

"I haven't long now, Ludovico, perhaps not even a day, and there are so many things that I would like to tell you, but the first, the most urgent, is of Yossef. He needs your help."

I lean over her, kiss her on her boiling forehead, hug her hard, but I don't relax my grip in time, and I feel her bones breaking, crumbling, turning to dust and splinters.

I leap back, as if scorched by flames, and look in terror at the pillows.

A pile of skin, ribs and nerves has taken the place of my love.

A gust of wind scatters everything.

During the second day, the old man alternates long intervals of unconscious peace with violent feverish rages. When the madness leaves him, he lies as if all his energy fled with it. Pale, cold, in a sleeplike state that is not sleep.

Hafiz goes on reciting the Koran. Mukhtar listens to him, motionless, kneeling on the prayer mat.

Every man's fate we have fastened to his own neck: on the Day of Judgment we shall bring out a scroll that he will see spread open. Read your record: Sufficient is your soul this day to make out an account against you.

Ali tries not to despair. He knows that fever, and he has seen Ismail shake it off and return to health within a few days. He gives him some lime tea to drink, and cools his skin with liquors and perfumes.

He wonders what he would do if Ismail died there, two thousand miles from home.

He thinks of Mokha, of the thousand tensions running through the city and finding a focus in the old man, a basin in which to mix, like raging but harmless floods.

He feels a void is opening, spreading through his heart, and everything is becoming futile. Ali curses his own lack of faith, and throws himself headlong into the *dhikr*.

"You're not thinking of having it printed in Constantinople, are you? Listen to your old bookseller friend, it would be pointless, you hear? These are things that need to be published in Europe, in the belly of the beast, to give it ulcers. If that genius Oporinus were still alive I would advise you to go to him, in Basilea, but the poor man died of gout two years ago, I don't know if you knew that. I had my little print works, in Ferrara, and then things took a turn for the worse. In the end the pope managed to impose his will even there, and people like me had to shut up shop."

Pietro Perna leans against the desk. His hair, the little he has left, is all white, but his shining eyes are the same as ever. He collects the papers and reads them out loud, quickly running through them with his little fingers. He lingers over a phrase, murmurs an enthusiastic comment, pulls grimaces of disapproval, makes annotations on some incomprehensible passages.

"This is a good time for me to be going to England. Things are good here in Constantinople; certainly they drink more wine here than they do in London and the sunsets are unforgettable, but you have to keep too many people happy, always licking someone's feet, kissing the hem of someone else's garment, and the third vizier of I-don't-know-where, the bey of Buggeration, and the pasha, the dragoman, the imam, the cadi, the favorite and her cousin, the black eunuch, the white one, the striped one, the Sultan's hundred pages, his gardener, the man who scratches his back, the one who rinses his balls: each one of them, from one day to the next, could rise up against you and remember the time you didn't greet him, that you published a book that insulted his grandmother, that you spoke ill of his tribe. The English are more concerned with the substance, you know? They don't rot your balls with this kind of nonsense."

Perna smiles, puts the sheets in order.

"But for now, get better, old fellow. The last few chapters are always the hardest."

Ali picks up a red and blue blanket, mutters something and arranges it over the old man's quivering body. It is dawn, and Ismail has been talking in his sleep, words that sound like delirium, and he is still fighting the fever. The disc of the sun is flooding the horizon with reddish light. Hafiz and Mukhtar have finished their prayers and come in to check on the course of the illness.

"Do you think our sheik will live?"

Ali tries to offer a drink to the old man, who doesn't recognize him. "If God wills it, Hafiz. What I think is that this man, now, is dead already. In fact

he speaks languages that belong to dead men, men of the past. If he opens his eyes and gets back on his feet it will be because God, He who resuscitates, dragged him from the depths of Gehenna."

Mukhtar kneels next to the old man and grips his hand, murmuring in a half whisper words in a language that is not Arabic.

What sign is it when a rainbow appears, when there has been no rain and the air is dry and clear?

It is that the earth is about to tremble and the whole world shakes.

Rows of horsemen gathering on the crest of a hill.

And the army of the humble has assembled, too, and the cannons vomit fire and flames.

People crouching in prayer. Eviscerated, butchered people, turned to smoke, wind, scraps as far as the eye can see.

What sign is it when the head of a man with a noble soul is exposed and paraded around on top of a pole?

It is that the battle is lost. Lost a thousand times, and the enemy gives no ground, because he never has and never will.

The horizon is moving, it is coming toward us. The horizon, black with armor, with horsemen, men of iron, men who make metallic noises and are already dead, the horizon that is Death, is advancing to crush me.

God. I see them now. The army of princes against the flock of the Lord. Blackened breastplates, helmets in monstrous shapes, grins behind the sallets, smiles from ear to ear, fixed in steel.

It is just dawn. I hear a voice crying, "Magister! Magister!" and it is mine, my own voice as always.

How old are dreams?

I see him on his knees, bent double. "Magister! Get up, for the love of God." I take him by the shoulders and try to lift him up. He is a leaden statue and I have to lift him. I try my best; I put one knee on the ground and try to turn him, to look him in the face.

There is no face. The features are meaningless.

I shout, get back to my feet, and my eyes seek the horizon that is now running toward us.

It will engulf us. It will drive us into the deepest of holes, the one that we call hell. Inside the flesh, inside the heart, a bitter place, intact after years, after a century, after a millennium, after all the time in which we have been drifting, paper boats, prey to the wind.

I'm sitting in front of a skeleton. It has a snake in its mouth, between its white jaws, and a rat is running around on the cap of its skull. Beneath the bones of its right arm, between the shoulder and the ribcage, it holds a guitar. It laughs. It jokes. It gesticulates with the bones of its other hand, it looks as if it has been delivering a speech for a long time. It tells me about its causes. It invites me to a wild party of death.

Ismail opens his eyes, looks around in the candlelight. Instead of his legs and torso, he sees layers of cloth. His body has disappeared; a merchant must have bought it in exchange for these coarse wool blankets.

He doesn't know what's happening. A man's dark face casts a shadow over his own.

Ismail lets himself drift back. Visions of angels, of djinns spilling from the earth in the form of distorted men and demons. Then his body returns, the empty skin filling like a sausage case being stuffed with mince, or as if someone were blowing into it. From his pelvis to his feet, his legs are constantly moving, his ribs opening and closing; his breathing is difficult; his limbs a willow's shaken by a raging storm.

I'm thirsty!

This is his voice. It is not from within his prostrate body that he can hear it. But it is his, he recognizes it.

Seventy palms, twelve springs. It is here that the weary Israelites took courage.

"I'm thirsty!"

It is his mouth, the one that is shouting. He sees it in the fragment of mirror, the one he brought with him from Yemen so that he would recognize himself at the end of the journey. The mirror hangs in the air, then falls like a snowflake.

The oasis of Elim. The people of Israel had their hunger assuaged by manna.

"I'm thirsty."

Ali holds the water to the old man's mouth, steadies his head as Hafiz finishes the prayer.

And when our signs are rehearsed to them with evidences their only argument is to say, "Bring our fathers, if ye speak the truth."

Mukhtar is unable to sit still, filled with childish excitement. The Sufi's face spreads into a tremulous smile as his eyes fill with tears. "You've come back, old man! God is great!"

Confused, Ismail asks where he is. "You were on the edge of the other world, and I was dejected because your infidel body would go on suffering, and suffering far worse, in Gehenna. But God, the Patient and the Eternal, must have other plans for you. And for us who follow you."

The old man's voice is thin but clear. "For how long . . ."

"Three days, Ismail, just like in Elim. Three days of fever and delirium. Hafiz has been reciting the Book all that time. Whenever you went to sleep, I was afraid it would be forever."

"I dreamed of a rainbow . . ."

"Now eat, old man. And thank God, a thousand times for each one of his names."

Part Three

Mağusa

21 Safar 978–23 Rajab 979
(July 25, 1570–December 11, 1571)

1.

As we awaited information about the fleet, fresh news came in from Italy. After months of difficult negotiations, Pope Pius V had persuaded Philip of Spain to join forces with La Serenissima, to face up to the Ottoman threat in the Mediterranean. The pontiff had contributed a dozen galleys, and the three Christian fleets had chased and waited for one another for weeks, from Zara to Corfu, from Otranto to Messina, finally meeting in Candia, whence they had set off together on the big expedition.

"Yes, but they aren't heading straight for Cyprus. Our whole fleet is there. You'll see, they'll strike in Dalmatia first, or in Negroponte."

I spent my days in the port and outside the Arsenal, waiting for firsthand news, aware that the distance was already making "news" old. Until that moment, in my job, I had always gathered information in the cities, where every event can be discovered in only a few hours. Now, though, I was interested in a world that seemed to dwell somewhere in the future, ten or twenty days on, the traveling time that separated me from Cyprus, and even more from the Adriatic.

In Constantinople two topics held the floor wherever more than three people came together: the makeup of the enemy fleet, and its chief aim. Everyone was convinced that the Christians had more ships than the Sultan. It was rumored that there were almost two hundred galleys and about a dozen galleasses. As to their target, a fortune-teller from Abkhazia told the wife of Muezzinzade Pasha that the Franks would strike at the mouth of the Dardanelles, and in the barbershops they were already studying a way to transport Orban the Hungarian's huge bombard across the strait.

Then, the same day, it was announced that Venice and her allies had thrust into the Dodecanese, making straight for Cyprus, but when they reached Castelrosso they turned back, after learning that Nicosia had already fallen.

The troops of Lala Mustafa Pasha had entered the Cypriot town after a furious attack on the bastions I had told them about, the ones that Savorgnan hadn't been able to reinforce. Nasi proposed to toast this news with the finest wine.

It was the eighth day of Rabi'at Thani in the year 978. Two hours after morning prayer, the occupation was complete. The great cathedral in Nicosia was stripped of bones and relics and turned into a mosque.

"I don't understand these Christians. They say that churches are the house of God, and then they fill them up with bones and dried-up corpses."

In Galata, fights broke out between Franks of various nations who accused each other of the failure of the Christian fleet. For a long time the *kahvehanes*

were full of tales of the atrocities committed in Nicosia, and the comments on those tales: "They're complaining that the pigs had their throats slit, but they're the ones who eat those filthy creatures."

The news traveled via dispatch riders, by beacon signal, on the wings of messenger pigeons, from the mouths of the returning wounded. Everyone seemed to have a friend, a relative or an acquaintance who had just returned from Cyprus. As I sifted what I overheard, even the vox populi finally came up with important details.

That was how I picked up the rumor of a Venetian reprisal. The peasants of the village of Lefkara had converted to Islam and placed themselves under the protection of the Sultan. The Christians had burst in at night, massacred the inhabitants and set fire to their houses. "Fanatics. Mad infidel fanatics," I thought for a while. If Venice could still punish people on Cypriot soil, it meant that taking the island from them would be harder than we'd thought.

Yet the Sultan's troops were already gathering around Famagusta. Mağusa, as the Turks call it: three miles of walls circled by a big trench. Apart from a single bastion, its system of defense was antiquated, no match for the new siege artillery. From the vantage point of Palazzo Belvedere, the fortress looked like a thin shell, which I imagined poised between a present full of expectations and a huge, radiant, tremendous future.

Lala Mustafa invited the captain-general of the stronghold, Marcantonio Bragadin, rector of Famagusta, to surrender. He sent him a bag of partridges, which was rejected. Then the pasha changed registers, and along with an order to surrender immediately he sent Bragadin the putrefying head of Niccolo Dandolo, governor of Nicosia.

When victory is near, it seems good to exalt the virtues of your enemies. So in the autumn, we were able to praise the hopeless courage of Bragadin and the few people shut up in Famagusta, because we were sure that the city would soon fall, just as we were certain that winter was close and that the Lord, from above, watched over the fates of men.

But even then, some said, "Brave? What do you mean brave, that fellow's just a fanatic. Did they send him a fleet? No. So why doesn't he just eat the partridges and go and digest them in Venice?"

I walked through the city, startled that every activity continued undisturbed. The comings and goings of human beings, business, prayers, the peace of Friday. The cycle was repeated without interruption; people seemed to be breathing normally, not raggedly as I was. I would have liked all obstacles to be past and ourselves in the safety of the kingdom that awaited us. I forced myself to stay calm, took deeper breaths, drank a glass in a tavern of the port, my ears pricked.

Often I found myself thinking of Dana, but made my mind drift elsewhere, lest I admit to myself that I missed her. I had given her up out of suspicion, fear, loyalty to Yossef Nasi and the cause of my people. I hadn't

repented; I just felt sad. Arianna had taught me a harsh lesson, and never again would I risk being betrayed.

The cold, the wind and the rain came, and began torturing Constantinople, as if she were the city that had to fall, rather than Ammochostos. "Emerging from the sands." The Greek name of Famagusta seemed to refer to the Sultan's fleet. Military operations were in abeyance, waiting for the season of fine weather to return. Most of the fleet came back from Cyprus to winter in the Golden Horn.

Nasi was spending more and more time at the Seraglio, trying to cement his friendship with Selim, and perhaps also to control Selim's moods, to lighten his spirit. The delay in his forecasts no longer seemed to worry him very much.

"In the spring, Manuel. In the spring," he repeated. In his voice I heard the same tension that had taken hold of me, but it was true, we had to be patient.

Donna Reyna was patient, anyway. After Dana's departure, she had been confined in her own part of the palace. I hadn't bumped into her for months.

Ismail also led a secluded life, on the opposite shore of the Bosphorus. When I asked Nasi what he was doing there, he approached the window and studied Asia, beyond the stretch of sea. Black clouds bared their teeth above the strait.

"He's waiting, as we all are. But not for news of the war."

"What, then?"

"To find the answer that he came here to seek."

We then discovered that the old man had fallen ill, a bad tertian fever, and he had lain in bed for weeks, convalescing, without letting us know. In that difficult situation I realized that Nasi really loved this man: He was worried, he went to Scutari several times and wanted his doctor to visit his friend, even though the danger was over.

The weeks passed, and winter reached its peak. Then, one day during Ramadan, the news arrived that sixteen galleys, on the orders of Gianantonio Querini, had surprised the port of Famagusta and managed to force the blockade, sinking three Turkish ships. They supplied the beleaguered town with food, ammunition and soldiers, then set off again, unmolested.

The ships of La Serenissima had arrived when no one expected them. Selim had the bey of Chios decapitated for not keeping watch over the waters of his island. He stripped the bey of Rhodes of the honor of flying the imperial banner on his flagship and keeping his lantern lit on the quarterdeck.

"Not that they did us much damage, mind you, but it certainly isn't a good sign for our Sultan." And other bad signs would come.

After months of preparations and a few sporadic attacks undertaken to keep from dying of boredom, as the blossoms unfurled on the branches our fleet resumed the war. In anticipation of this, the authorities of Famagusta cast out

the town's "useless mouths": women, children, the old and the infirm swarmed into the streets by the hundred. The besieging army let them pass, in fact it offered many of them food, either as an insult to the enemy, or out of pity.

The useful mouths remained on the walls: the mouths that spat fire. And a few days later they began to shout, and their roars shook the Ottoman armies.

On the twenty-second day of Dhu'l-Qa'dah, Lala Mustafa decided to view the troops from a distance that he considered safe: three miles from the city's bastions. The spectacle was intended to impress the besieged, show them the power of the Sultan's army: two hundred thousand men at arms, with skins and banners of all colors, and horses, and cannons, and swords glittering in the sun—a vast expanse of flesh and metal. The plain they trod must have been laughing with pride, superiority, the hunger for conquest.

Then, all of a sudden, came distant noises, a sound like hammering in the wind, and after a moment a rain of iron and stone, columns of dust and earth rising to the sky, bodies being crushed or hurled through the air. The Sultan's sublime army was suddenly clutched in the hands of a demon. The perfect order of the most powerful military force in the world had been shattered by Venetian cannon, whose shots had devoured the three miles of distance in a snap of the fingers, defying the boastfulness of the Turks. Shouts of enthusiasm from the distant loopholes had accompanied the chaotic retreat of the foot soldiers and the rout of the flower of the Ottoman cavalry.

It was more than sneering defiance. Coming after Querini's incursion the previous winter, it was clear to everybody that the Ottoman war machine was showing cracks.

"Old Mustafa's beard is falling out! Not even in Malta did things like that happen to him."

"Yet some people are clearly dragging their heels. Two hundred thousand soldiers against two thousand, two hundred cannons against fifty, and in seven months we can't make mincemeat of them?"

A few weeks later, I learned of the arrival of a delegation from La Serenissima, charged with the task of negotiating an exchange of prisoners with the Grand Vizier. They were led by the brother of the archbishop of Famagusta, who belonged to the faction in favor of peace and who had his supporters in both the Grand Council of the Republic and the Divan.

Don Yossef had said that the time for diplomacy was over, and yet Sokollu didn't seem to be of the same opinion. You could be sure that under the table he was plotting with Venetian delegates to forge an agreement over Cyprus.

I was filled with dull rage. For the first time I felt my faith in Nasi's plan wavering. Only the fall of Famagusta would put an end to the plots against us.

In fact it was another piece of news that sent the Venetian delegation back. It came on an afternoon of distant lightning that sounded like a battle in the middle of the sea.

2.

I ran all the way through the rain to Palazzo Belvedere. The news was doubtless going around the city, and I hadn't much hope of being the first to bring it. I looked for Nasi in vain in the library and in his rooms. The servants told me he was at the Topkapi Palace. I stood there dripping, steam rising from my clothes. Then I dropped to the floor.

When I heard him striding back in I got up, meeting him in the middle of the room, looking into his eyes. I didn't need to ask him if he knew; his grim expression said everything. He withdrew to the library, and I was about to follow him when the protecting figure of David Gomez appeared in front of me.

"Better to leave him alone," he said.

"Listen to David, Signor Cardoso. He knows my husband better than anyone."

We turned around. Donna Reyna had appeared beneath the portrait of her mother, as if she wanted to force us to notice the resemblance. The hostile glance that she exchanged with Gomez before he left didn't escape me.

"Bad news, I suppose."

"The pope and Venice have gained the support of other powers besides Spain," I replied. "Florence, Genoa, the knights of Malta, the Duke of Savoy . . . they have all sealed a pact. They call it the Holy League. It's a new crusade, and they say it's bound for Cyprus."

"So I'll be a queen in name alone?" Her tone rekindled the fury that had been smoldering in me for days.

"If you can't love him, at least try to respect him!"

"Who says I don't love him?" she retorted.

"You have an odd way of showing it."

She shook her head disconsolately. "Even if I wanted to, he wouldn't let me. You don't know anything about this family, Signor Cardoso. You see what appears on the surface, the face that everyone in this house shows to others."

"I see a man with a big plan, a stubborn man with danger on all sides."

Reyna sighed, and her shoulders slumped. "Go to him, since you can. And stay by his side." There was no rancor in her words, but there was a hint of bitterness.

I leaned against the library door. No sounds came from inside. I knocked but received no reply, and decided to go in anyway.

The map of Cyprus was spread out on the big table. Beside it, a jug of wine. Nasi was holding a glass. He looked up from the map and beckoned me in.

"Who am I, Manuel?" he asked.

I walked over to the table.

"You are Yossef Nasi, Duke of the Cyclades, prince of Europe, favorite of the Sultan. Future king of Cyprus."

"That's the question: What we will be tomorrow," he said, pointing to one of the shelves. "What do you see up there, Manuel?"

I saw an object that I knew: "Takiyuddin's optical tube."

"A gift from our Syrian friend," Nasi explained. "To see the Cypriot victory in all its magnificence. Nicosia had just fallen; conquest seemed imminent. How different it all seems now."

I had never seen him in such a dark mood. I struck my fist on the table to force him to look at me. "Why is Famagusta not yielding, Yossef? What if someone has been deliberately impeding the war? Have you thought of that?"

He sighed, as if he had seen that question coming. He said nothing.

"How can you stay here waiting while someone is trying to blow our plan sky-high?"

At last he stirred himself: "What do you think I should do? I can't fight the war instead of the Turks. Leaving Constantinople is out of the question. If I left, the coast would be clear for Sokollu to set Selim against me."

"Then send me down there." He seemed struck by this request. "We have to know what's happening," I added. "Let me be your eyes."

Nasi filled his glass again, and drained the wine in one gulp. A drop slipped into his beard and fell from his chin. His hand darted out to keep the map from being stained, and his elbow struck the jug.

The wine spread quickly over the drawing of the island. A shiver ran down my spine and an image rose up from my memory, a color, as intense as I had left it years ago. My father's blood. The blood-letting bowl overturning at my feet. I had helplessly retreated to the wall while the dark stain spread across the floor, as if pursuing me into that corner. The servant had hurried to throw a rag on the floor, and the surgeon had beckoned me over to him. I knew from his face that old De Zante was about to leave forever, as tormented by the treatment as he was by the illness. I put my ear to the pale lips that had kissed the cross a moment before.

"Always trust in God and in the strength he gives you."

Nasi got up and squeezed my shoulders, seeking in my face a confirmation of the determination that had animated my words. At last he said, "So be it. You will be my ambassador. But you can't go alone; you will need someone with you. Someone we can trust."

3.

The old man was fishing, sitting on the jetty holding his fishing-rod. He turned round when he heard our footsteps.

"Are they biting?" Nasi asked.

"Not at all," Ismail replied. The bucket beside him was indeed empty. He moved it to let us sit down.

"I'm happy to see you in good health," Nasi said, dangling his legs in the dark water.

"It's a day of peace," the German replied. "Yesterday I shed a burden. I've carried it on my back for many years, and now at last I've set it down."

"What burden are you talking about?"

"The story of my life. I've finished writing it."

"Will we be able to read it?" asked Nasi.

"I haven't yet decided what to do with it," the old man said. "I met a sage in Mokha; he came from the mountains in the north of India. He talked to me of sacred drawings made in colored sand. It takes hours, even days to draw them, then the wind blows them away and not a trace is left. Perhaps my book is like those drawings."

We sat there, absorbed in the tranquility of evening, observed by the gulls that poked about in the sand or floated on the water. The sun had already lowered above the Old City, and its glare no longer hurt the eyes. It was hot, but the evening was starting to take the depths of things away and to lengthen their shadows. Ours stretched thinly behind us, like the shadows of marsh birds.

"How is the war going?" Ismail asked, breaking the silence.

"Slowly," said Nasi. "Venetian pride is a hard nut to crack, and I admit that I underestimated it. They're still fighting, in hope that the Christian fleet will arrive soon."

Ismail said nothing. He stared at the spot where his line entered the water.

"The pope has achieved his aim," Nasi went on. "A holy alliance, as in the days of the Crusades. You know him as well as I do. Pope Ghislieri was Carafa's best pupil. One of those enemies with whom negotiation is impossible. We can only defeat him."

"You mean the Turks must do it in your place."

Nasi sighed and shook his head.

"It won't always be like that. In my kingdom the Jews will be able to create their own fates and defend themselves, once and for all, against the dangers of the world."

Ismail's tone grew slightly harsher. "With what weapons, João?"

"The most phenomenal in existence: English artillery. England will supply us with cannons in exchange for a trade base in the Mediterranean. Then we won't need the Turks anymore."

The old man didn't conceal his surprise. "He who plays on two tables runs a double risk."

"You and I have always taken risks," Nasi replied. "Listen to me: Who better than the Jews, who have been persecuted forever, can welcome the persecuted people from all over Europe? The kingdom of Cyprus will be able to give asylum to refugees, to free spirits, to victims of the Inquisition. It won't matter what their creed is, as long as they are willing to build our shared house. Tolerance and harmony will be the foundation of the New Zion."

"I have been to the New Zion," Ismail replied. "I have seen the prophets of the Kingdom at work."

"Are you comparing me to them? To the madmen of Münster?" Nasi dismissed the idea with a wave of his hand. A startled gull took flight, settling a little way off.

"Not with them," Ismail replied. "To myself in those days."

"We're living in different times now," Nasi said, "and I'm not looking for the apocalypse. Gracia understood, and that's why she wrote to you. That's why I'm here. Manuel is leaving for Cyprus with a message for Lala Mustafa. I want you to go with him. You used to go hunting with the general. He respects you."

Ismail's mouth shaped itself into a grin. Perhaps he was thinking of Nasi's words, of his relationship with Lala Mustafa or his former life in Constantinople. We would never persuade him like this. I decided to tell him what I thought.

"You won't find the answer you're looking for by staying here."

The two men turned and suddenly seemed to remember that I was there. I got up, stepping over them both.

"My mother's last wish was that I should grow up a good Jew. I rebelled against that for all of my life, until I became the opposite, a gadfly to my people. And yet here I am. Perhaps it was meant to be; perhaps I was fated to take such a long and tortuous detour. God's plan is unfathomable. We cannot know in advance what random events will make us what we are, or know if the means that we choose will turn out to be the right ones. What I do know is that big things are happening. Cyprus is the most ambitious plan that a Jew has ever come up with, and I'm fed up sitting here and waiting . . ." I aimed a finger at the old man. "Your defeats don't mean that there's no point trying again. You can choose to be useful to a cause again or to stay here trying to catch fish."

I nodded to Nasi follow me. It was the first time I'd told him what to do, and he obeyed me, albeit reluctantly. He walked behind me, resigned, and then Ismail's voice rang out in the evening air. "Have you thought of gifts?"

Nasi looked as if he'd been caught off guard, then stopped and replied, "Swords for the officers, silver spurs, harnesses for the horses . . ."

I saw Ismail shaking his head. "Something special for Lala Mustafa. He's a vain old man." Nasi thought for a few seconds, then his face brightened. "I've got exactly what he needs."

Ismail left his rod where it was. He picked up his stick and joined us. "Sieges are aggravating things, Signor Cardoso, I am aware of that. You won't like what you see."

"I'm not going there for pleasure," I replied.

The old man muttered something, then set off toward the houses.

4.

We plowed the waves fast and alone, during those July days. Nasi had put the flagship of his merchant fleet at our disposal, a *mahona* with an elegant, sinuous line, under the command of a Greek from the Peloponnese. When the wind swelled the sails and impelled the ship along, it seemed to ride the top of a great crest that rose and fell. When the wind subsided, the oarsmen took over. Their coordinated movements, the ancient gestures of pulling, rising, falling and pulling again, meant that we never lost speed. One way or another, the keel sliced the waves like a knife blade, heading south. The crew consisted entirely of *marioli*, salaried volunteers. No slaves or conscripts on a Jew's ship.

We carried a personal letter from Yossef Nasi and gifts for Lala Mustafa Pasha. *Fazte hermano kon el Guerko fin a pasas el ponte.* Become a brother of the Devil until the danger has passed. That was what Nasi had said to me as he handed me the gifts for the general, the man who had been Selim's tutor and who, unlike Selim, had been on the battlefield for months, amid the flying cannonballs, even though he was the same age as Ismail al-Mokhawi.

During the day we lived on deck, cooked by the sun like herrings set out to dry. At night the stars covered the sky to the horizon.

Hafiz and Mukhtar observed everything with worried eyes: the dark beauty of the sea, the clouds that passed above the mainmast, the flight of the gulls. Ali beguiled the time by roasting and grinding coffee beans, which he then brewed with cinnamon and cardamom. At other times he recited long prayers, or once more honed the blade of his scimitar, producing lugubrious sounds.

Ismail was the one least affected by the rigors of the journey. I struggled to believe that a short time previously he had been in danger of dying. The sea seemed to reinvigorate him and make him even harder than before. He was taciturn, and his friends respected his silence. One afternoon, on the quarter-deck, as he was looking out over the sea, I asked him whether in his long life he had ever been a sailor as well.

"No," he replied. "But I did trade in the northern seas. Plowing the sea is like crossing the desert. They are free spaces, open to a multitude of possibilities."

"And yet without the prospect of a landfall we would merely be drifting," I objected, but I received no reply.

One evening, almost at the end of the voyage, I realized that I hadn't exchanged a word with a living soul all day. The sun was setting slowly, red in

the sky. The men who weren't at the oars stopped to pray. It was the captain himself who led the worship on the deck, reciting the Koran. Hafiz and Mukhtar joined the others, along with Ali. The few Christians, a little apart from the rest, made the sign of the cross.

I joined Ismail behind the curtain, a place to which he had withdrawn a little while before. I found him naked to the waist, busy greasing his pistols. Drops of sweat shone on his chest, which was covered with white hairs, and on his belly, crisscrossed with scars. On his right forearm I noticed a strip of swollen flesh, perhaps a burn. Around his neck he wore a pendant; it looked like a pierced coin.

"Are you skilled with weapons?" I asked.

From a little trunk at his side he took a short sword in a leather sheath. He handed it to me. "Take this. Keep it under your jacket; no one will see it." He unsheathed the weapon, a handy, light dagger. The metal visibly bore the marks of time, but the blade had been recently sharpened.

A question formed on my lips. "Have you killed many men?"

He passed the wick into the barrel of the pistol. "Yes. I won't say they deserved it; it's not up to me to judge." He fell silent for a moment, then added, "And you? Have you ever killed anyone?"

"I was a servant of the state. The executioner got his hands dirty on my behalf."

My own words produced horrible noises in my mind, the echo of screams mixing with vivid memories: the pain inflicted in Venetian prisons. An altar of torment built for the security of the state. "Do you know what we're going to find down there, do you really know?"

He didn't reply. He bent over his weapons again and got on with the business of cleaning them.

The next day, in the light of dawn, we made out the dark line of the coast of Cyprus. Along with the two young Indians, I ran to the starboard side, where we found Ismail, as if he had been there since the night before. Young Hafiz said something in Arabic.

"What did he say?" I asked the old man.

"I'm not sure, but I think he said it looks like a fish."

"Not a fish," said Ali, who had just joined us.

The boy mimed the spouting of a whale.

5.

Even before the city was in view, bits of Famagusta came to meet us. Wreckage, charred planks, bottomless barrels. A woman's dress floated on the waves, along with a threadbare banner riddled with bullet holes. The body and golden wings of the Lion of Saint Mark could still be seen on it. Where the maned head and the book should have been, there was nothing but a gaping hole.

The distant outline of the city walls looked shattered: piles of stone in an arid, desiccated landscape. Clouds of dust rose up in the wind that blew across the land, and there were no trees to contain them. They carried a slow cadence to the ears, like a drum beaten in the center of the earth. It was the Turks firing at the city. Lengths of fortification collapsed, detritus rained down among clouds of sand. Surrounded by siege fortresses higher than the walls, Famagusta was still resisting. Far away, outside the range of the Venetian cannon, the tents and banners of the encampment seemed to be resting in the haze.

We were now close to the shore. We had met several Turkish galleys that were blocking access to the port, which was in turn obstructed by a long chain.

Having passed the port and rounded the little islands that closed it off, we moored in a place called Beach of Gardens, near the southwestern side of the walls. That section of the fortifications was in pitiful condition. The tower had collapsed: More than a building, it looked like a natural formation eroded by thousands of years of water and wind.

As soon as we disembarked, we were struck by the smell of Famagusta. Penetrating, hard to define. It was disgusting even to us, accustomed by now to the stench of the ship. It smelled of gunpowder and rotten wood, pitch and saltpeter. And of corpses, cooked by the sun and ravaged by violent death.

The Beach of Gardens was a barren place. Perhaps before the war it had deserved its name, but now it looked like a desert. The Turks had set up a service port there: a kind of shack, its walls cobbled together from planks and bales of wet cotton, rose behind a fortress; from the fortress, cannons bombarded the Venetian vessels still in the port. I found out later that there were three vessels in all.

An officer of janissaries checked our credentials. He read and reread them with affected attention, stroking his moustache with his left hand, then told an orderly to alert Lala Mustafa Pasha. He turned back to us.

"How many of you are going? You will need an escort to get your bearings in the trenches. The Franks are still firing, just a few broadsides a day. They're hitting targets further up, toward the encampment."

"There will be three of us," I replied. "Accompanied b two crewmen carrying the trunk."

The officer looked us up and down. "Have a wash first. Lala Mustafa Pasha can't bear bad smells." He paused. During that brief silence I heard a sound like a landslide, in the distance, and music. The officer resumed, "That must be one of the reasons for his ill humor."

After cleaning ourselves up, we entered the trenches. This was a labyrinth of earthworks and extremely narrow ditches, supported by wooden beams and planks, with storehouses and gun emplacements protected by gabions. The excavations were so deep that a man on horseback could pass along them without being seen from outside, and they twisted at sharp angles, first to the right, then to the left. Every suitable surface was covered with tiny script, most of it in Moorish characters. Perhaps messages to the next shift, or prayers, or curses. The human landscape that we slowly encountered, men who lived in this city of earth and dust, seemed to have been assembled by a madman. A bend, and here were infantrymen quartered in the most wretched conditions, torn and dusty uniforms, a terrified sentry peering through the loopholes. Another bend, and here were smartly dressed soldiers, blue and red uniforms a brave defiance of the soldiers at the tops of the walls. They must have been the next shift, newly arrived. In a roomier section, a group of musicians played warlike tunes dominated by the beating of huge drums. As we passed, the music suddenly got louder, and the wind instruments whinnied out of a kind of challenge, accompanied by crashing cymbals.

Further on, we struggled through the place where the wounded were assembled, many of them in desperate conditions. The stink of spilled guts and clotted blood was unbearable. The groans were a sorrowful, endless murmur. The dead were dragged away by the feet and piled up to wait for burial.

When we emerged at last, far from the walls, the smells were the first thing to change. The stench of men crammed together, but also the smell of wood and cooked food. This was the encampment, tents and fires as far as the eye could see, groups of cooks around huge pots. Lala Mustafa's tent was distinguished from the others by its size and the number of banners and standards that crowned it. Their letters, embroidered in gold and silver, were dazzling. The sky was a slab of blue.

The general's residence was protected by circles of sentries, who received the trunk from the hands of Hafiz and Mukhtar. Ismail gestured to them to wait, gesturing also to Ali, whose seraphic air seemed entirely unaffected by the almighty chaos all around us. An officer took charge of Nasi's letter and brought it inside the tent.

Ismail played nervously with the handle of his stick.

After a short wait, the entrance to the tent opened up and a janissary invited us to step inside. Lala Mustafa was seated on a bronze stool, with the letter in his hands. Standing impassively on either side of him were two huge

janissaries. The general invited us to step forward. He was older than I remembered from our audience at the Divan. The months of war must have tested him sorely. Nonetheless, he had the solid, stubborn air of the true man of arms. His voice was cold, formal.

"Nasi Bey's passion for this venture is such as to send you, his pupil, to pressure me to ensure that Mağusa falls as soon as possible." I was about to reply, but he cut me off, turning instead to Ismail. "But he didn't send you alone. For a moment I thought my eyes deceived me. But no, here is a man I thought lost on the borders of the empire." Ismail bowed, and Lala did the same, bringing his fingers to his forehead.

"The years of our hunting parties are a distant memory," said the general.

"Now you are pursuing rather larger quarry," Ismail replied.

Lala Mustafa laughed comfortably. "But I haven't lost my old passion."

He moved toward a corner of the tent and showed us two hooded hunting falcons on a perch. The general took some scraps of raw meat from a tray. Their beaks snapped and ripped the food to shreds.

"Remarkable specimens," said Ismail.

"The best. They come from Central Asia. If you wish, I may have the opportunity to let you see them at work." Then he seemed to remember me. "Show me the gifts, then," he commanded.

I opened the trunk. "Your entry into Famagusta will mark an important moment in the long tale of your exploits," I said. "And as you know, it will be an important moment for Yossef Nasi, too." I took out the front plate of a Milanese cuirass. Blue steel, of the finest quality, on which Nasi had had engraved words from the Muslim Holy Book. The precious object glittered. Lala Mustafa looked at it with interest. He nodded to the two janissaries, who took the cuirass and fitted it on their commander's chest. He stood straight on his feet, his arms outstretched, as the soldiers fastened the final laces.

"Important, you say. I have lost my son in this venture. But he was a soldier, and he has been rewarded with paradise. Has your mentor perhaps risked anything as precious?"

Without a moment's hesitation, I replied, "Yossef Nasi sent me. He asked me to witness the army's victory on his behalf. My eyes are his eyes."

The general looked at me with satisfaction, then demanded to be brought a mirror.

"We don't use steel breastplates," he said, "but I will gladly wear it to enter Famagusta, as Nasi Bey suggests in his letter."

He looked at himself for a long time, from various angles. "And don't worry," he added, before dismissing us, "I will show you everything from very close up."

6.

For the first part of the night I didn't sleep a wink. The Turks played horns and drums to stir up the besieging forces and unnerve their adversaries. I thought about what I would tell Yossef Nasi I had seen. I had in front of me an exhausted city, tattered like a worm-eaten scrap of wool, and all around an invaded, swarming countryside, turned upside-down by the hand of man, dug into trenches to provide shelter, heaped into bridges and embankments to be used as instruments of conquest.

Shortly before dawn, we were wakened by a handful of janissaries. Lala Mustafa, as he had promised, was inviting us to take part in his reconnaissance from above.

We got up and, still groggy, reached the pasha's tent, where he was ready to lead a short march, at its head, accompanied by a select guard. Lala Mustafa greeted us proudly and gestured to us to arrange ourselves around him.

To our rear was a muddy river of men. The agony of the fortress had attracted people of every sort, waiting to pounce on the leftovers, to gnaw on the bones of the prey. Lala Mustafa held a flask of perfume under his nose to mask the worst of the stench.

Hidden by the trenches and the wall of men protecting us, we reached the foot of one of the towers that we had seen from the sea. It was an old fortification in wood, like a ghost castle, made of planks, faggots, wicker baskets full of stones, the whole thing barely held together by ships' hawsers. The side exposed to the cannonballs was padded with cotton. Its bulk provided the only shadow for a radius of several yards.

Looking up from below, it seemed to me that the fortress was moving and about to fall on top of me. I worked out that this impression was created by the movement of the clouds.

We climbed the tower, leaving most of our escort at its foot. The wooden ladders led us easily upward. On the first floor stood falconets and culverins, ready to fire.

When we reached the top, I could see the entire city spread before me, no more than two hundred yards away. The Turks had opened various breeches in the counterscarp and climbed down into the moat. Lala Mustafa explained to us that covered pathways had been dug into it, so his soldiers could break down the defenses one stone at a time and lay mines without being shot at. They had raised barriers of masonry perpendicular to the moat and as high as the walls, to use as embankments and bridges, and as defenses so they could enter the

moat without being shot from the side towers. I saw men using hooks and picks to shatter, one stone at a time, the stretches of the barrier already broken by cannon shot, shielding themselves with tables covered with wet skins.

Only a few defenders remained on the walls, and they were further up, behind a high barricade of barrels, wood, and cotton bales, sheltered by big tables bristling with nails and daggers.

The arsenal tower had collapsed at various points. The Ravelin, Famagusta's land gate, was a terrifying pile of masonry. The city, inside the walls, had a desolate appearance, its buildings beaten down by months of cannonades.

Thick, black smoke rose outside the gates of Limassol. A huge, untidy pyre of planks and resinous tree trunks was being consumed by the flames, but I couldn't work out to what end.

Devastation, as far as the eye could see.

I was stirred from my thoughts by the voice of Lala Mustafa.

"Bragadin is an obstinate man. And his commander, Baglioni, is a smart fighter. Even so, they haven't a hope. Yesterday I made a request for surrender: They rejected it. Today I plan to dine on partridge pie." He held out his right hand, palm upward. "In there."

He lowered his arm and an explosion split the sky, shaking our emplacement like a fruit tree. A blast of rifle fire struck the ramparts and barricades that shielded the city's defenders. The Turks' war cries rang out three times.

Thousands of foot soldiers in leather and chain mail leaped from the trenches and launched themselves toward the walls.

The half-light of dawn faintly illuminated a vast and terrible scene. A sea of banners flapped in the wind and war music sounded, strident and monotonous. I thought the Cypriot defenses would collapse under the pressure. The rage of that first assault seemed irresistible. Columns of pikemen, of foot soldiers carrying light weapons, of janissaries were attacking the masonry of the Ravelin and the Limassol gates. The hair stood up on the back of my neck and the blood thumped in my temples.

As the wind changed, the smells of battle reached my nostrils. Pitch, turpentine, saltpeter. Blood freshly spilled and clotted, guts, roasted bodies, like the smell of a slaughterhouse. The sickly smell of piles of bodies already decomposing.

I looked and looked, even though the scene kept repeating itself cyclically, monotonously: assault troops passing over the torn bodies of their companions to keep their appointment with death; Famagusta, a relic abandoned in the sand, still resisting.

Behind the parapet that protected us, Hafiz and Mukhtar prayed along with Ali. Ismail stood motionless, leaning on his stick, his lower lip between his teeth. Lala Mustafa stopped frantically issuing orders and listening to information and turned to us. "You don't need to worry," he said. "This fort isn't a useful target for the Venetians. They have very little gunpowder, hardly any ammunition, and they've got to concentrate on the attack."

He had just finished speaking when a big boulder, after bouncing crookedly, raked a trench right below us, mangling legs and heads.

Bodies fell into the moat, slipped back into the dust, and others trampled them, stumbled and climbed toward the barricaded fortresses, where the enemy maintained its resistance in spite of everything: an enemy that had sent a whole generation to the other world on that hideous plain and went on fighting, throwing down fiery bucketfuls of pitch, shattering the masonry of the Ravelin with three-pointed nails, shouting *Long live Saint Mark* and firing again, and again preparing to fight with knives and swords.

A group of foot soldiers tried to enter at the side, where the fastnesses of the Venetians, though bristling with knives and daggers, seemed less well armed. A rain of bottles filled with inflammatory fluids drenched them, like sauce on cooked meat. The Turks fled in all directions, turned to human torches. Some of them dove into half barrels full of water. One headed straight toward us, running across the plain, under the sun, the fire disfiguring his skin and flesh. He looked as if he were swelling, growing. I saw his face devoured by the flames. His eyes were those of a living man, and they were screaming things that a mouth and lungs can't say. His body was impelled past its own inanition, like an automaton. Another few steps and he fell, face down. The fire finally consumed him.

Then, suddenly as it had begun, the battle ceased.

It must have been about one o'clock in the afternoon; the sun was high, more than halfway through its course, and the heat was suffocating. Breathing burned the lungs. The sudden silence, after hours of hubbub and shouting, hurt the ears.

Lala Mustafa was vexed. His plans for lunch had been thwarted. "In a few hours we will resume the attack," he said to us. "If you wish, you can still be my valued guests at the shacks on the Mount of Jews." He pointed to the first hill below the fortress and took his leave. I stood gazing, unable to take my eyes off the vision of the apocalypse.

At last we came down from the tower, escorted by our janissaries, and we asked them to accompany us to the Beach of Gardens, across the battlefield.

My eyes met those of a soldier who was yelling at his fellows, his right hand stretching upward, clutching a scimitar. I knew that veil in his eyes. Hashish. Intoxicating cannabis resin, the sublime ingredient of the sweets I had eaten with Dana.

I knew that warlike rage needed to be helped, sustained, induced. Behind the lines, if you act like a coward, punishment awaits you. In the front, the defenders rake the enemy and death is almost certain. I wondered what Bragadin was doing to lift the mood of his soldiers. The supplies of wine in there must have been endless.

We passed by the point where, until a few hours previously, the thin outline of the Ravelin had still stood. The Turks had filled the moat with earth and with the corpses of their own comrades. The unburied dead

numbered in the thousands. Some of them had lost their lives a few hours before; others had been dead for days. The stench of putrefaction was unbearable.

I could hear a faint buzz, getting louder. I didn't know what its source was, nor from what direction it was coming. Then I realized that it was climbing from the moat, just fifty yards away from us. Flies. A black whirlwind spinning over the corpses. The pestilential stink reached us with a terrible intensity.

I felt a desperate urge to vomit. Ismail took me by the arm and dragged me away, far from the stench of death. He fixed his gray eyes on me.

"Have you seen enough now?"

I didn't reply. I didn't know what to do. I started breathing again; I tried to stand firmly on my feet and turned around once more. Ali was a few feet behind us. He advanced through the carnage as if nothing were happening, as if he were untouched by events. Before he caught up with us, he knelt to close the eyes of a corpse.

I asked him what the point of that gesture was, in a hell like this.

He replied that it had a point to him, and that should be enough.

7.

We'd hardly reached the beach when cannons, arquebuses and human throats started roaring again. Lala Mustafa must have finished his lunch, albeit not where he had expected, and the assault began afresh.

We spent the rest of the day on the ship, without saying a word, listening to the noises of battle. At sunset, when the attack was over and the plain rang only with the wails of the wounded, a sudden explosion brought down the tower of the arsenal. The Turks must have detonated a mine below the walls. The rampart split in two, leaving an abyss. The southern walls were now broken at several points, and the city's hours were numbered.

I couldn't shake off that nauseating smell: Every pore of my skin was filled with it. I went down to the beach to swim in the sea, hoping that the saltwater might erase it. However much I rubbed myself with water and sand, it kept coming back.

Later, under the stars, I saw Ismail walking on the quarterdeck and exchanging a few words with the commander before he lay down.

I touched Ali, who was lying beside me, on the shoulder, and noticed that he too was awake. I didn't need to say anything to him.

"He's seen it all before," the Arab murmured. "Tonight he hates himself for being forced to live through it again."

"If he knew what we were going to find here, why did he agree to come?"

"Because he refuses to surrender. Even now, there's a struggle going on inside him. The same one that has inspired him all his life. I hope he finds peace one day."

I looked at the old man's dark silhouette, then got up and joined him, as I had done on the White Sea, when we went to enlist Mimi Reis. The mood couldn't be the same; the images of the day just past were still vivid, indelibly fixed in the mind.

Ismail's grim appearance would have dissuaded anyone from addressing him, but I did so anyway. "What will happen now?"

He didn't answer straight away, busy as he was studying the massive bulk of the dying fortress. Then he said, "Lala will give them time to decide. Whether to obey their pride or save those who can still be saved."

"Bragadin can't be as insane as that," I said. "He must know by now that neither God nor the Christian fleet will save him."

I was trying to convince myself.

Ismail stared at the stars. "It's not over yet."

The next day Lala Mustafa ordered a few half-hearted assaults, to wear out the last forces of the defenders, then suspended hostilities and waited. One more dawn and sunset, and then, on the ninth day of the month of Rabi' al-Awwal, a white flag appeared on the shattered walls.

I greeted it with relief and thought that Ismail might have been wrong, that the war was finally coming to an end. Fate had brought us there at exactly the right time.

Information started coming in quickly. To guarantee respect for the truce, Lala Mustafa established an exchange of hostages. Negotiations over treaties of surrender were under way.

We passed another day on the ship, at the mercy of the heat and our impatience. At last the conditions of the capitulation were made known. All the Italians were free to leave for Candia with their families and their belongings. The same applied to those Greeks who wished to leave. The Turks would put the necessary ships at their disposal, if the last three Venetian galleys weren't enough. On the other hand, those who had decided to stay wouldn't be subjected to reprisals or similar vexations. The Venetians had asked to take away their artillery and Lala Mustafa had met this condition with a denial. He granted the conquered men permission to have only five cannons of their choice. Finally, he ordered the evacuation of the fortress by the fifth of the Christian month of August.

I told Ismail that in my opinion it was a good agreement: it preserved the honor of the vanquished and permitted them a safe way out. The old man didn't reply, but went on thoughtfully staring at the defeated fortress, and I wondered whether he had noticed the anxiety in my voice.

From our mooring place, in the Beach of Gardens, we couldn't see the embarkation of the surviving population, which took place on the following day. The chain that closed the port was withdrawn, and the Ottoman ships entered the roads. That same evening, around a bonfire, a Turkish sailor told us of the exodus that he had witnessed. As far as he could tell, there were still a lot of "useless mouths" in the city, people who hadn't wanted to leave at the beginning of the year, unable to put their whole life behind them. A column of men, women and children, laden with bundles and goods and chattels, had embarked on the vessel. They would spend the night there, waiting to weigh anchor.

The next day, what remained of the garrison had to board the ship as well. Operations proceeded slowly, beneath a ruthless sun. The Turks carried water and food to the refugees, but their presence filled the air with a gloomy tension.

The worst moment seemed to be imminent when a gang of looters tried to slip into the city to set about sacking it. The Venetians took up arms, but it was the janissaries who reestablished order. I blessed the wisdom and the firm hand of Lala Mustafa.

Another day and at last it would be over. And yet I couldn't wipe out the river of blood that I had seen flowing; I would carry it with me for ever. We

would have to cleanse that earth and ensure that those men had not died in vain. Who could tell whether I really believed we could, as I formulated those thoughts, or whether I was just looking for a way to accept the reality of those deaths.

On the last evening I tried to look at Famagusta with new eyes. Once Jewish rule was established, we would rebuild the fortress. Under the enlightened guidance of Nasi, it would become yet more beautiful and more secure. The English cannons would crown the bastions, making them impregnable. Ships from all over the Mediterranean would moor in the port, laden with precious merchandise; trade would flourish. As for the trees, we would replant them, and the whole island would be a garden. I thought with regret of the carob tree. For just a moment I tried to convince myself that when the New Zion was sound and flourishing, perhaps I could . . . but no, no one can go back. It was forward that I must look, and I forced myself to do so, with a mixture of hope and trepidation that troubled my soul.

One more day. Just one day.

8.

The sun was already high when a janissary presented himself before the captain of the ship, asking for us. The pasha wanted us to join him at his headquarters, he said. I couldn't imagine the reason, but I was happy to get the request. I had had enough of watching from outside, and I couldn't wait for it all to be over.

In the morning there had been rumors of another band of irregulars attempting to sack the city. Again the janissaries had had to intervene to hold off these jackals, who were wandering around the city in little packs in search of easy pickings. Luckily, the embarkation operations were almost complete, and soon the ships of the evacuees would weigh anchor for Candia.

We followed the janissaries through the trenches and the Turkish encampment. The soldiers played music and danced. The raki passed from hand to hand in terra-cotta flasks, and the scent of hashish floated in the air. I saw tired men, happy to be alive, celebrating victory and the end of a life underground.

We reached the pasha's big tent. Once again, only Ismail and I were admitted into his presence. The others had to wait outside.

Lala Mustafa was washing his hands in a copper bowl, while the servants hurried to clear away leftover food. When he became aware of our presence, we greeted him with a half bow.

"Ah, here you are. You know, with all this business I almost forgot about you." He wiped his moustache with a cloth and combed it, looking at himself in a mirror held up by a servant. "Sealing the peace is much harder than making war." He seemed to be trying to find the right words. "It takes much greater skill." He dismissed the servant and threw out his chest. "Anyone who maintained that Cyprus would be a second Malta was mistaken," he said.

The reference to the Grand Vizier was obvious to everyone. Perhaps even to the two janissaries who took care of the general's safety. Lala Mustafa's aversion for Mehmet Sokollu was well known, and reciprocal.

"Nasi Bey," the general went on, "was one of the major supporters of this campaign. So I want his guests to witness the surrender of Vercingetorix in the presence of Caesar. Marcantonio Bragadin is coming here to hand me the keys of the city, before setting sail." He gave us a hint of a smile. "It seems that I will soon be able to put on the armor you brought me, and make my triumphal entrance into Famagusta."

At that moment an officer came into the tent and told us that the

delegation was arriving. He said the commanders of the fortress were there in force. Bragadin walked at the head. A servant walked beside him and shielded him from the sun with a red parasol. His escort consisted of 300 armed foot soldiers, with the wicks of their arquebuses lit.

Lala Mustafa exploded: "What do you think you're doing? You're coming to surrender, not to wage war on me. Disarm all these men and let only the captains step forward."

The officer stepped forward to execute the order. Lala Mustafa gestured to us to stand aside, on the edge of the tent, along with the orderlies and the guards. We found ourselves close to the falcons again. They were busy cleaning their plumage, heedless of events in the world. One of them met my curious glance for a moment before returning to its occupation.

The general's mood had darkened. It was clear that he was displeased by the information. The Venetian captains came in at last, escorted by a dozen janissaries. There were seven of them, and the one at their head must have been Marcantonio Bragadin. He was wearing a purple cloak and the hat of a city magistrate.

Lala Mustafa confronted him, and the captain-general of Famagusta bowed slightly. He was tall, with a gaunt frame. The most striking thing about him was the austerity of his face, tested by long months of hardship and by the gravity of the moment.

I saw Lala Mustafa's expression darken still further at the sight of Bragadin's bright clothes and haughty attitude. "I am pleased to meet at last the man who withstood my army for so long," he said. "People will talk of this venture in times to come, you can be sure of that, and I will be sure to recall the bravery of you and your men."

He waited for his words to be translated into Italian. Bragadin's reply came quickly.

"Our bravery, Signore, is born of our devotion to the Most Serene Republic, to the Doge and our Lord Jesus Christ. I received the order to save the city with all effort necessary, just as you received the order to conquer it. If I now yield Famagusta, it is because your forces are superior and it is impossible for us to resist you."

When the translator finished speaking, Lala Mustafa nodded. "Very good. Everything is ready for you to leave the island. But there is one point that hasn't been discussed." He waited for the translation and noted uncertain looks from the Venetians. "I have made my ships available to you so that you can reach Candia. What guarantee can you give me in return?" Bragadin exchanged a glance with the other captains before replying.

"You have my word."

Lala Mustafa took a half step toward them, his hands behind his back. "But give me a hostage. One of your captains."

His request was uttered nonchalantly. The glances exchanged by the Venetians began to look more anxious. My throat was dry, and at the same

time I felt the sweat trickling down the back of my neck and under my clothes. I wondered if Ismail, by my side, was also aware that there was something wrong with this discussion.

"Signore," Bragadin replied, in a tone extremely calm, "nothing in the agreement that we signed allowed for anything of the kind. Not a single chapter spoke of hostages."

With a brisk gesture, Lala Mustafa dismissed the objection and gestured to them to sit down on the carpets at the end of the tent. The Venetians sat down hesitantly, very close to the janissaries. "What the devil is he thinking of?" I wanted to whisper to Ismail, but didn't. Judging from his face, the old man wasn't happy about the turn things were taking, either.

"You want to split hairs?" Mustafa went on. "I know my agreement, Captain, and I can tell you that many things were omitted to ease your surrender and your exit from the city." The translator was in a cold sweat; he spoke quickly, but was careful to make no mistakes. At that point everyone had understood that in this confrontation there could be no misunderstanding, not of a single word.

"I don't know what you're referring to, Signore," Bragadin replied drily.

The pasha looked at him for a long time. Then he said, "For example, the two hundred Turkish prisoners who are still unaccounted for."

A deathly silence fell. Bragadin looked quizzically at the other captains, but none of them spoke. "I still don't understand, Signore."

His obtuseness irritated Mustafa even more, and he raised his voice. "We have the testimonies of three survivors who escaped the city at the moment of the surrender. They maintain that the Turkish prisoners have been massacred."

After listening to the translator, Bragadin turned pale. "That is incorrect, Signore. I have never given an order of that kind."

"So you will be courteous enough to tell me what became of those men," the general pressed.

"I have no idea, Signore. I spent the last days of the siege locked up in my rectory. I can tell you only that I never gave the order to murder the prisoners."

"And yet they were killed," Lala Mustafa shouted, "and thrown from the ramparts at night, is that not so?" He had risen to his feet, and his bulk loomed over the captains. "You didn't want to go on feeding 'useless mouths,' did you? You decided to eliminate the prisoners and keep the little remaining food for yourselves."

The silence that followed was thick with embarrassment. The captains looked at the ground. Only Bragadin met the pasha's fiery gaze. "I repeat that I never gave that order."

"Still, those men were under your protection," Mustafa declared. "Hence I put their death down to you." The general had come so close to his adversary that he was almost touching him. One of the captains leapt to his feet and sent the word *betrayal* echoing around the tent.

At a nod from the general, the janissaries obstructed the Venetians and tied their hands behind their backs. Startled by the commotion, one falcon uttered a shrill cry. I observed the scene with astonishment, and when Lala Mustafa gave the order to take the captains outside, I clutched Ismail furiously.

"We've got to do something!"

Outside, an ovation welcomed the Christians in chains.

We hurried from the tent, just in time to see the prisoners on their knees, with their heads lowered to the ground. Bragadin was held apart from the rest, and one of the guards held his head so that he was unable to look away. The prisoners were panting and snorting like beasts in a slaughterhouse.

Ali and the Indian twins came up behind us, questioning us with their eyes, but we gave them no reply. We had no reply to give.

Another nod from Lala Mustafa. The janissaries raised their scimitars. The blades glinted in the sun, then fell quickly and solemnly, severing the heads of the captains one by one. The cheers went up, even louder than before.

I gripped Ismail with all my strength. "It can't end like this. Not with violated agreements and the slaughter of men who have surrendered! Cyprus will be stained with shame for ever; this bloodshed will never be redeemed."

Ismail stood frozen.

Lala Mustafa ordered one of the soldiers from Bragadin's escort, who had witnessed the scene with horror, to be brought into his presence. He asked him which was the head of Astorre Baglioni, and the poor young man was forced to turn over the bloody remains to recognize his captain.

Lala picked up the head of the man who had been in command of the defenses of Famagusta and who had for a year opposed his desire for conquest. He held it aloft, so that everyone could see it, and then he approached Marcantonio Bragadin. The translator hurried over to him—carefully keeping his distance from the dripping trophy.

"Now look at your captain," said Lala Mustafa. "Did you perhaps hear me give the order to kill him? No. My soldiers know what I want from them. But unlike you, I don't hide myself." He threw Baglioni's severed head to the soldiers thronging around him. Then, with another gesture, he unleashed their fury against the Italian foot soldiers, who were overwhelmed and thrown into the dust. Severed heads rolled in all directions, kicked far from the general pandemonium. The earth turned red and then black, as blood gushed over it, then flooded it. I closed my eyes.

God.

My God.

When I opened them again, I saw it was Bragadin's turn. The executioner brought his blade down close to the captain's head, without cutting it off. A stream of urine ran into the dust. The janissaries sniggered. Another blow through the air, for the entertainment of the troops, and then two crisp blows close together. Off came Bragadin's ears. Where they had been, two red gouts of blood ran down his neck. The captain fell to the ground, writhing.

I felt my gorge rising. I gripped Ismail's arm again and forced him to look at me.

"Stop him! Talk to him! He'll listen to you."

He didn't even seem to hear me, lost as he was in his own nightmares.

I cursed and moved off, trying to get to the general, but one of his guards obstructed my path, his lance held across my chest. "I demand mercy for the prisoner," I said.

Lala Mustafa looked as if he wanted to incinerate me. For a moment I was worried that he would pass the same sentence on me.

"I represent Yossef Nasi, and I can guarantee that this man's life will be redeemed in gold."

Mustafa seemed amused by my offer and allowed me to approach him. "A ransom, you mean? How much do you think his life might be worth?"

I stood in front of him. "You set the amount."

He laughed and clicked his tongue. "Inform your master that not everything can be bought with gold. There are prices that are paid in blood." Before I could reply, Ismail's voice came from behind me.

"Lala Mustafa Pasha, listen to me." The old man stood firmly, almost without needing to rely on his stick. He had stirred himself and was coming to my aid. "Kill this man and he won't be Vercingetorix, he will be Leonidas," he said. "Do you want Famagusta to be the Thermopylae of the Sultan's army? Remember that the Christian fleet might already be on its way. Don't defy destiny. Send this wretch home and let the ships weigh anchor. The glory is yours."

Mustafa remained silent for a long time, meditating on these words, and I convinced myself that we would move him. *As a shepherd saves from the lion's mouth only two leg bones or a piece of an ear, so will the Israelites be saved.* The words of Amos rushed into my mind, loudly, and at terrible speed.

The general was about to utter his verdict when shouts and cheers rose up from the edges of the encampment. A little tide of men had begun to move toward the city. The looters had found a gap, and rumor of it was spreading rapidly. The janissary officer turned toward Lala Mustafa, waiting for orders, but the general said nothing.

"Stop them, my lord," I pleaded. "You can do it. It will be a massacre."

He, too, turned to look toward Famagusta. "A massacre, you say? Look down there. Fifty thousand Turks are lying on the battlefield because of this man's pride." He pointed to Bragadin, kneeling on the ground, drenched in blood. "He is to blame for everything." He turned to Ismail. "You are right. I won't kill him. I will go on making him die. He will never be a Leonidas, because I will make a puppet of him, a figure of universal mockery."

The officer of the janissaries was still waiting for the signal to make the soldiers intervene, but Lala said not a word. He withdrew to his tent. It was more than a retreat; it was the clearest order to break ranks. Now anything could happen.

I tried to find a prayer, just to know whether I had one left in my mind.

Ismail gave me a shake. "You want to do something? Then run."

"What are you saying?"

"Go on!" he exploded. "Fly to the Venetian ships. Tell them to set sail immediately!"

As he pushed me away, he whistled. Hafiz and Mukhtar came running, and kept running at my side. Because almost without noticing it I had started running with all the speed I had.

For the words of Amos.

For the Israelites, whoever they might be.

For those who could still be saved.

9.

The dust rose up in the streets of Famagusta, stirred by the wind and by people's footsteps. Only the blood-drenched ground was undisturbed by our passage. Ismail's words rang in my mind. I prayed to the Almighty that we would get there in time.

Turning a corner, we bumped into the disorderly troops. They were dragging away a broken door, furniture of little value, brass candlesticks, pieces of cloth. We faced each other in silence. Two young women and an old man were being kicked out of the door, their pursuers on their heels. The hubbub of the soldiers died down when they saw us. I caught the eye of one of them. The looter pointed at us with the tip of a knife.

"You. Find another house, this stuff is ours."

I trembled with rage and counted them in silence. There were more of them than of us. Hafiz touched my arm and gestured to me to go. We moved cautiously, giving them a wide berth, amid the sniggers and insults of the mob.

As we hurried toward the port, I trod in a pool of pitch. My feet stuck as I tried to run; I risked losing my shoes with every step. The ground, drenched in death, wouldn't let me go.

We reached the port. As if the walls that separated it from the city enclosed another world, a dazzling calm lay upon the water and the ships, the quays and the distant sea rocks.

The sun beat down, and the only shade to be found was on the water, beside the bulk of the ships, but no one was able to enjoy it. I walked over to a *mahona* that was laden to bursting, and still a line of men, like processionary caterpillars, was loading barrels, cases, wooden planks, bales of cotton. One was herding animals that had somehow survived against the odds. Goats, most of them. The pigs, unclean animals, had been killed and left to rot, along with the carcasses of many poor human wretches.

On the deck were men who looked as if they might be Venetian. I shouted, cupping my hands around the sides of my mouth.

"Weigh anchor, as quickly as you can! There's no time for more!"

Some of them leaned forward, craning their necks, demonstrating that they hadn't heard. The wind was blowing in my direction.

"Go, I tell you. Force your captains, you're in the majority."

A man shouted back, his voice carried clearly on the wings of the wind.

"We can't sail these ships on our own. Not many of us are seamen. Who are you? Why would a Turk and two Moors be worried about our fate?"

"I used to be a Venetian, and I tell you that you must go, right now. If you see no way, try and come up with something." The men looked at me in alarm, and then started talking excitedly to one another.

Mukhtar called my name. I had heard her voice very seldom, and was surprised, as if I'd been caught doing something wrong. Her eyes glittered, the color of honey. She pointed toward the fort that the Turks had built on the hill behind the port to check the embarkations.

A yelling mob was approaching. Armed men were also coming from the citadel side, a human landslide down the side of a mountain.

I drew my dagger and started cutting the hawsers that secured the ships to their moorings. Hafiz helped me with swift blows of his sword, running along the dock. I picked up a long pole, and together we tried to push the boat away from the shore.

The ship moved, and the gangway connecting the deck to the quay fell in the water with a great splash, but the vessel was too heavy and could not get under way.

Mukhtar called out again. As when a great galley bursts into flames in the quay the rats run along the hawsers to the dock, so the mob hurtled down from the citadel and attacked the ships, one by one, gradually drawing nearer to the place where we were standing. On the fort side, the charging men moved more slowly, and they still had a long way to come. The men on the deck of the *mahona* ran shouting towards the stern. They had worked out at last what fate awaited them.

I gesticulated and shouted at them again to leave, before Hafiz dragged me away, forcing me to turn my back on what was about to happen.

We climbed back up toward one of the minor access routes leading to the city. The Greeks who had decided to stay were being carried out of their houses. The screams of the women subjected to the law of the victors echoed heartrendingly from one house to the other. But many rapes occurred in the light of the sun, in the middle of the road. There was nothing we could do, and our knees buckled in despair.

Suddenly, behind a gap in a wall, we came upon a little boy. He was quivering, crouching like a rabbit, his face covered with dust, his clothes in rags.

Mukhtar held out her open hand. The boy shrank back and pressed himself even harder against the wall. I spoke Italian to comfort him. "Don't be afraid."

Lost, the little boy looked round. He must have been six or seven. Emaciated, eyes wide, skin diaphanous, almost spectral. He must have been in hiding for months.

"Hands off. This booty is ours," a voice croaked.

They had emerged from an alleyway, a dozen sinister faces. I recognized the man who had pointed at me in the distance with the tip of his blade. I threw myself between them and the little boy, my dagger in my fist. Hafiz bent his knees and drew his saber.

Mukhtar unlaced something under the sash around her waist. It was the weapon that I had seen glittering in Bandirma.

The looters were startled by the tangle of blades whirling toward them. A cascade of blades descended, and the blood spurted vividly. They laid hands on their weapons, but before they could draw, one of them was struck by Hafiz's curved saber. The young warrior moved like a beast of prey, crouching down on his legs.

The man who had spoken hurled himself at me. I parried, our blades giving off a grim clang. I tried to kick him in the belly; he repelled the blow. Then he tried to circle me to grab the child, and I brought down my dagger on his outstretched hand. He drew back with an animal cry, blood splashing his leather jerkin. He shouted something at those of his companions who were still capable of fighting, and they began to arrange themselves in a circle around us. The child's body trembled, leaning against mine.

We heard a shot, then another. The leader of the gang fell forward, followed by one of his companions. The circle of enemies opened up, spewing insults and curses.

I saw Ismail, his pistols still smoking, then Ali, his unsheathed scimitar flashing in the sun's rays, dealing murderous blows to any looters who came within range. The others scattered like jackals at the arrival of a lion.

I picked up the little boy, who clung to me with all the strength he had, and we hurried toward the beach. Only when we were outside the city did we stop to catch our breath. From a distance, we saw the horde attacking the last of the ships, the one we had urged to leave. It had managed to pull away from the quay, but not to take to the sea. The looters held it back with ropes and grapnels, and were climbing up the plank. In a furious voice, Ismail gave us an order.

"Let's go. There's nothing we can do here now."

10.

A massacre calls for revenge. Murder cries out for murder. Man washes out with innocent blood the blood the guilty shed, until a horrendous stain spreads over the earth.

After our failure to stop the carnage, after the sacking of the ships, Ismail withdrew into silence. We waited for the order that would allow us to leave the port, but Lala Mustafa had other things to do: tyrannize and humiliate Bragadin. He had had him shoved and kicked to the southern side of the walls, where the last attacks had taken place, and ordered him to fill the breeches opened by the cannon. The plain was still scattered with corpses; the stench reached our nostrils even on the ship. Bragadin shoveled and mixed, tortured by a pointless task, with black crusts where his ears had once been.

Lala Mustafa wasn't thinking about the ships on the Beach of the Gardens. He was thinking about pushing that exhausted man all the way down to the port and having him tied to the main yard of a galley. Then he planned to hoist him aloft, again and again, onto the stern of a *kadirga*, so that he could await the arrival of the Christian fleet on the horizon.

"So, Captain. No ship in sight?"

Better check again, and again, amid the shouts, laughter and insults.

Lala Mustafa wasn't thinking about us, the emissaries of one of the commanders of the venture. He was thinking of leaving this man, defeated and betrayed, in a tent, untended, with his wounds infected and flies buzzing around his head.

In the days that followed, a funereal calm fell upon the city and its surroundings, reduced now to misery. Men cling to life with all their might; they are like flowers or weeds that put down roots in the sparse soil on the rim of a ravine and hope that the next storm won't carry them off. The Greeks who remained in the city were trying to resume the course of their own lives, trusting that their new master would, in a time of peace, show a face less terrible than the one he wore in a time of war.

I was counting the days. What I really wanted was to leave the island. My soul was torn: on the one hand, what I had seen prevented me from feeling victorious in any way. The triumph I had been waiting for was a gimlet that pierced my heart. On the other hand, it was a start. The next generation would inherit a Kingdom.

Such reflections were pale attempts to heal my soul. I had never imagined a massacre on such a scale, and yet my eyes had seen it.

The little boy never spoke his name. Not to me, at least. I tried to talk to him on a few occasions, but he sat huddled under the ladder of the fo'c'sle, and wouldn't let anyone near him. Hafiz and Mukhtar took care of him; they brought him food and water, which he accepted without a word. The young man's presence in particular seemed to calm him; with Hafiz he was less wary. Coming down the steps, I sometimes spotted a pair of gleaming eyes, and thought of the burden of suffering that their owner had already been forced to carry.

It was a fate common to all of us. Everyone on board was facing up to the tragedy in his own way. I saw the Indian siblings, their faces weary, performing the rites of the Muslim faith. I, too, tried to pray, in my heart. But the words wouldn't come.

Ali prayed with the Indians, but his way of approaching God took a different form as well. In the shade of a bulwark, he sat ceaselessly repeating a formula. One day I asked him how it was that what he had seen didn't seem to have touched him.

He replied that, on the contrary, his heart was in mourning. All the people who had died or suffered deserved to be remembered. God was the master of righteousness.

"My old *shayk* took the words of the Prophet seriously: 'Go and seek knowledge, even if it's in China.' He traveled for years, beyond the boundaries of the Umma, the world run by the Muslims. In a place of idolaters, he had met a wise man and exchanged thoughts with him. God, He who embraces all things, could not have left those people completely deprived of his light."

A shadow passed across Ali's face.

"So the wise old man said to my *shayk*: hope and fear are like two thieves trying to slip into a house. Have you understood, my friend, what the house represents?"

I shook my head. Ali picked up the thread. "The house is man's conscience. If they find it full, the thieves will steal. If they find it empty, they are forced to leave."

Perhaps my keenness of mind had been dulled by the last events that I had seen, but I wasn't sure I had understood. I asked, "How did you interpret the story?"

Ali paused, then continued. "My only fear is to be displeasing in the eyes of God. My only hope is to be pleasing in his eyes. Other than that, my house is empty."

It was the last moral fable that Ali ever told me.

The next day, they brought Bragadin into the main square. His face was swollen, the remains of his ears reduced to rotting stumps. They kicked and

shoved him to the column. Two renegades undertook the task of torturing him; one of them was said to be Genoese. I saw him talking to the victim, but I didn't catch the words. The hubbub and the shouted insults subsided. Silence fell on the square.

The Genoese ran the blade of a big knife from one shoulder to the other, behind the head Marcantonio Bragadin.

They say he didn't scream.

They lie.

The Genoese and his assistant, with meticulous slowness, flayed the man. First his back, then his arms and legs, then his trunk and his chest, peeling the fat from his skin. The rector screamed, struggled and tugged at his bonds. Flies settled on his living flesh.

My companions and I couldn't take our eyes off him.

The rector was spared the sight of his own skin flapping off in front of his eyes. His head sank long before that.

The Genoese and his assistant put the man's skin in salt and then in vinegar. They stuffed it well with straw and cotton. They sewed up the pieces. They put two mother-of-pearl buttons where the eyes should have been. When the puppet that had once been Bragadin was finished, they dressed it the clothes of a magistrate, the ones he had worn on the day of the surrender. They sat it on a cow, protecting it from the sun with a little parasol. They sent it off among the streets of the city, so that even those who had escaped the horror in the square might see it.

Then they butchered the flayed body and scattered the pieces all around the walls.

11.

At last we were granted permission to leave the port. We took to the sea and never looked back. Opposing winds and a rough sea slowed our return. The ship struggled, apparently running through a medium denser than water. Men and things were empty, transparent, bubbles blown by a glass maker, mirages. Famagusta had attached itself to my soul as a long piece of seaweed does to your legs when you're walking on a beach.

During the days of the journey I exchanged few words with Ismail or my other companions. I had the captain assign me the tasks required to keep body and mind occupied, so that I could do nothing but gaze straight ahead when it came to reporting what I had seen, and demanding an explanation for it.

One day, when we were about halfway through our journey, I saw the little boy smiling at a silly face that Hafiz had made. I stood and watched the scene, to snatch some of the light given off by the two of them.

"You saved one."

Ismail was beside me, although I hadn't noticed him.

"Just one," I replied.

The old man nodded.

"It was what you were able to do, and that's what counts."

Yedikule, the village of tanners and slaughterhouse men, greeted me in its own way, announcing the proximity of the capital, just as it had done on the day when I first arrived. Less than two years had passed since then.

The day was gray, the sky milky. A cold wind came down from the Black Sea, the kind that heralds the end of summer.

When we disembarked, I knew that Ismail wouldn't follow me to Palazzo Belvedere.

"We've got to talk to him," I said to the old man.

"You know what you must do. I have finished here." He adjusted his bag on his shoulder and set off, followed by the others, in search of a boat for Scutari. Hafiz was holding the child by the hand.

Yossef Nasi welcomed me with a hug. "Welcome back, my brother. There's no hurry. Have a rest now; we will have time to talk."

David Gomez greeted me warmly, though with a certain awkwardness. The map of the New Kingdom was still spread out on the table, the wine-stain faded but still visible.

"Famagusta has fallen," I said.

Nasi replied that he knew. Many rumors had arrived ahead of me. He used the word *victory*.

"At what price, Yossef?"

Fields plundered and devastated until not a blade of grass remained.

Rivers of blood.

A vast cemetery all around the town.

As I advanced through the story, I saw Nasi's face darkening. Gomez looked at the floor. I continued undaunted. "Our ally Lala Mustafa revealed himself to be a bloodthirsty lunatic."

I told them about the violation of the treaties, the captains slaughtered just as they surrendered. About the Venetians pulled off their ships and enslaved, about the city sacked by dogs and murderers. Last of all, I told him of the torture reserved for Rector Bragadin, leaving nothing out, not a single detail. So I reached the end of my story, the empty, stunned expression of that terrible puppet still in front of my eyes.

Nasi cursed between his teeth. He looked as distraught as I felt. Gomez clenched his jaw, his face pale.

"Are these the foundations of the New Zion?" I asked. "Slaughter, torture and shame?" I didn't expect a reply, so I continued. "One day you said you wanted to heal the world, and I certainly didn't expect the suture to be painless. But now the wound is bigger than it was before, and infected, and I don't see what could cure it."

Yossef Nasi sat supporting his bearded chin with the fingers of his right hand. David Gomez shook his head in disbelief, muttering to himself. In that same room we had praised the courage of the defenders of Famagusta. Now magnanimity was only a memory.

"Marcantonio Bragadin was a fanatic," said Nasi. "He sacrificed everything to his own pride. If he had surrendered six months ago, none of this would have happened. Nonetheless, I shall say this to you, Manuel: There isn't a kingdom on earth that hasn't been born from the blood of the conquered. The first furrow in Rome was watered by an act of fratricide. The Lord's hand helped our forefathers to scatter and annihilate the people of Canaan. Their cities were destroyed and the inhabitants put to the sword."

I clenched my fists until my hands hurt. "At least our forefathers took the land themselves. They knew what they were doing, and they carried the weight of the dead on their own shoulders. We carried out our massacres through the janissaries, heedless of the evil that would come."

Yossef's voice assumed a feverish tone. "Manuel, Manuel, in a hundred years none of the young people of Cyprus will give the slightest importance to what happened. From today, this war is over. Our kingdom is the future. The future of all our people. I expect a summons to the Seraglio very shortly. Will you be with me?"

I didn't reply. I felt the need to go outside, to be in the open air. I reached

the garden and walked down the avenue, as I hadn't done for months. When I reached the little clearing surrounded by bushes, I stopped and sat down on the grass. A circle of disturbed and barren earth still marked the place where the carob tree had grown.

It was there that Nasi found me. He sat down next to me, to contemplate the same empty space. He gripped my shoulder to give me courage, but I had the impression that he was the one clinging to me.

He asked me about Ismail, about his reactions to what we had seen and experienced on Cyprus. I replied that the old man had saved my life. It was only thanks to him that I had come back.

"Gracia didn't call him back in vain," he observed. "May the Lord bless him."

12.

A sense of something imminent wore away at the hours, one after the other, from dawn till dusk, and again during the night, as we waited for the call from the Sultan. Instead, unexpectedly, we received one from the Grand Vizier.

Sokollu had never invited Nasi to a private meeting, and the novelty took us by surprise. Nasi asked Gomez to take charge of Palazzo Belvedere and wait there for news from the Seraglio. I would be the one who went with him to the audience. I was struck by that reversal of roles, and perhaps it didn't leave Nasi's trusted companion indifferent either.

Before I went out to join the boat, Gomez held me back. His olive face looked worried. "Stay close to him," he said. "You and I are the only people he can still trust."

I instinctively looked toward the east.

"There is one other. But he can't help this time."

Then I left him. I was about to meet the Giant again, and the thought didn't make me feel any calmer. I climbed aboard the boat, and Nasi gave the order to set sail. We crossed the Golden Horn without exchanging a word and continued toward the Grand Vizier's palace.

A page escorted us to the meeting rooms, watched over by armed men. We were introduced into a drawing room perfumed with incense and sandalwood. The Grand Vizier wore a dark green caftan and a white turban. Even when he was sitting down it was impossible not to notice his stature, which was such as to make the room around him look small. Beside him, at the desk, there was a short, slender man holding a roll of parchment under his nose, so long that it spilled over the edge of the table and covered his feet.

After the ritual pieties, the Grand Vizier congratulated us on the favorable outcome of the military expedition to Cyprus. Then he introduced the little man, who turned out to be the imperial Treasurer, and ordered him to read out the list of war expenses.

The parchment was rolled up again, and we listened in silence to the litany read out in the man's croaking voice. It began with the 54,206 fallen soldiers of the Turkish army. It continued with the sunken ships; the number of injured, the cost of their treatments and the overall days of illness; the number of animals lost during the campaign; the pieces of damaged artillery; the exploded ammunition and the drams of black powder; the arrows fired; the *cantari* of food and wood consumed. He went on to list the tents that had

been lost, the carts, even the wheels that had been damaged or broken during the year of siege. As the parchment unfolded at the treasurer's feet, that mountain of men, animals and objects became visible and grew in front of our eyes, reaching the sky, tottering like a monstrous pyramid built with the most diverse materials. The last expense listed was two million nails.

After which, silence.

Mehmet Sokollu didn't lose his old seraphic air for a minute. He merely welcomed the end of the list with a tilt of one side of his mouth. "Good. Very good. At the end of the day, Nasi Bey, your financial contribution to the Cyprus campaign covers only a tenth of what the imperial exchequer has spent on the venture. By our estimation, maintaining its current tribute to the empire, it will take Cyprus five hundred and two years to repay the entire sum." He allowed himself a moment to observe our reactions. I tried not to let mine show, though I had a knot in my throat and my hands were trembling.

Sokollu continued in the same calm, irritating voice, "I just wanted to inform you, so that in case you were to receive from our Sultan, the shadow of God on earth, the ruling of the island, you might act accordingly."

He paused again before continuing, "Although the military campaign has achieved its purpose, the war is not yet over. Our fleet is gathering at the mouth of the Adriatic to confront the Christian threat. The ships of the so-called Holy League are in the port of Messina, waiting to head toward the East. It's a considerable fleet, captained by an intrepid young man, Don John of Austria, Philip II's brother-in-law. Before putting himself at the head of their crusade, he showed his mettle by massacring the Muslims of Spain. Personally, I would have liked to send an expedition to their aid, but our navies were all busy with preparations for Cyprus." He let us savor the poison of his words. "I think that man was spoiling for a fight. There are Spanish, Genoese, Pontifical, Maltese and especially Venetian galleys under his banners. The only ones missing are the French and Polish, our good allies." He turned toward the treasurer. "We can consider ourselves lucky that England is no longer a power faithful to the pope and can't use this war as a pretext to poke its nose into the Mediterranean, don't you think?"

The little man chuckled, as my blood turned to ice. Why this reference to the English? Not so much as an accent in that man's voice was squandered at random. I noticed Nasi's unease; he too, like me, was busy trying to catch every nuance of the speech.

Sokollu went on speaking. "I do not doubt that our Muezzinzade Ali Pasha, with the help of God the Powerful, the Vengeful, will be able to stand up to the infidels and chase them back to where they came from."

He accompanied his words by raising his hand in a sign of reverence toward God. For a moment he seemed to be holding back a thought, as if he were jealous of it, and then he released it with ostentatious indifference.

"A shame we can't always face the Venetians on dry land, where the

superiority of our army is devastating. Their power lies in their fleet." He leaned forward slightly from his chair. "So we will postpone our accounts until we have also defeated their floating fortress," he concluded. "*As-Salaam 'Alaykum*, gentlemen."

The audience was over. No provision had been made for us to speak; he hadn't even had the intention to talk to Nasi. He had just informed us of how things were. He had put us in check with a simple calculation of expenses.

I thought that on paper Sokollu was on the losing side; after all, Cyprus had fallen. And yet he seemed sure of himself, and we appeared before him silent and with no chance of appealing his verdict, just as we had before Selim.

"He knows about the agreement with the English," I said, as we left the palace, heading toward the Golden Horn.

Nasi looked at me grimly. "He has suspicions and wants to put salt on our tails."

"Suspicions? You mean spies. Yossef, in your house . . ."

"Reyna doesn't know anything," Nasi interrupted me irritably. "It is certainly no secret that Ralph Fitch is my guest."

"Why do you trust her?"

The city passed slowly around us.

"She has done her duty by our family. She married me."

I cursed under my breath. I had very bad presentiments: I was sure there was more trouble to come. "We're missing something, Yossef."

"That's true," he admitted. "Sokollu is keeping me at a distance from Selim. He wants to convince him that Cyprus was a bad business. But the Sultan still needs me."

"Cyprus was madness," I said.

He didn't reply. I watched him from the corner of my eye, regretting having spoken.

For the first time, that great Jew struck me as alone and vulnerable.

13.

Hafiz and Mukhtar were washing their hands in the fountain. They flashed me a shy smile. A little way off, Ali finished his prayers, then got to his feet and rolled up his *sajjada*. They were here for their last farewell.

I had a great lump in my throat, and however much I tried to swallow, I couldn't get rid of it. In the whirlwind of my life, I hadn't had the time to understand, and it was only now that I realized, what they had become for me.

The people you go through hell with are friends.

The people you escape from hell with are friends.

These were my friends, and I would never see them again.

The bags were piled up in a corner of the drawing room. They covered the far edge of the mosaic: Sinai, Suez, the beginning of the Red Sea. I wondered if it was a coincidence or if they'd put them there for good luck. Among the bags and bundles sat the little boy. He looked less lost than he had on the day of the crossing.

Finally I saw Ismail. He was contemplating the portrait of Donna Gracia, as he had been the day I met him.

"So you're returning to Mokha," I said to his back. "It won't be easy to look at Scutari from the window, and think that Ismail and his friends aren't there any more."

"The center of the empire isn't a place for someone like me," he replied even before he turned round. "I'm going back to where I can be useful."

I approached, and we stood face to face.

"So you've had the confirmation you were looking for."

"I've had it, but I hadn't come here to look for it. I only tried to accept an invitation and honor a debt. I arrived too late."

"Perhaps we all arrived too late."

"Or too early, who knows. Perhaps men like Yossef look too far back, and see too far ahead. The present will always be a cage, for them and for the people who follow them."

Ali had joined him. They said nothing more, but I understood their mute request.

"I can't leave Yossef. Not now that things are taking a turn for the worse. He's done a lot for me. He killed Emanuele De Zante, and saved Manuel Cardoso."

Perhaps Ismail still had something to say, or perhaps he didn't. A servant arrived and told us that Yossef was waiting in the library. Our last conversation ended with my name.

Limping, the old man made for the bags. I saw him picking up a bundle and putting it under his arm. A few moments later, he slipped through the doorway to the library. I was left on my own next to Ali. Hafiz and Mukhtar looked at each other in silence. Then Mukhtar spoke. In Turkish, so that I, too, would understand.

"Ali, tell them the story of the *khalifa* and the parasites."

"Yes, tell it," her brother joined in.

Ali looked at the girl. "You tell it, Mukhtar. Our friend is fed up with the sound of my voice."

The warrior hesitated. "I'm not very good at telling stories."

"That's like saying you're not good at breathing."

"You have a lovely voice, Mukhtar," her brother said. Mukhtar blushed slightly and a cheerful smile appeared on her face. She drew a deep breath, and a minute later I witnessed a transformation. The creature I had seen dancing and killing, but from whose lips I had heard only a few syllables, began telling the story, backing it up with expressive gestures.

"One fine day, a *khalifa* encounters a group of men, all sitting doing nothing. He asks them who they are, and they reply, 'We're the ones who trust in the will of God. He, the Merciful and the Compassionate, will support us, because we have faith in Him.' 'You're just lazy parasites!' the *khalifa* says, shaking his fist in the face of the one who spoke. 'For people like you, I feel only disgust.' 'Why are you talking so harshly?' asks the one who spoke. 'He who has faith in God,' the *khalifa* explains, 'first plants seeds in the ground, and only then does he trust to His will.'"

Mukhtar declaimed the last phrase, gave the hint of a bow, then raised her head.

"And here ends the story."

"Thank you, Mukhtar," I said.

The idea came as an impulse. I rummaged in my pocket and took them out, the least expected objects. The dice carved at the mouth of the Po. I put them in Mukhtar's hand, an incongruous destination.

Mukhtar showed them to the others. Ali looked at the twelve faces, the Roman numerals I, V, III . . . "The Book prohibits games of chance," he said.

"Games of chance are over. I no longer consign myself to fate with my eyes closed."

Then I pointed to the tiny figure of the little boy, in the middle of the bundles. "What will become of him?"

"We'll take him with us," Ali replied.

"We've got another brother now," Hafiz added.

The little boy looked at us with confusion, as if he had understood that we were talking about him. I silently wished him good luck. I exchanged hugs with the others and started toward the door.

My throat tightened as I crossed the threshold. I swallowed hard, and it was right then that the tears started flowing.

14.

Many autumns before the Hejira, during the migration toward the hot lands, a family of ducks had taken a break on the waters of a river on the borders of Absurdistan. All the local animals had their own territory, and the ducks hadn't had time to settle anywhere before a snake or a frog came to reclaim the place and chase them away. The poor birds were about to resume their journey without settling again, when they saw a big tree trunk floating on the water. It was green with algae and moss, and because no one claimed it, the ducks chose it as their resting place, quacking contentedly, but immediately afterward they began arguing about who should occupy the most comfortable positions. They were so busily engaged in their disputes that only one of them saw the tree trunk open its mouth wide, but he didn't have time to escape. A moment later he and all his fellows ended up in the belly of the crocodile.

Gomez wasn't there to distill the words of the storyteller Meddah Masun for me, in the *kahvehane* on the Golden Horn where I had spent many afternoons, while I was still getting to know the capital of the empire. The Egyptian Yassir and a friend of his from Bursa tried to translate and explain, but I hadn't come to listen to fables about animals.

After Ismail and his friends left, I went back to walking the streets of the city, and Galata in particular, to listen to rumors and pick up information, the only medicine I knew to cure my obsession, the sense of loss that lurked in my soul, the suspicion that I was irremediably missing something.

I had frequented that café while waiting for my audience at the Divan, my first encounter with the Giant. Now I was coming back, after seeing him for a second time, and it was that old Bosnian who dominated my thoughts.

Sokollu Mehmet Pasha. I couldn't help thinking that the presumption with which he had received us, reeling off figures and reminding us that the war wasn't over, contained a threat. Since the day of our meeting, that suspicion had never left me. Every tiny detail I encountered spoke to me of him, reflected his face, like a skillfully positioned little mirror. Even the story about the ducks related by the storyteller.

The migrating birds were us, the Jews, the wandering people. The rotten tree trunk on which we would settle was Cyprus. Yossef Nasi was in search of a kingdom, and he had instead been presented with a list of debts. In seeking his island of vines and olives, he had financed its sacking and destruction.

Lala Mustafa and Piyale Pasha had also settled on it, in search of redemption for their defeat in Malta, but they had found only a Pyrrhic victory.

Cyprus had drained the imperial coffers. Now the grand admiral Muezzinzade Ali Pasha was preparing to face the Christian fleet, with the support of the Grand Vizier.

All of Sokollu's political adversaries were engaged in an expensive conflict whose outcome was uncertain. They had wanted it, craved for it, in the face of all his resistance. Now all they could do was take it to its conclusion. Just like me.

Sokollu knew this. He had let us all embroil ourselves in the fate of the military venture, and now he was waiting for the test of truth on the surface of the water.

He was the crocodile and I was the bird who saw him opening his mouth too late.

However, Muezzinzade Ali could still crush the Christians and consolidate the expensive victory of Cyprus. In that case, Yossef Nasi might yet have a hope of getting back into Selim's good graces and being readmitted to his presence.

According to reliable sources, the Sultan now had more ships than the Holy League. A little Ottoman boat with black sails had infiltrated the port of Messina at night and recorded that aside from the war galleys, the Christians had all kinds of vessels on the roads, anything that was fit to sail, even eleven Venetian galleasses. Venice had decided to put those clumsy giants back in the water, a choice that seemed strange to me.

But superiority of numbers might be meaningless. The Persian wars would have taught them that. Xerxes's army, the biggest of all time, had lost against little Greece and . . .

I felt a shock; my thoughts began rearranging and channeling themselves into a new direction. In Famagusta, Ismail had compared Bragadin to Leonidas.

After defeating the sovereign of Sparta, the Persians had faced the Athenian Themistocles. Thermopylae had been followed by the battle of Salamis. Xerxes's fleet was destroyed in that stretch of water. Themistocles lured them into the straits, where the skill of the Persian and Phoenician pilots proved to be useless. He allowed himself to be pursued there, pretending to abandon camp, before launching his surprise attack. Deception had been the key to victory. The Athenian *wooden walls* had resisted, as predicted by Apollo through the mouth of the Pythia.

I wondered which oracle Sokollu had consulted, which priestesses. I thought of the women, of the whirl of messages that flowed along an invisible bridge between Constantinople and Venice.

I picked up the kettle in front of me and poured hot water on the tea leaves at the bottom of my cup. I had had enough coffee, and the hubbub of my reflections was enough to keep me awake. I remembered the kettle in Takiyuddin's office, the one that turned the spit with its puffs of steam. Man can come up with strange machines. I remembered Nasi's quip: "Would you ever have thought that a kettle could roast chickens?"

I watched Yassir and his friend talking to each other and realized that I wasn't being the best dinner companion. I kept quiet, drinking my tea and pursuing abstruse lines of thought. Then I excused myself, left some coins on the table and went outside.

It wasn't yet dark, and Galata was already filling up with noisy crowds. I crossed the Golden Horn by the usual caïque and started to climb the imperial road. The Old City was more silent and tranquil, apart from the packs of dogs wandering about the gardens and alleyways.

I arrived near the hippodrome, where I had seen the army filing past as they left for Cyprus. I remembered the huge bombard that had closed the parade. The symbol of the power of Turkish fire, forged by a Christian engineer in 1453. It was said that Orban had offered his services first to the Byzantine emperor and after being refused had turned to Mehmed II, who without demur had agreed to finance the work. The frightened features of Anton Varadian, the Armenian I met in Venice, assembled themselves in my mind. He, too, had passed from one side to the other. Before establishing himself on the lagoon, he had served the Sultan. Craftsmen care little for the destinies of states, or for faith: They go wherever they will find a patron willing to subsidize their craft. Just so, Takiyuddin had moved to Constantinople because the Sultan wanted to put him under his protection and finance his contraptions. I smiled to myself, thinking again of his incredible kettle.

A moment later I stopped in the middle of the street, transfixed by a thought, oblivious of the passersby who were hurrying home.

Who would come up with the idea of using a kettle to make anything but tea? A man of ingenuity. An engineer. Varadian had left Constantinople because the Turks weren't willing to finance his experiments.

"Don't undervalue machines," Nasi had said when I arrived at Palazzo Belvedere. The phrase started buzzing incessantly around in my head. I noticed a mangy dog sniffing my leg, gave it a kick and started walking again, retracing my steps. Faster, this time, following the rhythm of my thoughts.

Varadian carried out experiments at the Lido. I had seen them. He was studying ways of making cannons more stable at the moment of firing. It was his obsession.

What had Fitch said when introducing his cannon? I tried to remember. His words were there, in my trained mind, and I just had to find them.

"You could arm a whole fleet with them, if it weren't for the recoil that prevents their being used on ships."

The recoil. The backward momentum of discharge. A cannon needs space, exactly what is missing on ships. The Turks aren't interested in that. The Turks venerate the Big Cannon, they want huge pieces of artillery, to be used on the ground, to blow out the bellies of fortresses.

But the Venetians are interested in recoil. "Their power lies in the fleet." Sokollu's voice quickened my pace still further, merging with Nasi's: "Where the force of an army can't reach, ingenuity can."

15.

I knocked vigorously until the door opened and I found myself face to face with Ralph Fitch. For once I hadn't tracked him down to the palace library, but had gone straight up to his room, at the end of one of the corridors on the first floor.

He greeted me, a little surprised by this sudden visit, and ushered me in. We sat down at a little tea table and he asked me if I would like something to drink. When I refused, he understood that something was troubling me and started listening. I knew him as a keen-minded man, and I knew that I could talk to him with the same candor that I expected from him. "I need your expert knowledge about artillery."

He smiled disarmingly, stroking his red moustache. "I am a merchant, Signor Cardoso. My interest in artillery is merely commercial."

"Nonetheless, I think you can be useful to me," I insisted. "In Takiyuddin's laboratory you said that because of the recoil, heavy cannons can't be used on ships. I'd like you to explain that idea to me in greater detail."

Fitch filled a beaker of wine. He sipped it, then set the glass down on the table and then seemed to forget it was there. He said, "That's easy. You see, normally on a war galley the cannons are on the stern and prow quarterdecks, and they fire when the enemy prepares to ram. Other guns can be placed on hanging decks along the broadsides, above the banks of oarsmen. But space is very tight, and obviously it's only possible to put little *pedreros* and falconets on them, since the recoil of larger calibers would cause the gun to fall back on the lower deck, and the oarsmen would be crushed."

I already had my next question lined up.

"So if someone found a way to reduce the recoil of cannons, larger calibers could also be put along the side?"

He raised an eyebrow, mulling over the hypothesis. "I suppose so. But that would require a great deal of very broad and solid hanging decks." He seemed to meditate on his own words, then added, "No galley of that size exists."

I leaned on the table.

"Let us imagine for a moment that it does exist. What kind of ship would it be?"

Fitch picked up his glass and sipped from it again. At last he replied, in the voice of someone explaining the obvious, "A massive, overladen ship, very difficult to maneuver." He paused for a moment, then added, "Have you ever heard of *Great Harry*? She was a slow behemoth that rarely plowed the waves.

I'm sure that vessels like that were never seen in this part of the Mediterranean. In any case, if I were to encounter a monster of that ilk, I would stay well away from it. It would be a kind of . . ." He sought the right words. "Floating fortress."

He must have read the puzzlement on my face, because he quickly asked me if I hadn't perhaps changed my mind, and whether I didn't feel the need to drink something.

This time I accepted his offer. I allowed the wine to sweeten my mouth as I tried to stay calm. *Floating fortress*. The same expression used by Sokollu. Except that now it was more than a colorful metaphor.

A whole wing of the Venice Arsenal had been dedicated to refurbishing the galleasses. A whole wing just to patch up the cargo ships that in wartime are used to transport food and ammunition, or to crowd arquebusiers into. Huge three-masters. Extremely heavy and immobile. Apparently harmless. But find a way of filling them with cannons, and you've turned an old kettle into a roasting jack.

16.

Night had fallen by the time I reached Nasi's bedroom, on the other side of the palace. He greeted me with a candelabra in his hand, and the worried expression of someone receiving a visit at an unexpected hour. He was dressed in a shirt and a pair of breeches in the European style. The only other light in the room was a candle on the desk, which illuminated a long goose quill and a sheet of paper. I hadn't woken him, then. I glanced at the big four-poster bed on the other side of the room, and it seemed to be still made up.

"I've got to talk to you."

He looked exhausted, his face weary, as if he hadn't slept for days. He beckoned me to follow him to the window and set the candelabra down on the windowsill.

"I'm listening."

Words seem very slow when thoughts are clambering over each other.

"This war is a big trick. We thought Sokollu was plotting to thwart it, we rejoiced when we managed to unmask him, and yet it was he who ensnared us in his plan."

I waited in vain for a reaction. "Sokollu knew he couldn't stop the war," I went on. "The other viziers wanted redemption for the humiliating defeat of Malta, Selim wanted a military triumph to demonstrate that he was a match for his father. And you wanted a Jewish kingdom. Sokollu understood that the war would be an opportunity to defeat all his adversaries with a single blow. He was the one who said so. The taking of Cyprus has already proven to be half a disaster. If the Ottoman fleet were defeated, the disaster would be complete. Selim's prudence would be praised to the skies, and we would be ruined."

"How could he have known . . ."

"That Famagusta would resist for so long? He didn't, but he fully expected that it would. He knows Venetian pride at least as well as I do. And I know he's waiting for Muezzinzade Ali to fall into the trap that the Holy League has set for him."

He leaned against the window, confused. "What are you talking about?"

I collected my thoughts, or tried to keep them from running away.

"When I knew that the Venetians had added galleasses to the Christian fleet, I thought it was a desperate move to make up for their lack of ships. Galleasses are very big, slow galleys, normally used for the transportation of supplies and troops. Then I remembered that the dry docks at the Venice arsenal had been enlarged specifically to accommodate those great beasts. The

Venetians don't spend their money on nothing." I took a breath before continuing. "A little way off, at the Arsenal foundries, the engineer Varadian works, and for years he has been studying ways to reduce the recoil of cannons. Not siege artillery, but medium-caliber cannons. You understand? These are the cannons that can't be put on ships. That's why he left Constantinople for Venice. Venice is funding his experiments, and meanwhile he's rearming the galleasses. There must be a connection between the two."

"In what way?" asked Nasi, stroking his beard.

"I think Varadian's cannons are on those ships, and that the Venetians have developed a big new fighting galley. A kind of floating castle, indestructible and with a level of firepower never seen before."

I read a sudden attentiveness on Nasi's face. "You were protecting the secrets of La Serenissima," he objected. "Don't you think you would have been informed of such a project?"

"This is a secret that could change the direction of a war. Not the kind of thing that Counselor Nordio would have shared with his underlings."

He moved toward the desk and sat down, staring at the floor. "That's only a conjecture on your part."

"But if I'm right, the risks are huge," I insisted. "I need a fast ship, Yossef. I need to join the Ottoman fleet and warn them of the danger."

"If you're right, it'll be too late when you get there," he said.

"But don't you understand? If I can put Muezzinzade Ali on his guard, we can still avert the worst. An Ottoman victory would blow Sokollu's plans sky-high. Otherwise it'll be the end!"

I had been shouting. Along the loggia, I heard a door opening and immediately closing again. I must have woken one of the servants.

Nasi remained silent. I thought he was weighing up my words, but I was wrong. When he spoke again, he seemed to be returning to himself. "My Aunt Gracia said a Jew always has to have his luggage beside the door. We are the wandering people. We must know when the time comes to set off on our travels again."

"Travels? Where to, Yossef? You've already traveled all around Europe."

He raised his head and stared at me. "I'm Yossef Nasi; I can always start doing it again."

Inside me, something broke. I wanted to cry, but on no account must I do that. "There's no time. There's one more thing to do and I'm going to do it. I need that ship."

He shook his head. He avoided looking at me, and I understood that I wouldn't persuade him. I could only try to save him.

"May the Lord protect you, Yossef."

I left the room, taking with me the image of a man trapped in a circle of candlelight.

In the loggia I found myself face to face with Gomez, standing by the wall, plunged in darkness. The love he felt for Yossef forced him to watch over him until the end.

"Good luck," he said to me.

He had understood; perhaps he had eavesdropped. It didn't matter.

We took leave of each other with a handshake.

Each minute was more precious than the last. I collected my few belongings together in a bag, gripped Ismail's dagger and hid it under my cloak. Nonetheless, the object that would be most useful to me was quite different. I dashed down the stairs and stepped into the library. The volumes were sleeping on the shelves, barely visible. I had spent whole hours, days, shut away in there, with my nose in pages that smelt of flight, of survival, running through ancient knowledge, the knowledge of my people and the peoples they had encountered on their long peregrination. If the New Zion was a utopian dream, the story contained in those books was concrete, made of flesh and blood, of lives lived, of hopes, tireless study and faith. Perhaps I had never been as close to the Kingdom anywhere as I was in there. Suddenly I gave a start: There was no time to lose. I searched everywhere until I touched the cylindrical object. Takiyuddin's optical tube. I slipped it into my bag and turned to look again at the library of the Palazzo Belvedere.

A beam of moonlight came in through the window and flowed over the table. Something on it attracted my attention. I stepped over and recognized the bundle that Ismail had had under his arm as he said good-bye. I cautiously opened it. It contained a manuscript. In the end the old man had decided not to consign those pages to the four winds. I couldn't help being pleased by his choice: He had brought them to the right place.

I closed the bundle again and quickly left the library. My footsteps echoed around the empty drawing room. I passed by the portrait of Gracia Nasi, but I didn't look up.

"You're leaving him, aren't you?"

Reyna's voice made me jump. I turned round and saw her sitting by the fire in a big armchair, hidden by its high back. That was why I hadn't noticed her. She got up and took a few steps toward me.

"I want to help him," I replied.

She came closer, near enough for me to see the pin that fastened her dressing gown: a red coral brooch. "Have you still not understood? No one can. Not even Ismail could. Not even my mother. And I . . ." She didn't finish the sentence. "That man would make a pact with Satan, just to pursue his obsessions." She took her eyes off me. "You never got to know him in the end, just to love him. I hope you will be wise enough not to come back here."

She turned her back on me and went to sit down again, invisible behind the chair.

I picked up my shoulder bag. "Goodbye, Donna Reyna."

I left without turning round again. I was in a hurry. By dawn I had to find a boat to take me to Bandirma.

17.

I sneezed so violently that I thought I'd broken the veins in my nose. I expected to see blood, and instead the leaves of tobacco expelled from my nostrils opened like strange petals before they fell on the deck.

Tobacco stuffed in the nostrils: that's the method they use on warships when the stench rising from the oarsmen's banks becomes unbearable. The crew wash with water and sand, bucketfuls of seawater are thrown amongst the benches to get rid of the feces, but there is nothing else to be done. The nose must be busy smelling strong, dense odors, if you want to survive the stench of a battleship.

The mind must be firm, if it is not to waver in the face of the task at hand, and the heart, too, must be a firm, if slender, vessel.

Mimi Reis passed me another handful of tobacco leaves. I would have liked a remedy as effective for the oscillations in my mind, and a drug as powerful for my thumping heart.

1 Elul 5331, 11 Jumada al-Awwal 979, October 1, 1571. The wind was warm now, as if summer hadn't ended after all. We had sailed the Sea of Marmara, plowed the northern Aegean, passed along the coast of Euboea, and now we were circumnavigating the Morea, in search of Muezzinzade Ali's fleet.

"Don't worry, Cardoso. We'll find him. These are my seas."

Mimi Reis opened a pilot's book and laid it out on a barrel. The outline of the coasts was an intricate arabesque, the names were oriflammes, the sand-banks tiny dots, the outlying rocks little crosses. "The latest information located the fleet in the Adriatic, off Zara, but I'm willing to bet that Muezzinzade Ali is already coming back, to intercept the crusades when they set sail from Messina." He ran his finger along a route that came down the Adriatic and entered the Ionian Sea until it reached Cephalonia and Corfu. Then he pointed to a route that came out of the Straits of Messina, passed along Calabria and arrived at the same destination as the other one.

I thought again of the mosaic in Palazzo Belvedere. There, it took only a few steps to cross the Mediterranean. I tried to focus my attention on the present again. Mimi Reis's finger was now pointing to a spot in the Gulf of Corinth, near a cluster of islands.

"Lepanto. If the Sultan's fleet wants to take on supplies, it will stop there. You understand? That's where the crusaders are going to pounce."

"We've got to persuade Muezzinzade Ali to avoid the galleasses at all costs."

I could see the concern on his broad face. "Muezzinzade is no *calascione*," he said in his Bari dialect. "He's not the type to shirk a fight. *L'acqua ca non ha fatte in ciele sta*—the water that hasn't fallen is still in the sky. God will grant victory to the deserving side."

Mimi Reis had reinvested the money he had earned in the Naxos enterprise by fitting out a galliot, the kind that the Turks call *kalita*. The Sultan's slender vessels are similar to the ships of the Christians, and they sail better even though they are built worse. They are arched, with bow and stern very high in the water, and more lightly armed. The crew—almost all Greeks and Albanians, a number of renegade Italians, a few Muscovites and Poles—were well fed, and were paid three *aspers* a day. Mimi Reis had chosen every oarsman personally. No slaves: He wanted to be sure that everyone would take up arms in the event of a clash. The wind was fair, the sea calm. The ship sped along the waves, and everything seemed propitious for the voyage, but premonition and concern hovered over our decks like a persistent and impalpable cloud. I slept little and badly, and not because of the usual worries of someone about to sail into the open sea.

No, what kept me tossing were the nightmares, their backdrop a city on the surface of the water, surrounded by breached and partly shattered walls. The scene incorporated all my life, all the faces and voices that belonged to my days. Arianna betrayed me every night, Dana waited for me in the shade of the carob tree and spoke Hebrew. Every night I reached a place that was Ragusa, and Salonika, Constantinople seen from the sea, and Famagusta surrounded by corpses.

That night Tuota wandered along the deck of the *kalita*. Or perhaps it was Ismail. I saw him closing his eyes at the sight of a battle-slain infantryman, and telling off our dog, Holy Ghost, for biting the feet of a corpse. At last he spoke.

The difference between the sleep of the just and the sleep of the idiot is that the idiot doesn't wake up again.

I woke with a start. It wasn't yet dawn. I got up, avoided the bodies sleeping in the hold, and began strolling along the deck, wondering whether Tuota wasn't actually with us on the ship. I spent the rest of the day helping the sailors with their habitual tasks and asking fate to let us accomplish everything in time.

In the bows, I stopped often to look at the bronze cannon, the chief weapon on the *kalita*. There were other, smaller guns, for which Mimi Reis showed a strange predilection.

"This one comes from Flanders," he said. "The other one from Brescia. They cost me an arm and a leg."

Metal. Copper and brass to make bronze. Iron. Gold. The fate of my people was bound up with English iron. The gold turned into cannons, and the fire and stone vomited up by these artifacts turned again, sooner or later,

into gold. *Solve et coagula.* Mimi Reis's cannon belonged to a game that stretched across the sea, over the oceans to the south and the west, to the very edges of the world.

The Puglian pirate had asked me only once for news of Ismail. I had had to reply that he had left, that he had gone home. Mimi, clearly, was displeased. When he saw me in Bandirma, and I asked him to join the Sultan's fleet, he had hoped that the old man would be coming along.

On the morning of 12 Jumada al-Awwal we encountered a Barbary caïque. Drawing up alongside, Mimi Reis asked for news of the fleets and received important confirmation: the Christian fleet had rounded the White Cape and was in sight of Cephalonia. The Turkish fleet, on the other hand, lay at anchor in Lepanto. Mimi Reis gave me a nudge.

"What did I tell you?"

He estimated that we would encounter the Christian fleet between October 17 and 18, in five or six days, near the islands of the Echinades, which the Venetians call Curzolari. Perhaps we would manage to slip past to warn Muezzinzade Ali and the other admirals before they took up the gauntlet.

We were drawing nearer our destiny. In my mind I ran through the speech that I had prepared, seeking the most important terms in Turkish, an appropriate rhetoric to address to those who must listen to and believe this Jew who insisted on interfering with their war. I was worried that they wouldn't believe me, and the closer we came to the moment of truth, the more desperate our mission seemed to me.

Over the days that followed our meeting with the caïque, I often heard Mimi Reis cursing the ship we were on for its slowness, which was beginning to exasperate us. Then, all of a sudden, his mood improved. I saw him walking to the prow, talking to his beloved cast-iron cannons, stroking their barrels and breeches with the palm of his right hand.

18.

On deck they were flaying a sheep, because the crew needed meat, especially the oarsmen, who had for many hours been helping the wind to spur us on our way. I was watching the blood forming a puddle and the flies swarming, when a voice shouted that there were sails in view. On the horizon, the fleet was a long black line.

Takiyuddin's optical instrument allowed me to review a whole side of the formation.

Western galleys, some Genovese, others Tuscan, many Spanish. There were also thin Venetian vessels. There was a huge galleass, pulled by other galleys, foists and galliots.

The galleass bristled with guns. They covered the whole of its perimeter— the bows, the sides, the high poop deck. I pointed the tube farther away and saw the Turkish ships advancing. A little beyond them, toward the coast, I could make out the bluish outlines of Oxia.

The Ottoman fleet looked like a forest emerging from the Gulf of Corinth. Closer to us, the Christians were beginning to maneuver. I had the sense that one flank was retreating, or else preparing for flight. I asked the captain his opinion.

Mimi Reis peered awkwardly through the tube. He looked up and returned his eye to the lens a number of times. "God is great," he murmured. Then he looked for a long time. At last he handed the instrument back to me. "Flight? They're getting into battle formation."

"Then let's go up to them. We can still do it."

He nodded and gave the order.

Under full sail, with all the oarsmen on their benches, the *kalita* started speeding toward the Ottoman fleet, passing beyond the right flank of the Christian forces.

"They're aiming at us. We're too close," I said.

"They're too busy looking at what's right in front of them, and even if they see us, they don't know who we are. And even if they do know, they're not going to break formation to follow us."

I heard a cannon shot. It was a signal from the Christians.

Mimi Reis ordered food and weapons to be carried on deck. Pikes, bows, arquebuses, leather corsets and helmets were piled up and arranged neatly along the whole of the ship, ready for use. So were biscuits, oranges, cheese, dates, dried figs, barrels of fresh water: Fighting drains the strength; you need

to have food and drink within reach. Then Mimi Reis hoisted a long black standard, Moorish characters embroidered on it in gold.

"What does it say?" I asked.

"*The Christian religion is a false religion.* But I would need to write it in Italian for that lot to understand."

He pointed to the left wing of the Ottoman fleet, and the closer we got, the wider Mimi's smile became. "Chin up, my friend." He extended his hand toward the open sea. "You see? All the best captains are over there. There's Ucciali, from Calabria. There's Caracoggia, and Commander Scirocco. There's the Muezzin's son; he's certainly no coward. And Mimi Reis will be there, too, *all'anima di chi v'ha mmuerte.*"

I pointed Takiyuddin's instrument at the Christian ships. The galleasses advanced first. They were allowed to advance on their own, far ahead of the rest of the fleet. Six fat morsels, bait to excite Muezzinzade Ali's thirst for victory.

A wave of unease surged through me. Now there was no way to reach the Ottoman flagship and warn Muezzinzade of the imminent danger to his fleet. I was late once again.

The sun was high in the sky by the time we found ourselves on the line that divided the fleets and saw the Turkish ships launching themselves forward. Clearly Muezzinzade's plan was to pass between the boats that seemed least threatening, and attack the heart of the Christian fleet. The Venetians' trap was about to snap shut.

Beside me, Mimi was waving his arms around as if he could be seen from the Ottoman flagship. "Head for the open sea, Muezzinzade! *Vattinn'!*"

I held my breath.

The ships of the first Turkish line arrived between one galleass and the other. The burst of gunfire nearly deafened us, the first shot immediately followed by a second, and shortly after by a third. The cannons on the sides of the galleasses crushed lifeboats, felled masts, smashed decks and gangways. I had never seen anything like it.

Mimi Reis spewed a stream of insults at the Venetians, calling down the rage of God and Saint Nicholas on them. I imagined the Turks' surprise, their grief, their rage. We were too late, we had to go on, leaving the most battered ships behind.

The Turkish ships that, however damaged, still managed to get through tried to ram the galleys in the first rows of the Christian fleet.

The galleasses floated lifelessly, slow and funereal, impossible to board, after imposing the first devastating blood tax on the enemy.

19.

The noise and the smoke extended all the way to us, far from the fray that had flared up in the middle of the lines. The right Christian flank and the left flank of the Muslims had begun to part, as if fearing a frontal collision. We saw the Turkish armies approaching and heading toward the open sea. Mimi Reis gave orders and commented out loud.

"Muezzinzade set them out badly. The right flank is too close to the coast. If things go wrong, the crews will desert to dry land, and who's going to stop them? I bet these boats you see here are Ucciali's galleys. He has something in mind. He plans to give them a wide berth, and take them from behind."

He turned around, and his face said more than words could have done. He ordered a break as soon as we were out of range of the Christian cannon. The oars were lifted, and preparations were made for prayer. The men performed their ablutions and spread out their mats. A young Albanian took charge of the prayers and the recitation of the Book.

No one paid any attention to me, as I clung to the parapet gazing with astonishment at the ships colliding at the heart of the battle. The noise of the cannonades was echoed by the sound of wood smashing and men shouting. Clouds of arrows flew from one deck to the other, while the arquebusiers fired from the sides. Smoke from a fire rose up in the middle of a floating forest of mainmasts. The water around the big ships filled with corpses, like the moat of a besieged fortress.

When the prayer was finished, Mimi Reis yelled at the top of his voice, "Let's go!" He commanded that the vessel veer to starboard, and then turned toward me. "Make sure you do your bit, because Saint Nicholas is with us here."

We headed for the meeting point of the fleets, where the tumult was being unleashed. Before us was a tangle of oars and lifeboats, two Christian galleys, a big Ottoman *kadirga*, one tiny hull wedged beneath the bow of the first, and other Turkish ships. I recognized them from their outlines, as one might in deep fog, because the colors of the standards were erased by the smoke from the cannon fire.

The hulls of the vessels had come together, forming an island of boats. A terrestrial battle was being fought beneath a vault of deafening noise.

A little Tuscan frigate obstructed our path, sweeping our deck with arquebus fire. The damage was minimal, but the crusaders had let a dinghy down into the water, in exactly the right place. It slipped below our oars on the

starboard side of the hull, and the ship halted its course and suddenly bore toward port.

We couldn't go on. Mimi Reis cursed in his dialect and gave orders to the whole crew, oarsmen included, to shift to that side. The ship swayed and its bulk loomed over the dinghy, which sank, by the will of God.

Our oars were free. Cries of excitement rose up from the crew. We made straight for the wooden island in front of us. I picked out a leather corset and a helmet a size too small. I unsheathed Ismail's dagger.

We were now within range, the bow cannon fired, but aimed too high. Our ship joined the confusion of hulls at a reduced speed. Its stem entered the knot of vessels, and we began to wheel to port, impelled by the movement of the other vessels.

The crew of what looked like a papal galliot was busy defending itself on the other side, where the Christian ship had fastened itself to its Ottoman neighbor, firing off a cloud of arrows. Some of them, shot from too great a distance, embedded themselves in the side of our ship. Only a few of the men on the Christian deck noticed our arrival, and even fewer worked out that we were about to board, taking advantage of the fact that our hulls had lined up side by side. Mimi Reis waited for the pope's arquebusiers in the gangway to discharge their arms, so that he could board the vessel under cover of the smoke.

The salvo went off. Mimi Reis grabbed his scimitar. "God is great!" he shouted.

He was the first to hurl himself forward, almost severing the head of the first adversary who came within his range. "*E iune!*" he cried, "One down!" as his men ran forward. I saw him running ahead once more, shouting like a man possessed, and threw myself after him. It was pandemonium; I found myself surrounded by gunfire and a universal thirst for blood. I ran in the wake of the charging men ahead of me. Fear, excitement, intoxication: We routed the enemy, the gangway turned red. From the other Ottoman ship, soldiers armed with maces and sabers emerged shouting. Attacked on both sides, the soldiers of Pius V surrendered. The field was ours, but we had no time to enjoy the fact.

A call went up. From our boarding side, past the *kalita*, the smoke dispersed and we were able to make out a big *bastarda* advancing towards us. The bow guns fired, the *cannone di corsia* fired directly at the deck, scattering debris all around me and throwing our barricades into utter disarray. The wreckage knocked me down and I fell. I got up, surrounded by corpses and the cries of the wounded.

Venetian cannons. By now the big galley was close enough for me to make out its standard; the maned lion held its closed book and its sword above our heads.

Mimi's broad face brightened: "At last." He turned to us. "*Uagliò!*" he shouted. "Lads! The Serenissima Repubblica is paying us a visit. Let's give her the welcome she deserves."

We started piling up rubble, bodies, barrels, gun carriages to form new barriers. Mimi looked like a wild cat, he darted with great agility from one side to the other, belying his stocky physique. By the time the fusillade began, the men were already in shelter.

Then the Venetians boarded.

As the first attackers climbed onto the deck, we fired and then immediately counterattacked with pikes and swords. A Venetian hurled himself at me. I merely held my arm outstretched. I felt the dagger plunging into him up to the hilt and the blood running through my fingers.

"Good man, Cardoso, *si fatte la fegura to'!* Nicely done!" Mimi Reis observed.

I hadn't even noticed that he was nearby. He had a word for everyone. He led us into the attack again, and we quickly crushed a unit of arquebusiers.

We fought for ages, acrid smoke and the smell of death filling our lungs. Mimi Reis's crew had mingled with the *sipahi*. True to their code, the *sipahi* went into combat with short swords, something that the Christians tried to avoid. The crew of the Ottoman galley, also under arms, had started hurling cooking pots and fireworks to make up for our lack of cannons.

The clash dragged on in a hideous balance of death, attacking, retreating, gaining a few feet of ground, with shouts, curses, prayers, insults, music, hissing arrows, roaring arquebuses, the smell of combusted bodies, of burnt wood.

I was caught up in a kind of dance. We had to come out of our shelters, seeking contact with the enemy, to take refuge again when the barrage resumed. We came out, we tried to get to the enemy, a salvo was fired, some of the men on our side lost their lives, sometimes we ended up hacking away in close combat.

The Ottoman archers had been fighting for over two hours by now. They were exhausted, in a terrible state. The Turkish bow is a fearsome weapon, but firing it many times takes a huge effort. Weariness fills your limbs, clarity of mind flees, a man becomes a coward. Fewer and fewer arrows were raining down on the Christians. More and more projectiles, fired from arquebuses, were striking our ranks.

I looked around for Mimi Reis: I missed his words of instruction. I saw him standing on a barrel, his left hand, held aloft, gripping a hawser, his right still clutching his sword. I couldn't make out what he was saying. Smoke engulfed the scene, but I could still hear him spurring on his men and railing at Venice. His voice came and went, according to the wind and the fluctuations in the battle clamor.

Close to me, a young sailor spoke. His face was stunned, his skin drenched with sweat, his eyes like lanterns. I thought I caught him saying that just as we'd left Lepanto, the Ottoman fleet had been marked by a bad omen. Crows. There had been a flight of crows.

A shot from a falconet shattered the wooden planks that sheltered us. The

ball struck the young man in the throat and tore off his head. Blood gushed over me, and I instinctively rose to my feet. I felt a very sharp pain in my leg and fell to my knees.

That was my salvation. I heard another bullet whistling where I had held my head a moment before. I looked at my calf; it had been pierced by a shot. The blood formed a little stream. I rested my back against the ravaged planks.

Cries of rage and desperation and insults rose from our ranks when we saw how the Christians were treating their prisoners. We peered out from above the ruins of our shelter. Blood formed pools on the deck.

Mimi Reis led the final sortie, followed by those few who were still able to fight, who were launching any missile that came to hand: pieces of wood, shoes, broken pikes, oranges and lemons. He had taken off his shirt, and you could make out the marks that etched their story on his skin even though it was blackened with smoke. The Muslims were fighting furiously. There were more Venetians, and they had more arquebuses. We began to lose our impetus. Mimi Reis waved his sword, disappeared amongst the bodies of his attackers, re-emerged, railed, gripped the throat of a Venetian seaman and yelled in his face. There was another salvo, aimed directly at us, a prelude to the final assault. The pirate was hidden by smoke.

Then I saw his face, twisted into a grin, high above the bodies and the drifting smoke. His severed head, dancing on a pike.

I don't know where my strength came from. I got up and dragged myself toward the side of the ship behind me. I heard cries and words of encouragement in Venetian, coming closer and closer. I rested my backside against the wall. With my hands, I lifted my injured leg over to the other side, along with my good leg. I dropped into the water.

When I resurfaced, I saw the gray mass of a galleass, in the distance, amid the fire from other ruined ships. It sailed slowly, like a massive turtle, indifferent to the slaughter.

Behind me I heard a cry of victory, and a chorus of voices giving thanks to Saint Mark.

Finale

Venice, December 11, 1571

Hawsers, scraps of sail, ropes, tree trunks, shards of shattered hulls, figure-heads, oranges, pages from books, a rosary.

I floated for a long time, among the living and the dead, amid the scum of war, a piece of flotsam among many others.

I could have rested in the anonymous silence of the depths, with the fallen of a thousand storms and battles, like one of Ulysses's companions. My death would have been worthy of the poems my father once read to me. Instead, the waves returned me to the world, so that my fate might come full circle. *Et stetit mare a fervore suo*, sated by the sacrifice of thousands.

They picked me up, the Venetians. Only to plunge me into this yet blacker abyss, the one reserved for the defeated and the traitorous, but not before cauterizing my wound with a red-hot iron. My cries must have been heard all the way here, announcing to everyone the arrival of an important prisoner. In fact it was not mercy that guided the surgeon's hand, but my name. It was just by chance that I was spotted by a convict condemned to a life sentence at the oars. He had risen from his bench and stretched out a filthy hand, the index finger pointing at me. His naked thigh still bore the violet scar from the bullet. Baldan is his name. I should have aimed for his heart, the day I decided to shoot at him to stop him from escaping across the canal. He couldn't have forgotten the man who had consigned him to a life of pain. For years, as he cursed my name with his every breath, he must have prayed that he might one day take his revenge, and inflict the same suffering on me. God heard his plea, putting him on the benches of the ship that picked me up.

That's the Arsenal assassin.

A Jew corrupted by Jewish money.

A traitor.

A murderer.

That's me. They didn't need to torture me to obtain a confession; I could have spoken the sentence myself. Denial would have been pointless, not after I'd plotted to obtain a war that left piles of corpses rotting in the sun and fattening the fish. A war whose fruits no longer belong to us. We only bear its blows.

They say that the Ottoman fleet was destroyed, that Kapudan Pasha is

dead, sunk to the bottom of the sea with his flagship. They say that only Ucciali, that shrewd pirate, got away, and that he will now be the Sultan's Great Admiral.

They say that Bragadin's stuffed hide reached Constantinople, and that it led Lala Mustafa's belated parade.

On the other hand, nothing is said of Yossef Nasi, as if he were an enemy no longer feared. And yet at my trial they asked me about him: Was it true that he was Selim's lover, that he had had children with his aunt, Gracia Nasi, that he worshipped the devil in the seclusion of his residence?

I laughed out loud at their stolid faces. A hearty laugh that echoed like a scandal around those dilapidated walls.

They brought me here, to this dark hole, where cold grips the limbs and tirelessly shakes them. Venice is cold as winter approaches, and this prison is even more so. My wound is a black lump of burned meat; I no longer even notice it. Not after being up to my calves in bilge for days and days, my feet tormented by water and chains, and then in this musty cell, reserved for the poor wretches I once locked up in here.

The Jews have been thrown out of Venice, expelled, all of them. I'm the last one, and a grand finale awaits me.

That's how I know he's coming. He won't be able to resist the temptation of seeing me before everything is done. I stay alert, I pace my spot to banish shivers and rats. I squash the insects that scrabble around under my clothes. It's strange how, even when the end is imminent, we go on repeating certain gestures, as if self-preservation were still a necessity.

In this blind intimacy, I can think about the ones I have left behind.

Tuota, whom I still imagine sitting bolt upright at the tiller.

Yossef, locked away in the solitude of Palazzo Belvedere.

Ismail, Ali, Hafiz and Mukhtar, together in the vastness of the desert.

Dana. I sacrificed our bond to the plan that should have returned me to myself, and instead it has only led me back to my starting point. I see again her face, her body, her hair; I hear her inviting voice. *Welcome to my garden.*

I stop on the threshold of the memory, startled at the rattle of the bolts. The door is thrown wide open and a torch banishes the darkness, showing the grim face of the jailer, bestial in the flickering light. I step aside to let him pass in.

He has aged. His hair and beard are grizzled. But his expression is the same: the face of someone accustomed to studying his neighbor.

"Good to see you, Consigliere."

Bartolomeo Nordio studies me for a long time. Perhaps he, too, is seeing the marks, or rather the ravages, that time has left on me.

"I didn't think you'd be so careless as to let yourself be captured. Not after getting away from me."

I shrug as I once wouldn't have dared to do in his presence. "Sorry to disappoint you."

He steps toward me and I notice that the wrinkles on his face are different, too. "Disappointed? On the contrary. You're my greatest success. I trained you to be my eyes, my hand. I put you to the supreme test, the sacrifice of your life, and you got out of it, you ran away, you became what I wanted you to be. A renegade, a traitor, a Jew. The truth is that you've never stopped being one of my agents. I turned you into what you are; you are more mine than a son would have been. But even so, you will go to hell, like everyone of your race, and you will be buried in unconsecrated ground. It's almost time."

There must be something that irritates him in my expression, something he didn't expect to find in this fetid hole. "Goodbye, De Zante."

He turns nervously towards the jailer, to be led out of the cell.

"There are men who would do anything to catch a hare."

The Consigliere stops and looks at me uncertainly, bewildered, as if he didn't catch my words. But in fact he did hear them, I'm sure of it.

"Men like you," I go on. "As I once was. Now you think you've been successful, and you don't realize you're clutching a carcass mangled by the same dogs you unleashed." I look into his eyes for the last time. "Keep this rag close to you. Because it's all you have left."

He stares at me again, his jaw clenched. Not understanding me is the biggest blow. He goes out without another word, and leaves me plunged in darkness once again.

Not much time is left. Enough to murmur a prayer and review all the faces of the people I have loved. I have stolen the last two years from fate: the best of a whole life lived backward over the course of a season, then hurled forward with the power of a dream, of home. Having tried to trace a difference future, having been freed to fly, even just for a moment, is what gives me the strength to confront what awaits me.

Perhaps that's why, now that they're coming to get me, I realize that I feel neither pain nor fear. Only bitterness at the disappointments inflicted.

The daylight hurts my eyes, forcing me to keep them shut. They drag me out, I struggle, I stumble, and am held upright. There's a crowd around me; shouts and insults fly.

Gradually I make out some shapes, as the anonymous multitude comes running over to see the great spectacle. My eyesight clears, and I look over the heads at the Ducal Palace, at the church of Saint Mark, with its great bulk and the campanile rising toward the sky. I think of all the times I have crossed this square as a free man, and go on losing myself in the details surrounding me, to keep them in full view. I don't listen to the magistrate reading the sentence. Each one of those accusations is false, and yet they sanction a just punishment. I have plotted against Venice; I have acted in accordance with her enemies. I have managed Giuseppe Nasi's money.

Yossef, I'm sorry. For me and for our island. We'll never know whether that hell on earth might have produced a paradise. And whether, though I doubt it, it is still worth the trouble of hoping and fighting for with all our

strength. If you were here, now, I would tell you without regret, Good-bye, my brother.

They tie my wrists behind my back, delicately, as if they were afraid of hurting me, a curious concern to show for a condemned man. The cap is placed on my head, with swift and expert movements.

My heart races, the sound of my breath drowns out everything else. Suddenly I recognize a figure in front of me, as it emerges from an ancient memory. It's my mother. She is young and beautiful.

She spreads her arms with a smile.

"Come, Manuel. Come on, come to me."

I'm small, I'm taking the first steps of my life to reach her, so that she can feel proud of her son and give him the prize of that warm embrace. Suddenly I realize that I'm not afraid anymore, it's easy, all I have to do is put one foot in front of the other and I can cover unimaginable distances. Even free myself to fly, high above the crowd, above Saint Mark's Square and the domes of the church, to see the whole city as if in a big fresco, and fly still further, faster, across the sea. To reach a faraway garden and rest, at last, in the shade of a carob tree.

Epilogue

Constantinople, 23 Rajab 979
(December 11, 1571)

The big hall is filled with the calm of evening. The sounds of the day and the shouting of the servants are far away; what remains are the rustle of water in the fountain and the crackling of the fire under the chimney.

The last light falls from above, through the glass, and by now the loggias are in darkness. Yossef Nasi sits on a stool by the open jaws of the fireplace, in the middle of the mosaic showing the *Mare nostrum*, from the Pillars of Hercules to the Sinai Desert.

He's been holding a roll of tobacco in his fingers; he has forgotten it is there. Perhaps he's been drinking wine, or perhaps, who knows, that was the night before. Pain distends time, it breaks it down into endless moments, each one the same as the next, until it blurs them together, until it makes you lose the meaning of the gestures that mark out the days, how to feed yourself, how to sleep.

He recognizes the footsteps behind his back and the warm, vibrant voice of David Gomez. "No news."

Another stab in the heart. Another pang of uncertainty.

"Keep on looking. Talk to anyone who came back."

"Yossef . . ."

"Please."

Gomez grips his shoulder hard, before withdrawing into the shadow that he emerged from. He will do what he's been asked to do. He will go back among the survivors of the catastrophe, as he has done every day, to question them, to uncover a clue, something, anything, that might illuminate the fate of the man who disappeared at sea. He will do it even though he knows it's pointless, out of the love that he feels, out of the fidelity that is his own.

The portrait on the wall is a ghost that mutely observes the passing of earthly glory.

The voice that echoes vividly in the mind is another one, that of the unsung victor. A true Giant, convinced that the future of the empire lies in the east, and that sooner or later he will sign a peace with Venice so they can return to their good prewar trading relations. Yossef Nasi sees the huge shadow rising to the ceiling and touching the corners of the room with its long fingers.

There's a moment in every game when one of the players is declared defeated.

There are men who can accept the verdict of fate without feigning, but you aren't one of them, Nasi Bey.

You believe that you can trick fortune and that every result can be turned into its opposite.

That much is proved by the letter you wrote to the King of Spain. These are your seal and your monogram. These are the words with which you offer your services to the greatest enemy of the empire, promising him to become a Christian in exchange for his favor.

How many times are you prepared to change face to save yourself?

I wonder whether Philip would have accepted. Do you think he might still need you? We will never know, because this letter will remain in my possession, as proof of your betrayal. It will be the guarantee that you will never again try to raise your head.

Even now Yossef can't repress a hint of admiration for Mehmet Sokollu. That man managed to make him fall into his own net. He waited patiently, he let his enemies organize their own defeat, leaving him master of the field at last.

Now he will rebuild the fleet and will steer the Crescent back toward Persia, India and beyond. A magnificent plan, even bigger than Yossef's own.

Your ruin is not in my interest, since Selim enjoys your company.

You will ensure that you please the Sultan for as long as God wills, and you will never again try to influence his will. You will be our court Jew once more, but you will no longer be in charge of imperial trade. Dr. Ashkenazi will take care of that. He has the right talents to do it, and above all he is a more loyal man than you can imagine.

You know, Nasi Bey, deep down we are the same, I esteem your tenacity. But unlike you, I have never committed the blunder of underestimating a queen. That's why I hold your life in my hands and declare you defeated.

He hears her approaching lightly, and when he turns round what he sees enchants him.

Her scarlet lips stand out in a face white as a statue's. There's something unnatural about her: her features are polished, her hair perfect, as if in a grotesque transfiguration. She wears a European dress that Yossef recognizes. It belonged to Gracia.

He wonders if she has come to confess or to accuse him, and suddenly he realizes that it makes no difference. Hard to say which one is the truly guilty party, he who wrote a letter to the biggest persecutor of Jews in the West, or she, who purloined it, prevented it from reaching its destination and handed it to the Grand Vizier. He has no wish to fight, he just wants to understand.

"Why did you do it?"

Reyna kneels in front of him and her skirt opens up like a corolla on the floor. He stares at her without rancor.

"All my life I have been what my mother wanted me to be. You and she

based your dreams on a sacrifice. Look at me, Yossef. I have no children. I don't even have a husband. She has always been your queen. When she died, you preferred to choose a loyal disciple rather than allowing me to serve you and love you."

"He's dead, and I should have died in his place."

Reyna brushes his hand. "Now you know you're not invincible. There are no more mirages to follow, or lives to sacrifice. You and I are the only ones left." She raises Yossef's hand and brings it to her face, coloring his fingers white. "My lord," she murmurs. "My king."

Yossef retreats from this painful homage and walks away, leaving her by the empty chair. He withdraws to the library, among the books, his sacred place where he breathes the smell of paper and parchment, as good and fragrant as the smell of freshly baked bread. He instinctively raises his gaze toward the hole in the wall, deluding himself that Manuel's eyes might still be there, but he finds it closed. No one is spying on his rooms.

On the table, instead of the map of Cyprus, there is a parcel of handwritten pages. Yossef runs the palm of his hand over them, as though testing their consistency.

Ismail's bequest, before leaving. The old man had understood. That was why he hadn't wanted to witness the final act. When he came to say good-bye to his friend, he gave him his memoirs, the ones he had worked on for years, pages that included the story of the battles and rebellions that he had been through. So his journey was not in vain; it had been useful for something.

Impossible to forget his friend's words before their paths parted for the last time.

Now I know why Gracia wanted me to be by your side. Not to help you to do what you've done, but to keep you from doing it. I understood too late, Yossef, and this is only the last of my defeats. If I didn't know you well, I'd tell you to come with us.

When the old man handed him the package his eyes were shining.

This is my story, which is also ours. Lest anyone forget that we were friends.

Manuel, Ismail. Too many good-byes for one old heart. Yossef holds back his emotion, brushes away a stray tear, and only at that minute does he become aware of the presence in the doorway of the library.

Ralph Fitch is in traveling clothes, and the sight of his young face revives the old man's spirit. Here is someone who still has much to see and do.

"I came to take my leave. My ship sails at dawn."

Yossef welcomes him with a handshake. The Englishman's tone does not conceal his regret. "What will you do now?"

Yossef Nasi spreads his arms, pointing at the space around him. "What I've always done. I'll protect fugitives." His gaze falls on the package. He picks it up and looks at it for a moment. "Accept a farewell gift, Master Fitch. These are the memoirs of a traveler, and I think a traveler should look after them."

The other man grasps his hands respectfully.

"Take them to England with you, along with my most devoted respects to your queen," Yossef adds. "Tell her I'm sorry."

"I will. Good luck to you."

"Farewell, Master Fitch."

The Englishman seems to be on the point of adding something, then merely bows and leaves. Now all that remains is to listen to the silence. The palace has never known silence so profound.

Yossef stands beside the big window and looks at the clouds drifting across Asia, where night is already falling. And yet it is a luminous image that forms before his inner eye. Dunes, and a track that snakes between scorched hills, to a city bathed by the sea.

Five outlines proceed in single file, mounted on dromedaries. At the head of the little caravan is a young woman, leading it toward the first of the houses. She is followed by an Arab with a long scimitar and a boy with a beardless, almost childish face. Clinging to her back is a little boy, with big, curious eyes. The old man brings up the rear.

There's a movement among of the houses: A flock of children comes from who knows where and surrounds the travelers with noise and laughter. Then men and women come out, even the oldest of them. When the old man climbs down from his saddle everyone crowds around him, giving thanks to God, He who reunites, for bringing him home.

Now there is no longer any reason to hold back the tears that mingle now with Yossef Nasi's smile.

Somewhere, far away, there will be rain and another season. The monsoons will return, the time will come to listen to the tales of sailors and pilgrims. And to admire once more the falcons' flight above the high plains.

Acknowledgements

This book owes a great deal to a great many people. We can only name a few of them here.

Roberto Santachiara, commander *en jefe*.

Severino Cesari and Paolo Repetti, for believing in us from the start, for following our every switch of direction, and for all of their advice.

Valentina Pattavina, for her patience, her teeth-gritting determination, her enthusiasm.

Ersan Ocak, for his personal interpretation of the term *tahammül*, set out one October afternoon, over a cup of coffee, in the Old Town of Damascus.

Andrea Lollini, for his valuable suggestions about Jewish culture.

Claudia Boscolo, for linguistic advice (and more besides).

Dimitri Chimenti, for his in-depth comments on the first draft.

Gaia De Pascale, for her overview.

The whole Polifonie group, for all the ideas flying around in that immaterial space.

Valerio, Giu, Giro, Alez, Filippo, Alberto and Carmilla's group.

Loredana Lipperini, for all her observations over the years.

Mario Boffo, Italian ambassador to Yemen (and author), for his kindness and helpfulness.

Omar Berakdar, for the discussion of Islam and the iconography of victors.

Dr. Balagan of Moorfields Eye Hospital in London, for filling in a dangerous pothole at the last minute.

Our partners Chiara, Chiara, Claudia and Giulia, for everything.

Our children Davide, Ismaele, Matilde and Sofia, because "everything" still isn't enough.

Luca, in fair and foul weather. This novel is for him too.

Everyone who, over the years, has shaped the fate of *Q*.

Appendix

[What follows is a "second prologue" to *Altai*, a long preamble in Mokha. We worked on this intensively in the autumn of 2008, but at a particular point we decided not to put it in the book, and to catch Ismail more *in medias res*. Here we tell of the bloodless reconquest of Mokha by the Ottoman fleet after the Zaydi revolt, and the part played by Ismail in the event. Basically, it was thanks to him that no blood was spilled. Then there's a gap; there was supposed to be a scene in which someone recently arrived from Constantinople hands Ismail Gracia's letter. In the last paragraph we show the old man, at home, reading her letter for the first time. Meanwhile, down in the street, a storyteller recounts the Sufi fable of the river that wanted to cross the desert, a fable that that is told (in different ways) at other points in the novel.]

Prelude

Al Mukha, 27 Dhu al-Hijjah 976

The Sultan's galleys came in sight of Mokha as evening fell. The monsoon breeze swelled the sails with sticky air, heavy as a tunic drenched in boiling water. On the shore, a line of white walls rose just above the sand, between the warm sea and the mountain backdrop from which the rebels had come down.

According to the information in the admiral's possession, the city had surrendered without a blow being struck. The inhabitants had refused to fight, the Ottoman garrison had fled, and the Indian merchants had sailed their feluccas to Abyssinia, on the other side of the Red Sea.

"We're half a mile away, Pasha," the bombardier informed him. "Where do you want to strike?"

The admiral unrolled a map and studied the coast once more. Mokha had neither gates nor bastions. The Zaydi gangs had taken the city on foot, with the complicity of a cowardly population. Both would soon know the price to be paid for betrayal. In essence, there were only two buildings armed with cannons.

"The Bey's palace is too close to the mosque," he said, pointing to the vertical of the big minaret. "Aim to starboard, at that isolated tower."

From the fo'c'sle the order echoed to the oarsmen's benches, and the galley maneuvered into firing position.

The gunner swabbed the middle culverin. Into its mouth he slipped the bundle of charge and a spadeful of sawdust, followed by six blows of the tamping rod. Then he picked up a sixty-pound ball and rolled it into the bronze barrel. He poured the priming powder into the touchhole, lit the fuse at the end of the linstock and waited.

"Elevation four," the bombardier commanded, as he was handed the incandescent scepter. In the meantime, five more gunners repeated the same operations with the lower-caliber weapons.

"Fire!" the admiral cried.

The explosion scattered a school of dolphins and startled the gulls. The culverin recoiled on the deck, coming to a halt against the mainmast. When the smoke dispersed, the tower they had been aiming at still appeared solidly in place. The other cannons were ready to fire, but no response came from the city: no gunfire, no shouts, nothing.

The admiral told the bombardier to stay prepared, then commanded that the vessel head farther down the coast and aim for the dock.

All of a sudden, beyond the pall of heat, dust and salt, the mirage of a banner appeared, flapping red against the wind, above the highest roof of the government building. Because he wasn't in the first flush of youth, and his eyesight wasn't what it was, he asked his second-in-command to help him.

"Captain, do you see that banner, too?"

The other man nodded.

"And do you recognize it?"

The captain leaned against the side and narrowed his eyes: three half-moons in a green oval on a red ground. "It looks like, I don't know, but, no, that's impossible, it couldn't . . ."

"So?"

"It looks like the Sultan's banner, Pasha. *Our* banner."

The old man sits at the table and writes. There is still enough light coming in through the window; the lamps are not yet lit. Once he has finished a page, he stacks it on the pile to his left: it's at least a hand's-breadth high, ten years of memories for each finger. Worn-out sheets of paper, ink-scarred, written in a threadbare Latin that the old man patches up with Turkish, Arabic, German, Venetian terms. Saint Jerome and Saint Augustine wouldn't recognize their language of choice.

He spreads a new page out in front of him, straightens his back and dips his pen.

"They're coming," a voice says behind him. "What should we do?"

It's Ali. The old man didn't even hear him coming upstairs. Old age and salt air are ruining his hearing. He turns around, his fingers stroking his white beard.

"How many?" he asks in Arabic.

"Eight galleys."

"Fine. Call the people. We'll go and welcome them at the customs post."

Ali is about to reply, but a distant explosion interrupts their conversation. The two men wait, motionless, like statues of flesh. Sounds of collapsing masonry burst through the window. The old man gets up, ignoring a pain in the small of his back. He looks up and sees, about thirty yards away, the smashed roof of a house, below the watchtower.

"It's a challenge," he announces. "If we don't respond, they won't fire again. That's the rule." He goes back to his desk and puts the manuscript back in a big leather bag. He picks up the ebony stick resting against his chair and, with the help of this, goes downstairs, with Ali walking ahead of him.

There were at least two thousand people crowding by the arch leading from the dock to the city. Veiled women holding babies in their arms, wrinkled old men in white robes, children naked from head to toe. Men and boys all had one protruding cheek, swollen with intoxicating leaves, and at their

waists they each wore a curved dagger, more as an ornament than a dangerous weapon. The only martial-looking young men were lined up in the front row: a group of about thirty Arabs, Indians and Africans, each wearing only a wide tunic.

In front of them stood a solemn-looking old man with his head wrapped in a turban. The admiral approached, followed by the galley captains. Once he was standing in front of the old man he looked him up and down like a camel he was thinking of buying.

"So it's true," he said at last. "You are . . ."

"Ismail al-Mukhawi," the other man cut in. "Welcome to Mokha, Pasha."

"A spy told us you'd stayed in the city with your men, and the Zaydis didn't dare touch you. So you liberated Mokha all by yourself?"

"They left at night, as soon as they knew of your arrival. There was no need to fight."

"And months ago, when they got here?" The admiral's voice was now quivering with indignation. "You didn't need to fight then, either?"

The old man spread his arms, as if to embrace the city and its people. "Mokha has no defenses, and there were thousands of rebels. No amount of resistance would have held them back."

"The fact remains that the captain of the janissaries ordered the inhabitants to respond to the attack, and he wasn't listened to."

Ismail rested a hand on his chest. "The responsibility is mine. I promised these people that the Zaydis would do them no harm. Events proved me right."

"Far from it!" the admiral roared. "You are a merchant, you think about business, and the mountain rebels don't seem like true enemies to you, because they produce the coffee you are so fond of. I, on the other hand, am a man of arms, and I think quite differently. Anyone who doesn't fight the Sultan's enemies is a traitor, and that is how he should be treated."

"If we were enemies, we wouldn't be here to welcome you, Pasha."

"Welcome me? As far as I'm concerned, you're here to surrender!"

"Even an old man like me can see that it isn't a white flag that's flying from the bey's palace; it's the Sultan's banner. And if it has returned to its place, it certainly isn't thanks to the governor."

With a sudden impulse of rage, the admiral turned round and ordered his men to load their arquebuses and have their bows at the ready.

The youths behind the old man brought their hands to their belts, as if to untie their robes. A moment later, every one was holding a pistol and, in the other hand, a whip of big metal strips as long as a man. Behind them, at the same moment, a hundred blades emerged from their scabbards.

The admiral drew his sword and put himself almost nose to nose with the old man. "Thank Yossef Nasi," he said between his teeth. "If it weren't for the fact that you represent him, I would make you repent for not fighting when it was time."

He took two steps back and raised the arm gripping his weapon. "Step aside, now!" he shouted. At a nod from the old man, the crowd divided in two and allowed the troops that had come from Constantinople to enter the city.

The uniforms filed past, accompanied only by eddies of sand and the sound of slippers on the beaten earth.

[. . .]

Night fell and the men of Mokha gathered to sing, smoke and tell stories, in the dusty space in front of the warehouses of Yossef Nasi, Lord of Tiberias, Duke of Naxos and the Seven Islands. The cups passed from hand to hand, full of *kishir*, the infusion prepared by boiling dry husks of coffee beans and cardamom seeds. In a city famous throughout the Empire for its *kahve*, the black liquid was reserved for the early morning, to clear the head of dreams or to make them emerge more clearly from the mind's torpor. Only the Sufi mystics drank it at any time of day, and Ismail, who frequented their monastery, had adopted the habit, every time he had to think.

The celebrations were taking place right under his window, but the old man had preferred the company of the letter that had just arrived. It was written in Flemish, forcing him to reread entire passages to be sure that he had grasped their meaning. The deep voice of the storyteller outside slipped in between one sentence and the next.

Born in far-off mountains, a river passed through many regions before at last it reached the desert sands. It tried to overcome the sands, but the further it tried to go, the more lost its waters became.

The old man got to his feet with the sheet of paper in his hand, in the hope that walking might help him to concentrate, but his knee, swollen with arthritis, forced him to hobble to other thoughts.

Summer is coming, he said to himself with his hand gripping his kneecap, *the damp summer of Mokha.* He blamed the place and the season, but he knew all too well that the hand of time would crush him in the end. Summer or winter, even in the most wholesome corner of the empire. But before that moment came, there was still life, there were still the obsessive memories and all those plans that had come to nothing.

It was then that a hidden voice murmured:

"If you rush in your usual way, the desert won't allow you to cross it. You will only be able to disappear or turn into a pool."

Gracia's letter wasn't the usual one, the one that arrived punctually every year, along with Yossef's ships loaded with fabrics and wood. It contained no lengthy reflections on the meaning of things, accounts of a thousand activities, ritual questions and others that were more heartfelt. The only common elements were the signature and the language of Antwerp. Otherwise, all the questions were condensed into a single request: Come back, as soon as possible. The news, too, had shriveled to a few words: I am ill, I am dying.

"The wind crosses the desert; the river can do the same, if it allows the wind to carry it."

Yossef, too, sent him letters every year. The surface of his words said: I miss you, I crave your wisdom, you would be more useful by my side, as in the old days. But the plea had become less and less heartfelt and the rhetoric more and more careless. Ismail ran his eyes over the pages; he wasn't really reading. He accepted the gifts that came with the letters; he handed them around. The true message that came to him from Istanbul was very clear. The City of Coffee was the right place for him.

But Gracia's invitation had been heartfelt, passionate, like his desire to hold her once more and comply with her last wishes.

Then the river sent its vapors up toward the welcoming arms of the wind, which lifted them and carried them to the east, letting them fall once more as snow on the peak . . .

The noisy voices that had served as a ground bass to the story grew until they drowned it out, then suddenly fell silent. A shout in Turkish interrupted the storyteller.

"Go back to your houses, admiral's orders. No gatherings after sunset."

Protests were heard in Arabic, curses, clumsy attempts to negotiate in the language of the soldiers. From the tone of the voices, Ismail understood that nothing untoward was going to happen. Not this evening.

He thought again of the words of the story. It was a Sufi parable, one he had heard many times, in many different variations, and he knew the ending: When the thaws came, the snow melted and the river became itself once more.

That had been his life, for many years. Allowing himself to be carried beyond the sands by the wind, and starting over when the rains came. Now he no longer feared being transformed into a marsh, and giving water to the desert seemed to him as noble as running between one's banks and irrigating the plain. Or perhaps that was what he liked to believe, whereas in fact his hearing had failed and his ears were no longer capable of hearing the voice of the wind.

Be that as it might, he could not return to Istanbul immediately, and it wasn't only the monsoon that kept him from doing so. He folded the letter again and began to undress for bed. The sands of Mokha were still in need of water.